Wildwood Creek

Center Point
Large Print

Also by Lisa Wingate and available from
Center Point Large Print:

Dandelion Summer

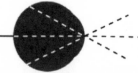

**This Large Print Book carries the
Seal of Approval of N.A.V.H.**

Wildwood Creek

Lisa Wingate

CENTER POINT LARGE PRINT
THORNDIKE, MAINE

This Center Point Large Print edition is published in the year 2014 by arrangement with Bethany House Publishers, a division of Baker Publishing Group.

The text of this Large Print edition is unabridged.
In other aspects, this book may vary
from the original edition.
Printed in the United States of America
on permanent paper.
Set in 16-point Times New Roman type.

ISBN: 978-1-62899-017-1

Library of Congress Cataloging-in-Publication Data

Wingate, Lisa.
Wildwood Creek / Lisa Wingate. — Center Point Large Print edition.
pages ; cm
ISBN 978-1-62899-017-1 (library binding : alk. paper)
1. Missing persons—Fiction. 2. Large type books. I. Title.
PS3573.I53165W55 2014b
813′.54—dc23

2013041063

Wildwood Creek

Prologue

Bonnie Rose
February 1861

I imagine the words as he's lookin' at me, hear the echo as he spies Maggie outside the door. It troubles me not so much for myself, but for my sister. . . .

She's little more than a babe, Maggie May. Just nine and a mite, yet she scarce remembers when the words were *angel, sweet one, daughter,* not *whore, burden, soiled one.*

How can a fallen woman be just a child? A wee girl, like Maggie May? Small for her age, arms thin as if they might break in a stiff wind. But she's stronger than they know. I must take her from this place, if there is a way.

He could be the way, this man.

But then come the words—those he speaks only with his eyes, with an upward tilt of chin, a slight pullin' away, as if the air's gone foul.

It's something I know, how they place the words on me. But how can they set them upon a child? None of it was Maggie May's doing. It was I who cut off the road to slip home through the trees. Who said, *It'll be shorter, Maggie May, come along.* I thought I'd such knowledge of the dangers, after only weeks in Texas. No longer did the Comanche maraud so far east. They'd been kept away by the tide of folk settlin' west of Fort Worth and on the winding Trinity River. Or so I'd been told.

It was I who decided all of it, not Maggie. Not Ma, or Da, poor little baby Cormie. My thinking brought the raiding party down upon us. My choice caused the shame, and the scars, and the pain, and the loss of all but little Maggie May and me.

Now this man . . . he knows of our shame as well. Stories travel like chaff on a bad wind here where we've refuged the four years since our ordeal, our story reaching as far as Elkhart and Crockett, seeming to find every plantation, settlement, and ferry landin' between here and Houston City.

He'll not be choosing me for the position, even though the good reverend and the missionaries have sent me here with a fine reference. I see the truth as the man slides his fingers over the silken collar of his jacket, rubbing long, slow. His eyes are dark, deep. Cold as the winter nights in Chicago before Da brought us away from the little Canaryville tenements. A better life is what he said we'd find in Texas. But instead, there was only death. Quickly for some. A shred at a time for Maggie May and me.

The man's eyes comb over me now, scratching

in like the teeth on a garden rake sharpened for planting. They tell me, as if I knew it not already, he *owns* things. People. The whole of a town. He sees in me a whore in his saloon, not a teacher for his school. It matters little what the missionary or the reverend have said to him about the plight of Maggie May and me. There is none of the grace of our Lord in this man. Or if there is, it's too spare to cover my sins.

His hands fall together on the desk, intertwine. In his chair, he leans away, watching me with the sad sort of curiosity I've come to loathe most of all. Never do I turn a corner here that the shame isn't walkin' before me.

"You seem very young," he says.

I rise a bit straighter in my chair, clutch my hands in my lap, the good fingers covering over the two that healed crooked. I've forgotten my gloves in my rush today, and I'm cursin' myself for it now.

I say, "I am eighteen, sir. I've taught two full terms at the mission school for orphaned children. I am qualified, I assure you." I speak the words very plainly, as I've practiced at the mission school. Not a hint of Irish, if I can help it. I have enough logged against me already. I fasten my gaze to this man very directly, and for a moment he's surprised by that. He blinks. His lips twitch slightly, but I cannot say whether toward a smile or a frown. "I am quite good with children, sir.

9

My recommendations are there in the parcel." I nod toward the wrapper on his desk—unopened, as far as I can see.

Leaning slightly, he peers into the hall, where Maggie May waits on the bench, quiet and meek. "And how old is she?"

"Only nine, sir. Just a child. We have none but each other."

This pleases him, if *pleased* is a means of describin' his expression. Perhaps it is more satisfaction than pleasure. No joy is in it, but I feel I've crossed some barrier I cannot see.

"I had the finest education at the mission school after . . ." They dangle like a hangin' noose, the words, quickly sliced through. Too late, I know where they were leading. All of life is *before,* then *after.* Before the shame. After the shame.

Two fingers straighten as he raises his hands, making the steeple on the church in a children's game. The fingertips are the folk inside the buildin'. Da played this game with us when we were small, and the remembering skitters through my mind like a dragonfly. It leaves a lacy shadow. Da's hands were big, his fingers a sturdy roof and steeple. A shelter.

The man trails the steeple along his bottom lip. "Yes," he says quite slowly, thinking the words in the speakin'. "Yes, you will do nicely, I believe." Again, a sentence drifts away between us, unfinished somehow.

I'm feeling there's more unspoken than's been spoken. I wish I could be asking, *Nicely . . . for what purpose?* But I've been warned. I've been warned to take care. By its nature, the position he's offering is one of few a girl soiled as myself might be considered for.

His gaze lingers there on my cheek, skimming as light as grass-feathers 'cross my ear, touching the skin at the edge of my collar. I finger the cameo locket the good reverend's wife has given me, then I tug the new bit of ribbon we've strung it on. I wonder if the scars show, red and anger-filled.

"You are not afraid to go into the wilderness?" he asks.

"I see no point in it," I say. "Fear changes nothing. A circumstance is still a circumstance."

"Fear motivates. In fact, I find it to be the most certain motivator of all." His long, thin fingers take up the pen and into the ink he dips, then signs a paper before pushing it my way. He turns the pen in his hand, extending it. "Sign here. I assume that you have no problem in working with Irish. Many of my laborers are Irish, which of course means that the whelps are Irish as well. The remainder in the settlement are Germans, for the most part."

"My parents were Irish. I was born there, but I do not remember it well," I say, though to be sure, he's seen it in my surname and in the look of me. It can't be missed.

I take the paper, begin to pen my signature.

After my first name and my middle adorn the paper, he stops me. I've lifted the pen to dip the ink. "That will do," he says. His lips curve again, and I feel that we're sharin' a secret together, but I've no way of knowing what it is.

"It is Bonnie Rose *O'Brien,* sir," I tell him, reaching toward the well of black liquid again.

He touches the pen to take it from me. "It is *Bonnie Rose* now." His flesh meets mine. Our eyes tangle. He is young to own so much. "It is better this way, don't you think?"

Suddenly, I've an understandin' of it.

I open my hand, let the pen slide through my fingers. A drip slips 'cross my skin, to splash on the desk. He takes a kerchief from his breast pocket. It's clean and white. Without a thought, he soils it beyond repair. The blackness seeps through and spreads as he strokes the linen over my palm. I can't help watching it.

He, instead, is watching me.

My wits gather up, and I look at him, then lose my composure at the meeting of our eyes. I've been offered something, but I neither know what it is, nor understand the terms of it. Anonymity? Absolution? A future for Maggie May?

What price does he ask to purchase it?

He smiles then, and this time I find some warmth in it. Or am I only seeing it because I need it to be so?

"I will expect you to be prepared for travel by the first day of the coming month," he says. "Arrangements will await you at the river port. I have ownership of a stern-wheeler that has made the run up the Trinity as far as Porter's Bluff thrice this winter, bearing both passengers and freight. You will travel with the *New Ila* as far as Trinidad, then overland with the ox freighter who transports my supply shipments." He rises, and I bolt from my seat, afraid even of smoothing my shirtwaist as he speaks.

"Set your affairs in order, Bonnie Rose. Pack well. It is a long journey to Wildwood."

Chapter 1

Allie Kirkland
February, Present Day

Even as a child, I was fascinated by my father's ability to create things that never were.

I'd forgotten so much about those little-girl years out in LA, my mother playing a bit part in the weekly soap opera, and my father working his magic. When the past is an amalgam of the painful and the sweet, sometimes all the mind can do is let the details fuse and blur. Maybe remold history a little, over time.

But somewhere in the muddle, there was always

the indelible feeling of sitting on my knees in my dad's canvas chair, looking through camera lenses and realizing he was willing to keep the whole world waiting while he explained shooting angles, and boom microphones, and lighting to an eight-year-old. Every little girl should have that moment with her dad, and no little girl should be forced to tuck away the crisp details of it. No little girl should be told she's better off ignoring the evidence in the mirror—her father's brown eyes, his penchant for daydreaming at inopportune times, the overwhelming hole where he promised he would be. Always and forever.

But some things just are what they are, no matter who tells you to overlook them. Along with the brown eyes and double-jointed elbows came my father's passion for all things related to film and live stage production . . . which made it hard to understand why the hairs on my neck stood up when I first walked into the old Berman Theater, just a few blocks off the University of Texas campus in downtown Austin. I couldn't pin the disquieting feeling on any one thing.

The building was cavernous and shadowy, rife with gold leaf and elaborate cornices, draped in heavy velvet curtains and gilded balconies, the frescos fading like an old woman's makeup slowly disappearing into aging skin. It seemed the sort of place where ghost hunters might come to do a show. The uneasiness it stirred in me was just a vague sense, like the one you get when you walk out the door in the morning, and the barometric pressure has dropped, and without ever having watched the weather you know a storm is coming.

I felt something . . . happening, but I didn't know what.

The sensation had been with me all day. My redheaded grandmother, who'd hauled me off to church every time she could wrestle me away from my mother and my stepfather and bring me to Texas for a visit, would've called it *the brush of angel wings*. To Grandma Rita, everything unexplained was either the brush of angel wings, or the touch of divine appointment.

The Berman Theater didn't feel like either one.

From the center aisle my roommate, Kim, sent a little finger wave my way, then nodded toward the balcony. The casting call line moved forward and Kim shuffled along with it, and I lost sight of her perky head. Goose bumps traveled over my arm and ran up my neck and into the little red curlicues that were probably sticking out of my ponytail by now. Luckily, I wasn't here for the casting call, but for another reason, and movie star hair wasn't necessarily required.

I slid into a theater seat near the wall, feeling conspicuously out of place. If I had to explain to one more person that I *was* allowed to be here, and that I was waiting exactly where the big, burly

15

security guy had told me to wait, it was entirely possible that I'd cave in and abandon this crazy plan altogether. If there was anyone else here seeking the production assistant's job Kim had told me about, I hadn't crossed paths with him or her. While Kim's line was progressing, mine didn't seem to be forming anytime soon.

Tucking my backpack in beside me, I looked for Kim again, but she'd been permanently absorbed by the crowd. Sooner or later, she'd make it to the front table, where hopefuls were turning in one-sheets, modeling cards, and eight-by-ten glossies that ranged from professionally produced to snapped in the backyard and printed on an inkjet. Tonight, when all the files were compiled, Kim's application and mine would mysteriously be moved to the top of the pile by a friend she had in the production company—at least, that was the plan.

My phone chimed in my pocket, and I scrambled to silence it before reading the text. People in the casting call line glanced my way.

The text was from Kim, wherever she was now. *Whoa! You see him up there? IDK, but think he's watching you . . .*

I looked for her again, then answered, *Who? Where? R U close to the front yet?*

Kim only responded to part of the question. Typical. Kim's train of thought ran on several tracks at once, jumping back and forth with no operator at the switchboard. *Look up in the first balcony! That's him, I think.*

I lowered the phone, peered upward, and made out a form. A man. Dark hair. Tall. Thin.

With the long coat cloaking his profile, he looked like Abraham Lincoln at Ford's Theatre. His face was hidden, but he was leaning slightly forward, watching, seemingly with curiosity, the activity on the floor below. For a moment, I had the strangest feeling that his eyes were locked with mine, as if through the darkness I could somehow see them. The uneasiness walked across my skin again, and I turned away, slouching over my phone.

Who? I texted.

The answer came quickly. *Singh. Rav Singh.*

Kim's friend, who was only a paper-shuffler from a temp agency, had heard that this casting call was related to Rav Singh—that he had signed on to produce the newest *Mysterious History* docudrama miniseries. It didn't seem likely, considering that Singh was known for box-office films, not television. But the psychological elements of *Mysterious History* did seem to fit his profile.

Singh's projects were rife with dark psychological stuff that tended to explore the worst side of human nature. He'd come from Mumbai and quickly made a name for himself in the American film industry. Maybe this was his way of capturing the American television market as well . . . or maybe the macabre elements of *Mysterious History* appealed to him. Along with taking a cast of modern-day adventurers back to a historical time period, *Mysterious History* projects always included a twist. For last season's show, forty people had been sent to live in, and staff, an English manor house. The twist was only revealed after they arrived—Hartshorne Abbey came with a gruesome history and a plethora of legendary ghost stories.

I glanced at the balcony again. The man was gone.

Kim didn't send another message. Apparently, she'd reached the front of the line. At least one of us might be getting a summer job today. As far as I could tell, I'd been completely overlooked. It was almost a relief. If I told my mother and Lloyd I'd found yet another way to prolong my impractical dream and avoid moving back to Phoenix to clerk in Lloyd's law office, they'd probably lock the front gates and hide the security code. They were still livid that I'd used my small inheritance from Grandma Rita to start a grad degree in film production at my father's alma mater, UT. I wanted to do what he had done—work my way up in the movie business. Austin wasn't LA, but it was a growing hub. There were opportunities here.

For Mom and Lloyd, the whole idea was

ridiculous. *Your grandmother never should've encouraged it. If it weren't for that, you'd be on track right now, like your brothers and sisters.* Lloyd delighted in pointing out that my three older stepsiblings, *his* kids, were tremendously successful people. Doctor, lawyer, engineer. Even the three Lloyd and my mother had together were science fair winners, kiddie chess champions, expert junior gymnasts. And then, there was me. *It's time to surrender this fantasy life you've created, Allison, and take up residence in the real world. . . .*

But that fantasy life, that universe within a story, was exactly what my father adored. Somehow, deep down inside, I couldn't help clinging to the idea that he would have adored *me,* starry eyes and all.

A shadow fell nearby and I looked up to find a woman there, her face rigid, exotic in some way, her dark hair slicked back in a bun so tight you could've bounced a quarter off it. A gray sheath dress made her thin frame look even thinner, and impossibly high heels gave her an imposing height. Standing up, I felt like a munchkin on the soundstage of *Amazon Women on the Moon.*

Her lashes lowered partway and I wondered if she was going to tell me to leave. She seemed unhappy about something. Decidedly.

"This way please." Her voice was strangely robotic, tinged with an accent that sounded slightly Middle Eastern and slightly French. I couldn't place it, and I was usually good with accents. The University of Texas being fairly global, Kim and I loved guessing where the strangers came from. This woman was far too glamorous to be shuttling people through a casting call in a dank theater building.

Which made me wonder if Kim might be right about Rav Singh. This exotic girl looked like she could be an actress out of Bollywood, a part of Singh's famed inner circle. He was known for keeping a tribe of loyal minions who fiercely protected his privacy . . . and the content of his ongoing projects.

I hitched up my backpack and fell into step behind her, feeling uncertain, awkward, and plain as we moved into the deepening shadows near an arched side-stage door that led into total darkness. A chill skittered past, and I conjured wild scenarios in which I was grabbed by the burly security guy, bound, gagged, and stuffed into a shipping crate. What would happen from there, I wasn't sure, but if I gave my mind a little time, it would come up with several possibilities. For as long as I could remember, my thoughts had worked that way. In scenes. Wild, unpredictable scenes.

"They told you I'm here to interview for the production assistant's job, right?" I asked.

She skimmed a look over her shoulder, the

way people do when they want you to know you're wasting your breath. Perhaps, schlepping applicants around wasn't her normal job, and she resented having to fetch me. Since we weren't going to talk, I focused on the bun . . . sort of a flawless blue-black cinnamon roll. A half-dozen hairs had escaped to trail along her smooth olive skin. The only rebellious thing about her.

The darkness fell like a veil and I was walking blind, following the *click, click, click* of her heels. My flip-flops slapped in response, the thready Bohemian skirt I'd grabbed before leaving the apartment, swishing in a way that was soft, yet audible against the dusty silence. We moved down a ramp, and the murmur of the multitudes faded until there was nothing but the echo of our passing. Not a soul was back here, as far as I could tell. Old wall sconces cast a dim glow along the corridor as we turned a corner, the arched plaster tunnels like catacombs reaching deep into the earth. She stopped at one of the dimly lit doors, opened it, then stepped aside, motioning for me to enter the room.

"In here, please." The request was polite, yet clipped. I glanced at her as I passed, and she looked me up and down in the way one alley cat sizes up another. What her issue could possibly be, I had no idea. Someone like her was under no threat from someone like me.

The room was small, with a desk on one end,

a leather chair behind it, and a cheap plastic cafeteria seat in front. One position was intended to denote importance and the other to emphasize subjugation. I had a sudden creepy image of what the production manager might be like, assuming I was here to interview with him or her. I envisioned the guard staff in an out-of-the-way Russian work camp somewhere.

There had been a meeting in this room recently—something having to do with costuming. Assorted fabric swatches lay strewn across the desk and there were sketches on a whiteboard—line drawings of men and women, the clothing seeming appropriate for an eighteen-hundreds reenactment, at least inasmuch as I knew about eighteen-hundreds reenactments, which honestly was not all that much. I'd taken a few classes in costuming as an undergrad and worked on many university and community theater productions over the years, but that was about it.

A scattering of résumés rested on the desk, along with design portfolios in neat black folders. Setting my backpack in the plastic chair, I sidled closer and peeked at the nearest ones. Clean dossiers printed on linen paper and accompanied by lists of coursework and various accolades. Qualified people had applied for the jobs here. Film and fashion design graduates who'd already racked up a plethora of industry experience.

I didn't have a prayer.

The door opened and I jerked away, then hovered by the cafeteria chair as a woman stepped in. Tall, leggy, smartly dressed in a formfitting white silk shirt and a black skirt with some sort of gold thread in the weave, she glowed. She was gorgeous. Bun hair, this time blond. She looked unfriendly. I was detecting a pattern here.

The door clicked closed behind her, as if it were afraid not to hop to its job, and she whisked past me on her way to the leather chair, a perfumed breeze traveling in her wake. "Sit," she commanded, pointing. I wondered if she had a dog at home.

Slipping into the seat, I set my backpack aside.

"Résumé." Her lashes swept upward, tugging cool sea-gray eyes with them as she adjusted a Bluetooth in her ear.

I hesitated, and she stretched a hand, fingers open impatiently. "You have brought one, I presume."

"Yes." I retrieved it and handed it over, though now it seemed pathetic. I noticed the wrinkles in the paper as she pinched it between her neatly manicured fingernails. Next to the other packets on the desk, mine was Cinderella after the stroke of midnight, realizing she doesn't belong at the ball.

I sat there waiting while the woman perused my credentials.

"You have experience sewing with commercial machines?" she asked without looking up. She was far back on the résumé now, to my high school vacations at Grandma Rita's in Texas.

"Yes. My grandmother owned a dry cleaning and alterations shop. I worked for her in the summers for years. I've worked part time in several fabric shops, and I've also taken fashion classes when I've been able, but of course my primary interest is production."

She blinked, the action completely, perfectly impassive. Her pale eyes were blank, her face android-like. "And you've applied for a position with us because . . ." She left the sentence open-ended, as if she were volleying the ball back to me and seeing what I would do with it.

"Film has always been my dream." For some reason, I decided to go for the personal approach, to see if I could melt the ice a bit. It'd always been a problem for me—desperately wanting to persuade people to like me. Being the odd man out in a blended family, you develop strange quirks. "My father was a director. My earliest memories are of being on set with him. He died when I was eight. I've always wanted to follow in his footsteps. Being in Arizona, there weren't many opportunities."

"Yes, I see you've completed your undergrad degree at some . . . this is a community college, I presume? I've never heard of it."

24

"I worked my way through. My parents were only willing to finance college if I studied something they considered practical, preferably law school."

"I see." For an instant, she and I were strangely, unexpectedly connected. I had the distinct feeling she knew all about having someone else pull your strings. Her eyes thawed momentarily, and there was something behind them, but I couldn't tell what.

"I have many qualified applicants for the production assistant's positions. Perhaps your skills would be better suited to one of the lay positions available—something on the cast. No experience in the film industry is required there, this being a reality-based production."

"I'm not exactly the on-stage type. I was the only fifth grader in the school production of *A Christmas Carol* selected to work behind the scenes, rather than in front. I love the inner mechanisms of a production. I've been involved in every way I could with theater—costuming, set design, whatever was needed. I know it's nothing compared to a full-scale film project like this one, but I'm willing to do whatever it takes to learn. No one will work harder than I will."

I scooted to the front of the chair, and she lifted a hand in a way that indicated she was accustomed to people freezing in place when she told them to. Her eyes darted toward her earpiece, and there was a quick headshake before her attention returned to me.

The interview questions then took a rapid right turn toward Terre Haute. "I would assume that you are not a superstitious type? There are some . . . myths and legends surrounding the town we intend to reenact. We are *not* looking for ghost enthusiasts, psychic mediums, and thrill seekers. We are also *not* looking for those who might be sniffing after a story or who intend to cash in by leaking details of the production to the media. Cast members *in* the reenactment village are, of course, not a concern, as they will be living on set for the duration, as part of the game. They will have no means of entering or leaving, unless they are dismissed from the cast. The location is remote enough to allow us that luxury. Support personnel, conversely, may be coming and going for months, though they will be housed in an onsite camp prepared for crew members. Confidentiality agreements will be required, as well as references and background checks. Would any of these caveats be problematic for you?"

Now I was thoroughly confused. Was she offering me a job? Or telling me why I wasn't qualified for the job? "I'm not superstitious and I have no problem signing confidentiality agreements of any kind."

Her attention drifted toward the door. Finally she stood, so I did too.

"One final thing," she added. "Are you familiar with the name Bonnie Rose?"

The interview had taken another hairpin turn. "No, not that I know of . . ."

"Very well," she said. "We'll be in touch."

Chapter 2

Allie Kirkland
February, Present Day

The evening after the casting call, I started having nightmares about the Berman Theater.

I was running through the darkened catacombs, but suddenly there were no doors.

Someone . . . or something . . . was in there with me. Footsteps echoed through the shadows. Closer, then farther away, then closer again, sometimes so near that I could hear breathing. I felt it on my neck, turned around . . .

Over and over and over, I jerked awake, then fell asleep again, compelled to return to exactly the same place repeatedly. Haunted by it. Only twice before had I been plagued by repetitive dreams. The week before my father died, I'd seen him driving off into a bright light. I tried to chase his car, but my eight-year-old legs weren't fast enough.

The week Grandma Rita was due to fly home

from her big Hawaiian vacation, I'd dreamed that I went to meet her plane, but it wasn't there. She was in the air on September 11, 2001, and the dream suddenly made sense. It was two days before she could send a message that she was fine.

I wasn't about to let Kim know about the Berman Theater dream. There was no telling how that would stir the waters. She was a basket case already, waiting for news.

"It's just . . . I'm going to be heartbroken if I miss this chance." She actually got weepy over Domino's Pizza as we sat outside our apartment. Our usual picnic spot was the stairway for our quad.

"It's not the end of the world if it doesn't happen. You only found out about this thing . . . what . . . a week ago?" Sometimes Kim could be so dramatic.

She ignored me completely. "I hope they saw how much I wanted it, but I don't know if they did. But I made it past the front table after Chase slipped my paperwork to the top. Of course, in the second room there were five people behind the table, and there was, like, a mirror *behind* them. I think it was a two-way mirror. I think *he* was back there watching them ask me all those psychological profile questions about whether I had any outdoor survival experience and what I thought would be hardest about living frontier style. It's all up to *him,* really. The committees are just a front. I did a great job on the psych profile—if there's one thing I know after all these counseling classes, that's it. I had that psychologist behind the table totally convinced I could tough it out as a wilderness pioneer. I just hope I convinced *him*." Kim was on a roll this evening, full of wild theories about Rav Singh again.

"Your OCD is showing." When Kim got her mind on a must-have, she could not, I mean *not,* think of anything else.

Maybe it was selfish, but I was starting to hope she wouldn't be offered a spot on the cast. There was something about my interview that still bothered me. I couldn't shake the sense that the android woman had wanted to warn me off, but was afraid to.

Kim stuck her fingers in her ears and started humming, as in, *La-la-la, I can't hear you.* Her face narrowed, and she squinted at me, her round, cherub cheeks and pert nose scrunching up. "Don't swat flies near the gravy, Allie. You'll ruin it." Kim came from my grandmother's little Texas hometown, which was how we'd met and become summer friends over the years. Just like Grandma Rita, Kim had more creative phrases than you could shake a stick at. Conversation wasn't just conversation, it was an art form.

I took a bite of my pizza. "Well, not to add to your gravy or anything, but weren't you the one who was looking forward to heading down to Galveston to hunt for hot guys on the beach again this summer?"

Kim frowned, setting down her pizza and resting her chin on her hand. "Yeah, whatever. We went there last summer, Allie, and what did it really get us? No guys and terminal sunburns. One of these days, we'll end up side by side, sharing a room in the nursing home, covered with Band-Aids where we've had sunspots lasered off."

"Well, now, there's an appealing picture."

Kim pushed her paper plate away, looking uncharacteristically somber. "I'm serious, Allie. I'm twenty-seven years old. I'm almost through grad school. Everyone I know is getting married. I'm so sick of wedding showers, I could spit. And what's gonna happen when I *do* graduate? I've put it off almost as long as I can. Eventually, unless I want to go for my doctorate in education, they'll give me a master's degree and kick me out of here. And then I'll be in some school where 95 percent of the teachers are *women,* and the other 5 percent are coaches. And coaches want *skinny* girls. Girls who look like they only eat Purina Rabbit Chow. I wanna *find* somebody, and this summer's my chance. I can *feel* it. There's the whole cast of the show, and then on top of that, there's the crew—all the grips and production assistants and stuff—*and* on top of that, there's all the people who eventually watch the show when it comes on TV. That's *a lot* of potential right there, my friend."

"*That's* why you want to do this so badly?"

Kim answered with a nod, her silky blond hair falling over her eyes. "And the whole idea of living like you're back in time for three months is kinda cool. Don't forget, I was a history teacher for two whole years before I went back to grad school. Just *think* about it. This thing is perfect for me. I love history, and those big ol' skirts totally hide the ba-donka-donk. I'm gonna look good in 1861. You should see the pictures of my great-grandmothers. They were some corn-fed German women, and they were both married before they turned seventeen. I'm living in the wrong millennium, that's all."

"I think you're getting way too wrapped up in this." For all her bubbly personality, Kim could go off the deep end in the worst way, then end up floundering when her plans went awry. Those periods of depression were not pretty. They scratched the dust off the times with my father that I didn't want to remember. Despite his brilliance, there was a dark side that drove him to his studio and kept him inside for days on end. The door locked, even to me.

Kim nudged me as Stewart Mulder exited the apartment next to ours, soundlessly as usual, his hat-rack-thin frame bent under the weight of an enormous backpack bulging at the zippers.

31

Stewart was a second-year law student who worked in the campus library and clerked at the DA's office.

Communication with him was always a little hit or miss. He was just as apt to walk by without saying anything, his face blotchy red with embarrassment under his unkempt mop of brown hair, as he was to stop and have an awkward conversation. Lately, he was into sharing the details of bizarre cases at the DA's office.

"Hey, Stew," Kim said as he checked and rechecked his door locks.

"It's *Stewart*." The thin cupid's bow of his lips compressed, the emotion impossible to read. "Stew comes in a can. I don't."

Kim wagged a finger at him. "That's a good one."

His mouth twitched a bit. He seemed pleased.

Kim swept pizza crumbs off her sweats. "So what's new at the DA's office?"

There was the strangest thing about Kim: Maybe it was the counseling classes, but she always had to engage people. It frequently garnered dating offers she *didn't* want. I had a bad feeling she was headed there with Stewart.

"We have been issuing warrants for out-standing parking tickets."

Kim's eyes widened. "Seriously?" She was famous for parking in places she wasn't supposed to.

I leaned over and stared at her. Sometimes Kim could be blond all the way to the roots. "Kim, parking tickets are city, not state."

Even with the hint, it took her a minute. "Oh, that's really a good one, Stew. That was kind of cold, though. You scared me."

An awkward smile teased Stewart's lips, and then he stood there looking uncomfortable before finally checking his door locks again.

Hooking his thumbs under his backpack straps, he exited down the stairs.

I turned to Kim after he was gone. "You know he has a crush on you. You know you're encouraging him, right?"

"What?"

"Just don't be surprised when Stewart asks you out for a date." In reality, Stewart had probably been sitting inside his apartment listening to our whole conversation about lack of male interest. I had a feeling that Stewart listened in on a lot of our stairway conversations.

Kim tipped her chair onto the front legs so that she could peer down the stairwell as Stewart lugged his backpack across the parking lot, his long, thin legs made even thinner by the black skinny jeans he always wore. Weaving through the cars, he seemed to sag beneath the weight of the books, or the weight of the world, or both.

"Puh-lease." Kim looked a little scared now.

"I'm just being nice. What do you expect me to do, be *mean?*"

"I'm just saying don't flirt."

"Okay, okay. I feel kind of sorry for him, that's—" Stopping mid-sentence, she pulled her cell phone from her pocket. "Holy cow! Oh my gosh, oh my gosh, oh my gosh!" She flailed a hand in the air, then pressed it to her chest and took a few deep breaths.

"What?"

"It's *them,*" she whispered, giving the screen a fisheye. "It's them! It's them! It's them! It's an LA area code."

Something lumpy and uncomfortable formed in my throat as Kim answered the phone, then quickly began taking instructions for a callback. Gesticulating wildly, she made writing motions and mouthed the word *pen*. I ducked in the door and grabbed one for her, and she furiously wrote details on the pizza box. When the call was over, she stood up, patting her chest.

"I made the first cut . . ." She stared at her bedazzled phone case, dumbfounded. "They really want me. Nine a.m. tomorrow, I go back in, and we do some more interviews, a medical profile, and some other . . . stuff. Oh my gosh, I can't even remember what they said. Some . . . something about a meeting again with their psychologist and doing some readings . . . and they're going to look at us, put us on camera and stuff. And then pick a second-round group."

The heaviness in my chest thickened. "That's really great, Kim. That's awesome." Why did this feel so . . . wrong?

Kim didn't catch my lack of sincerity; she was too busy squealing and running hamster circles around the landing. When she finally skidded to a stop, she noticed the stricken look I couldn't quite hide, and her face fell. "Oh . . . oh . . . they're going to call you too, Allie."

She had no idea that wasn't at all what was on my mind. I was thinking about the nightmares. The ones that seemed to come when I was worried about someone close to me. Were they a warning? "Kim, it's fine." All of a sudden I felt like I couldn't breathe, like I was trapped in those endless catacombs again. "You know that Lloyd and Mom would kill me, anyway. Maybe they're right about it being time to come home."

"The production is gonna *call,* Allie. Chase promised to do everything he could to keep your résumé at the top of the pile too, and besides, I've been having one of my *feelings* all week."

So have I. But the feelings I'd been experiencing had tied my stomach in knots.

Inside the apartment, my phone belted out an electronic jazz riff.

"There it is!" Kim squealed.

As I crossed to the door and answered my phone, the fine hairs on my skin rose, as if the cool air of the Berman Theater had found me from far away.

Perhaps, in a sense, it had. I recognized the voice on the other end of the call. "Hello, Miss Kirkland, this is Tova Kask, calling from Razor Point Productions. . . ."

Chapter 3

Bonnie Rose
March 1861

She's crying, my Maggie May, and as I come 'cross the field, I know the cause of it. There can be a grown-up wickedness in children, though they're yet small. It's young Joseph Bonham, and he's the worst of them. I've a notion to grab the little urchin up by the ear.

I can hear his words, even from a distance. It's a special meanness he's cooked up today. "You'll be got by the Injuns ag'in," he tells her. "You gonna go be a Injun ag'in, huh, squaw girl?"

She's pressed close to the wall, Maggie May, her hands fast over her ears, trying not to hear it. She's come to the headmaster's garden to take cuttings of the Seven Sisters rose we brought from the plot where Ma and Da and baby Cormie were laid to rest. I should've known she wouldn't leave without it. It's all we have of them, and I should've thought of it myself, but there's so much thinking to be done, my mind whirls like a wind ribbon on a stick.

"You'd best leave her be, young master Bonham," I tell him, wishing I had my rule stick along. He's a wicked boy and brash at only eleven years old, this one. It'll lead him to trouble one day, and more so with no ma or da to be lookin' after him. "It's a small man who profits himself from the trouble of others." Bending close to him, I remind myself that he has no parents, save the ones who left him on the street to shift for himself. "You remember that, Joseph Bonham. Be a good man as you grow, not a small one. It's a choice you'll be makin' in these next years."

I turn away, and he skitters off. Maggie May's still tucked against the wall, and I can see she's cut her hands to ribbons on the thorns. "Heavens me, Maggie May. What've you done to yourself?"

She's lookin' down at the blood then, noticing it for the first time. She can take her mind so far away, to a hiding place where she feels not a thing. I wonder, will she always be living this way now, with only a small part of her touching the world?

"It's time to be off," I say, and there's a rim of water 'round her green eyes. They float like clover in an ocean. Like Ireland, I think, but I don't remember Ireland clearly, and Maggie remembers it not at all. "It'll be well, Maggie May, you'll see soon enough."

I straighten her brown dress and dry her eyes, then clean her hands with the old linen from my pocket. It leaves behind the dust of chalk from a slate I've wiped while teaching lessons. I wonder what sort of students I'll be finding in this new place. I'll miss many of the little ones we leave behind—these so needful of love. I see their faces at the schoolhouse windows as I dip the cloth in the bucket by the gate and wrap the stems of the Seven Sisters.

I hold them so tightly the thorns come through as Maggie May and I cross the yard and offer our farewells, preparing to climb into the wagon with the good reverend. He'll transport us to the steamboat landin', then carry back supplies for the mission school on the journey home.

I think of the wagon returning and us not in it, and my throat tightens, so it's a labor even breathin'. The good reverend's wife hugs me to her, and she's the closest to a mother I've known these past four years, but still it's difficult for me. I'll not let myself be pulling away, but my mind has gone back to the noose again. I'm feeling it 'round my neck, a tightening strip of rawhide, and the only way to keep my breath is to match step with the Comanche pony on the far end of the strap. Once again, we're to be dragged from home, Maggie and me, but we've no other choice. We must make a life, and with this conflict between the states growing, less coin comes to the mission school by the month. Only a matter of time remains before difficult decisions must be made. We'll be two fewer mouths to feed.

The reverend's wife presses the cameo locket into my palm, along with a ribbon to string it on. I must always wear something to cover the scars, but mostly until now, it's been only a ribbon. "You poor, poor child. I wish I could give you more. It isn't of any value to sell, but it has been blessed with prayer. My grandmother gave it to me when the reverend and I came to Texas."

"Thank you, ma'am." I wish there were the love in me that she's owed in return, but there's a part of me now that will always shy away from touching, I fear. It's four years since the end of our shame, since we were ransomed from our ordeal, but that bit inside me is dead as ever. It feels nothin' but the need to run to the farthest dark place and hide away. I'm supposing by now that won't change.

I should return the locket to her, but I don't. I hold it in my hand instead, clenching it close as I take the seat next to the reverend and we ride away. My hands close tight, one filled with thorns, the other with the locket, both cutting into me in equal measure. All I can do is be still and let the miles pass . . . and try to keep breathin'.

In the wagon box Maggie May leans against our carpetbag and turns her eyes to the cloudless sky. I give her the rose cuttings by and by and tell her to tuck them away, and we'll hope they make the journey. They seem such fragile things, but they're strong enough to root in most any soil.

A horse whinnies in the field along the road, and Maggie May sits up to watch. They're livery horses, I think, but I cannot say for certain. Bays, sorrels, roans, grays. At least a dozen. The good reverend's wagon team snorts and quickens in reply. Maggie's eyes are pleasured, and she braces her hands on the side of the wagon to lean out and watch. I know what thoughts circle 'round in her mind now. She's remembering the horse herd in the Indian camp. So many you could scarce see clear across.

The woman who combed Maggie May's hair, and oiled it with bear grease and dressed her in a hide frock soft as silk kept a bay mare for her. A gentle old nag with four white socks and a pie-bald face. The one thing Maggie May had always wanted. She had Da's love for horses, though she could not remember the days back in Ireland, when there was a house and a stable and a field of horses to be sold in matched pairs for drivin'.

Maggie May could remember none of it. I could scarce call up those times myself, and even that was a blessin'. Far better to forget what's gone and be looking instead at what the new day has to offer. Da once told me that very thing. Yet he yearned for the horses back in Ireland, all the same. It was clear in the way he watched fine buggy teams pass by or colts frolic in the pasture. Maggie May is more like him than she knows.

The horses in the Indian camp were rangy and small, and it was no accident that there was a little mare for Maggie to have. In the woman's lodge was everything left behind by a child who'd been lost, a little one who must've been nearly Maggie's own size. It was a blessing that Maggie was young and they took her in as their own. It saved her from sufferin'. But not so for me, at thirteen. If not for the pleading of Maggie May, they might've killed me altogether, over time. It might've been a kinder thing.

The livery horses run to the far side of the pasture, and I send the past off to the corner of my mind, likewise. Instead, I look at the sky and hope to see tomorrow in it as Da always taught us. *Look up, Bonnie Rose,* his husky voice whispers like music in my mind. *Look up and out. Tomorrow is comin'. Can you see it, girl?*

I try to paint a vision as the miles plod by. Could a tomorrow of that sort truly come? One in which ten months of bondage on the prairie are no part of me, and my shame has been stripped away? Could there be such a home? Could it be Wildwood? The magical place in which Bonnie Rose O'Brien becomes only *Bonnie Rose?* No terrible past nippin' blood-hungry at her heels? No tiny piece of her birthed on the prairie and ripped from her arms and took away, leaving her no means of knowing whether it lived or died. Could there be no further need of caring, because that past doesn't exist any longer?

I ponder it until town is finally ahead, and with it the bustle of the riverboat landin'. For the first time since our ransoming, I no longer feel the leash of my tormentors. The noose is gone away, and I fill myself full of breath and imagine Wildwood.

Chapter 4

Allie Kirkland
March, Present Day

"Look at this thing! Isn't it beautiful?" My excitement bubbled over, even as I tried to contain it. My new boss, Tova Kask, didn't like excitement. I'd figured out that much in my first morning at work.

"I doubt costuming will use it," she replied blandly, swooshing a dismissive backhand at the latest delivery, an antique treadle-style sewing machine intended for the wardrobe department. "Have the man put it in the corner of the stitching room . . . or in one of the fitting areas, out of the way."

Costuming had been given several basement rooms for cast fittings, production, and storage of rented hats, shoes, and accessories. In the last few hours, I'd begun to learn the layout of the old theater—at least the parts we were using. Deliveries arrived via a subterranean loading dock, and my job as assistant to the production coordinator was to help Stevie, the downstairs production assistant, with shepherding arrivals to their destinations. Throughout the building, various departments were already at work on the setup of the pre-production facilities for costume designers, set designers, sound, lighting, and location specialists, as well as countless other members of the team.

Meanwhile, cast interviews and detailed psych profiles continued upstairs. No small expense was being spared to ensure that the people selected for the show could actually bear up under the rigors of pioneer life. Kim was hopeful. So far, she'd made the cut.

"Well, I know how to operate this thing if they do use it. We had one in my grandmother's shop." I instantly felt like a moron. I'd just expressed affection for the machine Tova clearly didn't approve of.

"Of course you do." She turned back to her iPad, muttering, "Things would proceed far more smoothly if he would refrain from encumbering me with things I do *not* need."

My skin went hot, and I had that old, familiar sick-stomach feeling that comes from knowing someone doesn't like or want you. Inside, I was nine years old again, the third wheel in my mother's new relationship with Lloyd and his teenage kids.

Pushing aside the inconvenient rush of insecurity, I focused on Tova's last words: *if he would refrain from encumbering me with things . . .*

Who was *he,* I wondered? Was *he* the explanation as to why, with my woeful lack of qualifications, I had been hired in the first place?

The question lingered through the rest of a very long workday. By 8:25 that night, I was sweaty and wild-haired, and I'd ruined a really cute new shirt that I thought would be adorable for work. Tomorrow, more casual clothes. There were a slew of tasks still to be done, including helping to organize Tova's lair and setting things up in the costuming area, which looked like a massive job. While some departments had a partial crew already in place to accept the deliveries, there was no one in costuming yet. I was supposed to do my best to arrange the layout of the work-rooms and the fitting rooms, so I had harkened back to Grandma Rita's shop. It wasn't that hard to create a logical structure for the design, stitching, and fitting areas.

The place was shaping up, if I did say so myself, and so was Tova's office area, which she had been absent from most of the day. I'd unpacked her boxes of folders, set up her computer equipment, tested printers, and put together office furniture and even gotten rid of the ugly plastic cafeteria chair. There was still much to be done, but at least the downstairs was greatly improved and now a workable space.

Tova found me cleaning up the last of the packing materials in her office when she came to dismiss me for the night. She stopped in the doorway long enough for a quick scan. I noted that her hair was still slicked into a perfect bun, her silk tank top was magically unwrinkled, and her linen skirt still hung smoothly from her hips.

I stepped back and waited for her to admire my hard work. I might've had my insecurities about a lot of areas of my life, but I was confident in my ability to organize. Hopefully, regardless of the circumstances of my coming onboard, Tova would now see that I really did know a few things, and what I didn't know, I was willing to work hard to learn.

I threaded my arms behind my back, having that giddy feeling you get when you've just handed someone their Christmas gift and you're waiting for the ribbons to be torn off. There were still crates to unpack, but this room looked 5,000 percent better than when she'd left it this morning.

"I suppose you will shape this up tomorrow."

She gave a dismissive wave, indicating . . . I knew not what. I had even collapsed and stacked the empty packing containers, rolled and folded the bubble wrap, and collected a bin full of recyclables.

Right now the place looked better than any of the departments I'd visited today. Upstairs, the Art Department was a zoo, and in the electrical rooms, the assistant to the gaffer was about to have a nervous breakdown. Because this production would be filmed in a re-created frontier far from civilization, the sound, lighting, and technical personnel had horrendous logistical challenges ahead of them. Between now and May, they had to come up with plans for placing and concealing hundreds of cameras, miles of fiber-optic cable, and a plethora of switches and audio devices, as well as the electrical network to run them.

Tova cocked an eyebrow, waiting for my response.

I forced out, "I thought you said to arrange the rooms down here? Maybe tomorrow you could show me how you want them to be?"

Her head twisted quickly to one side, giving her the countenance of a raptor catching sight of prey. Something primal inside me trembled. I sensed that I had come a little too close to being snippy. The smooth skin of her cheek twitched, and I realized that she was running her tongue along the inside her mouth, gathering the sour taste of restraint. There was something she wanted to say to me so badly right now, but once again, she couldn't.

We were locked in a battle, and I didn't even know why we were fighting. We were supposed to be on the same team.

"I have no time to worry about the rooms or shuttling deliveries to their proper departments. This is why I have *you* and Stevie, now *isn't* it? As Stevie is in charge of the delivery area, I've left this *small* job of organizing the basement area in your hands. However, if this is *problematic* for you . . ."

"It's not." I backpedaled like a Tour de France contestant about to go over a cliff.

"Then I will see you tomorrow at the same time, won't I?"

"I . . . umm . . . I have classes tomorrow morning." I loathed saying it, and I'd been avoiding the issue all day. I'd applied for a position as a part-time student intern. We hadn't really discussed that at either of our rushed ten-minute interviews, but surely she knew that I still had classes to finish this spring. The money from this summer job would be just enough to get me through another semester of school. I definitely couldn't afford to forfeit the courses I'd already paid for this term.

"I see." Again, she sucked in her cheeks, her

nostrils flaring slightly. "Well then, I will see you at what time?"

I quickly calculated how many minutes it would take me to get from class to my car, down to the Berman Theater area, into the parking garage, and to the basement of the building, including the two-minute stop at the front security check, where I was required to have my purse searched for camera equipment and leave my cell phone in lockup. This place was like Fort Knox already. I could only imagine how it would be once the production actually started. "I can get here by 11:35. Maybe 11:38 if there's traffic."

Her lashes lowered, shaping her eyes into blue half-moons. "Let's hope there is no traffic."

With that, my first day of work was over. I gathered my purse, reclaimed my cell phone from the guard at the front door, and limped out onto the street, gulping in fresh air like a tourist who'd been stuck in a high-rise elevator all day.

I hadn't made it five steps when the phone rang. Kim was on the other end. She was talking before I could get the thing to my mouth and speak into it. "Oh my gosh, it's about time you finally came out! I've been waiting forever. Did you see the cowboys?"

My mind stuttered slightly, processing the barrage of information. I was still mentally cycling and recycling the end of my day with Tova—rewriting it into a scene in which one of two things happened. In the first scenario, Tova found the basement rooms acceptable and was impressed with all my hard work, as well as my resourcefulness. In the second scenario, Tova aired her complaints to *him,* whoever *he* was, and by tomorrow, I didn't have a job.

"Allie, can you hear me?" Kim demanded. "My gosh, you look like a wreck. What did they do to you in there?"

My hand went to my hair. "What . . . Where are you?"

"I'm across the street. I was down this way anyhow, so I thought we could grab some dinner. I didn't know you'd be in there until after eight o'clock, though. I was about to give up."

I peered toward the little hole-in-the-wall Italian place nearby, and there she was, standing in the window waving wildly.

A rush of friend love filled me. Aside from Grandma Rita, there had never been anyone in my life who liked me just the way I was—quirks and all. Despite the lurking presence of Tova Kask, Kim and I were going to have the adventure of a lifetime this summer . . . if she landed a spot in the cast. I'd almost forgotten that today was her big day—the final decisions were being made. No wonder she'd been waiting for me to come out. She was probably about to explode.

When I stepped into the restaurant, she already had the waiter on his way over with a warmed-over half plate of spaghetti. She slid a Dr Pepper across the table along with the Parmesan. "You're lucky there's any left. It's really good, but I only ate half. I need to lose weight. Seriously."

Dropping my backpack, I collapsed into the seat and grabbed a piece of garlic bread all in one motion. "Holy cow, I'm starving. I think I died an hour ago." I stretched an arm across the table. "Pinch me so I can check, okay? I might be passed out in the theater basement, and this bread is nothing more than a really good dream."

Kim swatted my hand away. "You're so weird."

"You don't know what it's like down there in the basement. You can't *imagine* what it's like." I couldn't wait to tell Kim all about my day, about the sound and lighting equipment being delivered, and the five-thread sergers for wardrobing and the old treadle machine that was just like Grandma Rita's.

She grabbed a napkin and handed it to me. "Wipe that stuff off your chin. You look like old Tom Ball." Tom Ball had owned the store next to Grandma Rita's place. Nice guy, terrible table manners. All you had to do to find out the daily special at the café was take a look at Tom Ball's shirt.

"Thanks a lot." I laughed, the stress melting away.

Kim's lips pursed and her nose crinkled. "So, aren't you *ever* gonna ask if I got on the cast . . .

or should I say . . . in what *way* I got on the cast?"

"Sorry. There's no glucose left in my brain. So . . . wait . . . did you say . . . what . . . You're in? They told you? Is it final?" Kim seemed mildly excited, but not ecstatic. I wondered what that meant. Maybe her friend with the connections hadn't hooked her up as well as she'd hoped.

She released her hair from a binder clip, and golden strands cascaded to her shoulders. "Well, I didn't get a named historical character, like I was hoping I would. I wanted to play somebody I could research and learn about. Someone who was in actual historical records of this mystery town they're basing the show on. I was thinking that once they finally give us some details, I could dig around in the library, visit genealogy sites, learn about my person's life. Really get into the character and become *her*."

Now I was confused. "But if it's all supposed to be historically accurate, how can they just add people?" More than once today I'd heard team members on the phone ranting about how the structures, props, and fabrics had to fit the time period to the finest detail. Set design and costuming couldn't use anything with synthetic fibers or press-bonded details, whether it would be visible on camera or not.

The research assistants were digging like crazy. Makeshift desks were already strewn with photographs featuring groups of men posed around

51

old wagons, pictures of women in long gowns, an old tintype of immigrant masons building the high rock walls of a house, and a picture of a family standing beside an oxcart filled with belongings. I'd slowed down on my way through different rooms and looked at the photos, trying to imagine the everyday lives of those long-ago people.

"They explained it all." Kim sighed. "It's not like they can just pick up the Yellow Pages and *see* who was in the town. Records were sketchy back then, and in a boomtown, it was even more that way. A lot of folks came and went, and there's no surviving record of them. We *know* they were there, because of the businesses in the community, but they don't know exactly *who* the people were. You are looking at Bath and Laundry House Girl Number Three."

"Oh, Kim, come on." I almost choked on a sip of my soda. "This is supposed to be a semi-serious docudrama, not an episode of *Gunsmoke*. Did they hire Miss Kitty too?"

Kim blinked at me once, then again, then a third time—her attempt to convey that she did not appreciate my humor. "I wish I were kidding, but I'm not. Saloons, bathhouses, and laundries were part of the town. They liked me for the part because I look really young, and German. A lot of the girls in saloons and bathhouses back in those days were like thirteen, fourteen, fifteen years old. Which makes me really sad, when I think about it. When girls got to be that age, if their families kicked them out or moved away or couldn't provide for them anymore, the girls either got married or found some way to support themselves. They had to."

Her gaze drifted out the window. "So picture this: There I am standing in this room at yet another callback, and there are seven people behind the table, and I don't know who they all are, but they're having this discussion about me like I'm not even there. Then, at one end of the table, a guy points out that maybe I'm too fat. He asks me, right *in front of everybody,* what size I am. To my total and complete mortification, he goes on to guess about a size sixteen—which is *bigger* than I actually am. By this time, I don't care if I get a job or not. I just want to crawl off in a hole somewhere and go belly-up. Maybe this kind of stuff is pretty typical in Hollywood, but I'm not used to having people analyze me right *in front* of me. I thought the next thing they were going to do was ask to look at my teeth. I was so glad when it was over and they let me go back out to the hall. I almost just left."

"Oh, Kim . . ." Suddenly, I wanted to rush the doors of the Berman and thump some heads. How dare they!

Sighing, she rested her chin on her hand. "And then a few more people came and went from the

53

room. All girls about my age. There we are, trying to figure out who's the prettiest and who's the skinniest. It wasn't too long before they called me into there again and explained to me about the part. Then they handed me a packet of information for Bathhouse and Laundry Girl Number Three, including the schedule for costume fittings, legal meetings, and cast meetings. Then I had a pre-liminary legal debriefing where they threatened me with my life if I leak any details about the show. There's also a massive health question-naire to make sure I'm not likely to drop dead out there in the boonies, and then they sent me on my way. I tried to hang around and find you, but a security guy nabbed me and said I should check my packet for my *designated times* to report downstairs. I tried to chat him up, but even my considerable folksy charms had no effect on him. I know you find that hard to believe, but it's true."

She pushed her empty glass to the edge of the table, so the waitress could pick it up. "How was your first day as a great big production assistant?"

"Scary." It was the best way I could think of to describe it. "I'm telling you, Tova Kask neither eats, nor takes coffee breaks. She hates me and wishes I weren't there, but other than *that,* there were some really neat things about the day. . . ."

Chapter 5

Allie Kirkland
March, Present Day

Work. Day four. Complete insanity.

When I arrived at 11:42 after morning classes as usual, the corridor outside the costuming rooms was piled with boxes of fabrics, ribbons and notions, fasteners, vintage buttons, hats, gloves, shoes, and accessories.

"What do you mean by telling me the costuming crew cannot report here until April *ninth?*" Tova's voice echoed down the hall. "They must take charge of their area now! How am I to accomplish anything when he has saddled me with a part-time, *untrained* college girl and a full-time *ninny* at the loading dock, as well as costuming personnel who will not report for *two weeks?* And now this edict to hire pre-production help locally? Where am I to find *qualified* people in this *backwash* of a town? I need underlings who know what they are doing. I haven't time to nurse-maid them. I have already been given one of his *pets* to look after, and now *this?* It is impossible even for *me!*"

The slipknot in my stomach yanked tight. I considered running the other way, but there was a man waiting with a large crate down there. He gave me a look that said, *Lady, I've got a wife and kids to support, and I need this job. Please don't make me go in there and ask where she wants this.*

I skirted Tova's door and met the deliveryman at the end of the hall. Neither rain, nor snow, nor sleet, nor a tyrannical boss was going to rob me of the opportunity this summer could provide. Strange though it may be, this was my dream.

I routed the delivery, then went back to Tova's office to make sure she knew I had arrived on time and started work. Dread circled as I walked in the door.

Tova had just finished her call, but she was still clutching the cell phone, trying to strangle the life out of it. "It is eleven *fifty-eight*."

I thumbed over my shoulder toward the other rooms. "The installer was in the hall with the CAD system and the pattern plotter for costuming. I figured he was waiting for you, but I didn't know how long you'd be, so I took care of it. I hope that's okay."

Despite the fact that her cheeks were red with emotion, she looked fresh as a daisy . . . or a pitcher plant—something attractive to look at, but deadly. "Please, do check with me when you wander in, so I can help you to prioritize your tasks." Standing up, she dropped the cell phone into a suitcase-sized Coach bag before slinging it over her shoulder.

"I'll be sure to do that in the future."

She began gathering notebooks. I hesitated, unsure if I had been dismissed or if I should wait to be insulted some more. The office looked like a storm had blown through. Where in the world had all the new stuff come from?

She looked up suddenly, the way people do when they realize innately that you've been analyzing.

"Is there a purpose in your hovering there, Allison?" As far as I could remember, it was the first time she'd addressed me by name since the interview.

"I was just wondering . . ." *If you have a pulse.* "Should I go back and help the installer, work on the costuming rooms, or help with routing the backlog at the loading dock? It looks like Stevie's got more than he can handle. There's stuff piled at the end of the hall." I'd already noticed that Stevie, the full-time production assistant, spent as much time upstairs as he could. "Or is there something else you want me to do?"

"Yes, that will be fine." She returned to her notebook, dismissing me. "I will be leaving shortly for our first team meeting at the airport Hilton. The principals are flying in, and our time is limited." Her fingers trembled as she sought the opening on a plastic sleeve, then gave up and stuffed loose papers into the binder. "Just try not to screw anything up, Allison.

That will be enough of a task, now, won't it?"

"I'll do my best to manage." The smackdown smarted, but it was my own fault for walking in like a little lamb once again, hoping to make friends.

A glance at her watch seemed to heighten her frustration. "Take care of the costuming rooms, and I want to see the loading dock deliveries in order when I return."

She whooshed past me, leaving me alone to contemplate that last request. *Ohhh-kay. Yes, and while I'm at it, let me realign the earth's axis, conquer world hunger, and come up with a detailed analysis on that global warming thing too.*

"Oh, man," I muttered as I walked back down the hall to look for Stevie. With Tova gone, the atmosphere in the basement was considerably brighter, but the loading dock was worse than I'd ever seen it, and Stevie was nowhere to be found. A quick junket through the building clued me in to the fact that he'd officially turned in his badge at the theater office and walked out the door an hour ago, muttering expletives. The loading area was a mess for a reason.

"Okay, okay, just chill." Leaning against a crate tacked together from multicolored recycled wood, I pulled in a breath. "It's just a job. Think it through a step at a time." My college counselor's advice punctuated the dialog in my mind:

Organization and analysis prevents paralysis.

"You can figure this out . . ." On the side of the crate, a set of roughly carved numbers caught my attention: *6-14-55*. I traced a finger across them, a sense of wonder sprinkling over me, washing away the silt of the day.

Grandma Rita had always promised that life was filled with divine appointments, if you looked for them.

June 14, 1955, was my father's birthday.

For a moment I imagined that this bit of lumber had been salvaged from the old school in nearby Buna, Texas—that my father had carved these numbers himself, probably while his mind was drifting off, spinning a story. Just like mine.

He'd be so happy I was here this summer, even if I was just a small part of a big project. In my mind, he leaned close to my ear and whispered the same thing he had years ago when he'd placed me on a stool behind the camera: *You can do it, Allie. You can do anything you set your mind to. Never be afraid to try. . . .*

The tension ebbed as I sorted, pushed, pulled, and scooted containers into groupings by department, then decided to take some invoices upstairs to the guys with the dollies.

A noise from the other side of the loading area stopped me just as I was rounding the corner. Footsteps. That half of the building was completely unused, yet the steps were undeniable, slow and measured. The kind made by long legs in no hurry. A man's boots.

That strange sensation slid over me—the one I'd had the first time I walked into the Berman Theater. Heebie-jeebies rattled my shoulders, shaking loose a couple of invoices. They seesawed gently to the floor, the paper crinkling amid the echo. A sound I understood against one I didn't. The footsteps seemed to flit off the arched ceilings and come from everywhere. I walked a few paces to the left, and the noise vanished. Then it returned, originating from the vicinity of the costuming rooms. In the opposite direction.

No one could move from one end of the building to the other that quickly. . . .

Gooseflesh prickled, and I wondered about all the people who may have come and gone from this theater in its lifetime. The place had probably been here since the days of speakeasies. What was its history? What things had it seen? What human dramas, both real and imagined, had seeped into these walls?

Were there hidden entrances? Secret passageways?

My mind went wild imagining.

A chill crept up my back. I wished Stevie were here, or Tova. Even ghosts would be afraid of Tova.

Not that I believed in ghosts. I didn't. At all.

The footsteps changed sides again, returning to the unused corridor, seeming to travel toward an old storage area filled with theater props, gray with dust and draped with lacy spider webs.

I tiptoed closer, stopping near the corridor's entrance, the invoices clutched to my chest.

"Hello? Is someone down here?"

The walking stopped, but no one answered.

"Can I help you?"

No answer. More noises, behind me this time, in the costuming hallway. I whipped around and looked. No one. A door creaked open, then slammed shut. That was *not* my imagination.

A man murmured, the sound passing overhead like smoke, seeming real at first, then fading into what could've been only pipes groaning.

I had three choices—pursue, ignore, or make a run for the stairwell and the security guy in the box office. If he came down here and didn't find anything, I'd look like a nut. Word might get back to Tova. She *had* made the point in my initial interview that they weren't looking for people who were superstitious. No ghost hunters allowed.

And I wasn't one. I did *not* go in for that kind of thing. Not, not, *not*.

Old buildings do make noises. . . .

A shadow slipped past the doorway. At least I thought I saw something, but no one was there. The footsteps went silent.

The adrenaline of fight or flight surged through

my body. One final step, and I slid around the hallway corner. Nothing.

Closing my eyes, I let my head fall back as the air conditioner clicked on overhead, eclipsing any sound. *The ventilation system.* Of course. The building had probably always made these noises. Most of the time, the climate control units were chugging away constantly, but today the temperate weather had caused them to kick off. That could explain why I'd never heard . . .

"Pardon me, ma'am?" The voice struck a reflex point. My hands flew up, I spun around, and invoices went everywhere.

With the lights behind him, all I could see was his outline. Tall, slender, wearing a long-sleeved shirt, jeans, cowboy hat.

Real enough, thank goodness.

The lump of cotton in my throat wouldn't let me force out a sentence at first. Finally, I managed, ". . . help you?"

"Yes, ma'am." He was polite at least, which was always a good sign, in terms of unidentified intruders. "I'm looking for the costuming department. Need to drop off some papers real quick." He emphasized the words *real quick* and offered up a couple of half-folded sheets. "Where do these go?"

A strange vibe rolled off him as he came closer. Maybe it was the body language or just the fact that the cowboy hat shadowed his face, but he seemed nervous about being there, which made me nervous.

"Are you bringing in a delivery?" He didn't look like any deliveryman I'd ever seen, and he hadn't buzzed at the dock door. How had he gotten in?

"Just these papers."

"What are they for?" I didn't move closer. My life had just flashed before my eyes, and now all of a sudden, here was this guy, mysteriously able to enter the basement, and not wearing a crew badge? Security wouldn't even let Kim come down here.

Maybe he was an interloper of some sort, snooping for information. There was a reason for all the confidentiality agreements I'd had to sign for this job—the production company didn't want curiosity seekers and rubberneckers discovering the location of the reenactment set, which was being constructed, even now, somewhere in the hills of central Texas.

The stranger stepped into the orb of yellow light cast by the sconce overhead, and my thoughts hitched momentarily.

He was a really . . . good-looking . . . cowboy interloper. Kim would've loved him. Tanned skin, medium-brown hair neatly trimmed around the ears and collar, hazel eyes that were goldish in the centers, a strong chin with just a hint of a cleft in it. Right now it needed a shave. White cotton shirt, freshly pressed, and his jeans had the long, narrow lines down the front that indicate a man who has his dungarees starched at the cleaners—something I had learned about while working with Grandma Rita. Cowboys take their go-to-meetin' jeans seriously.

This had to be one of the guys Kim was talking about . . . dreaming about . . . obsessing about. One of the reasons she was dying to spend the next few months in the wilderness. His gaze darted toward the ceiling, then sideways to each wall, as if the place had him spooked too. There was a fine sheen of sweat over his skin, and under the tan, his cheeks were flushed. I hadn't noticed that at first.

"They told me to bring these down here." He turned from polite to impatient in the blink of an eye. "Listen, I've gotta go."

I took the papers, looked at them. Nothing more than a couple sheets torn off a yellow pad, wrapped around a postcard. The postcard was from a tuxedo shop, and it had tailoring measurements on it.

Was he here . . . trying to apply for a position in the cast? With two sheets of notepaper and the sizing card from his last tuxedo rental? Maybe he was in the wrong building altogether and thought this was . . . a bridal shop or something? Maybe he was supposed to be in someone's wedding . . . maybe even his own. Lucky bride. But he had mentioned costuming. "Ummm . . .

the main office is upstairs, they can help . . ."

He shook his head, slid his fingers into his pockets, and shifted his weight from one foot to the other, his cowboy boot scuffing along the floor. "Everything's there. How tall, how wide, all that stuff you people asked for. In case you need more, that card is from one of those wedding rental places. Hasn't been all that long ago. Information should still be good. That oughta be enough."

"Enough for what?"

He angled his body toward the stairway door. "Making some kind of clothes, I guess. They told me to bring that thing down here before I left. That's all I know." He looked up and down the hall, took a backward step. "What's the quickest way out of this place?" His boot heel landed on one of the invoices. He didn't even seem to notice.

"Hang on a minute. I don't know anything about this." If I let some guy walk in here and hand me measurements on a slip of paper, Tova would kill me, and then she'd fire my dead body. She was already beyond irked at the costuming crew, whoever they were, and now I'd have to tell her that her full-time assistant had walked out this morning.

"I'm not sure who sent you down here, but the costume shop isn't operational, and won't be for a while yet. They haven't even come on staff. My boss will be back later today if you want to wait. . . ."

The sentence was still dangling half-finished when he turned on his heel, slipped on an invoice, then caught his balance and retreated up the hall as fast as he could go.

"Wait a minute!" I called after him, but he just disappeared around the corner without looking back.

I was left with no choice but to put his strange delivery on Tova's desk and hope she didn't blame me for it. Since I knew she probably would, I hurried upstairs, found the guys with the dollies, and went to work frantically trying to make some headway with the pileup Stevie had left behind.

Hours later, when Tova reemerged from her meeting across town, I had managed what felt like impressive progress on both the loading area and the costuming rooms, considering the monumental nature of the task. I'd been so busy, I hadn't even realized it was almost eight o'clock again. Given Tova's devotion to duty and the fact that casting had been working nearly around the clock, I didn't suppose that would impress any-body all that much.

Tova stopped at the costuming room door. "Why do I still see things in the hallway, Allison?" Her hands settled on her hips, her elbows jutting out sharply.

I motioned to the piles of fabrics, rented costumes, notions, trims, and accessories presumably ordered by the yet-to-arrive designers.

"We've had so many deliveries today, especially for costuming."

Her lips squeezed together. "And this is taking so long because . . ."

"I've been routing all the deliveries *and* trying to work in here. You told me to—"

"It is not your job to route the deliveries. I asked you to assist Stevie and then ensure that these rooms are fully organized so that when *qualified* persons *finally* arrive, they can go to work promptly. Their time is valuable. Do you understand that?"

"Yes, ma'am, of course. But Stevie . . ."

"Don't *think,* Allison. Just do your job. And do not call me *ma'am.* Ma'am is for hillbillies and bellhops. I would assume you are neither one. You may call me Ms. Kask."

She was studying the room now, her eyes acute. "What have you done in here?" The question was flat, no undertone giving indications as to her meaning. I chose to assume that she was pleased with what she saw and quickly began showing off my organizational system, beginning with the cardboard barrels I had found near the loading dock, dusted off, and stacked on their sides with the openings facing out, creating fairly convenient, and rather fantastically funky, shelving that worked well for fabrics on rolls. After that, I moved to a thread rack made from a strange multipronged rake-like thing I had found languishing in a closet. It was rusty and old, and just the kind of treasure I loved to repurpose. It gave the room a feeling of history and held forty-eight spools of thread.

Considering that I had little more to work with than the old industrial shelving that was built into the room, the place was practically a masterpiece. Thanks to all those years of helping Grandma Rita, I knew how to arrange an efficient workshop for garment alteration and production. I couldn't remember the last time I had labored so hard physically and mentally for this many hours all at one time—on anything.

Tova didn't comment immediately. Dared I hope that she was . . . impressed to the point of speechlessness? "And you've been finding these . . . shelves and whatnot where?"

"In the warehouse by the loading dock."

"And how did you bring these things up here, might I ask?"

"I just . . . carried them." I sensed a sudden darkness, a cloud slipping over the sun, chilling the air.

"Where are the bolt racks and the role racks, the spool holders and the adjustable shelving?"

"The . . . what?" I stammered. Maybe those things were in some box somewhere, and I had failed to locate and unpack them, thereby creating a bunch of unnecessary work.

Uh-oh . . .

"Is it not your job to arrange and outfit these rooms?"

"Yes, it is my job."

"Then why have you not ordered the necessary hardware to do so?"

"What? I didn't . . . realize I . . ."

"I was under the *impression* that you knew how to do this job. I think you gave me the impression yourself, as a matter of fact, when I interviewed you." Her hands found her hips again, her fingernails sinking into the fabric of her skirt. "This is *not* university theater, the community playhouse, or the kindergarten Christmas spectacular, Allison. This is a production with a multi-million-dollar budget. Do you really think we drag supplies out of the trash heap to organize ourselves?"

"Well, no, of course not. I . . ."

"Then if you needed equipment, why did you not send in a requisition for it?"

Because asking you anything is like conferencing with Attila the Hun, and by the way, Stevie quit. I wanted to say it so bad, I could almost taste the words . . . almost. Instead, I tasted the salty sting of tears. I had worked so hard in these rooms, and all I'd managed to do was screw up again. I could hear my stepfather in my head: *For heaven's sake, Allie, don't you ever think?* "I'm sorry."

"Don't apologize, Allison. Just take care of it.

Rent or buy what is needed to properly equip the room before the costuming crew arrives. We will also need pressers, steamers, and so forth. With your experience in dry cleaning, I assume you know about these things."

"Yes. No problem."

"Any other questions?"

"No. None. I can handle it." I swallowed the beach ball in my throat. "Stevie quit this morning."

She didn't even flinch. "There are twenty more waiting for the opportunity. He'll be replaced by tomorrow." She wagged one perfectly manicured red fingernail toward my repurposed thread holder. "Leave that. I like it."

And then she was gone.

I scurried to the computer table to grab a piece of printer paper and begin making a list of the supplies and equipment I was supposed to requisition. There was so much to do.

I'd barely had time to start before she was headed my way again. When she turned the corner, she was holding the yellow paper with the cowboy's measurements on it, and she did not look happy.

"What, might I ask, is *this*?"

Chapter 6

Bonnie Rose
March 1861

In sleeping, I travel back. I'm drifting, same as the dead leaves on the river passin' along the white hull of the *New Ila*. The leaves turn in the foam of her stern wheel, trapped before they're spit out to drift down the river, not knowing where they're headed.

My dreams churn as well. I see Ma and Da. They're tilling the garden, and Ma, she's looking up and smilin' at me. Then she turns away, and it's the baby she hears. She's left him in the house, no doubt. Then, she's gone back to working as if she didn't hear the wee one at all.

I walk then, and it's the Indian camp all around me. I hear the cries, and I'm wondering if it's my babe, the tiny girl torn from my body and taken from me in this cursed place. There's not a soul will tell what's been done with her.

I find only emptiness in lodge after lodge. And then I spy a babe inside one, hanging in her cradleboard, all wrapped up safe and warm. I want to take her down and loose the rawhide ties to see if there's a strawberry mark on her leg. It's all I know of her, the birthmark.

A loud sound comes then, and I'm pulled awake. The sun shines in my eye. I hear the chuggin' of the *New Ila*'s engine, and the breeze dances by, carrying the smoke of her stacks. All around, the crew is scramblin'. They've brought us up to a landing to take on cordwood again. It's cut and stacked by farmers along the riverbank, always left at the ready.

The landing is on the opposite side of the boat, and I don't go to watch it. The takin' on and dischargin' of cargo and wood is a troublesome matter. Done by Negro roustabouts, it's difficult and burdensome work. The first mate is a disagreeable man, with the temperament to strike the slaves as they struggle at navigating the gangplank bearing their heavy loads. I've not been party to much of slave owning and its ills in my years, but here there's no avoiding it. With this conflict growing between the states, there will soon enough be no avoidin' it in any place, I fear.

It's all the talk among the passengers—the owning and working of slaves. There've been troubles in the dining room over it, those having first-class passage on the boat bein' on both sides of the slavery question. Upon the deck, the immigrant folk fare not much better than the slaves on this river journey, but they can be cruel as all the rest.

For my part, I can't be watchin' it. When I do, the scars burn against my skin. I know what it is

72

to be deprived of my liberty, to be beaten and shamed and made less than human.

Maggie May hangs over the railing on the river side of the boat. She's down the way near a stack of grain sacks piled under a canvas. The *New Ila* is traveling heavy-laden, carrying almost four hundred tons, her captain, James Engle, tells us. The deck is packed with household goods and supplies for farming, as well as immigrant folk themselves. They haven't staterooms, such as the one Maggie May and I have been kindly given. It's surprisin' to me, this fine treatment of us, but I'm grateful for it. I've even managed to gain a little pot of soil in which to root Ma's roses.

I've kept up our clothes as best I can, and I'm thankful that no one seems to know us here, but the confinement on the boat is a struggle for Maggie May. I hurry down the rail to her now.

"Mind your skirt, Maggie May!" I say. She's bent so far over the rail, her dress has blown up and under her petticoats her pantalets show. She's kicked off the shoes that are too small and pulled off her stockings, and hooked her feet over the rail to climb higher. It's a spectacle the fine ladies in the dining room would be turning their noses at, if they saw it, though they seldom come on the low deck when the ship is landin'.

Thank the Lord they cannot see my young sister this minute. "Maggie May! Down from there this instant. Are you hearing me?" I glimpse the captain up in the captain's house then, and I am reminded of my elocution lessons with the good reverend's wife. I must be certain I'm speaking properly at all times.

"Horses!" Maggie points, and I run to her and grab her skirt to be sure she doesn't tumble off into the water.

"Come down now," I say, but her mind has fled to the riverbank. There's a herd of horses come down to water. Wild ones, from the look of them. They've hidden in the thicket. They snort and paw, wide-eyed, wishing to return to the water. Along the shore, one of their young lies mired in the mud. A little bay with a stripe on its face. It calls to its ma.

I feel a sickening inside me. The foal has struggled for some time. Its slick brown coat lies streaked with mud, sweat, and foam. "There's naught we can do for it now," I whisper to Maggie and wrap my arms around to pull her down. "Come and put your stockin's on. What if Mrs. Harrington were to see?"

Mrs. Harrington watches us in the dining room at night. Asks questions. She's wondering about Maggie and me. She's wondering how the likes of us can go first class, for one thing. She's wondering also at the captain's constant attention to us. I'd be wonderin' myself, but this ship and the slaves and much of what's carried on board belongs to the selfsame man who has hired me to Wildwood. Mr. Delevan's riches are beyond my imagining. I've no way of knowin' what to make of our treatment so far.

Maggie May fights to wiggle free as I bring her down to cover her legs. She'd rather let them go bare. There's a wildness in the girl, like the horses on shore, and I fear it will never be gone from her.

"You'll be stopping this now, Maggie May! Do you hear me?" I drop the stockings and grab her shoulders, shaking her hard. "You'll not be behaving this way." My voice comes in a hiss. So much venom, it surprises me. The days are difficult on board *New Ila*, as she labors her way upstream with the shoals rubbing her belly, her hull scarce able to move around logjams that could split her open and sink us all. The evenings are no easier, trapped in the dining room with the fine folk and the captain. Given my choice, I'd have traveled with my own kind. But even they are no longer my kind. The immigrant folk look at me as if I'm a creature crawled from beneath the boat, pretending to be the queen.

I have no *kind* here, but for my sister. And even a bit of her lives in another place.

"Is there trouble, Miss Rose?" The captain stands over my shoulder now. I feel the blocking of the sun before I turn to look his way. And there I am, standing with Maggie's bare foot in my hands.

"No, sir," I say and roughly pull stockings

over her skin. I give her a wicked look. I've had enough, and I want her to know it. "She's spied the horses on shore. There's a foal bogged in the mud. She loves animals, this one. Horses especially."

Maggie shakes her head as I'm saying it, her eyes wide. She doesn't want the captain to take notice of the animal. Twice, we've come along stray cattle mired down and left behind by drovers. The boat paused long enough for the men to put the animals out of their misery and bring back fresh meat for our tables.

"Maggie, it will only suffer," I say to her. She can't be making a spectacle with the captain so near. We mustn't take the chance, much as my heart hurts for the poor bogged creature. I love the horses as my da did, but there's nothing to be done for this one.

The captain moves to the railing, braces his hands, and looks over. I manage to secure Maggie May's shoes before I free her.

I turn, and the captain cuts a fine figure there. He is a bull of a man—Norwegian, with broad shoulders and a thick head of straw-colored hair. He seems a decent type, which gives me hope for my eventual destination and the man who employs the captain as well as myself. Would a good riverman devote his life to the employ of one who's unworthy?

Maggie finds the rail again, her boots slipping

on the wooden rungs, the breeze lifting her skirt. She leans too far once again, and the captain clamps a big hand over her arm.

"Be easy there, Maggie May Rose." He has greater patience with Maggie than I can muster these days. But life on this boat is normal to him. He has no secrets to keep. "Will you dive in there and rescue him yourself?"

"Don't shoot him," she pleads.

"Maggie May!" I scold. "The captain has a boat and passengers to see to. He cannot be worrying about . . ."

The captain turns to me then, his eyes the bright blue of the sky behind him. "It is one of God's creations, Miss Rose." He searches me, but for what I cannot say. "And a helpless one, at that. We are to aid the helpless, are we not?"

I sense that he may be talking, instead, about me. I wonder what he would say if he knew all of my story, but I won't be telling it. "Yes, of course that is so."

He lifts my sister down then and sets her at my feet in the gentlest of ways. "Mind you, stay away from the railing, though. Or we'll be rescuing you *and* the foal." Then he strides away, and in short order three slaves have been removed from their duties loading cordwood and sent off in a skiff to see after the foal.

Of those in the skiff, one of the slaves is the man called Big Nebenezer. In size and strength, he is equal to two men. I imagine that the first mate, Mr. Grazide, isn't pleased to have Big Neb and the others gone from their task. I'm hoping he won't learn that Maggie was the cause of it. The first mate is a rough fellow. He dislikes the look of Maggie May and me, and he loathes the captain's attentions to us, that is plain enough. It matters none that it's not my doing. If it were my way, we'd have no attentions here at all. I want only to be left alone to scratch out whatever life we can manage. I know that no respectable man will look my way with any decent sort of intention, not once he learns of my shame.

No sense in fighting what is, Bonnie Rose, Da told me in Ireland when the horses were gone and the house was taken, and there was nothing left to do but go. *Best is to accept your lot, then get walkin' forward.*

The captain returns to the railing down the way now, but the first mate has come up, and there's an argument brewing. The first mate pulls his pocket watch up by its chain, and points to the time.

The captain puts the first mate in his place quickly enough. I can tell it without hearing the words. The first mate grips his fists behind his back, like he's wishing he could go to fisticuffs, but the captain stands a good head taller, and he is the authority on this boat. Such an act by the mate would be mutiny, and Mr. Grazide knows it. Finally, he turns away, but as he does, he gives a narrow look at me and then at Maggie May. He has discerned what's happened.

Fear creeps over me again.

Meeting my eyes, he adds a quick jerk of his chin, as if in his mind he's casting Maggie May off into the water. I know I can't be leaving her to wander the deck alone again. No more sleeping with both eyes closed. Whatever it may take, I must see us safely all the way to Wildwood.

Down below on the bank, the men have brought up the skiff near the mired foal. The horses skitter off into the trees, but a mare runs to and fro, nickering and stomping. She wants to fight for her babe, but she cannot do it.

One of the men tosses a rope over the foal's head from a bit away, as Big Neb wades in through the mud and water. He moves under the backside of the foal, bracing his shoulder down low. The men pull and Big Neb strains hard, letting out a cry that rents the air. Almost single-handedly, he pushes the foal out of the mud as the rest of them pull, and when it's over, the man, his clothes, and the horse are all the same color.

There's a cheer from the deck overhead, and I see that some of the passengers have come out to watch.

"Lovely! Just delightful!" A woman applauds as the foal trots off to its ma.

"Hear, hear!" seconds one of the gentlemen.

They've had a good afternoon's entertainment,

courtesy of Captain Engle. A little cheer for brightening up this slow, overburdened trip upriver.

The passengers are still glowing over it that evening at dinner, the ladies in their gowns and the gentlemen in their silk jackets and high starched collars. Amid all the color, Maggie May and I appear like poor relations.

Tonight much talk is given to the captain's kindness, but not a thing is said of Big Neb, whose strength and labor freed the foal.

"And what do you think, Miss Rose?" Mrs. Harrington addresses me now, calling attention my way, no doubt because she knows I do not want it.

Mrs. Harrington's grown son, Jeffrey, turns with an interested eye. There's not another young lady on the trip unescorted, and I fear he finds me of slight fascination. It is a fortunate thing his mother keeps him within an arm's length. I can only imagine the trouble it would be if he were to make advances. "Yes, tell us what you think, Miss Rose. Is it worth the time and the risk of three slaves to save the life of one scrappy wild pony? The stallion could have come out of the brush at any time and gone after the men."

It's surprising sometimes what the fine folk don't know about horses. Da was right—there's many a gentleman hasn't a thimbleful of sense about what pulls his carriage or stands beneath his saddle. "I'll wager the stud wouldn't go near the bog, sir. He's survived a good long while by knowing better."

Mrs. Harrington pats her collar and turns away at the mention of the stud. Such a word wouldn't be coming from her gentle mouth, I suppose. I turn my eyes to my plate, since I've given an answer.

But young Jeffrey hasn't finished with me yet. "So it is your opinion that it was worth the trouble to rescue the little scrapper from the mud?"

I fold my hands in my lap, hold them tight. "It is not my decision, sir."

"But if it *were?*"

I wonder what the talk was this afternoon among the gentlefolk—perhaps a debate as to the captain's wisdom regarding the foal. Doubtless, they saw the argument with the first mate. Tempers on the *New Ila* run high at this point.

The first mate has spoken not a word all through supper, but he's lookin' at me now. I feel that something has tumbled from bad to worse. We've an enemy here, and now this has rubbed him crossways.

I look up, and the captain is watching me through curious eyes, waiting for my answer to Jeffrey's question.

I straighten in my seat and say what is right to say. "It is one of God's creatures, sir. And God's creatures are meant for our kindness, surely as not. I do not suppose a kindness is ever wrong."

"Hear, hear!" Mr. Searcy, a gentle mill keeper, lifts his glass. "May we have the patience of Job, the strength of Samson, and the countenance of Solomon."

The others raise their glasses, and I do as well, but the sip of wine slips sour down my throat.

At the far end of the table, it is whiskey in the first mate's glass. But he does not drink of it.

Chapter 7

Allie Kirkland
April, Present Day

I saw the mystery cowboy again the day before the first big meeting of cast and crew was scheduled to happen at the Berman. On Tova's orders, I'd ventured out to do some errands. With the costuming personnel arriving next Monday, it was suddenly critical that there be a coffee machine, as well as various foodstuffs and a standing order for a deli tray to be delivered to the basement each day. Given the condensed time frame, there was concern as to whether the costume designers, stitchers, cutters, and fitters could accomplish the dressing of over seventy cast members in slightly under eight weeks.

My assigned mission for today was to finish equipping the basement with anything else needed to make it as self-contained and efficient as possible. Since that task brought me above ground, I was thrilled.

And then, suddenly, there was the mystery cowboy. Blake Fulton—I'd learned his name from the tuxedo rental card that was still taped to Tova's wall. I rediscovered him, of all places, in the little city grocery store just down the block from the Berman. He was at the deli counter, ordering salami on rye. My mind stumbled over itself, trying to place his voice when I heard it. Then I recognized something about the way he was standing.

The mystery man, in the flesh. Making sandwich selections. Go figure.

Slipping around a display of Granny Smiths, I listened in on his conversation. For the better part of two weeks now, the paper he'd given me hadn't been touched, and after being horsewhipped with the thing the day Tova found it, I wasn't about to mention it again. From time to time, she brought it up as a case in point—I was not to overstep my bounds and do anything that she had not *specifically* instructed me to do. In other words, I was not to think for myself . . . unless it was a case in which I was supposed to think for myself, such as the ordering of the fabric racks and shelving.

Now suddenly, here was the man. He liked mustard, lettuce, tomato, and a frightfully large helping of jalapeño slices on his salami sandwich. Yuck.

The girl behind the counter was flirting like crazy, and he was into it. Contrary to our encounter in the theater basement, today he seemed relaxed, friendly, and in no hurry. Right at home, even. The deli girl knew just how he took his coffee. "So how's the work going on the building?" She paused to deliver a *come hither* look as she put the lid on his cup and handed it over the deli case.

Building? I wondered. *What building?*

"Going fine," he answered amiably. "No problems with the rain."

The deli girl took a minute to clue in to the joke. The last few months had been mercilessly dry in Texas, especially considering that it was spring. She giggled. "You're funny."

He favored her with a dazzling smile, straight white teeth, twinkling hazel eyes, and then a little wink. The whole cowboy enchilada, so to speak.

"Just right," he said after tasting the coffee.

Bracing a hand on her waist and jutting her hips to one side, she struck a pose, getting her groove on as best a girl can in a hairnet and plastic gloves. "So which building did you say you were working on? The Berman, wasn't it? That's such a pretty old place. I'd love to go inside there."

The Berman? What? I stepped back so quickly

84

that a trio of apples rolled off the edge of the display and fell onto the floor.

Blake Fulton turned, saw me there, and registered surprise. I'll bet he was surprised.

"Funny you should mention the Berman." I picked up an apple and tried to put it back on the display, but it rolled back into my hands again. "Remember me?"

The deli girl shot a concerned look back and forth between us, but Blake Fulton quickly moved from surprised to flirtatious again. "How could I forget?" He graced me with one of the slightly off-center smiles that had been working so well across the sandwich counter, then he moved to the navel oranges, tested a few, and selected one for his lunch. "Orange?" He offered me one too.

What kind of game was he playing? There was *no* remodeling going on in the Berman. Surely he realized I was aware of that. One thing was for certain: He'd caused me no small bit of agony at work, and this time I wanted some answers. "You know, you got me in trouble with my boss. She thinks you either wandered in off the street, or I made you up. Anyway, she would love to meet you. She's got a few questions about those documents you gave me."

I imagined bringing the mysterious cowboy to Tova, thereby redeeming myself. "We could walk down there now. She's in the office."

"Did she call the number on the top sheet?"

"What number? There was no phone number."

He actually looked surprised. "I must've forgotten to write it on there." He was already reaching for his cell phone. "Hang on a minute. I'll get it for you."

"Get *what* for me?"

"The phone number for you to give to your boss, Allie." He looked at me when he said my name, his eyes bright in the neon glow of the deli lights. I was mesmerized for a moment before it occurred to me to wonder how he knew my name.

Then I realized I was still wearing my Razor Point Productions employee badge . . . with my name on it.

He tore a piece from his lunch sack and jotted a number on it. "Just have your boss call. They'll explain it." In one smooth movement, he retrieved his lunch and tried to hand me the scrap. No way was I falling for that trick again.

"I'll just let you give that to her yourself. You know what they say about shooting the messenger."

"Would if I could, but I've got a three o'clock flight to make." He flashed another *aren't I adorable* grin. "Sorry I got you in trouble. See you in eight weeks, Allie Kirkland."

Underneath all the obvious thoughts about this ridiculous cat-and-mouse game, there was another one—stealthy and slightly insidious, like an undertow. *He didn't even look at the badge again.*

He remembered my name. Some annoyingly girly part of me liked that.

Taking my hand, he put the paper in it, then folded my fingers over the top before he sauntered off, leaving me momentarily stunned. He'd almost made it out of the produce aisle before my mind kicked into gear, and I hurried after him.

Rushing around the seedless grapes, I headed him off at the pass, hemming him up against a giant box of Rio Grande watermelons. A brilliant maneuver. "Now *listen.*" I shook the paper with the phone number on it. "How stupid do you think I am? You just told that girl at the deli that you were doing renovations on the Berman building. And now you want me to deliver *yet another* message to my boss? No way, mister. Who are you really, and *what* is going on?"

His gaze tangled with mine, and I couldn't tell if he was irritated or just amused. He glanced at his watch. Then, as calmly as if he were opening the door and stepping onto the front porch, he settled his hands on my shoulders and gently moved me aside. We were suddenly in close quarters as he slipped through the space between me and the watermelons, leaning close as he did. "Take the number to your boss, Allie. Tell her to call it. It'll be all right."

I felt his breath on my ear, and a jolt of electricity traveled down my neck, sliding under my T-shirt and raising an unfamiliar prickle there.

Suddenly, there wasn't one intelligent sentence in my entire pea brain, so I just watched him stride to the cash registers, pay at the self-check, then head out the door.

He was way too big for me to tackle, anyway.

My iPhone rang as I was juggling packages on my way out the door. I grabbed the call without looking, thinking it might be Tova with more instructions for me. Instead, my mother was on the other end. "Allie, how are you, sweet? Your father and I were just going through the summer calendar." I felt the usual stab that came with the *your father* reference to Lloyd. Maybe it should've seemed natural after sixteen years, but it just never had been. Hard to say whether that was because the term had been forced on me before I was ready, or because my relationship with Lloyd was always more *miss* than *hit*. He just didn't like me very much and never had.

"Fine. Good." A knot formed in my stomach. I hadn't told them anything about my new job. Day after day, I'd convinced myself that, given the typical lifespan of downstairs production assistants in the Berman, I should wait a while to fight the family battle. Any given day, I could end up getting fired. "Working on wrapping up another semester."

"We're making summer schedules," Mom said. That explained the unusual midday call. "I'll be gone to Coronado Island with Whit, Ashley, and the grands the week of May 17, and Lloyd is scheduled to fly to Taiwan for merger talks with one of his clients. The twins have been invited to train at an invitation-only day camp with an Olympic-level coach. Their gymnastics team just swept the regionals. Emerson brought home gold in two events and Madison took the overall. The camp is an opportunity too important to miss. If they're seen by the right people, it could mean scholarships and . . . well, who knows."

"Sounds awesome." I had that sinking feeling that comes with realizing major family milestones have been reached and no one even bothered to share them with you. "Tell them congratulations for me, okay? Actually, never mind. I'll send a text."

"It's a little after the fact now." The answer was sharp, and I could only guess at the meaning . . . perhaps that I would've been there for all the family happenings if I hadn't chosen to run off to grad school in Texas.

"Guess so."

"I'm hoping you'll be home by that May 17 week, at least?" Mom got back to the point, and that explained the call, in a nutshell. Emerson and Madison weren't old enough to shuttle themselves to their invitation-only camp. They needed a driver while Mom and Lloyd were away.

I sat down on the bench in front of the store, let the grocery load rest beside me, and contemplated a homeless woman pushing her shopping cart down the sidewalk. Did she have a family somewhere? People she'd left behind because it seemed like every contact ended painfully?

"When is your flight?" Mom pressed. "I need to add it to the calendar. Lloyd says he'll just go ahead and put you on salary at the law office the week you're looking after the twins. Logan's going to the beach with me. He doesn't have soccer camp until the next week."

"So, I'm the nanny while you're gone? That's why you're in a hurry for me to get there?" I pressed my fingers to my mouth as soon as I said it. The little burst of venom burned, but I couldn't stop it. Over and over and over our conversations led to something poisonous.

"Don't be crass. You need the money, Allie, now that you've frittered away the little nest egg your grandmother left you. In truth, you'd have been better off if that money had never come along. We all have to grow up and settle into real life sooner or later. Lloyd and I are trying to help you."

"I'm not coming home this summer." There. I'd said it. It was out in the open. "I actually got a job on a project that's filming here in Texas. It's really exciting. We're re-creating a—"

"A job as what . . . a runner, a tech, a secretary, a production assistant? You forget that I do know this business, Allie. They take in young starry-eyed kids, work them to death, pay them almost nothing, and send them on their way when the project wraps. That's how it's done."

Tears welled and the street scene blurred. *Breathe, breathe, breathe.* "It's what I want to do. It's a starting place. Why are you always trying to make me into something I'm not? Why can't you just be happy for me, for once?"

Empty air dangled between us, an impenetrable curtain separating two points of view. I pictured Mom slowly growing red from the neck up. "It's a dead end, Allie. That's why I can't be happy about it. This . . . obsession of yours needs to stop. It isn't healthy. What happened to your father wasn't your fault, and you have to stop trying to atone for it by . . . by . . . becoming him."

"I'm becoming *me*." Why couldn't she understand? Why didn't she ever see it? "And the real problem is that Lloyd doesn't like *me* and he never has. I'm sorry I don't fit in, Mom. I'm sorry to be such a disappointment." I needed to just end the call before it got any worse. I knew I did, but I couldn't push the button. I couldn't stop hoping that, just this once, she'd say something more like Grandma Rita would have. *Run after your dreams while you're still young, Allie. You've got all your life to settle down and start making compromises.*

My mother's answer was a disgusted snort. "Don't be melodramatic, Allie. For heaven's sake, show some sense. Come home while there's a still a good job available for you here. You do realize that Lloyd is doing you a tremendous favor? That he has stuck his neck out with the partners . . . for *you?* Thirty thousand dollars a year with your kind of qualifications is nothing to sneeze at, and if you'll go back to school and *at least* get your paralegal . . ."

I couldn't think of anything more dismal than spending the rest of my life in Lloyd's office. "It's just . . . not what I want." My voice cracked, and even though I hated the weakness in it, I couldn't muster anything stronger. When would I ever get past the point of wanting her approval? Of begging for it and ending up wounded when it didn't happen? "I already committed to the job. I won't be coming home."

Chapter 8

Allie Kirkland
April, Present Day

By the evening of the big cast and crew meeting, I'd almost put the phone conversation with my mother out of my head . . . almost. It's amazing how much power your family has to either build you up or tear you down, to make you question everything about yourself.

"Don't let them do this to you," Kim said as I waited for her to unlock her pickup truck so we could drive to the Berman together. The meeting had been set for late Saturday evening, so as to accommodate people who were working day jobs until it was time to move to the set and begin the three weeks of pre-production training in cooking, livestock care, safety, and all things nineteenth century. "Don't let your mother rope you in with the guilt card."

"I'm not." But I was. And I knew it. And I couldn't stop it. My mother had managed to make me feel like I was ruining everyone's summer, as well as my own future.

"You're an adult, Allie. You have a right to your life, and just because you're not *like* them doesn't mean there's anything wrong with you." My best friend rolled a pointed look my way. "A black sheep is a black sheep, but he's a sheep too. And the Lord loves sheep, and the Lord loves you."

A puff of laughter pressed out. "Where did you come up with that one?"

"Vacation Bible School. Fifth grade. My teacher taught it to us. Guess who she was talking about?"

"I can't imagine."

Kim's expression turned serious as she settled her hands on the gearshift. "Don't back out on me this summer, Allie, and don't you quit on your-self, either. We need each other for this adven-ture. It all just hit me when I was signing the mega-pile of final documents. This isn't a joke. It's really gonna happen. They sat me in a room and made me read and initial every single paragraph, and believe me, it was down to the gory details. I could fall off a cliff, be run over by the livestock, set myself ablaze while I'm cooking over an open flame, have a heatstroke living with no air conditioning. . . . The list goes on and on and on. What if I get out there in the boonies and I'm not tough enough?"

A feather pillow popped in my chest, itchy and tickly all at once. I was a slim half inch from saying, *You know what, let's go for frozen yogurt and forget this whole thing.* "Come on, you're a country girl. Remember all the summers at Grandma Rita's, when you dragged me down to the creek to catch tadpoles and fish for those nasty old whiskery catfish, and we played *Little House on the Prairie* and stuff?" I tossed my purse onto the floor, and Kim caught a breath when it landed on something.

"Eeek. Don't mess up the periodicals. They're from the library, and they're *not* supposed to be checked out. Stewart brought them to me." Wide-eyed, she delicately covered her mouth with her fingertips. "He *broke* the rules. But don't tell anyone. I promised I would scan the articles over-night and have the stuff back to him first thing in the morning."

She rescued a couple books from the floor, holding them up so I could read the titles. *Frontier Texas at Work* and *Women of the West: Home-*

steaders, Harlots, Mothers, and Missionaries.

Under my toe was an old magazine with a cover article entitled, "The Texas Cowboy: Mystery and Mystique." I squinted. "You got Stewart to take things from the library that weren't supposed to leave the building?" Stewart was a stickler for rules of any kind. Obsessive-compulsive about it, actually. Around the apartment complex, he was always reporting infractions—from parking violations to trash bags left outside front doors overnight. He drove the apartment manager crazy.

"I begged," Kim admitted. "Nobody's gonna miss it tonight. Besides, it's good for Stewart to live on the wild side a little bit. He actually hid the contraband in a recycling cart and carried it down the back stairs while the other library clerk was taking her break."

Poor Stewart. He was probably holed up in his apartment nursing an ulcer and waiting for the library police to come after him by now. "You really think it's a good idea to be asking Stewart for special favors? He'll probably be awake all night, worrying about it."

"Don't be so dramatic." Kim snatched the magazine and moved everything to the back seat, where a pile of similar materials sat in a jumble.

"What's all that?" With Kim, you could never tell, and between finishing classes, my work at the Berman, and Kim's preproduction appointments, I'd barely seen her these last couple of weeks.

"It's research. And clues. I think I've figured it out. I know where the reenactment is going to take place, and what bit of *Mysterious History* we're reenacting. Wait until I tell you. You're going to totally flip out."

I had that queasy feeling that sometimes came from being privy to one of Kim's ideas. "Okay, you might as well spill, but I really think you should leave it alone. Remember that giant confidentiality agreement in that pile of paper-work you signed? They don't want anyone to know ahead of time where we're going. Cast members aren't even supposed to tell each other what frontier counterpart they've been given."

Kim rolled her eyes and huffed. "Don't be such a drone, Allie. So . . . I did get a few things out of the security guard the other day, and between that and what I *might* have overheard while I was in for my psych interviews, I've got it narrowed down. Based on my brilliantly gathered clues and my astounding powers of deduction—and the fact that the security guard let it slip that his uncle *in Cleburne* had been hired to bring horses for the docudrama, and they would be trailering *said horses* about *thirty minutes* from home—I know that we're going to be somewhere in this vicinity."

She snagged a photocopy from the pile in the back seat, laid it on the cup holder, and pointed to a portion of central Texas along a thin, winding river. "I also *might* have overheard mention of *a river* and *Moses Lake* here and there around the Berman during the health screenings and such. We know that this project centers on a boomtown that existed *before* the War Between the States. That narrows it down a bunch. There wasn't a whole lot in that part of Texas before the war. So then you have to think about what makes a boomtown. Back in those days, it was either shipping locations on a river or trailheads for settlers moving to the frontier . . . or the discovery of natural resources, like gold and silver."

Her fingernail scratched a slow circle on the map's surface, then stopped where the river emptied into Moses Lake. "Of course, this lake is man-made, so it wasn't there in the eighteen hundreds, but Stewart helped me identify a small boomtown that was here before the Civil War. There never was much gold fever in Texas, but it did happen a time or two around the Llano uplift region and farther north. One place was right here, where the river meets a little creek. It's gone now, but there was a town here called Wildwood."

I looked at the map and a cold sensation inched over me, raising goose bumps—the same feeling I'd had that first day in the Berman. Why did that name seem familiar? "Kim, we'd better go before we make ourselves late." Given Tova's mood when I'd left work a couple hours ago, I didn't want to do anything to make trouble for myself. "Besides, you were planning to get there ahead of time and scope out the guys, remember?"

Kim pitched the map into the back and proceeded to pilot us to the Berman via the shortest possible route, her attention suddenly focused on getting there in time to watch the rest of the talent walk in. When we arrived, though, the Berman was already half full. The crew-members had taken seats in front on the left, while the cast members were still milling around in the aisles, scoping each other out and pretending not to be comparing notes on the details they'd gathered so far. The level of secrecy and security maintained around the building had clearly led to some wild theories and no small amount of nervousness, especially for parents who were not only signing up themselves, but their children.

On the way in, Kim fluttered here and there like a honeybee, greeting people she'd met during her comings and goings from the Berman—in particular, the single men.

"Well, do you see him here?" She leaned close after sharing a quick greeting with the Wall family, who, I gathered, would be stepping into the docudrama as the owners of the dry goods store. Sometimes, it amazed me that Kim hadn't already gotten herself fired, with all her snooping.

"See *who* yet?" I scanned the crowd. The atmosphere was electric today, the air a storm of whispers.

"The mystery cowboy. The Blake Fulton guy

you told me about. I'm *dying* to get a look at him." Kim wheeled her hand as in, *Keep up with me here.* "If he doesn't show today, that tells the tale, I think. They said in no uncertain terms that anyone who didn't come to today's meeting would be replaced. They have a standby list a bazillion people long; I got that information from the lawyer when I signed my papers, by the way." She stood on her toes and glanced around. "So, do you see the scrap-of-paper guy anywhere?"

"Shhh!" I looked for my boss, who did not, repeat *not* need to be reminded that I'd delivered yet another mysterious message. "Tova hit the roof when I brought her that phone number yesterday. If she wasn't having so much trouble keeping help downstairs, she probably would've fired me on the spot. And if I never hear that name again, it'll be too soon."

"Oh, come on, where's your sense of mystery?" Kim's eyes sparkled with fascination. "I want to *see* this guy. I'm dying to know who he is and whether he's legit. What if he's a spy, like, from the tabloids or a competing network or something? All these big secrets have my mind going crazy. I couldn't even sleep last night."

"Me neither, hon!" A brightly dressed red-haired woman in jeans and cowboy boots stopped beside us. "I was on pins and needles, just as hoppy as a cricket on the woodstove, and Genie was up calling my house before the rooster." The woman smiled at her companion, a sweet, gray-haired lady who at first glance reminded me of Grandma Rita.

"I couldn't even close my eyes last night. Could ye-ew?" Genie's southern drawl stretched the last word, plucking a familiar twang.

"No, I couldn't," Kim answered, then leaned close to divulge the forbidden details she'd ferreted out. "Genie and Netta are the matronly sisters in the big house—the relatives of our town founder in the big mystery town."

Netta made the motion of bolting her lips and throwing away the key, then winked at her friend, who snorted and adjusted her glasses. "I hope that lock's triple-titanium, elsewise it don't have a prayer of lastin' long."

The two of them giggled as we made formal introductions. Watching them, I wondered if that would be Kim and me someday far in the future, laughing about this experience. I also wondered how two women in their senior years were going to survive all summer without air conditioning. In general, the cast members were younger, more in the twenty-to-forty range.

"Listen, I'd better get over there to my side." I shrugged toward the crew area, scoping out an empty seat. "It looks like they're about to start." On stage, a folding table had been set up with microphones and five chairs, as if this were a formal press op, but other than a guy standing by the side stairs with a flip cam, there were no cameras present.

The crowd hushed as five people emerged from the stage wings to take the seats—Rick Meyer, the associate producer Tova reported to, Cheryl Pierce, the location manager, Regan Willis, the electronics engineer whose job was to work with sound, lighting, and cinematography to make those things as nonintrusive as possible, Chevis Arteuro, the casting director, and Carson Clay, the lead historical expert.

The casting director took the microphone and welcomed attendees to the meeting. Chevis was a good-natured guy who spoke with an East Indian accent and a slight lisp that made him seem younger than he was. Even so, he was young to be in a key position, but unmistakably brilliant. "We stand at the brink of a most excellent adventure," he offered, a wide white smile reflecting in the theater lights. "Chances are, after traveling through the paperwork and the screenings, you feel as though you have surmounted the greatest test of will already. Some of you may have wondered, during the psychological interviews and the panel interviews, why you, in particular, were chosen? Why not another?"

A murmur of agreement from the cast seats answered Chevis's question.

"Or perhaps that thought was crossing your

mind when you received the final call. It would have been much easier, no doubt, for our crew to have shopped for the cast of this docudrama series among experienced reenactors, survival special-ists, or even farmers and ranchers accustomed to living very close to the land. While we have included some of these persons in the most excellent demographic of our cast, our directive was to create a sampling that does realistically represent the population of a frontier settlement of the American West, and in particular the town in question. Smaller docudrama miniseries projects have, in the past, reenacted the lives of individual pioneer families, and indeed we ourselves at *Mysterious History* have re-created the life of an entire English manor house, a Scottish castle, and the crew of a Viking ship. But nothing of this magnitude has ever been attempted, even by us."

Chevis paused to let that sink in. This time, there was no murmured response from the audience. Only silence and a sense of awe, or fear, or both. More than seventy people, traveling back into the shoes of our ancestors, for three months.

"We are, much like those we seek to re-create, pioneers." Chevis went on. "And much like those whose lives you will step into, you'll find yourself in foreign circumstances, forced to cultivate new skills, pressed to adapt in order to survive. This is our reason for choosing many of you who have no prior survival experience. We must typify those who, over a century and a half ago, sought their fortunes on the rugged frontier. Indeed, in casting this production, we have matched our participants as closely as possible to the backgrounds, physical statures, and known details of the inhabitants of the original town. You, my esteemed friends, will not only become that place. You already *are*."

A collective exhale went out as that knowledge seeped over the room. Suddenly, the plans for this summer became real to me. I'd known for weeks, as much as anyone at the lower levels did, the sketchy details of this thing we were attempting, but I'd been somewhat removed from it. Now, listening as Chevis went on to describe the set under construction—high tech in its abilities to record ongoing life in the town, yet by all appearances, a frontier settlement of 1861— I felt as if I were already there.

"With that, I would like to introduce you to the panel, allow each of them to speak of their particular areas of interaction with you, and then open the floor for questions. As you know, however, we will not be revealing the name of the settlement, nor the location until the ceremonial surrendering of the cell phones as we move to the set. Buses will transport the cast and crew. No communications devices will be permitted. All interaction with the outside world will be via the village post office, which will operate in a time frame most appropriate for the frontier of 1861."

Around me, hands went self-consciously to purses and pockets, which would have contained cell phones and electronic tablets, if they hadn't already been surrendered to security at the box office.

This summer would be like nothing we'd ever experienced. If Kim was nervous before we got to the Berman, she was probably scared to death now.

I turned around, scanned for her blond head, and found her trading cell phone numbers with the guy beside her. She probably hadn't heard a word Chevis said, and maybe that was a good thing. If she really contemplated all this, it could make for a very long weekend. Right now all I wanted to do was finish a project due in one of my classes and catch up on some sleep before it was time to head back to the Berman on Monday.

As usual, Monday came sooner than I wanted it to. I slept right through my first class, made the next two, then hustled off to the Berman. When I arrived, Tova was already in a meeting with what turned out to be the key players in the Costume Department—a tall, skinny guy with a gray ponytail and two women. They were dressed in a funky, casual style, and like most of the people in the departments upstairs, they looked . . . sort of . . . relaxed and fun, compared to Tova.

"This is Allison," Tova said blandly, motioning me in the door.

I lifted a few fingers and did a little wrist wave, still clutching my backpack, a box of refills for the Keurig coffee maker, and a bag full of cups, plates, and plastic utensils.

The introductions were quick. The guy with the gray ponytail was Randy, the costume designer, and the two women, Phyllis and Michelle, were his costume supervisors. All three were in their mid-forties, and they seemed friendly enough, which made me wonder if they worked with Tova very often.

Tova gave a backhanded wave in my direction, then turned her attention toward an abundance of sketches laid out on the desk. "Please feel free to use Allison in *any* way she can be of service to you. I've been told that your stitchers will be here in the morning. Our preproduction schedule is horrendously short, as you know, so I am once again asking you to do the impossible, which of course is nothing new. So, if you have personal matters you need to attend to and have not already done so, it would be best to wrap them up now."

Bracing her hands on the desk, she pushed to her feet, the wheeled office chair skittering backward and bumping into the wall. "I am due at a meeting with the accountants and the lawyers. Allison will show you around the building, make certain you know where to find the various departments, then take you to the space you've been allotted. No doubt, you will need to rearrange it to make the shop operate efficiently."

Crossing to the door, Tova glanced my way, seeming to relish the taste of the words. I had devoted every spare minute the last two weeks to making that space as close to perfect as was humanly possible, and she knew it. Now she'd just set everyone up to dislike it before they'd even seen it.

Don't say anything. Don't say anything. Don't react. My molars shifted like tectonic plates as she passed by. When she was gone, Randy, the costume designer, smiled at me. "Welcome to the jungle."

Phyllis and Michelle snickered, and I decided right away that I liked them.

Dumping the groceries, I took them on a tour of the building, introduced them around upstairs, then held my breath when we returned to the costuming rooms, now fully appointed with the latest in shelving, fabric and notion racks, the electronic pattern plotter, cutting tables, dress forms, and the endless bolts of muslin for making dummy garments. I had set up the sewing machines and equipment for the cutters, fitters, and stitchers in a second room.

A nervous little pulse thrummed under my skin as the three of them discussed the accommodations, the work ahead, and how they would set up production. Somewhere along the way, I began to clue in to the fact that they weren't talking about changing everything. They actually seemed happy with the arrangement just the way it was.

Finally, Randy braced his long, thin hands on the braided belt that seemed the only thing holding up his pants and turned a full 360, surveying the room one more time.

"This looks good." He smiled at me. "This looks very good. From what Tova said in the meeting, I expected much worse. Someone has put just a bit of time into this place."

"Just a bit," I admitted.

"It's a magnificent job." He surveyed the territory again. "Yes. This will work. We can do miracles here."

Somewhere in the distance, I heard angel song. Despite everything, I had gotten it right. Even better, there were now three people in the basement who were . . . nice to me. The road to my future suddenly seemed exponentially brighter. Maybe Tova was determined to squash me like a flea, but Randy, Phyllis, and Michelle were willing to give me a chance. That was all I needed. A chance to prove myself. A start.

Randy homed in on the Computer Aided Design system and the pattern plotter. "State of the art. Even *I* haven't worked with one this new."

"He can afford the best," Phyllis remarked.

"It's a pretty amazing machine," I admitted, suddenly feeling comfortable, as if this were my domain, and they had come in as guests. "The technician gave me a lesson while he was troubleshooting it."

Phyllis leaned over the plotting printer, her spiky hair casting an uneven shadow on the paper roll. "Well, that may come in handy, because Randy's known for botching the technology."

They bantered back and forth, and I gathered two things. They had been working together off and on for years, and they knew who was backing this production, but they weren't saying. *He can afford the best,* Phyllis had said. She was talking about the executive producer. Whether that was actually Rav Singh or not, it *was* someone big, and that was the reason these three people, who clearly had contacts all over the film industry, were here in Texas, in the shadowy basement of an old theater, working with Tova Kask.

Randy paused, looked at me, and scratched his stubbly chin. "What else does Tova have you doing around here . . . besides this, I mean?"

"A little bit of everything. Mostly managing invoices and helping to make sure the loading dock deliveries go to the proper departments." *Should I mention the three full-time downstairs production assistants that have come and gone already? Probably not.* "The deliveries have slowed down now, though."

"She did say we could make use of you in whatever way we want, right?"

"She did." At this point, I was up for almost anything, especially if it involved the new costume shop.

"Then I think we're going to steal you." He pulled a set of keys from his pocket. "There's a white Suburban down in the parking garage. In the back, you'll find a huge box of notebooks. Those are the costume diaries for our show participants. We've been working on them hodge-podge while finishing a film in Canada. Do you have any experience with historical research?"

A giddy feeling started somewhere near my big toe and fluttered upward, lightening my entire being. Costume diaries detailed everything about each character's wardrobe, from historical examples in old photographs to layer-by-layer descriptions. Fascinating stuff, and much higher level than what I'd been doing here so far. Upstairs, the historical experts and the Art Department were knee-deep in similar research for the props and building interiors on the set. "I do. I've worked on a lot of community and university theater projects."

"Perfect." Randy slipped the keys into my hand, and I closed my fingers over them. "Then you're our girl. We'll turn the costume diaries over to you. I'll let Tova know about it. Scamper off, now. We're on a timeline."

"I'm already gone." I was trying for dignified and professional, but I'd only made it a few steps out the door before a giddy squeal erupted and echoed down the corridor. *Today . . . notebooks. Tomorrow . . . hello, Hollywood. Here comes Allie Kirkland.*

I couldn't help thinking of my dad again. Maybe he'd started with a job just like this one. It would make sense that he had. For most people, the film business was about working your way in. I didn't really know my dad's trajectory, other than the fact that he was successful and people in the industry respected him. Being ten years older than my mom, he was already directing feature films by the time I came along. His career success, I had a feeling, was one of the reasons my mother was willing to hitch her wagon to an artistic type. Despite my father's quirks and some epic fights, the two of them were in love. Mom had been in denial of that ever since. Perhaps she thought it would hurt Lloyd's feelings, but I remembered things the way they really were.

Down in the parking garage, Randy's Suburban was stuffed to the gills. I found the box, set it on the ground, peeked inside. Atop stacks of notebooks was a list twenty pages thick—the master spreadsheet of cast members and their historical counterparts, beginning with generic cast positions like Kim's and continuing on to actual people whose lives would be assumed by modern-day replacements in less than two months.

The information within was fascinating. Names. Ages. Known facts about each person, place of birth, links to photographs in genealogical documentation on the Internet, physical traits if they were known—hair color, eye color, height, weight, distinguishing characteristics, build and facial structure, ethnicity. There were details on how each individual fit into the community—employment, place of residence, position in the social structure. I ran my fingers along the rows, read a few of the descriptions, felt the presence of bygone lives.

"Unbelievable." This was the Holy Grail for a girl who'd been imagining characters and stories her whole life. But these people weren't just characters. They were real. They had lived. Now they leapt off the page and lived again in my mind.

Clarence O'Day, born May 1, 1838, Irish, a stonemason and carpenter by trade, husband, father of two, brought family west on the promise of employment erecting housing and other buildings in town.

Sam Horn, born December 1830, ethnicity unknown, survivor of the Battle of San Jacinto, unmarried, gold prospector.

Ella Lively, born June 10, 1849, Irish, indentured servant, cook in the Delevan household, brown hair, green eyes, known description: *a child of slight build, and quiet, accommodating nature. She was indentured to the Delevan household for seven years to pay for her passage.*

Ella's place of birth was Durban, Ireland. She'd been orphaned at the age of eleven. She'd be nineteen by the time she finally earned her freedom . . .

But it never happened.

Her date of death was listed as May 27, 1861. There was a cause of death, as well, and the word on the page caught me unprepared. *Suicide, unexplained.*

My throat tightened, and suddenly I was grieving a little girl I never knew, a child who lived and died over a century and a half ago. I felt her disappearing in my mind, like a sketch being erased, the outlines first, then working inward, the brightest detail—her green eyes—disappearing last. Finally, she was gone altogether.

Shaking off the emotion, I flipped to the last page to see how many characters were listed in total. Over eighty soon-to-be time travelers at this point. The cast was even larger than I'd known. Getting these costume diaries in order was such a big job. I could in no way tell Kim about this. She'd be pumping me for details like crazy. But this, putting together the costume diaries, was the real thing. And Randy was willing to trust me with it.

He wouldn't be sorry. I'd make sure of that. These would be the most complete costume diaries in the history of film, maybe in the history of the world.

Chapter 9

Bonnie Rose
April 1861

Something I've eaten on the boat hasn't settled well. I'm surprised by that, considering there should be nothing more offensive to the stomach than the scraps tossed me during my time in Indian camp. But nonetheless, I've been abed for two days now, feverish and not able to keep down even the bit of broth and bread brought by the quiet little Negro girl with the doe eyes. More than once, she's cleaned up the slop pot and the mess I've made.

She's embarrassed that I keep thanking her for aiding me, but I do it in any case. *Essie Jane.* I've learned her name, at least. She isn't many years beyond Maggie May, perhaps thirteen or so.

I'm wishin' I could tell her I know what it is to be lashed and bound, to be living as a slave, but I can't be saying it, of course. Bonnie Rose O'Brien has been left behind. There's no place for her on this boat that's making its way up the winding river, fighting the shoals and the snags that grow more dire by the day. Often now, the *New Ila* sits still in the water while the men clear a tangle to allow us passage.

They're at it again today, and I'm feeling a touch better. Maggie May troubles me to let her up on deck. It's made her bearish, the confinement in this tiny room without windows. Her spirit fights against walls. There's that part of her that wants to break free and run again across the wild lands where there's not a solid thing, save what God made.

She'd have me turn her out to wander the boat, if I would. But the first mate is on my mind, and the only good result of my being ill is that it's given us reason for keeping away from the others. Essie Jane has let me know that we anticipate making our destination tomorrow noon, and I'm feeling the relief of finally leavin' the boat.

But there's a tightening in me too. The trip overland awaits. The caravan of wagons and supplies taking us to Wildwood will be travelin' well-guarded, but we'll be moving through untamed country from here to there. I know what can happen in such a place.

"I want to go up and look for the horses again, sister." Maggie crosses her arms over her chest, in a fitful humor again. Then her eyes take on a pleadin' look. "Please, Bonnie Rose."

"What've you been told about callin' my name

that way?" My nerves are edgy, worn from the sickness and made raw by worry. There's little more to do, lyin' abed than feel the worry-devils nippin' at my flesh.

I move 'cross the room, lay a hand on Maggie's head, looking her full in the eye. "What have we been practicin'? *Bonnie,* and Bonnie *only* when you're speakin' to me now. *Rose* is the surname. Like a game of *we pretend,* only we're playing it all the time. Day and night, Maggie May. And when we arrive in our new home, there's not a soul who'll be knowing of our shame. And we'll not tell a thing to nobody. There'll be no more boys like that Jacob, thumbin' a nose at you. It's a new life for us, Maggie May, but you can't be forgetting yourself. Not so much as once. Are you hearin' me?" My voice sounds like Ma's—so much so that it wrenches my heart like a fist reaching in. That's how the grievin' becomes after a time. You've tossed off the black blanket, but scraps of it fall on you unexpected, your life always a quilt with a dark patch or two. The Good Lord uses those to show off the bright colors, I think.

Maggie's eyes are wide and clear, filled with more knowing than a girl of nine should be having. "If we go to the deck, I won't forget. I'll be behavin'. I promise, sister."

"Well and good, then. Only for a bit, though. I've not got my legs under me full well yet, but if

I stay in this room any longer, I'll have cottage rot myself." The men are occupied with clearing the snag for now, and no doubt Mrs. Harrington and the other passengers are on the upper deck, fanning the heat off themselves and watching the progress. There's little else to do for entertainment other than stitching and gossip for the women, and card play for the men. But even those pursuits grow tiresome. All are ready to make our landin' tomorrow and set feet on dry ground.

I follow Maggie from the cabin and up to the deck, where we might watch the men work, but after so many days in the dim stateroom, the bright afternoon sun is more than my eyes can bear. I've forgotten my bonnet.

"Stand here and don't wander a bit, Maggie May," I tell her. "I'll hurry down and fetch my brim. Don't be climbing on the railin' while I'm off."

She nods and whispers, "Yes'm," in that quiet voice she uses if others are nearby. On the lower deck, the workers are milling, and nearby, young Jeffrey Harrington and his da watch the clearing of the snag, so it's well enough to leave her here a moment.

Nearby, an osprey skims the water for fish. Maggie points to it, gaspin' as it swoops past.

"That's a pretty thing, now, isn't it, Maggie May?" I stop in the doorway to watch a moment before hurrying in for my bonnet. By the stair, I

116

pass by Essie Jane with a bundle of table linens. "It is a beautiful day, is it not, Essie Jane?" I ask. No doubt she's happy to see me up and around. She won't be having to clean up after me anymore.

"Yes, miss." She smiles, her doe eyes inching up only as far as my chin, but she's a tall girl for her age and could just as easily look me in the eye.

"I've forgotten my bonnet to go on deck," I say by way of making conversation, but I know there's no sense in it. Essie Jane keeps to her business as if her life is dependin' on it. Having seen the treatment of the male slaves on deck, I wonder if it might be. I question whether Mr. Delevan condones such treatment of living, breathing persons, or if he is unaware of it completely.

"Yes, missus," the girl says and slides away, eager to let me go to my stateroom. She thinks I'm an odd sort, I'll wager. To most on the boat, she's not visible unless they've need of something.

The bonnet isn't where I'd remembered it to be. It's been lost in all the rubble of my sickness, and I'm a moment finding it. I hope Maggie May is behaving herself on deck. There's a happiness in me as I go out the door and move toward the sunshine again, and I let the bonnet dangle from my fingers, swinging it as I hum a little tune beneath my breath. For some reason, I'm thinking of Ma and Da and how they loved dancin'.

Before we came west, there were parties here and there about the neighborhood, and weddings too. There's nothin' like a good Irish gathering for music and dance.

"Well, now, if this isn't a spry young lass." The voice surprises me, and I know before looking up that it's the first mate, Mr. Grazide. He's just come out a door up a bit from our own. I stiffen as I pass by, wondering at his business in a passenger's room. And then I catch a glimpse through the openin' and see a Negro woman inside, gathering up her mop bucket and her dress all at once. She turns her head away, hiding her shame, and I feel my stomach rising to my throat.

I grip my bonnet strings tighter, my arms straight as bits of wood. Is he wondering if I'll speak of this to the captain? I most certainly will. I know what that poor woman is feelin'. My heart pounds inside me now, ringing like a hammer on an anvil, molten splinters shooting out. I want to tell him what I think of this, but I pretend I've noticed nothing out of the ordinary.

I think I've gotten by him when his hand catches just above my elbow, his fingers closing tight enough that it hurts. He whirls me around so I'm facing him with my back to the wall. There's no place for me to go.

Behind him, the Negro woman slips out the door and hurries down the hall with her bucket, glancing back, her eyes large and fearful as she rushes 'round the corner.

I pull away, but he doesn't release me, and my mind tumbles wildly back in time, like leaves caught in a scatterin' wind. For a moment, I'm frozen, and all I can think is, *Not again. Please, Lord, not one more time.*

The memories rush over me in sharp shreds, a scattering of glass. I open my mouth to scream, and he covers it with his hand. Over my nose as well, so that I can't catch a breath.

He leans close, and I smell whiskey, sour and thick. "Tell, and I'll say it was you who asked for it. Who do you think they'll believe? You think these fine folk can't see what you are? Little Irish harlot?" His fingers rake into my hair, pulling hard, and I struggle with all that's in me, but there's no use in it. His weight hems me to the wall. I turn my face aside, catch sight of Essie Jane standing just down the corridor, her eyes wide. I blink, and then she's gone.

His free hand trails down my neck as I'm trying for air. He presses hard, so I'm choking and coughing against his palm. "Try to make a fool of me at the dinner table, did you?" His fingers slip inside the ribbon 'round my neck, his finger-nails scratching jagged over the scars.

My mind is running then, bolting like so many times before, looking for a place to hide from the *now.* Somewhere inside, a voice screams, *Fight back! Find your backbone, Bonnie Rose. You cannot endure this again.*

But still, my body stands frozen.

"It'd be a shame if anything happened to that little sister you watch after so careful, now, wouldn't it?" His chin rubs hard against my hair, twisting my head aside so the pad of his palm can slide the ribbon down and press into my collar. The ribbon slips loose, and I hear a seam of the dress tearing a bit.

My mind dashes farther away—to that place again. That place where nothing stays but darkness. There's no feeling there. In my wilderness time, it was the only place I could run to.

He stops his perusal unexpectedly, cranin' his neck up and away from me. *Please,* I whisper in my mind, daring for hope, though so many times on the prairie, the same hope went unanswered. The same plea went unheard.

"What've we got here?" He pulls the collar hard. The thread loops pop open. He combs along the scars with his fingertips, soft at first, then harder. "You've been in the hangman's noose." He shakes my head hard against the wall. A shower of lights explode behind my eyes, brilliant as the Chinese fireworks over the Harbor Bay in Chicago. Beautiful for an instant, then fading into darkness. "Look at me, girl! I said, you been in the hangman's noose? Where'd you get this?"

He slowly releases my nose and mouth. I gasp a breath. His eyes bore into me. "You holler out, and that little sister girl is gonna pay. You savvy?"

I nod, cough for air, try to form the words *Yes. The hangman's noose.* Is a lie better than the truth? I am branded either way. Will he find one more repulsive than the other? The questions rush, swirl, wanting answers.

Of a sudden, he is ripped away from me, tumbling backward, his boots drumming the hollow floor as he staggers, then crashes to the wall, unable to find his balance. It is the captain standing over me then, his eyes fierce and wild.

Behind him, Mr. Grazide staggers to his feet, wiping a drop of blood where his forehead has hit the timber. The redness seeps over his brown hair. There's a softenin' in his posture as he lifts both hands. "Now, Cap'n, sir, what's a man to do when a fiery little strumpet offers herself up, willin' and waitin'? I know you been fancying her for yourself, but—"

Before I can comprehend what's happened, the captain's sidearm rises. "Back away, man, or I will shoot you where you stand."

Mr. Grazide's mouth hangs open in horrified surprise. "But, Captain, sir . . ." He lowers his hands slowly, lets them hang motionless at his sides as if he no longer knows what to do with them. "There's been no crime committed here . . .

just an invitation offered, and I'll wager it's not the first time, for her. I've seen her plying her wares toward the young Herrington boy. She's not some helpless schoolmarm, this one. Have her show you. She wears the mark of . . ." He's reaching toward his neck, mimicking my scars, glaring at my collar, where I've grasped it together and pulled it high, covering myself with that and the bonnet. Beneath, the skin goes hot as coals in a billows.

My stomach rises up, and my head whirls. I taste the bile of the small meal I managed this noon. There's movement down the hall, little more than a shadow. Essie Jane is there. It is she who's saved me, I know it.

The captain cocks the hammer. "I said stand down, Mr. Grazide."

My mouth fills. I clamp my hand over it, turn and run, the muscles beneath my ribs tightening in spasms, the bonnet slippin' from my hand as I reach the door of the stateroom. I barely make the chamber pot before I'm retching and retching.

When I'm finished, I slide down the wall, limp and trembling, hot then cold.

Will my life never be my own again? Will it always belong to the shame?

What's the use in living this way?

My heart cries out to God, and I wish He'd taken me along with Ma and Da and baby Cormie. This life, this world . . . I've no place in it. Pain and shame and surviving. That's all there is for me now.

A hand strokes over my hair, small soft fingers. I reach for it and clench it beneath my cheek, thinking it's Maggie May. But she kneels down and wraps herself around me, and I smell her scent of mop buckets and hard work, the sharp lingering of lye. I know it's Essie Jane.

I cling to her, this living soul who's come into the circle of pain. She whispers against my hair. "Shush now, shush now, miss. Cap'n gone put dat man off the boat." Her voice stirs my hair as it coos. "Heard him say dat myself. Say he ain't gon' have no such on the *New Ila*. Cap'n a good man, miss. Ain't gon' let nothin' happen to you."

When my senses creep back, she fetches water and the basin and cleans me up, then puts me abed as if I'm a child. It's then I remember Maggie May and the fear strikes me again.

"I've left Maggie May by the railing." How much time has passed? I've no notion of it. Mr. Grazide's threats ring in my ears.

Essie Jane presses me into the blanket. "I gon' go for her. I go for her, miss." Off like a rabbit, she is then. And even though I'm ashamed by it, suffering the humiliation of my own weakness, I curl into a ball atop the bed and cry.

When Maggie May slips in with Essie Jane, I pretend the sleep has taken me off. It's clear Essie

123

Jane told her nothing but that I took ill again.

When we're alone again, I instruct Maggie that we'll not be leaving the room until the *New Ila* comes to her final landin'. Then I close my eyes and wish away the snags and the wicked currents of the water, and pray we make it swift to the end port upriver.

The day passes, and then a night filled with fitful dreams. I'm running through the trees, clutching Maggie May's hand, dragging her behind me. Her fingers slip from me then, and I feel the breathing of something fearsome on my neck. Then I'm being pushed down. I fight with all that's in me, fight for air, fight for life, fight to be free. But the weight is too burdensome. Time and again, I wake up with screams hanging in my throat.

And then I'm lying in the dark, looking deep into it, and thinking I hear whispers. They all must be whispering by now, knowing what happened, askin' and wonderin' and supposin'. The captain putting his mate off the boat won't go by without notice.

In the morning, we stop to take on cordwood. Maggie May pleads to go atop and watch, but I'll not allow it. The captain comes to ask after me himself. I send Maggie May to the door to tell him I've gone sick again. In the corridor, he's bidding her to assure me that he has removed Mr. Grazide from the boat at the cordwood stop. There's naught for me to worry of now. We'll make our final port by dark today. A last dinner will be served on board, and those who choose to may sleep the night here before leaving off in the morning. Our party, departing for Wildwood, will strike away, first light.

"Please tell your sister I will hope to see her at our final dinner here on the *New Ila*," he relays to Maggie May, doubtless knowing the doors are thin and I hear him well enough on the other side.

Coming in again, Maggie doesn't bother repeating the message. She knows we'll not be going to dinner.

Overnight, we pack what little we have and wash and scrub our hair in the basin, sleeping while it dries. It's well before first light when we wake and dress, making ourselves as presentable as can be.

I'm clinging to Maggie May as we make our way up. Outside, the mornin' air is thick with fog, the day just beginning to blow soft breath on the river. Sounds bustle all around, driving the wild beating of my heart.

Porters cry out.

Metal clatters against metal.

Iron wheels squeal, tearing the morning air as loads are brought up and down the gangplank on hand rollers.

Slaves groan beneath heavy loads. Horses whinny and snort, waiting at the docks. An ox bellows, goats bleat, a rooster crows, singing up the sun.

I lose myself in it as we come to the railing. Along the dock and down the street into town, wagons loaded with freight wait to be unloaded and transported, while empty wagons wait to receive cargo off the *New Ila*. There's a feeling of excitement in the air, and it catches me. I see nothing of the other passengers, and I'm glad of it. Perhaps they've gone on to their business already. Perhaps they're waiting to leave the *New Ila* after her cargos have been exchanged.

Maggie May and I are to find the supply party that's traveling west to Wildwood, but there is a great clamor on the dock and I realize I've no way of knowing which party should be ours.

"Come along, Maggie May." I squeeze her hand. The fresh air and the excitement all around has got into me. I feel it, like the answer to the desperate prayers in the black of midnight. *Hope.* It moves anew, soft and silent as the morning light. "We'll go and find our wagoner."

We circle the deck, but goods are transferring up and down the plank, obliging us to wait until it's clear. I let Maggie free, and she climbs onto a crate, so as to better see the town.

Myself, I look beyond it, far into the distance.

Now's the end of Bonnie Rose O'Brien, I promise. I gaze west beyond the town, where the countryside spills into a sky still dim enough to allow the moon and the final stars a showing. I grip the rail, lean over and close my eyes, and whisper thanks to God for bringing us here safely, for whisking us far from the shame. Surely, that is a miracle only the Almighty One could forge.

"You're looking fine and fit this morning, Miss Rose." The captain's voice brings up short my thinking and romancing and praying.

I feel a sudden heat creep up my neck. My cheeks go flush. "Thank you, sir." I straighten my shoulders, and I'm wondering what I would see in his eyes if I were to look, but I cannot do it. He is, perhaps, one of the finest men I've ever chanced to meet. And one with a good and honest heart. "I've caught the excitement of setting off over-land, I think."

"It's a fine day for it." But there's nothing of admiration for this fine day in his tone. Instead, it is grave. There's a worry there. I risk a glance his way and notice that he's looking out also. A shadow dims his blue eyes as he watches the preparations on the dock. I wonder if it's anything to do with me, or if he is only fretting the return trip on the river. There's been no more rain, and the water's only gone lower. He's a fine captain, I think, devoted to the *New Ila* and its cargo, but he cannot make it float over sand. It's a risky venture, bringing a stern-wheeler this far upriver.

"I wish you a fine journey back." I should

thank him for saving me from Mr. Grazide, but it's not in me to be speaking of it. "I am grateful for the help you've been to Maggie May and myself on our journey thus far."

"It is your journey from here that concerns me." I feel him looking at me now. He's come 'round to his point, I know. This is what he's been wanting to say to me—why he's here alongside me now.

I fold my hands tight against my stomach inside the gloves that hide the burned flesh and the two crooked fingers.

"The frontier is an uncertain place and not a proper location for a respectable young woman alone, and with charge of a child, no less."

I wonder then, has he not discerned anythin' of my past? Most surely Mr. Grazide would've told what he had seen on my person, by way of excusing his foul actions toward me. Hangman's noose—or rawhide loop tied to the tail of an Indian pony—it matters little in which manner scars came to be there. Both condemn me.

Yet the captain's face holds tender concern, as if he feels a responsibility for me, even though I'm to leave his boat today.

For a moment I sink into his softness and strength, stepping into his eyes like a pool, the water flowing over me, and with it are a yearnin' and a wantin' I thought I had banished long ago. I dare not entertain it. It's the kind of hope that will lift me too high for falling. Yet it grips me hard.

I push it down deep again and lock it away. My life isn't to be the girlish thing I'd once dreamed of. He only looks at me in such a way because he doesn't know.

I turn toward the dock again. "We are to travel with the supply wagons, well-armed, is my understanding. I am assuming there will be other settlers leaving out from here as well. The settlement is growing fast, with the finding of the gold. It is a grand opportunity for me. The children need schooling."

The captain sighs, placing his hands on the belt of his uniform, looking down at the deck as if there might be an answer there. "You seem determined to go."

Part of me cries out to tell him what is true—that I can see no other way for Maggie May and me, than this one—but instead, I say, "I have made a commitment to it, a signed contract with Mr. Delevan himself."

Another breath swells his shoulders, then rounds them as he releases the air. "I have been instructed to send Big Neb along with the supply train, as well as Essie Jane. Please request of them anything you need in the way of aid during the journey. I have told Big Neb to watch out for you. He is a good man. Loyal."

"You needn't worry after me, Captain. Maggie May and I come from strong stock." If only he knew what we've survived, a journey across the frontier with the supply train would seem a small thing.

"But I do worry after you, Miss Rose." I chance to look at him again, and he gazes down at me. A smile plays upon his lips, but a sad one.

I'm filled with wonder and with fear. "We'll manage well, sir."

"James," he says, offering his given name.

It is too familiar for two persons in our position, but I accept the name, take it in and speak it. "James," I repeat.

For a moment, we are bound together this way, looking into each other's eyes. I wonder what he sees, and I fear what he might discover.

Along the deck someone calls for him. Before the spell is broken, he reaches for my hand, cradles it in his palm, seems to take no notice of the crooked fingers within the glove. Or if he notes it, he cares not a bit.

Only the thin linen separates us, and I can feel him through it, a pulse beneath his skin, beneath my wrist, beneath my own heartbeat. "If it is not as you expect it to be, Bonnie, send a message to me in any port, in the care of the *New Ila*. If you need me, Bonnie Rose, I will come for you."

Chapter 10

Allie Kirkland
May, Present Day

Randy regularly referred to my costume diaries as "works of art," and Phyllis and Michelle jokingly dubbed me *Wonder Girl*. If I did say so myself, the costume diaries were extraordinary, thanks to hours and hours spent in the university library. Over the past six weeks, I'd been slipping in there every chance I got, and each time I arrived, Stewart had a pile of carefully selected research material waiting for me. He'd taken it on as a personal project, almost an obsession, and he did know his way around the dusty book stacks, as well as all the far-reaching online resources available via the library network. We made a rather spectacular, if odd, research team, and it hadn't taken us long to determine that Kim was right about the target site for the docudrama. It was Wildwood. I, quite wisely, hadn't revealed that fact to Kim.

Stewart had compiled so much material about the settlement itself that I'd finally taken all the extra copies and given them to the research crew upstairs, where the historical experts and admins in casting were creating biographical journals that detailed the life history each participant would be stepping into. Even Tova seemed a little less flinty toward me now. Clearly, she respected Randy's opinions—either that, or I had helped to make her look good with the upstairs crowd. In any case, it was a win.

"I think I'm wearing her down," I whispered to Kim when she came in for her final fitting. "I'm convinced that she hates me a little less every day."

Kim's giggle reverberated off the walls of the small dressing room. "Well, I guess that's a little victory." She angled a narrow look toward the door while wiggling carefully out of the cotton blouse and knife-pleated skirt that had just been fitted to her—a work dress she would wear at the bathhouse. "But I still say, you should just let me wait for her out in the parking garage. You say the word, and this Texas gal'll open a can of whup-up on that skinny woman. I've ridden horseback over every hill and valley south of Austin. I know places to hide the body where *nobody* will ever find it."

Our laughter filled the room as I carefully moved the costume to a garment cart.

"That thing makes me look huge, by the way." Kim curled her lip at the costume. "I'd hang around and rib Randy about it, but Stewart came by again. He had some new materials, and he really wanted you to see them *today*. I told him you had to work late, so you couldn't go to the library. He was pretty disappointed, so I thought I'd just go pick the stuff up and bring it home. By the way, you're a pooh for keeping secrets all this time. He told me you two figured out *weeks* ago that I was right about Wildwood."

"Kim, don't ask him to smuggle stuff out again. Last time, you made him a nervous wreck. And I didn't tell you about Wildwood because I knew this was exactly what you'd do—get all obsessive about it. When you board the bus to head for the set with the rest of us, they'll give you your character journal and the whole mystery will be solved, anyway. Why not just wait? Think of it like a . . . a Christmas present."

"I peek at Christmas presents, thank you. Doesn't everybody? And Stewart is enjoying himself. All this research is the biggest thing to hit his life in forever—look how into it he is." Kim finished dressing, and we left the room.

"He's *too* into it," I told her as we walked down the basement hall together. "I've told him, like, three times that I'm done with the costume diaries, and I really don't need any more research material. With work and finishing classes for the semester, I don't have time to read anything extra."

"I would've read it." A plaintive frown came my way as we stopped outside the costuming room to deposit the garment cart. "If you weren't such a pooh-head secret keeper."

"Yeah, whatever. More like keeping you out of trouble. I do not want to end up in the woods alone this summer."

Kim put on a happy face as she poked her head in Randy's door. "You're gonna put super-stretchy spandex in my costume, right, Randy? Like built-in Spanx, okay?"

A few gray hairs escaped Randy's ponytail and fell down his thin cheeks, surrounding a smirk. "You're about a hundred and forty years too early for spandex, sweetheart, but I do have a period-appropriate alternative for you."

I snort-chuckled, knowing what he had in mind as he crossed the room. I was already laughing by the time he presented her with a corset. "The nineteenth-century alternative to spandex. Wear it with pride."

Brows knitted with concern, Kim investigated the hooks in front. "Well now, this'll be like putting ten pounds of taters in a five-pound sack. Do you have a bigger size?"

Randy turned the thing around, showing her the laces in back. "It comes with a dual-expansion slot. But don't worry, Kim, you're smaller than you think. And once you get this thing on, you'll look like Vivien Leigh in *Gone With the Wind*. Or Melanie Wilkes. Wasn't Melanie a blonde?"

Kim gave Randy an adoring look. "I love you. That's the best thing a man has said to me in forever. If you weren't already married, I'd be after you like a hen on a grasshopper."

Randy chuckled. "Well, now, there's an attractive picture. I'll let Miranda know that she has competition for my affections." Randy had a wife on the West Coast somewhere, but like many couples in the industry, they didn't end up working in the same city very often.

I felt a little sorry for him. After growing up in a household where my mother and stepfather ate in different rooms, watched TV in different rooms, and most often slept in different rooms, I'd made up my mind that if I ever did find somebody, I wanted the kind of marriage where we actually did things together in the course of a day. Normal things, like coffee in the morning, a surprise sack lunch in the middle of the day, a trip to the park just because the weather was nice, evening talks beneath the moonlight. . . .

It was all just a dream, a fantasy, but it was a nice fantasy. I couldn't help clinging to it, no matter how impractical it was for a girl like me. Given my lack of luck in the dating world, it didn't seem super plausible, but it was good to believe that someday it would just . . . magically . . . happen.

I turned to walk Kim out, and all of a sudden, there was Tova, standing behind her in the hallway looking morose, as usual. My stomach dropped, bounced off the soles of my shoes, rebounded somewhere into my chest, and then sank into place again, which was my usual reaction to Tova.

Her icy, narrow eyes slanted back and forth between Kim and me. "And pray tell, what are *you two* doing loitering around here together?"

"Fitting." I pointed to Kim, so as to make it clear that this was a legitimate visit, and I was in no way breaking the rules, nor would I ever *dream* of it.

Tova studied each of us head to toe, taking in everything from the frosted tips of Kim's hair, which would have to be dyed back to the natural color before we moved to the set in less than a week and a half, to the measuring tape strung around my neck and Phyllis's favorite fabric scissors protruding from my pocket. I'd picked them up in the fitting room to return them to their normal place. One of the Costume Department's requests was that I quell the daily tide of clutter and misplaced materials, so things could keep running in maximum overdrive.

Tova turned her attention to Randy. "Wren Godley will be here at 3:45 for her final fitting. Apparently the child was sick this morning or some such. I do not know why her mother has my number rather than yours, but now you have been told. Please make sure to give her your card so she will have the correct contact when next they have an issue with keeping their appointments."

"Will do," Randy answered, then flipped through his schedule to see who could handle the fitting. "We'll work her in somehow. I'll call upstairs and tell the guard to let her come down when she gets here."

Tova's cell phone rang, and she left without another word.

"Well, I'm gone." Kim gingerly set the corset inside the door as Randy slid into his office chair and rolled toward the phone. "I've got a couple errands to run yet this afternoon, and also a guy called about the ad I put on Craigslist for my truck. Maybe I'll get lucky and he'll buy it, and I won't have to pay the insurance and the payment over the summer." Kim had devised a clever plan to sell her current vehicle, since she wouldn't need it for the next few months. In the fall, she planned to use the savings, plus her earnings from the docudrama, to buy a new set of wheels.

"See you at home later—but if you're meeting the guy about your car, make sure you do it in a public place, okay? Maybe you can get someone to go with you. Creepy people troll those online lists."

"Yes, *mother.*" She finger waved over her shoulder on her way down the hall. "Don't work too late. Maybe we can go out and celebrate the sale of my truck tonight."

"Sounds good," I said, but I should have known better. As always, the afternoon became a blur of phone calls, meetings, and general panic. In the end I had to cover the Wren Godley fitting, of all things.

Randy literally shoved her costumes into my hands and said, "Here, deal with this. She's been fitted. Her wardrobe shouldn't need anything but fine adjustments. Just pin the hems."

Wren, I quickly discovered, did not fit her gentle-sounding name. At. All. She was a tiny redheaded, blue-eyed terror. The sort that gives redheads a bad name and makes it tough on the rest of us.

Checking her wardrobe took twice as long as it should have. While I worked, Wren wiggled, whined, complained, and blackmailed me for cookies and sodas from the break room. Her mother was constantly in my way, commenting, advising, and insisting that Wren's costume should be designed so as to best accentuate her features. Having previously had small parts in several Austin-based plays, little Wren was a star in the making—at least according to her mother. I finally determined that Mom was more than a little over the top and possibly on a high dose of medication, and she had some sort of personal connection with someone on the production who had pull.

By the time she walked her soda-bloated eleven-year-old down the hall and out the door, I was convinced that parenthood would never be for me.

When I finally left the Berman, it seemed like days had passed since I'd been home. Trudging up the stairs to our apartment, all I wanted to do was climb into the shower, wash off the grime from crawling around on the floor, and sink into bed. Unfortunately, I had finals to study for this week.

A dark form suddenly appeared above me at the top of the stairs, and I gasped and staggered back a step before realizing it was only Stewart.

"You scared me." I exhaled loudly and started up the stairs again.

Adjusting his backpack, Stewart plodded past without glancing my way. "You shouldn't leave pizza boxes outside your door, Allie. It attracts vermin."

"Sorry. That must've been Kim. I'll get her to clean it up." At this point, I couldn't count how many times Stewart had flagged us for stairwell offenses.

"I took them to the trash for you. So you wouldn't be in violation . . . if they spot-check the stairwell areas."

"Thank you, Stewart. Sorry about the pizza boxes." But he'd already headed for the parking lot.

When I opened the apartment door, Kim was sitting on the sofa with a stack of cash beside her and her laptop balanced on her knees.

"What's all this?" I asked, though I was afraid to know.

"I screwed up." She didn't bother to look at me but remained bent over the laptop screen, wildly scrolling. "There's food in the kitchen. Oh man, I screwed up so bad. Stewart's going to kill me."

"If you mean the pizza boxes, I saw Stewart on the stairs. He actually carried them down to the trash in case there was a *spot check*."

"Don't mention *Stewart*. If he finds out . . . oh man." She slapped a palm to her forehead, pulling upward until she had the bug-eyed look of a Pekingese dog with its topknot rubber-banded too tight. "It was just a CD pack of audio recordings that were made back in the thirties and forties—interviews with people who'd lived through the Civil War period, I think. I remember putting them in my truck, and I thought I brought them back into the apartment before I met the guy who answered the Craigslist ad. I know I did, but they're not here. Stewart just came by to ask if I'd given them to you, and I lied and said you were listening to them."

She cast a miserable, guilt-ridden look my way. "I didn't mean to. I just panicked. You know how seriously Stewart takes things. I must've accidentally thrown the CDs away when I cleaned all the junk out of my truck at the car wash. And I even called down there, and they'd already had their trash hauled away. So now I'm trying to figure out if there's anywhere I can buy copies."

I walked to the table, set my stuff down, and rested my head against the divider wall. "Kim, you lost some of the things you convinced Stewart to smuggle from the library? Please say no."

"I've got it under control." She huddled closer to the computer. "I remember the name— *American Voices.* University of Nebraska. I'll replace them, and nobody will ever know the difference. Don't worry, okay? Heat up some of the leftover pizza and come sit down. I've gotta tell you about the guy who bought my car. We sat out in the parking lot talking for *three hours,* and then we ordered pizza and talked some more. I think I'm in love."

Chapter 11

Allie Kirkland
May, Present Day

"I can't believe it!" Kim moaned as we finished breakfast. "I finally meet a guy I really like . . . a guy who might be *the one,* and now I'm headed into a communications blackout in the middle of nowhere for months. It's just not fair."

Three days before the cast was to report for transportation to the set, Kim's relationship drama and the stress at work were driving me to the brink of insanity. "Yes, but look on the bright side. You found a good home for your truck, you met a nice guy you can get back in touch with in the fall, we're off on an adventure for the summer, and we have almost no living expenses for three whole months."

What we had here was a case of serious role reversal. I was actually looking forward to moving to location, while Kim suddenly seemed to be dreading it. She'd been with the truck guy every night since the Craigslist deal. I had yet to even meet him. "Kim, if it's really meant to be, then it'll last through a few months apart."

She hadn't mentioned the docudrama or cowboys in days. I had a sickening feeling she was thinking of backing out. "After all, he's known all along that you would be gone for the summer, right?"

"Well, of course. I told him when I was selling the truck." Pausing, she sniffed a vase of red roses that had arrived over the weekend. She had the moony look of a girl in love.

"And he decided to like you anyway, right? So, when do I get to meet this guy? You know, I haven't even given my approval yet."

She rinsed a dishcloth and then started wiping the counter, her lips straightening into a somber line. "I don't want you to yet. I'm scared he'll . . . meet you and decide he likes you better. I need time to cement things, but the problem is, I don't *have* time. I'm not going to *be* here." She lifted her hands, slinging a fine spray of water across the kitchen.

"No, seriously . . . why are you really not letting me meet him?" With Kim being so secretive, I wondered if something weird was going on— like this guy, Jake, was twenty years older than her and she didn't want me to know it, or he was one of her professors or something.

"I *am* serious." She went back to work, scrubbing at a stain that had been on the counter since the day we moved in. "You're just so . . . skinny and tall and pretty, Allie. Everywhere we go, guys look right past me to ogle you. And you don't even *care,* which makes me want to choke you sometimes, even though you're my best friend and I love you. Jake is . . . perfect. He's a decent guy, he comes from a little town like I do, his daddy is a deacon in the Baptist church, and he is . . . okay, I'll admit it . . . *so* good-looking. I just want to keep him to myself for a while, okay?"

Sometimes Kim's way of thinking amazed me. "Okay. But you're wrong about the other thing. You're the one with all the trophies and tiaras. While you were winning all that stuff, I was walking down the hall with bad hair, braces, and my mouth practically wired shut while the mean girls pointed and made fun of my lack of fashion sense."

A sardonic snort answered. "You need to take a

good, hard look in the mirror, Allie. I think that's why Tova gives you so much trouble. She feels threatened. You're younger, and you don't even *try* to be pretty. You just are."

I went back to my breakfast. Sometimes I wished I could see in myself the things Kim saw. Life would be a whole lot easier if I could shuck off that girl in the braces and the headgear, the one who disappointed all the family expectations.

"What I really wish is that I could be *here* for the summer." Kim dumped imaginary crumbs into the trash can.

My stomach and my heart collided with a painful, queasy thud. "Kim, you signed a contract."

"I know . . ." Dropping the dishcloth in the sink, she started toward her bedroom. "I'm excited about the pioneer life thing. I am. When I went in for my final paperwork yesterday, I just came right out and asked the guy if our town was Wildwood, and he just smiled and said, 'You didn't hear it from me, though.' The more I read about the real town, the more fascinated I am by it. When I bought those CDs online, I also picked up a DVD about mysteries of the Civil War. Jake and I just watched it last night. Wildwood was, like, legendary. Nobody really knows anymore what's myth and what's fact, but in the summer of 1861, people from the town just started randomly disappearing—like into thin air.

"After a while, there was some kind of mass hysteria. Families were running off in the night, hiding in caves in the woods and things like that. Some people apparently just jumped off the cliffs into the river and drowned themselves. Then there was a giant storm. Whenever outsiders came to the place again, all the people were gone. Not one single soul left in town—just empty buildings. Now, *that's* a history mystery, and it makes me even more convinced that the big, secret executive producer of this thing is Rav Singh, by the way. This totally sounds like one of his horror flicks. And it's fascinating to think about—how could a whole town of people disappear? I just wish I could be in two places at once, that's all. I can't stand the idea of being away from Jake. Especially when we're so . . . new. All I want to do is be with him. He's the first thing I think about every morning."

"Well, I can't tell you how to be in two places at once. If I were smart enough to figure that out, I could be home to take the twins to their gymnastics camp next week, and my mother wouldn't be pretending I don't exist right now." I instantly wished I hadn't brought it up. I wanted to put the family issues out of my mind, but I couldn't.

Kim sighed. "I know. I'm sorry. I understand that people have real problems. I do. You just need to ignore your mom and her emotional blackmail, Allie. This summer is your big chance, and the people who care about you should want it for you."

Kim wandered off to her bedroom, and I finished breakfast, then got ready for work. There was a full day ahead at the Berman now that the school semester was over. The good thing was that I was gaining so much experience this summer, and in so many different areas, that I really did believe Kim was right. This summer was not only an opportunity to scratch together enough money to float another semester of school; it was my chance to make the connections I needed.

Kim caught me in the stairwell as I was headed out. She was wild-eyed and excited, still in her pajama pants and socks. "Oh my gosh I've got it!" The sentence came in one big rush of words. "I figured it out. My iPhone. My iPhone!"

"Shhhh!" There were three other apartments on the quad with ours, and it wasn't yet seven in the morning. If we woke Stewart, he'd be calling the management. "I have to head for work, okay? I'll talk to you tonight."

"No, but wait. I've got it figured out—how to be in two places at once." The volume started in a whisper and inched upward. "My iPhone. If I have it *with* me this summer, I'll be able to keep in touch with Jake. It won't be the same as getting to see him, but I'm telling you, Allie, I don't want to lose this guy. I can't explain to you how I know he's the one, but I know this is it. I really do."

Poor Kim. I hated to remind her of the obvious, but somebody needed to. "Remember the techno-turn-in that's scheduled to happen as we move to the set? No driver's licenses, no folding wallets, no cigarettes, no plastic *anything*. They're *not* going to let you take an iPhone. It's all in your contract. The only communication is the village post office—remember that? You and Mr. Right will be courtin' the old-fashioned way. It's kind of romantic, if you think about it."

"It's barbaric." Kim held out her beloved iPhone. "*I* can't take my cell phone, but *you* can take it *for* me. Even if we're so far out in the boonies that there's no cell phone signal, they're bound to have some kind of satellite Internet and wireless in the crew camp. These are important people. They have to do business. There's no way they're going to be out of touch all summer."

I pushed the phone away gently, pressing it against her body. "Kim, they've already told us *no cell phones* unless it's company-issued. Randy is about to have a heart attack, and he's only going to be up there for the first month or so to help with any dressing disasters." Actually, the communications blackout bothered me too. But when the opportunity is huge, so are the sacrifices.

Kim extended the phone my way again, and we played a quick game of push-me-pull-you.

"You could hide it," she said finally. "You'll be traveling up there with mountains of . . .

production stuff. How hard can it be to smuggle in one itty-bitty gadget? I won't use it that much, I promise. I'll just sneak off in the woods to text, email, or talk to Jake every few days. The battery will last a long time. You'll only have to recharge it for me once in a . . ."

"No *way!*" I protested, my surprise escaping into the stairwell and echoing off the nearby apartments. No lights came on, thank goodness. "Kim, I am *not* getting involved in this, even for you. You know how quickly this could get me fired? Both of us, for that matter. They'll make you into one of those nameless citizens who jumped off the cliffs into the river. You know, that's what they do when cast members break the rules. They kill off your character."

"Allie . . . *please* . . ."

"No. No way. No how. Nada. Nope. I'm not doing it. You and Mr. Wonderful will just have to keep in touch long distance, like our ancestors. It'll be a great story to tell your grandchildren someday. I have to go to work. Good-bye."

I turned away and left Kim there in the stairwell—mad, sad, or whatever she was right now.

The love bug was one of those things I was afraid I'd never really understand. I wanted to, but I just didn't. Maybe there was something wrong with me. Maybe I was so damaged by my father's death, by everything that happened afterward, that I'd always be living solo in a world full of people, always keeping up my defenses, hiding behind the mask. What if I never found a place, a person, a life that . . . fit?

It was too hard to think about, so I shook it off during the short drive to work. In my mind, Grandma Rita offered one of her famous Texas wisdoms: *Can't never could, won't never would, and shan't probably should.* Basically, it meant, stop whining and get busy doing. *God gives every bird his worm, but He doesn't drop it in their mouths once they're big enough to fly.*

Grandma Rita had a saying for pretty much any occasion.

By the time I walked into the Berman, I was feeling good. I took the back stairs and ducked into the assembly room, where the stitchers had not yet arrived at their sewing machines. The scents of fabric, and machine oil, and thread surrounded me, familiar and comforting.

A little tingle passed through me, and I had the bittersweet anticipation of a parent realizing it's almost graduation time for a beloved child. In three days all the costumes would leave the Berman and through them, a bygone world would emerge. I'd never been part of anything this massive before, and just thinking about it filled me with gratitude and a sense of wonder. My coming here wasn't an accident. This was a gift, but if I wanted this new life, I was going to have to be bold enough to work for it.

"Hey, *rojito*, you better not let the big kahuna find you there looking all tranquil." Randy stopped in the hallway outside the door. "Some kind of edict came down from on high this morning, and our fair production supervisor is *not* in a good mood. She's looking for you, in particular."

I groaned, my little bubbles bursting one by one, swatted out of the sky by the ugly claws of reality. "Am I in trouble?"

Randy gave me a smile and a wink. "I think she's got an errand for you. She's in her office now. I heard her on the phone a minute ago." As if on cue, Tova's voice echoed down the hall. I couldn't make out the words, just the rapid pulse of aggressive sound waves in her particular range.

Randy frowned. "That's . . . the familiar noise of something unexpected coming up. With any luck, that errand she has for you will be off-site."

"Guess I might as well find out." I took a deep breath and headed down the hall. In the office, Tova was still engaged in a phone conversation. I waited near the door, out of sight.

"What do you mean you are sending him down here? Do you realize we are on the verge of moving to location? Randy's crew is packing everything for transport today, not creating garments for . . ." Short pause, and then, "But . . . there's no possible . . ." Pause. "He cannot just . . ." Pause, a little longer this time. "Yes. Yes.

Yes, of course they are capable of it, but . . . Very well. Yes, I will see to it myself, of course."

I stepped in the door just as she was ripping the Blake Fulton scrap of paper from the wall and giving it a look that could have fried an egg. So, the mystery cowboy had somehow reemerged. Had she finally called the number he'd given me in the deli, or had someone called her?

I didn't even want to know . . . and then again, I did. I found myself hoping my unnamed errand had something to do with finally learning the truth behind that piece of paper and the guy in the grocery store. Who was he, really?

"*There* you are. Finally." Tova snatched a shoebox-size container off her desk. "Someone must do advance placement work at the set today. Delivery locations for materials from the costume shop and props not already in place must be clearly marked with the labels enclosed in this folder, and *even then* we will be fortunate if the transport service gets *half* of it right. It was my intention to go myself, so as to label things clearly, but it looks as though I will be . . . otherwise occupied. Since I can spare *no one* at this point, I am sending *you*. Here are the markers."

She thrust the box into my hands, and I grabbed it just in time to keep it from landing on the floor. "These are directions to the location, maps of the set, and detailed instructions." She slapped an overstuffed accordion folder on top of the cardboard box, and it slid sideways, landing against the crook of my arm. I shifted and clamped my chin to the stack to keep from losing it. "The keys to a production vehicle should be waiting with the guard at the box office. I have already signed for it."

When I looked up again, Tova was staring at me like a serial killer about to go on a rampage. "Do not screw this up, Allison. If you do, I will make certain that not so much as the *smallest* community theater in the *minutest* backwash at the *farthest corner* of the map will even *consider* hiring you in this business. Do you understand?"

I felt my life flashing before my eyes. I hoped it didn't show. "Yes, of course. You can count on me. I mean it. Whatever it takes," I babbled out. A muscle knotted in my neck, and I realized that I was unconsciously recoiling from Tova's murderous gaze, dragging the folder with me.

"If I had anyone else to send, Allison, I would *not* be sending *you*."

"Yes, of course, I know that." *Wrong thing to say.* Now she thought I was being a smart aleck. Her mouth twitched on one side, nerves and sinew straining for control.

"Follow the instructions to the letter. Do not deviate. Do not stop to admire the wildflowers. Do not linger over the blue, blue sky. Do not even *consider* sharing the information in that folder with *anyone,* or taking *any* stowaways along with you." Of course, by *stowaways,* she meant a certain roommate, whose name we would not mention. "Are we clear?"

"Absolutely." *Holy cow!* She was sending me to the set. *Me!* Through the haze of fear and the wild static of nervous adrenaline, it was just starting to dawn on me as I glanced down at the label on the folder.

I'd just been slated for the granddaddy of all production assistant errands.

A batch of butterflies hatched in my stomach, and it was all I could do to keep from grinning ear to ear. I struggled to appear appropriately miserable until Tova finished threatening me one last time, then left the room.

A muffled gasp slid out once she was gone.

I was headed to *Wildwood!*

Chapter 12

Bonnie Rose
May 1861

I find myself longing now for my first sight of Wildwood, no matter how great my uncertainty of the conditions that will be meeting us there on our arrivin'. There's not a soul in our party can tell me what we're to be expecting, save for the master of our wagon guard, Grayson Hardwick, who travels with shipments being brought to Wildwood and other settlements on the Texas frontier. Other than Mr. Hardwick, the whole of the party are like myself, never havin' seen such country as this before. Even the territory up Weatherford way, where we'd settled with Ma and Da, was not so rugged and uncivilized as this land west of Waco Village. The sharp hills of limestone rock and live oak have a beauty, to be sure, but there is also a lonely desolation and far too much cover for a raiding party to lie in wait.

Altogether, twelve men accomplish the drivin' of the wagons, seven working as a way of providing for passage to Wildwood. It's clear enough this is an arrangement that's been employed by Mr. Delevan many times before—the trading of passage for labor. Upon arrivin' at Wildwood, the men who haven't money to purchase land will work mining claims for Mr. Delevan, in hopes of earning their way to a stake in the gold strike area.

In our travels thus far, we've made our way past only a small village or two, and thrice, we've been visited by Indians as we went. They were Tonkawas each time, and friendly, but Mr. Hardwick kept Maggie, me, and Essie Jane under canvas in a wagon during his communication with them. I'm gathering that it's not the first time there've been women along with the ox carts and the mule wagons for this journey, but Mr. Hardwick is not one for talking. He is a tall, lean, and hard-edged man who seems to know his work and keep to the business of it.

Now his patience is worn thin, as we've been camped here for days along the banks of the rain-swollen Brazos, near the ferry landin' at the home of Samuel Barnes and his wife, Elizabeth. There was talk in the house last night that the Tonkawa have seen parties of Comanche about the area. "It's the ones you don't see you'll favor yourself to worry about," said Mr. Hardwick as he finished the coffee and sweet biscuit Mrs. Barnes had offered up. He seems not perturbed by the news, but today I'm noticing that he wants to be across the river and so do the other men. Having only just come west, they've no experience with hostiles, and they're not lookin' for any. Four of them have wives and children they hope to bring at a later time, and the other three are brothers— Ryan, Jack, and Sean, only a few months off the boat from Dublin.

The river's currents swirl wicked, but it's the mood of the men that's concerning me most. Mr. Hardwick seems the type to fear nothing of man nor beast in this world, yet it's clear enough he's troubled. He's paid the ferryman extra to bring us across, against the better judgment of Mrs. Barnes, who's lived by the river many a year now, after starting the ferry with her first husband, a man who died in the river when a boat swept over, spilling a wagon and a team of mules, as well as all on board.

But Mr. Hardwick has his mind set on it today. There's no more time for delay, he insists. The weather looks ill off in the distance and despite the dry and brick-hard ground, if rain falls upstream, we could be held here a week or more, yet. Mr. Delevan won't have it, is Mr. Hardwick's final reasoning, as if he believes that even the river would not dare overtake something belongin' to Mr. Delevan. If we can accomplish this crossin', we'll push hard and make Wildwood in four days or less, regaining a bit of the schedule we've lost.

So our decision's been made, and while we're gathering up the last of the camp, Maggie May says her good-byes to two of the Barnes children she's come to fancy as friends. I find Big Neb hiding in the shade of the live oak grove, down on his knees in the leaves. His eyes are closed, and his lips are movin'. Beads of moisture glitter on his mahogany skin. He's praying, I see, so I wait. He hears my footsteps and climbs quickly upright, fearful that I've found him here, off to himself.

"I hope you've prayed for the both of us," I say, and smile to let him know I wouldn't speak a word of this to Mr. Hardwick.

"Yes'm," he murmurs quietly and skirts me,

like a horse that has known torment from one hand, and sees the self-same potential in all.

He stops at the edge of the brush, looking toward the river. The line of his jaw trembles like a wee little child's.

"Mr. Hardwick intends you to cross on the raft with the bay mules, to hold them quiet," I tell him. It was Mr. Hardwick who sent me to discern where Big Neb had gone off to. The second mule team has been difficult throughout the trip. Not so skittish as horses, but worse by far than oxen. My father taught me enough about mules that I know there's no foolishness in them. They look after their own hides, despite what their masters ask of them. A mule won't run himself to death under the whip, as will a horse. The bay mules won't like the river crossing, I know it. They've too much sense for it.

Big Neb seems to feel this same way. The closer we walk to the ferry landin', the more the quivering spreads over his body, until even his breath trembles in and out.

"We'll make the crossin' in fine shape." I wish my words could bring a sureness of it, but there's none to be had. The noise of the river has begun filling my ears, the rush working its way inside me. I wonder if Mr. Delevan would be having us risk our lives this way, if he knew of it. Would he be insisting that we hold to his schedule?

I stop along the bank, and Big Neb continues

on. Mr. Hardwick has spied him now and calls for him. Maggie waits down by the landin', watching the proceedings as the ramps are set and preparations made to bring across Mr. Hardwick, his saddle horse, and the three young Irishmen, Ryan, Jack, and Sean, along with various packets. Once across, they'll help work the lines from the other side and manage the packets of provisions that've been taken off the wagons for transport on the ferry.

"Big Neb don't swim none," Essie Jane tells me. She's come from nowhere, as she tends to do. "Got 'im a pow'ful fear a' the river."

"We'll make the crossin' well enough, all of us." I feel the need of promising it again.

"I don' swim none, neither, miss," Essie Jane whispers, her voice little more than air passing. "Them what live in the house here say they's bones un'er dat water. Bones a' animals and men, hid down in the deep-dark. Bones a' the missus' firs' husband, even."

Her words sink through my skin, kindle the fear that's been lit inside me for days now as I've watched the river. "I won't be hearing talk of that sort, Essie Jane." My voice comes out hard, and she ducks away as if I might strike.

I yearn to share words of comfort and prayer, of the God who shall protect us in the wilderness, but what good are lofty words from one soiled as myself? Despite all that the good reverend and the missionaries have said, I fear that God must esteem that which men esteem, and despise that which men despise. That He, too, knowin' of my shame, must surely despise me.

I slip my hand between us and wrap my fingers around Essie Jane's, taking comfort in the bond of flesh to flesh. "We'll cross on the same raft together. I'll make certain of it. I'm a strong swimmer. Like a codfish, my da always told me, rest his soul."

Essie Jane regards our fingers in surprise, a circle of white flesh over brown. Her hand remains rigid, unbending. Perhaps she's only minding her place, or perhaps she knows that even a codfish would have trouble in this river.

We stand watching from the hill, while below the first raft makes it over, is unloaded, then returns empty with the ferryman. Mr. Hardwick returns, as well. He oversees the second load—the one with a wagon and the skittish bay mules. Big Neb stands at their heads, his hands wrapped in the harness reins, clinging on for the life of him. His fear creeps up the riverbank like the comin' of a fog. I won't catch a breath until he's safe across, I think. It comes to my mind that Ma's roses are travelin' with him, tucked in the box of the wagon. I say a special prayer, biddin' Ma and Da be asking the saints to watch over the roses and the men and the crossin'.

Beside me, Essie Jane whispers a prayer of her

own. Some part of the Twenty-third Psalm, but it's short by a few words. She repeats over and over again the parts she knows. "The Lord, He be my shepherd, He takin' me to the green pasture. He makin' me a place by the still water, and the water don' overflow me. . . . The Lord, He be my shepherd, He takin' me to the green pasture. He makin' me a place by the still water. . . ." Her fingers tighten and cling to mine. I don't think she knows it.

The raft bobs low in the water as it sets out, the current splashing over the mules' feet. A parcel slides, and pushes them from behind. Mr. Hardwick catches the box, straining to stop it, then pulls hard on the reins to hold the mules from going over Big Neb and turning the raft in the water. The ferryman yells to the men onshore and the lines are tightened. The sun glistens against Big Neb's head and the coats of the sweat-soaked mules. Muscles tremble beneath their hides as they're forced back a step and the raft is righted again. All who are watching send up a cheer as the boat reaches its destination.

I catch my breath as the raft is unloaded, the nervous mules being brought off and lashed quickly to a tree. On the opposite shore, the Irish boys begin reloading the wagon until it's time to take up the ferry lines again for another crossin'. Mr. Hardwick comes to the water to board, bringing Big Neb along.

"He be comin' back again," Essie Jane whispers, and before I know what I'm about, I'm running down the hill waving my arms, yelling for Mr. Hardwick to leave Big Neb on the other side. He's made the crossin' once, and once should do. If the mules had pushed him in just now, he'd be dead surely enough. A man of his size and weight wouldn't have a chance of surviving this river, unable to swim.

Captain Engle put Big Neb and Essie Jane in my charge upon our leavin' the *New Ila*, and I feel that I'm responsible for them. I cannot help but think, were the captain here, he wouldn't force a man onto the ferry repeatedly, knowing the man is only inches from death. The animals and supplies are of importance, but are nothin' compared to a man's life.

Mr. Hardwick looks my way a moment, but goes on with his plan. He and Big Neb come 'cross with the empty raft again. I find myself thinking of Captain Engle—James—and wishing once again that he were here to look after us. Many times I've thought of that last moment I saw him on the deck of the *New Ila*. What if I'd made the other choice and stayed behind when the supply train struck off for Wildwood?

As the ferryboat makes shore, there's a fire in me, and I'm storming toward the river, words spillin' out of my mouth. Mr. Hardwick has barely a foot on land before I've set upon him. "I'll not have Big Neb brought across again. Did you not see me asking you to leave him on the other side? The man can't swim. If he falls from the raft, it'll be to his death."

The men managing the loads stop to look at me, as do the half-grown children of the ferryman, who've been scurrying about, each with a job to be done here. Down the way, I see Maggie May watching, wide-eyed. Essie Jane is beside her now. They're drop-mouthed at my ranting. I feel my hair pulling loose from its ribbon. In the excitement this mornin', I've forgotten to re-bind it. Red curls fly around me like licks of fire. I imagine I'm making quite a spectacle of myself. Nothing a proper lady would do.

Mr. Hardwick's narrow face says as much. The faint scar beneath his eye twitches. I wonder how it came to be there, and then I'm afraid of knowin'. His lashes flare over angry gray eyes and his fists clench, and I'm wonderin' if he might strike me. He's a rough sort, this man. The sort to have lived a life on the frontier and done what was needed for surviving.

"You'll mind yourself, Miss Rose. And I'll run my supply train my own way." The scar beneath his eye twitches again, and he leans close to me, adding in a whisper, "Cross me one more time, and you'll find yourself in the river."

But words have come in my mouth, and they fly out wild as the whips of hair slashing across my skin. "Big Neb and Essie Jane were left in my charge by Captain Engle upon our leaving the *New Ila*. I'll see them brought safely to Wildwood, and if not, I will be certain that Mr. Delevan is made well aware of the reasons."

Anger and fear mix a strange brew inside me. Mr. Hardwick's eyes search my own. I haven't an inklin' what he's looking for—my resolve, perhaps? I keep my gaze steady. He'll not see me waver. Truth be told, I've no way of knowing if my words would hold any sway with Mr. Delevan. For the most part, it is only my hoping that makes him into a decent man. My hoping, and the fact that he would take me into the teaching position at all, knowin' my story as he does. Who but a good man would go to such trouble and expense to bring me so far and provide a new life for Maggie May and me?

Mr. Hardwick blinks once, slow. He shakes his head the slightest bit, and I think I've bluffed him in this game of cards we're playing.

"Then pray the raft doesn't turn," he says, and walks away. Below, they're loading the ferry again. A team of oxen this time and several packets, but no wagon. Three more men will cross on the raft. One of them kisses his rosary, holding it up to the light before he tucks it away. Big Neb is again put in front to hold the oxen steady.

They make the crossin' without incident, and then Mr. Hardwick returns on the raft with Big

Neb again, as I feared he would. There's no profit in confronting him, so I keep silent.

Supplies and wagons and livestock move across, raft by raft, and I'm holdin' my breath each time. The current pulls the raft sideward, playing with it like a naughty little boy handling a toy made from sticks and string. An ox team pins Big Neb hard against the railing, and his deep voice cries out, the rail looking as if it might break and spill him into the water with the animals atop him. Beside me, Essie Jane gasps, and Maggie May throws her hands over her eyes. She knows the power of the river. When the Indians were moving their encampment, we saw the drownin' of a girl and her baby brother. The horse slipped from under them, and there was naught could be done about it. Afterwards the keenin' and cuttin' of hair and skin was terrible to behold.

Mr. Hardwick manages to move the oxen off, and I close my eyes and wipe the moisture from my hair, pushing away the memory of the Comanche children drownin' in the river. I cannot let myself relive that time. Bonnie Rose O'Brien is gone now, and her memories must go with her.

Overhead, the sky darkens. Thunder rumbles, and a mist of water spits down, threatenin' to bring rain and leave us trapped, half on each side of the river. The men heighten their speed, and the boat crosses even more heavily laden.

It returns again, and it's the sorrel mules, along

with whiskey boxes and kegs of gunpowder next to go. Mr. Hardwick decides it is time for Essie Jane, Maggie, and me to make the trip. We walk down the shore like prisoners heading to the gallows. Essie Jane is frightened beyond her wits and snivelin', poor thing. Her whole body trembles. I sit her next to a barrel that isn't heavy, and pull her hands to the ropes lashed 'round it. "If anything should happen, you hold to this. It will float in the water. Kick your feet hard like you're chasing at flies, and try to make shore."

"Yes'm," she whispers, leaning against the barrel and closing her eyes. Tears seep under her dark lashes.

"Don't worry, now," I tell her. "We'll be landin' on the other side before you know it." I move to Maggie then, and do the same with her, settling her in next to three barrels that have been bound together.

The wind comes up, whistlin' over the water, rocking the raft hard as we set off. Maggie sits upon her knees and casts a worried look my way, and Essie Jane tucks her head low, whimpering into the shoulder of her dress. Nearby, Big Neb holds the mules. They are an older pair that has made this trip many a time. They're not expected to offer trouble.

Beneath us, the decking of the raft rocks and sways as we leave the landin' behind. The wind pulls crests from the waves, splashing over the boat, and the mules stagger on the water-soaked logs. Their small, sharp hooves clatter and slide as the boat rocks and sways. I stretch my arms 'round the barrel, gripping Maggie May's hands on the other side. Her fingers, in turn, clutch my sleeves, and we hold on. Maggie whispers the Lord's Prayer. *Is our Lord hearing it now? I wonder. Is He watchin' over the river?*

A wave shoves hard against the raft. The mules stagger back left. "Hold them steady!" Mr. Hardwick yells above the wind and the storm. "Hold them steady, or I will split your worthless hide!" At the rail, Big Neb struggles to keep the mules from bolting forward. The storm's got them sorely frightened. Mr. Hardwick attempts to brace his feet and lean against the reins, but his boots only slide. He slips on the deck as if it were ice, and he hits hard against the railing, off his feet. The mules sit back on their haunches, giving to the sudden weight of a man against the bridle reins. They throw their heads, the iron bits cutting into their mouths. One goes down on his haunches, and the harness pulls the other mule so he's scrambling wild as Mr. Hardwick tries to get his own feet.

"Turn 'em loose!" Big Neb yells above the din. "Turn 'em loose, sah. I holds 'em!" His groan splits the air as he struggles to pull the mule back to its feet again. The side rail cracks and bows against the burden. The heavens open overhead, and rain rushes down, so thick I can't see. Of a sudden, the load begins shifting, tipping the boat into the current. The water grabs it, and I feel the logs rise beneath me.

"Hold tight, Maggie May!" I dig my fingers in, determined that I won't let her go. Our bundle slides, then stops, hanging by a rope tied fast. The raft tips far enough that I feel the bottom of the keg lifting off the floor.

I wonder, *After everything, this is the way we die? Never havin' reached Wildwood at all? Our bodies down below with the bones of men and animals whose crossin's were upended? Who never saw the other shore?*

Essie Jane's scream rends the air. I feel something slide past, catching my dress a moment, pullin' hard, then tearin' loose. Through the downpour, I've a glimpse of the girl's face—a single, frozen moment—all eyes and open mouth, terror-filled. I turn loose of Maggie and reach for Essie's Jane's hand, but she's too far. All I can catch is the end of the rope trailin' by, and it slips through my fingers, wet and slick. Essie Jane is scramblin' now, trying to get loose of the barrel. She slips sideways 'neath the railing and goes off into the water, screamin' out the death wail.

"No!" The wind cuts my voice away. Something strikes the raft. I see it dark against the rain, an upended tree, the roots sticking out like fingers. It pushes the boat up, forces the low end above the water. Big Neb pulls the mules to their feet in the instant it gives us.

The ferry rights itself, and the ferryman yells, "Hold them mules still!"

Through the rain, I see Mr. Hardwick over the railing, in the water, clinging to the barrel and Essie Jane.

Next I know I'm scramblin' across the deck, my skirt catching under my knees, splinters of wet wood pushing through my gloves. I hook the toes of my boots between logs, and stretch until I'm lying on my belly across the raft, trying to grab for Mr. Hardwick. In the water, Essie Jane is flailin' all over him, panicked to keep her head above water.

Mr. Hardwick struggles to cut the barrel free of her, and when he finally slices it loose, he brings his hand back and strikes her hard across the face, and then she's limp. I grab for her as he struggles to hand her up, and I pull her back across the deck. Mr. Hardwick drags himself from the water and falls on board, coughing up the contents of the river.

The water quiets as we're nearing the shore. The mules tremble where they stand, and overhead the wind retreats into the trees. But for the look of us—and the barrel floating off down the river—no one would know we'd struggled with the crossin'.

When we're safely onshore, Mr. Hardwick

demands to know why Essie Jane was lashed to the barrel. I take the blame for it, though it was none of my doing. It'll go easier for me than for her, I suppose, but it must've been she who tied herself there as we were departing the shore. Mr. Hardwick is in a wicked humor about the loss of the gunpowder. I assure him I'll stand the cost of it when I begin receiving my wages.

We speak no more of it, as the last of the crossings is accomplished with neither loss of man nor beast.

When the loads are put in place again and the teams harnessed up, we move on from the river, wet and cold and sufferin'. It's a quiet evening in camp that night, all of us realizing the difficulties of the journey are near an end now. Wildwood is just days overland. The final river as we reach the town is an easy ford this time of year, according to Mr. Hardwick.

In the night, I dream of the crossin', and then I'm flying over the river like a bird on the wing, far, far upwater to where the *New Ila* steams along, her stern wheel turning peacefully. And then I'm standing on deck with Captain Engle. *James.* His blue eyes smile at me.

If you need me, Bonnie Rose, I'll come for you, he whispers.

In the morn', it's his name on my lips, but Mr. Hardwick's face hovering over my camp bed. I don't know if he's come to wake me, or if he's been there a time. I rise without speakin' and tend to the morning business. We make a meal of only hardtack and water, and soon we're on the trail.

It's a bright fair day for travelin', and the men are of a fine spirit, each knowing we will reach Wildwood soon.

The sun is low on the horizon on the fourth day when finally we see the place with our own eyes. The coyotes come out, howling like a chorus of demons as we top the final hill and move along the bluffs toward the river ford. The smell of woodsmoke salts the air, and we see the fires of Wildwood below. A cheer goes up among us. Even with the fading light, we can accomplish the crossin' of the ford.

We've reached our journey's end now, at Wildwood.

Chapter 13

Allie Kirkland
May, Present Day

By the time I turned off I-35, south of Temple, I wished I'd broken the rules and taken Kim with me on the trip to the set. She probably would've agreed to hide in the floorboard of my loaner vehicle, just to get a look at the place. In fact, she probably would've insisted on it. Which was exactly why I hadn't called before I struck out. It would be just my luck that we'd get caught.

The farther from the interstate I traveled, the more rugged and deserted the territory became. A company pickup truck is a far cry from a horse-drawn prairie schooner, but a lonely, uncertain feeling closed in as civilization faded in the rearview mirror. I couldn't help imagining what the journey must have been like for those early-day pioneers whose shoes our cast members would soon try to fill. The idea that the people in our costume diaries and biographical journals had traveled these very paths was both awe-inspiring and disquieting. The sensation stayed with me as I wandered along ribbons of two-lane highway, snaking through limestone hills and slipping under the branches of massive live oaks that must've shaded wagons in days of old.

Along the roadsides, vibrant sprays of wildflowers painted foamy colors amid seas of green: the yellow and crimson of Indian paintbrush, the soft pinks and whites of primrose, the bold yellow blooms atop prickly pear cactus, the deep purple of wine-cups, the azure of fading bluebonnets, the lavender of wild phlox.

The names sifted from the corners of my mind, a pleasant residue from Grandma Rita's habitual Sunday drives into the country. Each year when I arrived at the beginning of the summer, we bonded over wild lantana, Indian paintbrush, and the Seven Sisters roses that grew near what had once been pioneer homesteads. Grandma Rita taught me so many things, but above all else, she taught me to respect the dreams that bubble from the wellsprings of the heart. *Those dreams that find you in the quiet of yourself, those are the truest of all, Allie,* she'd told me. *Making a hope come true takes faith and smarts, and hard work. Follow your dreams, but always take your brain with you.*

A tingle of excitement crackled as I topped the final hill and saw the glistening waters of Moses Lake in the valley below. Nestled among seemingly endless folds of spring green, dusty sage, and the milky flesh of limestone, the lake was breathtakingly beautiful, a fathomless deep blue, the water capturing the early afternoon light in shattered pieces. Here and there, boats skimmed the surface and sun-drenched docks bobbed in the current, providing shade for the lazy paddling of mallard ducks.

A squirrel dashed across a live oak branch overhead, then stopped and stood on its hind feet, seeming to wave a greeting as I passed a weathered sign at the edge of town. Comprised of ancient-looking rock pillars supporting a few rustic strips of board, it read, *Welcome to Moses Lake! If you're lucky enough to be at the lake, you're lucky enough.*

Moses Lake seemed like the kind of town where people might come to get away from it all, to bring the family for a woodsy, watery vacation and happily let the world pass by. Billboards here and there offered everything from fishing guide service to cabin rentals to canoe trips down the river. I followed the signs to the Waterbird Bait and Grocery, searching for somewhere to buy gas and grab lunch. Situated on a patch of gravel uphill from the lake, the rambling tin building didn't look like much, but as I pulled up to the gas pumps and stepped out, something definitely smelled good. The aroma of fried food was thick in the air. Downhill near the docks, a pair of fishermen was headed toward the store, one carrying a gas can in hand. When they reached the parking lot, they were deeply engaged in a conversation about fat bass and lures.

"I'm tellin' you, Burt, it's the green fire tail worms in the spring, and the red fire tails in the fall. That's what I caught that lunker bass on last year down by Caney Cove."

"Nester, as I recall, you didn't catch that supposed lunker a'tall. It ain't caught till it's in the boat. There's no proof you ever had you a lunker on the hook in the first place."

"Don't you even start up with me, Burt Lacey. It ain't a figment of my imagination. You saw the broke pole that thing left behind. . . ." Nester looked my way and held up the gas can. "Pumps out, down the hill."

"This one seems fine." Actually the numbers on the dial were moving faster than a Vegas slot machine. Now I understood why Kim never had any money and why she was in such a hurry to sell her pickup truck. Fortunately, a company credit card for gasoline had come with the loaner pickup.

Nester set down his gas can, craning to get a look at the jumble of boxes and assorted antique tools in the back of my truck—things I'd been instructed to drop off at a warehouse outside of town, where the set designers could pick them up as needed. "My daddy had a old hand billows like that one. Haven't seen nothin' like that in years." He leaned over to examine the tools.

Burt abandoned the pump opposite mine and came over to take a look. "Well, that old saddle is sure a dandy. I don't think I'd be ridin' that one, worn as the leather is, but it's somethin' to see. That a family heirloom? Got any idea how long ago it was made?"

"Pre–Civil War, is my understanding. It's just a prop. Nobody's going to be riding on it."

Bert and Nester eyed each other, then Nester eyed me. "Yer one of them movie folks. Shoulda known it by the plain white truck with the number on the side. It's a rental, ain't it?"

"It belongs to the production company. I'm not

sure if it's a rental or not. Actually, this is my first time to the location. Do you know how long it takes to get there from here?"

Burt and Nester shared a bit of silent eye conversation, and I wondered what that meant. They looked like two kids who'd been caught selling bubble gum on the playground at recess. "We've been sworn to secrecy, ma'am," Burt finally answered. "But if I *did* know where that filmin' set was, exactly, I'd tell you it's closer to get there crossin' the lake than it is to go overland. To drive it in a truck, you got a good hour of hills and dirt roads waitin' on you. You know how to operate the four-wheel drive in this thing? It full time, or you gotta lock it in?"

No doubt my cluelessness showed. The pump had just clicked off, and I was staring at the seventy-dollar gas bill in complete shock. *Seventy dollars for gas? All at one time?* "Four-wheel drive . . . huh . . ."

Nester *tsk-tsk*ed under his brushy gray moustache. "Oh, darlin', you don't want to be like that other bunch that come high falutin' out here from Hollywood. Tow truck had to go pull them out *after* they spent the night in the woods and scared theirselves half to death. Fools got two cars and a minivan high-centered at Bee Cave crossin'. That was back in the spring, when they started construction on the town site out there. They quit the minivans and started sendin' trucks after that. Now, if they would've asked us local folk, we coulda told them that in the first place. You don't want to be takin' chances on them roads up in Chinquapin Peaks. Can't always get cell phone service up there, either. Comes and goes, dependin' where you're at."

"Oh . . ." My glittery sense of excitement and adventure melted quickly into the uncomfortable squiggle of fear and trepidation. Maybe I needed food and extra water . . . just in case I found myself stuck in the mountains like one of those tourists who takes a wrong turn during the off-season and ends up fighting for survival. Maybe Tova had sent me up here on purpose—a clever way of finally getting rid of me.

Nester's gray mustache twitched upward. "Let me give it a closer look and make sure you're all set for the roads in Chinquapin. Now, you do know that the Wildwood town site is on fifteen thousand acres of private land owned by the power company, right? You got a key to get in that place? Because otherwise, you'll be slap outta luck. The construction crew already finished everythin' and left yesterday. I hear the movie folks changed the locks soon as the crews left, so no one could get back in. They're keepin' that place a Class-A secret." He smiled and winked at me. " 'Course, I guess they never thought about the fact that *if* the fella has a boat and *knows* his way to the cove along Wildwood Creek, it ain't hard to get there by water."

Bert elbowed Nester in the stomach, and Nester let out a soft *oof.* "Nester, you're gonna get us arrested. How would that look? Former principal of Moses Lake High School and the head mechanic at the bus barn, thrown in jail?"

Nester waved off the concern. "I'm tryin' to save this young lady from driving all the way up there for nothin'. If she don't have the key, we could call Mart McClendon and have him let her in. Game warden has the key to the old electric company gate next to the new one. He could get her on the place."

I quickly assured them that the combination had been given to me along with my traveling instructions for the day. An analysis of the truck and a rudimentary lesson in four-wheel-drive operation followed, and then I went inside to grab a soda, a chicken finger basket to go, and a precautionary six-pack of bottled water. Nester and Burt accompanied me in—apparently I was the most interesting thing happening in Moses Lake at the moment—and while I waited for my food, Pop Dorsey, the owner of the place, encouraged me to sign the Wall of Wisdom. Offering a Sharpie, he indicated the rear area of the store, where visitors had been leaving signatures and favorite bits of wisdom since the store's inception in the 1950s.

"It's good luck to sign the wall," Nester urged.

"Means you'll always come back to Moses Lake."

Since I needed all the luck I could get, and I did want to come back to Moses Lake—both today and at the end of the summer on my way home —I felt obliged to add my two cents. After thinking for a minute, I decided to leave that bit of wisdom from Grandma Rita.

Follow your heart, but always take your brain with you.

I signed it with both of our names. *Allie Kirkland and Rita Lane Kirkland.*

Now we were officially part of the Moses Lake Wall of Wisdom, along with such clever quotes as *Early to bed, early to rise, fish all day, tell big lies.* And *Never test the depth of the water with both feet.*

After I was finished, my new friends showed me the way to a massive old cotton barn the production company had rented to house props and construction materials. The barn lay along the lakeshore, behind a massive Greek revival house that had been converted into a bed-and-breakfast. The property owner there, Blaine Underhill, unloaded the boxes and tools into the barn, where buggies, wagons, buckets, tin pots, huge iron kettles, and all manner of other antique materials waited.

I stood in the doorway, admiring the sheer magnitude of the collection, my blood quickening with the whispers in the dusty air. The stories these things could tell . . .

If these were just the props, I couldn't imagine what it would be like to see, for the first time, Wildwood itself.

Chapter 14

Allie Kirkland
May, Present Day

I parked a few spaces down from the SUV and sat in my vehicle for a moment, watching for signs of anyone nearby. Along the hillside to my right, the crew camp seemed basic, but efficient— a few dozen plain vanilla, industrial-looking trailers on newly plowed gravel pads. They sat scattered among some stone picnic tables and rock build-ings that looked like they might have been part of a campground or ranger station at some time in the past. Electric wires and white plastic pipes crisscrossed the ground everywhere, creating a web of connections that eventually ended at nearby power poles.

To the left of the newly leveled parking lot, old stone steps and a freshly mown path led uphill and past several massive stone blocks that must have once formed the corner of a building or fence. Weeds, trumpet vine, and mustang grapes had overgrown the remains of the structure, making it seem a part of the natural landscape, but for its shape. At the trailhead, a scrap wood sign simply read *Wildwood* in slapdash letters. According to the map in Tova's folder, the old town site, now the location of our newly built restoration, was just on the other side of that ridge.

A sudden breeze whipped a dust devil along the parking lot, then died at the edge of the gravel, and everything went incredibly still as I stepped from the truck, the folder clasped against my chest. Goose bumps rose on my skin, and I had that uncomfortable, wary feeling that comes in dark parking garages, empty stairwells, and silent classroom buildings after-hours. Something inside me, the sort of sixth sense that warns of danger, wanted me to leave.

"Is anybody here?" My voice disturbed the afternoon stillness, then echoed into the distance as I stood listening for an answer. Nothing. Silence. Who did the other vehicle belong to? I'd come through a locked gate. If anyone was here, he or she had to be a member of the crew. Another person with the key code, maybe a member of the security team.

Atop a nearby electric pole, a camera in a white metal housing was pointed my way. Who could say whether it was operational and whether I was being watched, but thanks to a wrong turn on the largely unmarked dirt roads leading here, I'd already arrived much later than planned. The afternoon shadows were lengthening, and one thing was for certain—I wanted to finish the job and get out of here before evening set in. This place was eerie, even in broad daylight.

The tree shade fell inky and cool against my skin as I crossed the parking lot and started up the path marked by the *Wildwood* sign. Alongside the walkway, the tumbledown cornerstones rested amid a tangle of brambles. I stopped to look and made out a word, etched in and moss-covered. *Delevan.*

Harland Delevan. Randy had been working on his wardrobe for weeks, based on the costume diary I'd put together. As the founder of Wildwood and a member of a prominent early-day Texas family, Delevan was easier to document than the nameless immigrants who eventually found themselves working mining claims on the massive land grant secured by the Delevan family. Building Harland Delevan's costume bio was relatively straightforward. Understanding the history of the town he founded was not.

Even with hours and hours of library work, Stewart hadn't been able to satisfy his obsessive need to know how real or far-reaching the Wildwood gold strike may have been. Some amount of gold-bearing ore was pulled from the hills around Wildwood Creek and assayed, but from what we'd managed to determine, the reports printed in Eastern newspapers, boasting of "a strike of remarkable and promising character both in richness and extent of ore, so as to leave no further doubt of the existence of a gold-bearing belt in the land along Wildwood Creek" amounted to a little more than hype and speculation.

It had crossed my mind many times, while watching the wardrobing crew create fine silk and brocade clothing for Delevan's modern-day counterpart, how ridiculously out of place those clothes must have seemed amid the trappings of struggling immigrants, frontier shopkeepers, prospectors, farmers, trappers, freighters, and the slaves brought to the frontier by Delevan as his empire expanded. Against the rugged backdrop here, Harland Delevan, his mother, and his aunt must have been peacocks among yard fowl.

In my mind, the man was a faded image from a tintype dated just a year after the ill-fated end of Wildwood. He'd been photographed as a Confederate colonel in the Third Texas Cavalry, a striking, dark-haired man, posed with one hand resting on the hilt of his sword, and the other on an officer's field desk that must have been set up as a prop inside a photographer's studio. Behind him, the portrait of a sweeping plantation house stretched out in romantic, misty shades. His head was tipped upward, his carriage one of innate arrogance, his lips a thin, unyielding line, his eyes a fathomless black. Less than a month after the photo was taken, he would be dead in battle at Iuka, Mississippi. Stewart had unearthed an account of his death and the defeat of his Texas-based regiment.

Despite Stewart's intricate research, Harland Delevan had been little more than a spreadsheet of costuming details and production paperwork in my mind. A character. Now the name on the old cornerstone sent my thoughts tumbling end over end. The reality of this place was a wild assault, unexpected and impossible to process. These people were *real*. I'd scratched the surface of it during those long hours in the library, but I hadn't *felt* it. Suddenly the citizens of Wildwood were drawing breath, whispering, moving all around me.

What had happened to them?

Walking up the hillside through the trees, I heard their whispers. They'd lived in this place, left footprints on these paths. The massive live oaks on these hillsides were so large I couldn't have reached halfway around their gnarled trunks. These very trees had seen the citizens of Wildwood pass by—perhaps sheltered those who first arrived in the town, shielded young lovers as they sneaked away from prying eyes, or provided climbing castles for the children who lived here.

Children who'd vanished, it seemed, off the face of the earth.

What happened here?

I crested the ridge, then stopped as a breath caught in my throat. Nestled along a limestone bluff on a sloping hillside, the village tumbled downward toward the river basin. The rush of seeing it was indescribable.

I'd been imagining it for weeks, but now it was real.

The small main street ran parallel to a spring creek by the bluff, the buildings constructed of stone, log, and roughhewn wood. On the high side of the street, several structures squatted close to the mountain. On the low side of the street, rock foundations propped up buildings constructed of log and chink, as well as bare lumber. It was impossible to tell, at least from this distance, if any parts of the town were original or if it had all been freshly constructed for *Mysterious History*. Undoubtedly, the wooden structures were new construction, but they had been skillfully built and carefully cosmetically aged by the art finishers. The buildings looked like they'd been there all along.

"Amazing," I whispered. Above the treetops, Moses Lake peeked through in the distance. Prior to the building of the dam in the 1950s, the area that was now submerged had been a vast, fertile valley. One of the filming challenges here would be avoiding capturing the lake on camera, since it was not authentic to the time period of Wildwood. Work had been done to create a natural-looking shield of brush on the other side of Wildwood Creek, preventing accidental views of the lake through the trees.

More than anything, I wanted to slip my iPhone from my pocket and start taking pictures so I could show them to Kim and Stewart. Kim would have a fit when she found out where I'd been today—that I had actually set foot in Wildwood. She probably wouldn't believe me. No one could believe this place without seeing it.

Just one little picture, temptation whispered. *They'll so flip out.*

I looked around, wondering if there were more remote cameras nearby. Because of the desire to create an authentic experience, very little of the filming would be done with handhelds. As much as possible, life in Wildwood would be recorded by tiny robotic cameras embedded seamlessly in the set—something that had never been tried before to this degree. In Wildwood, Big Brother really would be watching you. Creepy to think about, even now. Despite its amazing appearance of authenticity, the place was a high-tech fishbowl. Within the village, there was no way to play to the cameras. They were everywhere.

Which meant someone really could be watching me right now.

I stopped with my hand halfway into my back pocket, nixing the idea of doing anything I wasn't supposed to do. Kim would just have to wait until she arrived on the bus with the rest of the cast. Maybe that was a good thing anyway. It wouldn't be right to spoil the moment of climbing the ridge and taking in the initial view of Wildwood. It was magic—hidden cameras or not.

Opening the folder and finding my site map, I proceeded down the hill and located my first target—the blacksmith shop on the low side of the street. Like most other businesses in the town, it was owned by Delevan. In the small, shed-like building, he used slave labor and charged exorbitant prices for horseshoeing and iron repair work. A slave known in surviving documents only as Big Nebenezer or Big Neb toiled here, sweating over a forge in the summer heat. I'd met his modern-day counterpart, Andy Blevins, during a costume fitting. Nice guy, getting his masters in history at the university. A former hometown football star.

How would he feel about spending the summer here in this rudimentary dwelling? While the history of my own Irish ancestors wasn't always pretty, as evidenced by the treatment of the immigrants who'd labored in Delevan's town, Andy's history was even more difficult. He was a sixth-generation Texan, and while historically Texans were divided on the issue of slavery, Texas had ultimately joined the Confederacy.

In real life, Andy drove a BMW his parents had bought for him. How would he adapt to the tiny nook at the back of the lean-to shop? He'd be surviving with little more than a cot and an open pit out back for cooking. Around the room, the set designers had placed a variety of labels to specify the locations for delivery of everything from tools, to lanterns, to cooking utensils and food-stuffs. I followed the blueprint and added the tags for placement of his wardrobe and personal items. It didn't take long. The show's historians had given Big Neb little more than the clothes on his back and a job to do.

Beyond the blacksmith shop, I continued along the lower side of the street, placing labels in the Baum home, the Forsythe home, the Miners Exchange, and the Assay Office. Then I walked through the trees along the network of footpaths that led into the woods where canvas shacks and modified cave houses would serve as homes for those portraying the recent immigrants to Wildwood. I couldn't imagine the kind of fortitude it must've taken for people to come here, to scratch out a shelter from the unforgiving hills and try to survive. On hot days, this life would've been an exercise in swatting mosquitoes and sweating. On rainy days, the humidity would seep in and dampen everything, runoff from uphill creating a quagmire on the floors. How did people keep their clothes dry, their bodies clean?

I'd never considered the trials of my ancestors. I knew so little of my own history. Grandma

Rita's grandmother had lived on a small piece of land outside Lufkin, Texas. She'd cooked at a boarding-house while my grandfather cowboyed on a ranch somewhere. Grandma Rita told stories about her mother, my great-grandmother, hearing the wolves clawing and growling outside their Piney Woods house at night. *My mama used to say she was mighty afraid when her daddy was away, but her mama did whatever it took to protect her babies and their land and their animals. It wasn't much, but it was all they had. If they lost it, they didn't survive. Wasn't any welfare system back then, you know.*

Wildwood gave me a sudden appreciation for that story. I might've come from hardy pioneer stock, but I had a feeling that the genetics had been watered down somewhere along the way. As much as the Wildwood project fascinated me, I didn't want to live anywhere that wasn't within proximity of a hot shower and a well-stocked refrigerator.

After placing all the tags in the low-rent district, I crossed the street and continued up the hill to the high side of town. The wood and limestone buildings there were a marvel of modern set design. Even with tags everywhere and many of the props not yet in place, entering each of those buildings was like walking into a time capsule. They were authentic down to the finest detail and the concealment of the robotic cameras was incredibly well done. High-tech equipment masqueraded as baskets hung on walls, coffeepots strategically placed beside woodstoves, even a child's rag doll sitting on a windowsill. The only sign of modern technology were well-hidden camera lenses and wires that disappeared seamlessly into walls or floors.

Halfway along the upper street, I veered into the small alcove of bathhouses and laundries tucked along a spring creek at the base of the bluff. Kim's future quarters were nothing fancy, that was for sure. Two girls to a room, two rope beds with hand-stuffed mattresses, a row of pegs in one corner for hanging clothes, a tin basin and pitcher for washing. And a chamber pot.

Kim would love that one.

She couldn't hide a cell phone in this place if she tried. There was definitely no room here for privacy. I wanted to snap a photo, but I resisted the urge and placed tags instead. Time was running short.

Shadows stretched across the main street as I left the bathhouse area, and the light waned into the soft shades of evening. Some sort of animal rustled in the woods, the sound standing every nerve in my body on end.

"Okay, Allie," I whispered, looking up and down the street toward my two remaining targets —the small stone schoolhouse and the two-story home at the top of the hill, which would provide lodging for the Delevan family as well as their household workers and slaves. "Time to wrap this up and leave the creepy, empty town behind."

It seemed prudent to knock out the bigger job first. The Delevan house would take some time: there were literally pages of tags. Vaguely unwelcoming, the two-story clapboard structure stood massive and shadow-covered. I had no idea what, if any, provisions had been made for lighting on the reenactment set after dark. Nor did I want to find out. One way or another, I was going to finish this job before the last of the evening sun disappeared behind the bluff.

Something rustled in the woods again, as if to punctuate the idea. "Yeah . . . ohhh-kay . . . definitely time to finish and get out." This was all starting to feel way too real. Grandma Rita's wolves-clawing-at-the-cabin story came to mind.

I double-timed it up the hill, climbed the steep porch steps to the Delevan house, and let myself in through massive front doors, which seemed ridiculously ostentatious for a settlement where much of the community still had dirt floors.

The interior of the place was equally luxurious, furnished with ornate velvet fainting couches, heavy Renaissance Revival chairs, and a mahogany table large enough to seat eighteen. A gorgeous walnut plantation desk and leather chair graced Harland Delevan's study, and shelves filled with books stretched to the library ceiling. In the women's parlor, wooden embroidery hoops, sewing boxes, and baskets of needlework waited near ladies' chairs crafted with wing seats wide enough to accommodate the hoop skirts of the day. The house even had indoor plumbing of a sort, running water being brought in from a cistern attached to a spring-fed windmill beside the kitchen house out back. For 1861, this was luxury, but as interesting as it was to see, the heavy velvet drapes cast a spooky pallor over the place, and I was happy to finish attaching the wardrobe tags for the three members of the Delevan family and their cast of house slaves.

I couldn't leave the Delevan residence quickly enough.

A crow flew off the porch railing as I stepped out the front door. I jumped out of my skin, then crawled back in again. "Okay, okay . . . just one more building." The daylight was leaving way too fast, evening cloaking the main street of Wildwood in a murky gray vapor that seemed part fog and part shadow. It followed me as I hurried to the school and went inside, leaving the double front doors open for light. From the center aisle, the building, with its high, whitewashed wooden ceiling and rows of pews appointed with flip-up school desks, appeared surprisingly quiet and peaceful despite the gathering darkness outside. The antique wooden surfaces bore the evidence of use and miscellaneous attempts at refinishing. Their history seemed to travel through my fingers as I touched them. Hairline cracks and fissures testified to the fact that these pieces had seen the ravages of wind and weather. Where had they come from?

Outside, a wooden shutter fanned the wind, playing with the amber light over one of the pews as I opened the folder to look at the map and the tags.

"Just seven? Just seven in here?" I continued up the aisle to the pulpit and teacher's lectern, which were one and the same. Wooden cabinet doors on the front wall concealed an antique blackboard that had undoubtedly seen countless years of lessons in whatever classroom had originally housed it. On the teacher's desk, inkwells and slates lay already in place. As in the Delevan house, the designers had done a fantastic job of satisfying the finest details.

Strangely enough, I had only a few tags for the two apartments built onto the back of the school. I had researched the young schoolteacher, Bonnie Rose, with special interest, as Tova had mentioned her name to me during my first interview with Razor Point. Hers was the apartment on the right. The apartment on the left appeared to be vacant. There were no tags to place, but curiosity urged me toward the door and through it.

The room was the ultimate in efficiency apartments—a small woodstove in the rear corner for heating and modest cooking, a stuffed mattress on a rope-tie bed along one wall, a tiny table, a foldable wooden chair of the style that was used during the Civil War, and a dark mahogany combination dresser and wardrobe cabinet. One oil lamp for light. Near the table, a door with one tiny four-paned window led directly onto a back porch that faced the limestone cliffs behind the building.

Not much of a view—outhouse, cedars, live oaks, and the cliff face. Somewhere down the hill, the spring cut its way through the rocky soil, hidden by the underbrush. The light in these rooms would be muted even during the middle of the day. Sort of a dingy place to live, but still a step up from the workers' quarters in the bathhouse district or the shanties in the hills. No doubt the tent homes on mining claims further out would be even worse. On top of everything else, those participants would have to construct their dwellings themselves, just as their impoverished ancestors had.

Across the adjoining wall, but only reachable by returning to the main schoolroom, the teacher's quarters were a mirror image, other than a larger wardrobe cabinet, a separate dresser with an oval looking glass on top, and two rope-frame beds. The room was arranged to give the appearance that both Bonnie Rose and her younger sister, Maggie, were living here. In reality, the underage cast members whose parents were not part of the reenactment, like Wren Godley, would be living up the hill in crew camp. Regulations and child labor laws governed working hours for the kids on set. This room was no place for a child, anyway. Too dark. Too confining. Along the back wall, a tall eight-paned window looked toward the bluff. The lack of a door to the back porch gave the place the feeling of a prison cell more than a bedroom.

I stood for a moment after placing the tags for Bonnie's belongings—including a bonnet, a cameo locket, two pairs of ladies' gloves, and three dresses. The remainder of what she owned, she would arrive in. Bonnie's costumes were being rented from a production warehouse, so I hadn't even seen her wardrobe or met her modern-day counterpart.

Standing now where the real Bonnie Rose would have stood, where she'd lived what—by all the evidence—was the last summer of her life, the sadness of her story struck me. She was just a girl, barely out of childhood when she came here to be a teacher. What were her thoughts as she sat in her tiny room? What did she dream of? What did she hope for?

What brought her here? Judging from its history, this town was no place for a young woman alone. Why did she come?

The mystery tugged at me, but came tinged with

a palpable sadness. She'd lived and died with almost no record of her life left behind. In our research, Stewart and I had uncovered the one solicitous newspaper piece written by a reporter for a Chicago newspaper. The words made Wildwood sound like the path to wealth and good fortune. In the article, the newly constructed school was touted as a selling point for the town's "most civilized society." *Wildwood,* the words boasted, *will soon be sporting an opera hall and a reputable gentleman's club, as well as a school and house of worship, staffed by a clergyman of great faith and morals and a cultured and dedicated teacher educated in the finest manner.*

Other than that small bit of information, it seemed as though the schoolteacher's short life had never been. Her trail and that of her younger sister began and ended in Wildwood. Stewart had tried to find out more about them, but nothing existed.

I closed their door behind me on the way out, then stopped at Bonnie's desk, ran my hands along the wood, and realized with a sense of pride that, if nothing else, the young woman who had come to this place would finally have a voice through our work this summer.

She deserved that much.

"People will know who you were, at least," I whispered into the empty room, touching her ink-well and slate. Emotion choked my throat. I wasn't sure why. Maybe because Bonnie Rose was so young. If only the foundations of this old building could talk, tell me her story . . .

A chill slipped over me. I felt the air shift in the room, the coolness of evening slide in. Uneasiness teased my senses, and with it came a feeling that I wasn't alone.

Instinct caused me to spin around, and I gasped at the silhouette of a man in the doorway. My heart lurched upward, then froze momentarily. With evening light shining from behind, he was little more than a shadow. The air in my throat turned solid, the moment seeming to warp and stretch as I floundered for reality. Was all of this a dream? My trip to Wildwood only something my mind had conjured while I was fast asleep, safe in my own bed?

"And who was she?" His voice was deep and smooth, confident, almost emotionless, bearing just a hint of an accent, the origin of which I couldn't guess from only those few words. "Who was Bonnie Rose?"

He was real at least, the man in the doorway. I wasn't having some sort of strange mental breakdown, inventing people out of thin air.

"Pardon?" I managed to croak out. The SUV in the parking lot crossed my mind, and I had a mental flash of the license plate. *RAV-5.* The silhouette in the doorway bore a remarkable resemblance to the one on the balcony the first time I'd entered the Berman Theater, the man Kim had insisted was Rav Singh.

It all made sense now . . . in a paralytic sort of way.

Was this him in the flesh? Because if it was, I feared I would faint. This could be the biggest moment of my career, my life, and my meager existence on the planet. Had he been here, somewhere nearby, the whole time I'd been working?

Thank goodness I hadn't succumbed to the temptation to snap a photo or two.

He moved farther into the room. Two lanky, easy steps. He was tall enough to be Singh. He fit the profile Kim had dug up on the Internet. In school in India, he'd followed American basketball and dreamed of one day playing in an American college. Instead, life had taken him into a directing and producing career in Bollywood.

"Who do you think she was?" he asked again. "Who was Bonnie Rose?"

I touched my fingertips to the desk and steadied myself against it, my mind racing like a hamster on an out-of-control wheel, round and round, going nowhere and everywhere all at once.

The right answer. What was the right answer? What would make me sound like I was intelligent, competent, good at my job? Respectful yet not the sort of pathetic underling who would shamelessly grovel to earn brownie points? "I couldn't find very much of the research on her, other than what was already in the costume diary when it came to me." *Stupid answer. Stupid answer.* That made me sound too lazy to dig deeper.

Come on, Allie. Think. Why couldn't he have asked me about someone else? Someone we'd actually found more material about? I hadn't looked at Bonnie's costume diary since Stewart and I gave up on tracking her any further. "She was young. Too young to be taking on the responsibility of a job while raising a younger sibling, and moving to a strange place. I can't imagine having that much on my shoulders at eighteen." *Great. Well done. Way to make yourself sound like an immature slacker.* "But I guess you do what you have to do to survive. I guess we don't know what we're capable of until we're tested."

I ventured across the open space at the front of the room and stood near the pulpit, trying to gain a better view. I wanted to see his expression, to discern whether I was getting any of this right.

He turned sideways, almost as if to conceal himself from me, then leaned against one of the pews, crossing his legs and threading his arms, gazing into the rafters. "Do you think we can really understand it, that desperate struggle to survive? We, who have been softened by a world of privilege? Where water flows from a tap and food comes in neat plastic containers? Where we can create light and darkness at the flip of a switch?"

I took a moment to digest the question, to measure its depth. "I don't know. There's Maslow's Hierarchy of Needs, I suppose." *Thank you, Kim, for making me quiz you on all that counseling homework.* "Once we know our basic physical needs will be met, we elevate from survival to more complex emotional needs." Suddenly, this felt like a psychological profile. It was an odd first conversation to have with anyone, much less your boss's boss's boss . . . if that's who he was.

"And what do you think *survival* meant to her?" He waved a hand, indicating the desk behind me. "Bonnie Rose. What did she desire? What did she fear? What *drove* her?"

I'd been asking myself almost the same thing only a few moments ago, but trying to answer it under pressure made my mind trip over itself. "Well . . . she was a teacher. I suppose she must've cared about children, been devoted to giving them the skills to achieve a better life. Wildwood would've been a place where she was desperately needed. Maybe that's what drew her here."

He turned slowly, and I could just make out his features. Angular chin, thin nose, dark hair grown long enough to bind with a rubber band at the back of the neck, somber eyes. This was definitely Rav Singh. "Or maybe she was running from something. Maybe this ragged little settlement on the frontier was the last place she could hide. . . ." He spoke the words as if they were more than just a theory, as if he knew something I didn't. Like he was enjoying baiting me with little morsels.

"Running from what?" The image of Bonnie Rose shifted in my mind, and then shifted again, struggling to solidify into one thing. None of this was among the smattering of biographical information in the costume diary. If Singh knew more, why hadn't he shared it? Why keep it to himself?

"Who else would she have been?" I asked.

"A seductress? A murderess on the run, living under an assumed name? A woman who doesn't seem to have existed in any historical record before or after Wildwood? A bewitching beauty who fell madly in love with the richest man in town, so much so that she killed, then killed again in an effort to secure his affections? Who was so driven to achieve the social position that marrying him would provide, that she manipulated others into doing her dirty work? A woman who masterminded a string of unsolved crimes that eventually drove the town into a sort of mass hysteria?"

"She was *eighteen* years old." For whatever reason, his portrayal felt vastly offensive. "An orphaned girl with a younger sister to raise. It seems like quite a stretch to believe she'd be capable of manipulating an entire town. I mean, she—" I bit off the sentence, realizing that I'd gotten more impassioned then I meant to.

But the idea of using a girl who'd most likely died at eighteen, who couldn't defend herself, to add some sort of dark plot twist to this summer's production both made me queasy and lit a fire inside me. Given Rav Singh's usual bent toward warped reality shows—and the sometimes-twisted nature of *Mysterious History* projects—it didn't seem outside the realm of possibility that the intentions for *Wildwood Creek* went well beyond the factual representation of the town. In fact, given Singh's reputation, his questions about Bonnie Rose seemed a likely answer to why someone like him would take on a project like this.

He was completely unbothered by my protest. In fact, he didn't look my way. Instead, he continued speculating toward the whitewashed ceiling. "There were some accounts given after Wildwood was abandoned—claims made by citizens who'd run from this place before its last days, taking almost nothing with them. They told of strange happenings, people jumping off cliffs into the river, people disappearing without a trace. A sort of hysteria among the citizenry. There was talk of some sort of mythical river people who tempted victims from sleep, dragging them to watery graves in the dark of midnight.

"It has been said that the events began not long after the arrival of Bonnie Rose. Shortly following her installment as a teacher here, a young woman —reportedly Bonnie's rival— hurled herself to her death. Harland Delevan gave an account of these things to a field reporter during your Civil War. Did you know that? Even as he was dying in a field hospital, he did not change his story. He claimed that Bonnie Rose was some sort of witch—that it was all her doing. Why would a man lie on his deathbed?"

"Maybe because he wanted the truth to die with him." My explanation made more sense than his, considering his had to be pure fantasy. "But I don't believe an eighteen-year-old girl was responsible for the demise of an entire town. I don't believe in witches, ghosts, and river people either. There's a logical explanation— there always is."

"What do *you* think happened? What do you believe? I know you've done a fine job of researching the place."

I hugged the folder against my chest, the shadows falling thicker now. Outside, an owl hooted long and low, and suddenly the conversation, the village, and Singh's presence were more than disquieting. I wanted to leave. "I haven't really thought about it. I mean, I've just focused on my job. Speaking of, I'd better get back to the Berman. They'll be wondering where I am, and it's a long drive to Austin." So much for making brownie points with the big boss. I was outta here.

"There was a song about her, sung in Civil War camps and on cattle drives of the time. 'The Ballad of Wildwood.' Have you heard of it? The lyrics, for the most part, seem to have been lost to history, other than oral tradition among some of the locals."

"I don't think I saw anything about it in the research."

And lays them down in sweet repose,
The milky hands of Bonnie Rose . . .

The words whispered through my mind out of no place. Had I read them somewhere?

Above the cliffs, alone she stood,
The bitter maiden of Wildwood . . .

I blinked, stopped a few steps from him in the aisle, but no more words came.

Singh hadn't moved, but he was watching me as if he either expected our conversation to continue or intended to stay after I left. I studied him without wanting to. His features were emotionless, his fathomless dark eyes probing, seeming to be searching for something in me.

I slipped a hand into my jeans pocket and took out the keys. "So . . . I'd better hit the road. I'll never find my way out of these hills after sundown. It was nice meeting you."

He smiled slightly, but it didn't reach his eyes. It was more a look of assessment, a measuring. "It does get very dark. I spent the night here last night."

Heebie-jeebies danced over my skin. What in the world was I supposed to say to that? "Oh." *Not me, mister. No way I'm staying in this place alone . . . or with you, if that's what you've got in mind.* I took another side step toward the door. "Well, I definitely don't want to miss the last of the light." *Outta here. So outta here. Whoosh. See that dust trail? That's me. Gone.* Kim would have an astronomical freak out when I told her about this conversation.

The creep factor right now was off the charts. In fact, part of me wanted to reconsider my whole decision to spend the summer here. But with more than a hundred cast and crewmembers, it would surely feel safe enough, even after dark.

"Not a trace of ambient light," he mused, now surveying the window. "The stars so close, they are just beyond your fingertip."

"It sounds . . . awesome." *Please, God, help me to extricate myself from the situation in some way that is not ridiculously ungraceful. Now. Please, now.* "I'll have to watch on the way home." *Far, far from here. By myself.* I took another step toward the door. One, two, three. I was almost there.

"I want *you* to become her." The words stopped me on the threshold. I turned slowly. Maybe he had me confused with someone else. One of the cast members, perhaps?

Maybe he was just . . . talking to himself . . . or

to the ghosts he thought were here. Maybe he was completely off his rocker. Creative types tended to teeter on the ragged edge sometimes.

He hadn't changed position. Instead, he was leaning slightly over his crossed arms, seemingly deep in thought, studying an expensive-looking pair of black boots. Actually, I realized now that he was dressed from head to toe in black. Black boots. Black slacks. Black button-up shirt in some sort of slightly iridescent fabric that caught the fading light. Silk, most likely.

"Excuse me?" Sometimes the smartest thing you can do is play dumb.

He nodded slowly, as if he were establishing something in his mind. "I want you to become Bonnie Rose."

The keys slipped from my fingers and clattered to the floor, disturbing the dusty air in the schoolhouse.

Singh looked my way then, his head swiveling slowly. His gaze started at my feet and traveled carefully up my body, past my eyes, and then back down again in a way that made me feel more than weird—as if I were a new car or a slick polo pony he was thinking about buying. "You're perfect."

In most instances, *You're perfect* feels like flattery, but in this case, it just felt . . . bizarre. I fumbled for a response. What were the right words in a circumstance like this? I finally settled for "Oh, I'm just in production. An assistant . . . Well, sort of an intern, really. I'm not part of the cast. I work for Tova. Tova Kask? I have several years' experience in community and university theater, and I'm working on my masters in film. This summer is a dream job for me."

I was babbling now, and I knew it. I tried to pause, to see if he would jump in, but he wasn't saying anything, so I felt compelled to babble some more. "I love research and costuming, especially. I really do. And I've learned so much this summer from Randy, Phyllis, and Michelle. It's been a fantastic experience so far. And I'm working my way through school, so I needed the job. It's always been a dream of mine . . . film . . . But behind the scenes, I mean. I flunked out of being on stage in the fifth grade. Totally. Complete stage fright. They had to carry me off. I was the only kid assigned to work with the teacher, helping with costumes and props. I didn't mind it though, because . . ."

The intensity of his gaze stopped me. My mind went completely blank. "I know who you are, Allie Kirkland." He pulled his lips between his teeth, tilted his head slightly to one side, regarded me the way a portrait painter might take in a subject he's about to render onto canvas. Some-thing inside me shuddered. I'd never had any-body look at me with such intense scrutiny. "I make it my business to know everyone who works for me. Your father was a director."

The uncomfortable quiver inside me radiated outward, crawled over my bones, and slipped into the air. What in the world was happening here? What would he do if I said no—*when* I said no—to this insane proposition? "Yes, he was," I answered tentatively. "My earliest memories are of film sets. Behind the scenes. I've always wanted to follow in his footsteps, see if I have what it takes. My father's work ended way too soon." If he knew everything else about me, he probably knew that as well. It didn't matter now. My purpose was to convince him that I was much more valuable in a support capacity, that I could pull my weight and then some.

It occurred to me to wonder whether Tova had set this up. She was the one who'd sent me here today, alone. Maybe this was her way to avoid being stuck in a crew trailer with me all summer. But I had done a good job so far, hadn't I? I'd worked like a dog in the basement of the Berman all these weeks. I was the one who knew how to fix the machinery, who knew how the files were organized, who knew many of the costumes seam by seam, inch by inch. She had to realize that. Would she do this to me now? Was she really that heartless?

Singh's eyelids lowered slowly to half-mast.

Sweat dripped beneath my shirt, despite the fact that the evening air had cooled noticeably.

"What if you could have that dream, Allie? What if, by doing what I am asking of you, you could guarantee yourself the funds for not *one* semester of film school, but all of it? What then?"

I lost my balance, staggered a step, my tennis shoe landing on the raised threshold so that I fell backward and ended up catching my footing on the porch outside, which was just as well, because that put me farther from Singh and closer to an escape. Even so, I stood frozen.

"What exactly are you . . ." I paused to collect my thoughts, if I could find any. Now wasn't the time to speak without thinking. I had to be careful. Singh did not look like the kind of man who was accustomed to being told *no*.

"What am I saying?" He finished the question. "That's what you were about to ask, correct? That's the thing you want to know?"

I nodded.

"Simply, that you assume the life of Bonnie Rose this summer. For three months. That's all that's being asked of you. And then I will see that you have what you need for film school. I hold sway over any number of scholarships and admissions boards. This *is* a business of special favors. Should I make it known to the right people that we had an exceptionally bright and capable young intern serving us in *Wildwood Creek*, you could quite quickly find yourself stepping into the life you've always wanted. Law school is, of course, admirable, if it's what you desire in life . . . but if it's nothing more than a family expectation, then it amounts to enslavement of a sort, don't you think? What is enslavement, if it's not the forcing of your labor toward a life that has been chosen for you?"

I stood staring at him, unable to formulate anything other than a three-word response, which seemed rather pointless now. "But why me?"

His fingers slipped under the flap on his shirt pocket, reached in, and slid something out. Pushing off the back of the pew, he walked forward to hand it to me. An unconscious retreat moved me a half step before I forced myself to take what he offered. A photograph. A tintype similar to many of the ones Stewart and I had scrounged off the Internet or copied from books and magazines for the costume diaries. But this one was original.

I turned it slowly in my hands . . . a picture of a school. *This* school. Children were posed on the steps. A dozen or more. All ages, from no more than five or six to as old as fourteen, wearing everything from nicely made dresses and stockings to what looked like flour sacks cinched at the waist with twine, bare feet sticking out the bottom.

Standing beside them was their teacher, Bonnie Rose.

Tall, slender, with long ringlets of hair that were

probably red, she looked only slightly like the sketch Randy had rendered in her costume diary.

She was startlingly familiar, though I'd never seen her before.

If the picture hadn't been taken over a hundred and fifty years ago, she could have been my sister.

Chapter 15

Bonnie Rose
May 1861

"You'd best be marching up the hill now," Mrs. Forsythe says to me as I pass through her kitchen. "Take your sister along with you, and she'll not trouble me this aft." Her eyes narrow in her meaty face, and she looks pleased to be sending us off again.

Daily, Mrs. Delevan holds a ladies' tea and sewing circle in her fine home on the hill, but it's not an invitation the womenfolk of Wildwood are thankful to be receiving. Mrs. Forsythe knows this as well as I, and that's the cause of her satisfied look today. It's the better part of a month now, during the buildin' of our room aback the schoolhouse, that Maggie May and I have been underfoot of the Forsythes, and it's hard to know whether remaining here or participating in one of Mrs. Delevan's odd tea parties is worse.

It's not as though I'll be refusing Mrs. Delevan's invitation, of course. With the town fair to burstin' from so many folk arriving each day, and the one small hotel operated by Mr. Hollis always full, it's easy enough to see how fortunate Maggie May and I are to have the kind patronage of Mr. Delevan. While others go wanting, we are put up in the Forsythe home. They've ousted their two daughters to give us the space, and it's clear that Mrs. Forsythe was told to do it. Angry whispers hiss through the walls as we lie abed at night. Her daughters sleep in the hay above the wagon shed out back now. The lady of the house is not happy to be feeding extras, either, not one bit. Goods run a pretty penny at the Unger Store, when they can be had at all.

But as with everythin' in Wildwood, the Delevans hold the mortgage on the mill where Mr. Forsythe earns his daily bread. So he keeps us as boarders whether it pleases his wife or not.

She smiles behind her hand as I gather up Maggie and go. It's a small bit of satisfaction to her.

On the trek uphill, Maggie complains again. She's not allowed into the ladies' teas, and she's loath to sit on the steps aback the Delevan house by the hour, waiting for old Mrs. Delevan and her addle-minded sister, Peasie, to tire of their guests and set us free.

"I'll stay at the schoolhouse. I'll not wander a

bit. . . ." Maggie pleads as we pass by the small buildin', where, to date, we have only seven children in grades from first to sixth. They come for classes from morn until just past midday. We'll add seventh and eighth grades later, if there's a need for it, but by the upper ages, most children here are helping their parents to open crosscuts and sink shafts in the hillsides of Chinquapin Peaks. The immigrant families, having risked all to come here, live in hopes of striking the deep veins that generate the gold-bearing ore found near the surface. There's barely a man can't tell of some color scratched from his claim, yet none have amounted to much thus far, it seems. After the portions owed Mr. Delevan's Miners Exchange and his store are paid, they have even less.

For the most part, those who've come with dreams of wealth have found themselves living in homes built of anythin' they can scratch up. The womenfolk turn their hands to keeping their broods fed and washed, but growing table fodder in this rocky soil is no small matter. Those operating businesses in town at Mr. Delevan's direction fare somewhat better. They seem to be German folk mostly, and the claim seekers being mostly Irish. The Irish are known for the dreamin', much the same as my da. It's nothin' to them to take on a risk. They haven't much awaiting them back East but hard labor and low wage.

"You'll be coming up the hill with me, Maggie May. And no complainin' about it," I say to her as we pass by the Unger Store and the climb grows steeper, up the high side of the street toward the Delevan home on the hill. "And mind your manners, on the chance that old Mrs. Delevan should look out and see you there. Don't be making trouble for Essie Jane and the others."

Five slave women work in the Delevan home— so many they seem to be stumblin' over one another. With only the two older ladies and Mr. Delevan to care for, the slaves spend their time scrubbing the corners of the house, then scrubbing them again.

On tea days they help with dressing the ladies. It's an odd ritual I wouldn't have been believing, if not for seeing it with my own eyes. Mrs. Delevan will have nothin' of dirt off the streets brushed over her carpets, or common clothing sitting on her fine chairs. Before entering the home, each of the women is brought 'round back to the kitchen house, and there helped to shed her own frock in favor of something pleasing to Mrs. Delevan. The clothing is laced, or bound, or given a hasty stitch as need be to fit it to the wearer, and then the women are gathered and proceed to the front to pretend to be just arriving at the Delevan home.

It's a strange thing, to be sure, old Mrs. Delevan poised there in her son's fine parlor, delightin' herself over the dresses and hats, pretending never to have seen the garments before. A grown woman, playing at a game of dollhouse. No one says anythin' about it, and there beside her, Peasie looks on quiet and meek but just as delighted, her countenance that of an overgrown girl.

I've wondered if Mr. Delevan knows of these things, but he's been gone away on business since my coming to Wildwood. With shots now fired between the Unionists and the Secessionists at Fort Sumter, and Texas having voted to join the Confederate cause over a month ago, there's much talk and whisperin' and meetin' taking place somewhere outside Wildwood—I've gathered that much, though our information here is slight. Wildwood not being on the path to anyplace else, few come here, unless it is to stay.

I've no way of knowing whether this folly with Mrs. Delevan's tea parties will continue on when her son returns to take up the reins of his household, or whether it may end. He seems a more practical man than this. The womenfolk in town have work to do—children to tend, meals to scratch up, businesses to look after with their husbands.

"Please," Maggie whispers, tuggin' on my arm. "I won't wander if you leave me here." She looks back to the schoolhouse, but I worry over letting her stay behind. The Reverend Brahn, who makes his home in the boardin' room next to one being finished for Maggie and me, seems a drunken and slovenly old man, and I've my suspicions as to whether he is a reverend at all. He's been no help in starting the school or in persuading families living in their dugouts of canvas and timber that there can be advantage in educating the young. Only the town children have come, thus far— those from the German families. But dozens of families live out in the wood. The few I've seen are a scrappy, ragged lot, their clothes in tatters, their feet bare, and their hair matted. They are as hardscrabble as the hills themselves.

A wagon rolls along the street past us and stops beside the Unger warehouse, and four men scurry to do the unloading. The driver jumps down with a leather-bound packet 'neath his arm, and I know his lanky walk before we come close enough to see his face. I've not crossed paths with Mr. Hardwick since he delivered me to the Forsythe home a month ago now. What I have heard of him is that, upon leaving Wildwood, he manages his living by the constant transportation of goods to other settlements downriver.

I find myself quickening my pace, though I'm not certain why. The man did bring us safely across the unsettled country, but I've not forgotten several insufferable moments on our journey. Not the least of which that river crossin', which almost took us all. Doubtless, he has neither forgotten me.

He casts eyes my way, and I'm a bit taken aback when he pauses to tip his hat, pleasant enough. "Miss Rose."

"Mr. Hardwick."

He studies me with a keen interest then, and I'm surprised by it. "You're looking well, I reckon. Finding life in Wildwood agreeable so far? No more rivers to cross, at least." A slight smirk follows the question, and I feel myself bristlin'. Perhaps he thought he would find me at this point, simperin' and babblin' and pleadin' for deliverance from this place. Just last week, a young woman ran the length of the street screaming and moaning and tearing at her clothes. Mrs. Forsythe did not even move from her wash line. "There's some womenfolk can't bear up," she said, sending a hard look my way.

Now Mr. Hardwick seems to be entertaining the same thoughts of me.

"Some matters are difficult," I answer and meet his cool, gray eyes. They remind me of the water in the river, a glassy surface hiding secrets beneath. "But that is, of course, to be expected. While it is a bit of slow going, persuading the families living out on claims to surrender the labors of their children to an education, I have faith that it can be accomplished in time. For now, we await the arrival of books and materials . . . and a room to be completed for Maggie May and me aback the building. I look forward to no longer imposing on the hospitality of Mrs. Forsythe."

"I've never known her to have any," he remarks and smiles then, and I am again surprised by him. He is at least a decade older than I, perhaps made to look more so by the scar beneath his eye and his thick head of hair gone early gray, but his smile suddenly seems that of a young man. A man who was playful once.

A laugh pushes up my throat, despite the bad manners of it, and I stifle it into my glove, pretending to cough.

Beside me, Maggie giggles straightaway. "She steals the bread off our plates, and says we ate it, and then she feeds it to her daughters."

"Maggie!" I reach across and grab her arm hard.

Mr. Hardwick is surprisingly charmed. I've never supposed that he could be. He leans close to Maggie, touches a fingertip to her chin, and says, "Could be because her daughters aren't near so pretty as you, Maggie Rose."

I tug Maggie's arm, shifting her away slightly as she favors him with a smile. I've come to be leery of the sort of men here in Wildwood. Though none have offered any trouble to Maggie and me, they are rough-cut and many in want of a woman. Mrs. Delevan will not allow saloons and the like in her town and insists that the bath-houses do only respectable business, but just down the spring creek in Red Leaf Hollow lies a place where gamin' and drinkin' and all manner of debauchery is said to happen. The girl who ran screaming through the street had come from there.

Mr. Hardwick straightens to his full height and looks over his shoulder toward the wagon. "Reckon I've got some of your books and slates in the crate there. I'll deliver them up to the schoolhouse after I've taken the mailbag to Unger's."

"I could help you," Maggie offers, and her forwardness is surprisin'. Perhaps being here in this strange place has made Mr. Hardwick's face seem more like that of a friend than it should be.

Even more surprisin', Mr. Hardwick appears somewhat agreeable to it. Before I know what's happened, he's taken the mail pouch from his arm. "Reckon you could trot this in to Mrs. Unger, and I'll walk up to the smithy to see about new shoes on my red mule? Then we'll take the books down to the church house." He turns to me, finally. "Reckon you'll be hankering to see what's in the crates as soon as they're opened too."

His gaze darts toward the wagon and then to his hands, almost bashful. It's a bafflement. Does he mean to invite me along? Of a sudden, he seems nothin' of the hard-edged man who delivered us here. I find myself blushing and tripping over my words. "I've been called up the hill for tea. There's never any telling how long it'll be."

He nods without looking at me, seeming unsurprised that I've answered in the negative.

"But I suppose it will be well enough if Maggie

goes along." I'm stunned to find myself saying it, and it surprises Maggie as well. She catches a breath, smiling for the first time in a fair bit. She's happy to escape the big house today.

It's just as well not having her there, I decide. Essie Jane has learned far too much from the slaves in the kitchen house, and she shares her new knowledge. Maggie's been privy to more than she should know about that place in the wood at Red Leaf Hollow and what sort of sinful behavior happens there. Even the women slaves don't go that direction along Wildwood Creek when they're out gathering mushrooms, nuts, and herbs for cooking.

I turn to Maggie. "But no slipping off to the wood or around town when you finish helping Mr. Hardwick. Are you understanding me, Maggie May?" She has a wicked curiosity in her mind about that place, Red Leaf Hollow. I've seen it in her eyes when she whispers about what Essie Jane has told her. She's wonderin' after it, even though Essie Jane and the kitchen women's purpose was to warn the young girls never to stray near.

"Yes'm," she answers, then bounces on her toes as she clutches the mailbag to her chest. It's no small thing that Mr. Hardwick is trusting her with it. She dashes for the store, and Mr. Hardwick takes his leave of me. I'm wishing I could share their afternoon, rather than partake of the one assigned me.

My mind remains with Maggie May and the new schoolbooks as I make my way to the Delevans' kitchen house and proceed to change into finery that must be pinned up at the back, as it's too large in the middle and the breast for me. Asmae, the eldest of the kitchen women, finishes the task by arranging my hair in curls atop my head and securing a green wool felt hat with a pin that comes just short of drawing blood from my scalp. She's impatient with the silly task, and I don't blame her in the least. When it's all finished, the only things I've left of my own are my gloves, unmentionables, and the locket I wear on a thick length of ribbon coverin' the scars. I am careful always to hold it in place during the dressing and the undressing so none of the other women can see what hides underneath it. Coming to tea today, along with me, are four others whose husbands operate businesses in town.

We make our way 'round to the front to be presented properly to Mrs. Delevan, me lagging behind, as the slippers are too snug on my feet. I feel as if I've got my toes caught in the black-smith billows, and Big Neb is pushing down with each step. I long for my ankle boots, which wait in the kitchen house.

We've barely made our way inside the house and to the ladies' salon before there's the sound of someone new coming in the door, and in a wink, Harland Delevan himself stands in the entry, observing the tea ladies. He's dusty from travelin', but his mother seems to mind not a bit. His aunt Peasie smiles and claps her hands together, and Mrs. Delevan's eyes fill with her son as he moves across the room, then bends to kiss her cheek. He greets the rest of the ladies properly, before calling for me to leave the room with him.

"Pardon, sir?" I say, a fierce heat under my skin. I'm already imagining what the ladies will be thinking.

"I've something for Miss Rose to see," he explains to his mother, not to me. She excuses me straightaway, and I rise from my chair. My passing through the room echoes, no other sound to disturb it but the ticking clock on the mantel. The regard of the ladies follows me until I'm gone, and then Mrs. Delevan resumes the conversation about whether a periwinkle should be sewn from a shade of blue thread or a shade of purple, or both.

In the entryway Mr. Delevan says to me, "I trust you'll forgive me for removing you from the afternoon's festivities." I flutter a glance at him, half expecting a wry twist of his lips, like that of Mr. Hardwick earlier on, but there is not a hint of his humor at the moment.

I merely nod and say, "Certainly." I find myself looking up and down the hall, wishing for the kitchen women to come with teacups and trays, but there's no one. Again, I wonder what it is about this man that sets me so ill at ease. He's shown us nothin' but kind treatment thus far.

He leads me to the door and opens it, and it is a relief when we step onto the porch. On the street below, people move about. It's clear that Mr. Delevan means us to walk down the hill, and it's crossing my mind that I've the silk slippers still on my feet. My toes are hemmed up like tube sausages, and aside from that, the slippers will be soiled, should I wear them below. We've had a bit of rain yesterday and the milk-colored caliche streets are damp yet. I'm afraid to make mention of this, not knowing whether it would be better to delay Mr. Delevan's plan or risk the slippers.

Finally I merely walk along beside him. He seems in a rush. I hope the kitchen women will wash the slippers before returning them to Mrs. Delevan's collection of tea clothing.

"My mother is most pleased with you," the man says to me as we move single file along the stone path leading down the hill, myself in front of him.

"I hope it, sir." I can't help wonderin' what he thinks of the eccentricities of his mother and his aunt, and if he has lived all his life under such behavior. What an odd thing to be strapped with womenfolk who've not a bit to occupy their minds but their own frivolous entertainment. Perhaps this is the reason he's come so far from civilization to make his living? Perhaps this is the reason he has no wife in his home?

If he's bothered by it, he doesn't say. His mood seems fine enough today, though I wouldn't know for certain, havin' only spoken to the man's face the day he hired me to my position. These past weeks, I've seen him once at a distance, and then he was gone away again. Even in his absence, he has made certain we were looked after, and I am grateful for that much.

"And how do you find our town of Wildwood?" He steps up beside me now, as the path grows wider near the head of the street.

"Quite well." So many things I yearn to mention, but I sense I should not do it. "Though I've found little time to spend about the community, truly. I've been quite occupied working to bring the school to order. Not all of the children are warm to the idea, nor are their parents, but they seem to be slowly coming around to it."

"It is my mother's desire, the school. To bring a measure of culture to the town." He clasps his hands behind his back as he walks, his chin turned upward, taking in the hard line of buildings against sky. I'm conscious of the sound of hammers striking wood, the clink on the blacksmith's anvil, a barking dog, and many eyes turning our way as we walk. Embarrassingly so, though Mr. Delevan seems not aware or bothered by it.

Mrs. Unger watches from the store window as our reflections melt over the glass, mine like a

223

brightly colored bird, all pinks and purples and the green of the hat. But it isn't the reflections I see—it is the grave look on the Unger woman's face. I wonder what is meant by it. She's been kinder to Maggie and me than most.

"I will make a success of the school with time. I remain confident of it," I say, fearing Mr. Delevan might become discouraged with the idea, as it is apparently his mother's and not his own. "What is worth having is worth the investment of hard work." It's a quote of Da's, the sort of determination that enabled him to start again in a new country.

The man turns then, his eyes resolute beneath the brim of his fine black silk hat. "Yes," he agrees, his lingering gaze raising color in my skin. "I find that it is."

Two women step aside into a horse alley and watch us pass. I've been with both of them at Mrs. Delevan's tea parties, but neither one offers up a greeting.

It remains likewise as we move along the street, and I'm more than uneased by it. I feel their eyes over us, sense their whispering. It must be the schoolhouse we're headed to, down the hill on the high side along the spring creek. Perhaps he's bringing me here to show that the books have come.

He speaks of his plans for the town as we move along. An opera house here, a smelter there, another hotel, a waterworks eventually. "More housing, of course, at some point. But they're a lazy lot, these Irish. Will live in tents and dugouts in the woods forever if I'll let them. Beggars and vagabonds. Most of them little better than gypsies, really. Not with the sensibilities to appreciate the hallmarks of culture in a town, certainly. Not given to thinking for themselves or advancing themselves. Drones. Much like worker bees in the hive, wouldn't you say?"

I cannot bring a word from my throat. Inside, there's been a torch lit to the pitch pot, and it's boilin'. My hands grip Mrs. Delevan's borrowed skirt so tightly it'll likely be returned with scorch marks in it.

He leads me up the steps to the schoolhouse, not seeming to notice I haven't replied to his question.

The room is empty when he opens the door to admit me in. Where could Maggie May be now? Still about town with Mr. Hardwick? There's no sign of the crates with the schoolbooks—just the room as it was when I ended class and sent my students home a full hour early, as I'm forced to do when I'm called upon for ladies' tea.

I pause to check the street, yearning to catch a glimpse of my sister. I hope she's not gone wandering the woods while Mr. Hardwick busies himself at the blacksmith shop. I hadn't thought to look on the way past, to see if the man was still there with Big Neb.

"Come," Mr. Delevan says and traverses the center aisle of the schoolhouse. I've no choice but to follow him to the door behind my desk. Until now, it's been closed and sealed over with an oilcloth to keep out the dust and noise made by the workers constructing the room for Maggie and me.

Mr. Delevan pulls the latch and the door falls open, and he smiles at me for the first time. I'm caught in it for a moment. His smile is a bit of rain in the heat of summer. Something you're aware won't come often or be long-lastin'.

"Come and see, Bonnie Rose," he bids me again.

I do as he says, and when I cross the threshold into the room, the air catches in my mouth. I taste wood dust, fresh linen, and whitewash. The room is small but lovely. Everythin' inside is clean and new. White beds with turned posts for Maggie and me, feather mattresses, and linens and quilts on each one. A table and two chairs for dining, a corner cabinet to house our foodstuffs, an indoor stove for cooking, which is more than so many here have. Along the back wall is a small door with a four-paned window in it. Soft light shines through the lace curtain, revealing the path to the spring creek, the privy, and the stone face of the mountain not forty yards beyond. A fine breeze will slip through the room when the door is open. We'll plant our starts of Ma's roses there by the porch, Maggie May and I, and enjoy their scent comin' in once they've grown. The roses have taken root in a pot already.

"It is a lovely home for us." The words are followed by tears as I step past him to better see the place. We've a dresser with a mirror and a cabinet for our clothing. Not since the loss of Ma and Da and baby Cormie have we had a place of our own.

"I am most pleased that you find it to your liking." He advances a few steps farther into the room, and I'm conscious of his coming close behind me. Of a sudden, I feel everythin'. The scratching of the pins at my waist, the binding of the slippers, the dampness where the mud has seeped through, the rustle of his breath.

A mockingbird flies off a tiny tree near the porch. The poor creature sails hard into the glass, and I jump.

"It hasn't yet learned where the walls stand." His voice is low, but not soft. "Some will beat themselves against the windows until it is best just to snap their necks and do away with them."

There's a turnin' in my stomach. "I'm certain the poor thing will learn it in due time. It's one of God's creatures, and it was the bird who made his home here first, after all."

"Of course," he agrees, and he is closer behind me now. I feel his breath on my skin. "Forgive my mentioning something so . . . unpleasant. This color is most becoming against your hair. Emerald green. I suppose it should be. Mother selected well for you."

A racket comes then, unexpected. The front door in the schoolhouse blows open and strikes the wall, as it will do if one doesn't remember to catch it first. Maggie clatters through it, her voice echoing to the rafters as she enters. Another set of footsteps follow hers, adding a long, heavy, labored sound.

"I can put this on her desk, and then I'll help you," she chirps, cheerful as a summer day.

"Reckon I've got it." Mr. Hardwick's voice. A cool rush of relief strikes me. "Put that where your sister will find it, and then we'll try our hand at unpacking these for her."

I gather myself, turn, and smile at Mr. Delevan. "They've brought the books."

The man holds for a moment, as if he's of a need to show me that it'll be his say when we leave this room, no matter who's come in the schoolhouse door. Finally he steps aside, and there's little choice but for the two of us to depart together.

Mr. Hardwick lowers the crate, and then spies us leavin' the boarding room. His look is first one of surprise, and then of emotions I cannot read. Dismay, anger, accusation, or disappointment—or some mixture of all. I feel the stain of shame, so familiar in my skin. Regardless of how far we travel, it discovers and rediscovers me. The past is never gone. There is always someone who knows, and Mr. Delevan knows. I fear that fact will be the undoing of this new life of Bonnie Rose.

He gives an impatient tip of his hat my way and proceeds toward the front door. As he passes along the aisle, he pauses only slightly, long enough to say to Mr. Hardwick, "I will expect you when you finish here. Come to my offices, not to the manor house. As much as Aunt Peasie may find you fascinating, I'm afraid that mother considers many of my . . . business associates . . . distasteful. I trust that you've made it through with my shipment intact this time. No missing kegs of powder?" He walks on, not waiting for an answer.

"I trust that I have," Mr. Hardwick replies in his long, slow drawl. An eyetooth flashes at Mr. Delevan's back as the man strides off into the sunlight.

Mr. Hardwick's friendliness of earlier is vanished when he turns my way again. I know what he thinks of me. There's not a thing I can do to help it.

Maggie May remains unaware of the currents in the room. She takes something from the desk and shakes it, disturbin' the air with the clear sound of a bell. It is heavy and made of iron, and she holds the polished wooden handle in both fists.

"Big Neb made it for you. We helped him finish it," she tells me with a smile, then wags it once more. The bell speaks so loudly that it seems to be rattling the windows all about the room. "For calling the students in. Big Neb says he'll make you a larger one when he's able."

She extends the gift to me, and I touch its smoothly polished surface through my glove. "It is lovely, to be sure." The bell is crudely hammered from scrap, with a length of chain and a bolt as a striker. I hope that Big Neb hasn't overstepped his bounds by crafting it. Iron is in short supply here.

From the corner of my eye, I'm aware of Mr. Hardwick looking me over, and for the first time I notice I'm still dressed in the borrowed clothes. I'll be forced to return up the hill to reclaim my own. Maggie makes mention of it, then, and I'm desperately wishin' she'd hold her tongue.

"I'm well aware of that, Maggie May," I snap before reining myself in.

Maggie's wispy smile falls.

I swallow my temper and touch her shoulder. Her bottom lip quivers. We're always striking and defending without meaning to, Maggie May and I. It is so difficult, this life of only the two of us, I at once her mother and her sister, and so many strange and bitter memories between us. Not the least of which, her throwing her small body over mine and begging our captors to beat me no further. Such was the love of Maggie's Comanche mother for her, as to give Maggie what she asked in the moment. My young sister may well have saved my life that day, but I wasn't grateful for it. I screamed at her to let me be, so wretched was I as to wish for my own death.

All of it rushes through me now, when I look into her eyes. There's not another human soul connected to me as my sister. I pray I haven't chosen badly for the both of us by comin' to Wildwood.

"Mr. Delevan has just shown me our new room," I say, as much for the benefit of Mr. Hardwick as for Maggie. "Go and see. We've a lovely home of our own now, nicely made. A place for ourselves. When the books are unpacked, we'll go to the Forsythes' and fetch our things. We'll sleep in our new beds tonight."

The news cheers her, but it does not change the mood of Mr. Hardwick.

He scoops up his hat, which has fallen to the floor beside the crate, leaving his thick hair to tumble unkempt around his shoulders. In one quick, impatient movement, he resets the hat on his head, and he's moving to the door. "I'll leave you to your unpacking, and your trip back up the hill to fetch whatever you might've left there."

I feel his words digging in sharp, making evident that the clothes on my back are not my own. I've allowed myself to be little more than a puppet, or worse. Mr. Hardwick is a puppet to no man, I suspect. But a man can make his choices, while a woman has none. She must eat, and she must feed those who cannot feed themselves.

"But I thought you were stayin' to help us," Maggie protests before I can stop her.

"I reckon it's better if I leave it be," he answers, then disappears through the door without a backward glance.

Maggie and I go on with the unpacking of the books, and I make certain to wait long enough that the tea time will be finished, Mrs. Delevan having retired to her private rooms, before I go up the hill. In the kitchen house, Old Asmae has my clothing awaiting me when I arrive there. She helps me into my things, then takes the soiled shoes without a word and tosses them into the kitchen stove for burning.

"She ain't gone miss dem, but she don' like no muddy shoe. Be da devil to pay." She favors me with a long, slow look after smoothin' my skirt over petticoats that're little more than rags. But they're all I have. Her old eyes are cloudy 'round the edges, yellow and worn, and she cocks her face to see me through the centers. "You know what you doin' here, Miss Bonnie? You know what gone on 'round dis place?"

Her gaze puts a shiver in me somewhere deep. "No, Asmae. I do not."

She shifts upright, cocking an ear to the door, to the sound of Mr. Delevan's voice somewhere about the house. Not meaning to, I grab onto her apron, afraid of something without knowing just what it might be.

My bodice is only half buttoned, and my feet are yet bare. I realize I'm looking 'round like a kitten when the dog comes home, searching for a corner to hide myself. I recall our conversation behind the schoolroom, his closeness to me. I don't want to be found here at his home, particularly in this condition. Asmae hesitates, then swings open the back door between two large stoves that cast off an unwanted heat, lit in anticipation of supper for the big house.

Her dark, gnarled hands shove my shoes and stockin's at me, almost rough. She takes her eyes from mine. "Go on dis way, chile. Be a path through the wood and 'long the crick. Be on, befo' the dark settle in down the holler and the wolf, he come scratch 'round. Get restless this time a' the evenin'." She clutches up my shoulders, turns me to the door so quick I'm stumblin'. The only thing holding me is herself. For an old woman, she is a strong one. "Hurry 'long. Git gone. Set a bolt tonight. Keep he-wolf ou'side the do'. He gone prowl in dis full moon. Off now, befo' you make trouble somebody else got to pay fo'."

I am out the door then, and she's closing the latch behind me, pulling up the string. In the house, Mr. Delevan raises his voice and something crashes down. I don't wait to see what it is —the back path Asmae has told me of now seems a wise choice. I cradle my shoes in one fist, scoop my skirt higher than's proper, and dash over the grass, barefoot like a woodsprite. It would be a freedom-feeling if not for the fear of being seen. I pray no one might peer out the back of the house. I've not an inkling of what excuse I'd give for such a display.

I've almost made the trees when a glimpse toward the side porch shows Aunt Peasie there in her rocking chair with her ever-present needle-work.

Please, Lord of heaven, make me invisible to her, I pray, but she's looking my way, and I know she must see me. She doesn't call out, and I pretend I've not noticed her. I bless the saints, every one, as I make the woods and run past the outhouse shed where the slop pots are piled for washing. I don't stop until the brush has me well hid, and even then I'm afraid to pause for my shoes. If I'm found here, using the path the slave women use, what would I say about it? I cannot tell them Asmae has sent me this way. She'd be the one to suffer for it. Mrs. Delevan is loath to anythin' that is improper. A grown woman dashing through the wood half fastened, and without her shoes and stockin's is anything but. I've no means of explainin' why I would leave this way, rather than by the front path.

The trail travels downhill to the stream bed and then alongside it. And with the town out of sight, even though the shadows now fall in the hollows, I feel safer. There's no one gathering water just now. Not a soul. But it is the time of day for watering horses and milk stock before being home for supper. Any of my students could come here, doing their daily chores.

And just as I'm thinking it, I hear a rustle in the leaves and ahead, a man leads his saddle horse down to water. Too late I see him there, and too late I realize it is Mr. Hardwick. He spies me before I can disappear into the brush. His regard travels over me, from the skirt still clutched above my knees, to shoes and stockin's in my hand, to the buttons loose at my bodice. I can imagine what he must think. I've learned long ago there's no dissuading people from believing the worst if they're bent to it, so I don't trouble to try. I only run past him and keep on until I've reached the schoolhouse. I let myself in the back door and throw the bolt behind me. It's only then, as I'm gatherin' myself together, that I realize I've lost a stockin' on the way.

I decide I'll go after it in the morn', and since it's the only pair of stockin's I have to my name, I wrap my foot in a rag before I put on my shoes and fix my appearance. I find Maggie May, and we walk to the Forsythe home to collect our things. We take a last meal at their table, and Mrs. Forsythe sends us away with a basket of goods to get us by, though she makes it clear that it's only something she's done because she must.

Leaving her house, I carry the starts of Seven Sisters roses in my hands and feel I'm finally breathin' for the first time in weeks. Even the queerness of the afternoon leaves me when we return to the school and settle our things and plant the roses. We enjoy the new books for a bit before the Reverend Brahn comes in. His round cheeks are flushed, his eyes red, and he staggers as he closes the door behind himself. It's clear enough that he's had a nip or two again.

Why, I wonder, would a man of God feel the need to keep himself in such a state? So many here could benefit from his leading, if he were in any shape to give it. Instead, he preaches nonsense on Sundays and few attend. I've heard that the faithful meet for secret worship in the wood, so as to maintain their faith without risk of insulting Mr. Delevan. The Irish gather in one place and the Germans in another. Maggie and I, of course, are forced to sit through the reverend's drunken rants on Sabbath days.

Tonight he staggers off to his room, and we retire with the books and finish settling in. Soon enough the Reverend Brahn's snores can be heard through the wall, and we laugh together.

"It's as if I'm bedded down in a cave with an old mother bear," Maggie remarks, her blue eyes sparklin' as I sit on the edge of her bed and pull the quilts to her chin. The blankets smell of clean water and lye and lavender oil to keep the vermin away. The kitchen women have laundered them fresh for us, I suspect.

"An old he-bear. Gone into winter sleep in the summertime," I tease, and we chuckle again. Before long, she's driftin' off with her book still in her hands.

She's just begun breathin' deep and long when a knocking comes at the back door. I think that, perhaps, one of the Forsythe daughters has come by with something we've left behind. I've no notion of what it might be. We have little between us.

When I open the door, it is Mr. Delevan standing on the other side. He seems out for a stroll, his silk vest unbuttoned and his white shirt no longer fastened high at the collar. I turn my eyes away and pretend I haven't noticed it.

"We've settled in quite nicely," I say, my nerves on edge. What is his purpose here? "And Maggie May has quickly gone off to sleep, enjoying her new home, I think." I give a small nod in her direction, and he moves closer a step, across the threshold now. I hold my ground and grip the door, so as not to make any invitation. Surely he won't be asking for any, with Maggie asleep there, and the Reverend Brahn, drunk though he may be, just on the far side of the wall.

Mr. Delevan holds an object up between us, compelling me to look his way again. "You've left something behind on the path to the river, I believe." His eyes fasten to mine, and I see it's my stockin' he's holding. I try not to imagine where he might've found it, and I refrain from asking. I take it and fight a shudder when his fingers touch mine. His hands are so cold.

"Thank you for returning it," I say. "I only missed it just a bit ago. I cannot guess how it must have come to be in that place. Perhaps one of the dogs snapped it up and carried it off." The town is filled with wandering dogs. They hunt after the rats and rabbits and watch for predators after dark, or for Comanche or Tonkawa who might be sneaking about.

"Come out and see the night sky, Bonnie Rose," he says, and it doesn't feel as if he's askin'.

"I couldn't, sir." I'm flounderin' now, like a sunfish flipped on shore, not knowing which way is to safety. "Such a thing would never seem proper. I must set a fine example for my students. And Maggie May is asleep, just there. In a new place tonight. She'll be frightened if she wakes alone."

His tongue glides along the tip of his teeth. It is not his custom to be told no. He's decidin' what should be done about it. He likely thinks those to be foolish words, coming from a woman soiled as myself. Doubtless, he feels I should be expectin' this, and he's been patient enough.

He casts an eye toward Maggie, lyin' abed in

her night shift, the quilt thrown partway off already. In the candlelight, her skin is milky and smooth as a babe's.

A shudder travels over me. What is he thinkin' of?

Somewhere in the wood, a panther screams, the sound like a woman crying out. I gasp without meaning to, shrinkin' back at the noise. It's all I can do not to close the door with him still in it.

I think of Old Asmae's words. *Set a bolt tonight. Keep he-wolf ou'side the do'. He gone prowl in dis full moon. Off now, befo' you make trouble somebody else got to pay fo'.*

"I'll run the creature through and hang the skin to dry before morning, not to worry." Mr. Delevan studies the night now, hungry-eyed in a way that drops slivers of ice inside me. "I have no patience with things that trouble me."

He turns and descends the porch without another word. I watch him stroll down the path to the spring creek, disappearing in the direction of Red Leaf Hollow. When he's gone away, I close and bolt the door, then blow out the lamp and slip into bed with my clothing still on my body. This room hasn't the feel of home tonight.

In the morning, as I read over the lessons, a knocking at the door surprises me. It's barely a sound, and at first I think I'm imagining it. Who would call so early the sun has scarce graced the sky?

239

I open the latch, and it's Essie Jane on the other side. She's pressed close to the wall, not wanting to be seen here. "Asmae send me out after the hens dat's got out from the coop dis mo'nin'. Gone be trouble, dey fin' me here." Her eyes dart round into the mist that clings low along the bluff. "Gots to be sho' you and Miss Maggie is well."

"Certainly," I say, but the mist creeps up the porch and over her feet, and a chill winds along my legs. I think of Mr. Delevan, standing here last evenin'. Is this why she's come? "Well enough. Maggie's abed yet. Why has Asmae sent you to ask after us?"

She shakes her head. "Asmae gone skin me too, I be foun' here. She say, 'You leave they bid'ness to theyselves. Massah catch you, he cut you up good.' But, Miss Bonnie, you gots to know it."

Her gaze lifts and for a wink, I'm seeing her slide off the ferry raft into the water. That's the sort of fear in her now. "What is it, Essie Jane?" The words come as little more than a breath.

"They done fin' a body dis mo'nin', float down river," she whispers. "Girl from Red Leaf Holla throw herself off'n a bluff. She been Massah Delevan fav'rit, befo' you come. People sayin' she gone 'cause you be makin' it happen."

Chapter 16

Allie Kirkland
June, Present Day

"I wish I could have your spot. Being on the cast would be the ultimate dream," confided Stacy, my replacement in Tova's department, resting her chin wistfully on her hand as we sat at the computer in a production trailer.

For twelve days now I'd been working mornings up the hill, training Stacy for Tova, then spending the rest of the day down the hill in what had lovingly become known as *Pioneer Boot Camp*. So far, the training in livestock care, meal preparation, wood chopping, and nineteenth-century personal hygiene and etiquette were grueling. The more I learned about the daily life of the real Bonnie Rose, the more I admired her—and the more I realized that, physical resemblance aside, I was thoroughly unqualified to become her.

"I wish you could too." I'd just sneaked a hot shower in one of the crew trailers, and it was amazing how much one little convenience could spoil you all over again. In my tiny apartment behind the school, washing up involved lugging water from the springhouse by the creek and using a washbasin in my dressing area—a small corner of my room that was hidden behind a hanging quilt.

Stacy frowned sideways at me. "I take it you're not excited about this afternoon, then?"

"I think it'll be neat to see the whole village in period clothing for the first time. But let's face it—that stuff is an endurance test. Twelve pounds of hot, sticky garments do not go on the body without a fight." When I finished with Stacy this morning, she would help me into my Bonnie Rose clothes so that I could attend afternoon safety classes. The historical specialists wanted to make sure we knew how to avoid catching ourselves on fire, tangling our skirts in wagon spokes, and stepping in front of moving horses while wearing bonnets. Women died that way, it turned out. The gruesome details of yesterday's lecture had made a believer out of me.

"I'd go listen in, if I could. I've got a minor in history, but some of this stuff you never even think about." Stacy looked longingly toward the window again. "The everyday things the trainers know fascinate me."

"They are pretty impressive." Our historical life specialists were a skilled combination of nurse-maid and drill sergeant. They were friendly and patient despite stupidity, whining, and occasional lack of pioneer spirit. "They haven't committed mayhem on Wren Godley yet, which, I have to say, is pretty amazing."

"Ohhhh, that kid." Stacy rolled her eyes. "I cannot imagine why they cast her. There had to be some other little redheaded girl they could've gotten. One that doesn't come with a momzilla attached. Every time I pass by that woman, she gives me some list of gripes and wants me to pass them on up the ladder. What does she think I am, nuts? I've already got Tova breathing down my neck all day."

Poor Stacy. Tova had made her cry at least two dozen times in a dozen days. I could've told her the Blake Fulton scrap-of-paper story, but even that probably wouldn't compare to the dangers of being an intermediary between a maniac stage mom and Tova. "Listen, I'd avoid being the messenger for Wren's mom or anyone else on the cast, if I could. Just a word of advice."

Wren, as Bonnie Rose's little sister, was my (less than delightful, I might add) part-time roommate when she wasn't up in crew camp, lounging in a trailer with her mother. Of all the kids I'd spent time with in the schoolhouse this week, while learning to conduct classes 1861-style, Wren was by far the most difficult. In addition to arguing with everything the trainers told her, she liked to rub in the fact that she and her mother had been given a fairly nice trailer in the crew camp, since her mother was not part of the cast. When it was time for Wren to leave the village for the day, she'd invariably smile, scrunch her pert, freckled nose at me, swipe the back of her hand across her little forehead, and say, "I hate cooking on a fire. Don't you? I can't wait to go put my shorts on and sit in front of the air conditioner in my trailer. I think I'll have a Dr Pepper and some Bluebell ice cream when I get there. Doesn't that sound good?"

At that point, I'd resist the urge to stick out my tongue, because teachers aren't supposed to do that. Especially not teachers in 1861, when propriety mattered above all else. Nineteenth-century womanhood came wrapped in layers upon layers of rules.

Stacy rolled her eyes. "Yeah, I keep telling the mom I have absolutely no clout here, and she has to give her requests to casting, if she needs something. She insists she should be able to go straight to Tova. That woman's got some serious connections here, apparently—she as much as told me so—and that makes it a bit of a tight-rope."

"Hang in there," I said, and we both laughed at the pun before returning to the massive spread-sheet of nineteenth-century foodstuffs that Stacy had been working on all morning.

The computer screen froze, refusing to upload the data. "Great. Just great." Stacy let her head fall into her hand. "The Internet's down again, and this order needs to go in this morning. If I don't get it done before eleven, not only is Tova going to kill me, but the entire village will starve to death within a couple weeks."

"Wait, I'll go for the backup." The wireless Internet in camp was ridiculously cantankerous, and if production couldn't do its work, *everything* in the village and in crew camp eventually ground to a halt. "Let me get my cell phone out of lockup, and we can use it as a hot spot again." Stacy and I had been forced to improvise this way before. Fortunately, security's techno-gadget holding area was next door. It had gotten to the point where Sean, the security guard, barely even stopped reading his magazine when I came and went.

Today he was engrossed in a particularly interesting edition of *Deer Hunter* when I passed through his office. "Internet's down. Cell phone," I said.

"No prob," he answered.

I was back in the production trailer in under three minutes and just about to resume my position beside Stacy, when suddenly there was Tova, looming large in the doorway.

"Allison!" Her voice propelled both Stacy and me to attention. A stack of papers was shaking in Tova's iron grip.

On occasion, life down the hill in 1861 didn't seem so bad. This was one of those occasions. That frantic, murderous look in Tova's eye could only be a sign of some unpleasant surprise that would rock the day off its axis.

"We were just using this as a hot spot," I babbled, lest she think we were making phone calls to the outside world or doing anything else strictly forbidden.

"You'll be driving back to the Berman today." Tova crossed the room to her desk, frenetically sorted through more papers, and finally came up with a set of keys.

Stacy and I exchanged stunned looks. "Wha . . . but I was supposed to go back down the hill for . . . We have safety in period clothing the rest of the day."

Tova thrust the papers and the keys my way impatiently. "Do not give me excuses, Allison. Just do as you're told. A number of things that should have been brought here by various departments were left behind. Here is the list. You know your way around the place. Find all of these items. Bring them here. But most importantly, there is a *red* jump drive somewhere in my basement office. Most likely it is in my upper left desk drawer. In any case, I *must* have it. And *that* is to be kept strictly between us." A predatory look swept in Stacy's direction, then returned to me. "Under-stood?"

"Yes. Oh . . . okay."

She was gone as quickly as she came. Stacy and I stood for a moment, just blinking back and forth at each other.

"I guess I'm out of here," I said finally.

"Guess so." Stacy sagged in her chair, looking hopeless and defeated as she turned back to the computer. "Well, the Internet's back up again, anyway. Don't worry about the spreadsheet. I'll figure it out somehow."

"Sorry to leave you in a bind." We both knew I didn't have any choice, but I still felt guilty about it.

The guilt traveled with me only as far as the parking lot. Within minutes, I'd retrieved my purse from lockup and was rattling up the dusty camp road, leaving Chinquapin Peaks and 1861 behind, just as easy as that.

On the way through Moses Lake, I spotted Burt and Nester outside the Waterbird. They were hanging around the gas pumps again, this time talking to a visitor in a ball cap, camo pants, and a khaki T-shirt. They waved as I passed, and I stuck my arm out the window, suddenly feeling like a local. The guy in the ball cap glanced my way, and for the barest instant my mind tripped over itself. He smiled and waved, and even from a distance, I would've sworn he looked familiar.

Moses Lake had faded away in the rearview mirror before I came up with the right card in my random deck of memory.

Blake Fulton? Could that have been him?

Surely not. I hadn't heard one word about him since Tova snatched that paper off the wall a couple days before we packed up and moved to the set. His name was nowhere to be found on any of the cast lists.

My mind wandered over the question as I drove on, and finally I just let it drift away. The farther I went, the less it seemed to matter and the more my thoughts smoothed. Maybe a visit back home to Austin was exactly what I needed. Each mile I felt more and more like myself.

Even the dark, silent halls of the Berman, now housing only a few support personnel, seemed strangely welcoming when I arrived. With the place nearly empty, it wasn't as hard as I'd thought it would be to round up the items on Tova's list. Thankfully, the red thumb drive was exactly where she'd told me it would be—waiting in the upper left desk drawer next to a tube of lipstick.

I was back in the company truck in record time. Lying in the seat, my cell phone beckoned, lighting up with a text message notification from Stewart. The man was a bloodhound, and much like a bloodhound, he didn't seem to want to give up the scent trail of Bonnie Rose. The times I'd grabbed my phone from lockup, there was usually some tidbit waiting. I'd tried to explain to him that, at risk of my job, I really couldn't be in touch anymore.

Contact me when you receive this. Urgent, the message read.

I sat with the engine idling for a minute and

thought about it. Maybe it wouldn't hurt to stop by for just a minute to thank him for all he'd done to help. The day we'd locked up the apartment and left to board the buses at the Berman, he'd been nowhere to be found. Kim and I had to deposit our little box of thank-you cookies on his doorstep, along with a note.

Aside from that, there were a few things in the apartment that might help me to survive the summer . . . if I could smuggle them into Wildwood. Just small luxuries I really couldn't do without, like toothpaste and shampoo. There were plenty of places in my quarters to hide them. No one would ever know. And I wouldn't be the only one. I'd smelled minty-fresh breath here and there around the village and caught the scent of Herbal Essence.

It felt deliciously rebellious, weaving through the familiar streets, pulling into the parking lot, trotting up the steps, slipping in the apartment door, stealing through my rooms like a thief, gathering up a Wal-Mart sack full of goodies, snitching one of Kim's Dr Peppers from the refrigerator.

"Mmm," I moaned, taking a long swig of sweet nectar as I walked out the door again. "No one should have to live before soda. . . ."

"Allie!" Stewart's voice caught me by surprise, and I sent a river of soda splattering over the doorframe.

"Oh, Stewart!" I tipped the can up, saving what was left. "I was just going to look for you. You scared the bejeebers out of me, though." The last phrase was a loaner from Kim, who was undoubtedly in safety class far, far away right now, wondering where I was and pining for her newfound love. So far, she'd spent most of her time writing letters on the backs of the survival papers she should have been studying.

Stewart ducked his head awkwardly, a frizz of curly brown hair falling over his eyes. "I . . . didn't think anyone was authorized to be in your apartment. I thought both of you were gone. I came over to check on things for you."

"I am gone. You didn't see me here." The attempt at humor was wasted. Stewart was sweet and incredibly intelligent, but hopelessly odd. "You didn't see me with this, either." I patted the little bundle of necessities. Total contraband, in the form of toiletries, Band-Aids, capris, a T-shirt, a few unmentionables made from fabrics oh so much more comfortable than those available in 1861, a decent toothbrush, and a pair of tennis shoes I figured I could get by with wearing on my morning trips to the springhouse at least, since they were hidden under my skirt and ninety-nine petticoats. I'd only tried on the Bonnie clothes for short periods, but I'd learned that nineteenth-century ankle boots were beyond uncomfortable.

Stewart frowned at the sack as I slipped my

wrist through the handles and made sure the apartment door was locked. "I just got your text. Did you need something?"

He shook his head. "I didn't send a text today."

We exchanged confused looks. "Oh, well . . . maybe it was hung up in the system. The cell phone service is really spotty up there in Chinquapin Peaks. But, listen: I won't be able to use my phone anymore after today. I guess we'll see you at the end of August. Wish me luck."

His shoulders sagged, and he looked down at his feet. For the first time, I had the feeling he'd be lonely here this summer without us.

"We left you a note and some cookies before we headed out. Did you get them?"

"The ants discovered your package. Too many people leave their trash bags in the corridors." He frowned, watching as I stopped my toothbrush from slipping through a hole in the plastic sack.

I rolled my eyes and smiled. "Thanks again for all the research help. You're a miracle worker. When we're back in the fall, I'll replace the cookies, I promise. Hold down the fort for us in the meantime, okay? I'd better hit the road before I get myself in trouble."

"I can still help you. . . ." Stewart took a quick step forward, blocking my path. Suddenly, I felt bad about leaving him there. He'd become so involved in the project through the research and now he was just . . . out. "I found materials pertaining to Bonnie Rose . . . I think. I have them on order. You know I have access to private collections all over the planet—letters, old news-papers, census reports. Unpublished accounts. I have even secured a reproduction copy of Jane Eyre for you via eBay. Leather bound. Published only a dozen years or so before Bonnie Rose's time period. It would have been the reading of the day, and Jane's story may well be much like Bonnie Rose's. Brontë's work does not shy away from the brutal realities of life in the era."

There was no way I could hang around and look at whatever Stewart had found, and the fact that he'd now bought something on eBay made me feel that much more guilty. "I'd love to see it, Stewart, but I can't stay. If I'm not back soon, I'm dead. I wasn't even supposed to stop by here at all. I'm sorry you went to so much trouble for me. Can you save the eBay receipt? I want to pay you back."

Brushing hair out of his face, he rushed on, "I could bring things to you there . . . as they come in." He looked away, his lashes shielding his eyes, his cheeks flushing, the color turning fiery red and extending down his neck.

His crestfallen look sent a wave of guilt splash-ing my way. "Thanks, Stewart, but it's not possible. It's high security out there, remember? The only way in is through a locked gate . . . unless you want to swim across the lake. The copy of Jane Eyre might get through to me if you sent it via the village post office—if the cover isn't too modern, that is—but they won't let the rest of the things through. They're not appropriate to the period."

"I could scan and email things to you as I find them." Dropping his backpack, he squatted over it, his knees poking upward like cricket legs in his black skinny jeans. "Here. Write down your email address on this paper. I'll keep in touch that way. You can include the appropriate postal address, too."

My guilt swelled even further. He was so invested in this. "I have to leave my phone in the lockup at the security trailer when I get there. I won't have any way to check email once go-live starts." Unconsciously, I laid a hand on my back pocket, where my iPhone lay cuddled close to my body. If I got caught trying to smuggle it into the set, I would be fired and escorted off the premises. Aside from that, Kim would kill me. Her phone was still sitting in the apartment, since I'd completely refused to even consider sneaking it in for her.

If I took Kim's phone with me now and turned it in at the security trailer, then kept mine with my contraband, no one would ever know. . . .

Before I'd even processed the thought, I was giving Stewart my email address along with the address for the village post office. "You know what . . . send me anything you find in the next few days, and I'll try to sneak off and check email a few times until the battery dies. But don't go to a lot of trouble for me, okay?"

"I will be in touch." Squatting over his backpack again, he carefully replaced the pencil, then began meticulously folding the paper, taking pains to get it perfectly straight each time.

I didn't wait for him to finish but grabbed Kim's phone from the apartment, locked up, and said good-bye before heading for the hills with my iPhone transferred hastily to the little sack of luxuries I intended to strap under my bulky skirt, underskirt, petticoats, and chemise after Stacy helped me get dressed. One of the few advantages of nineteenth-century clothing—you could hide a small pony under there. If Yankee Doodle had been a woman, it would've looked like he was walking into town.

Even so, later that afternoon as I left the modern age behind in the back of the production trailer, I felt like a drug smuggler hauling in a load of cocaine. My heart leapt up when Tova surprised me on the front steps. The Wal-Mart sack strapped to my leg emitted a plastic rustle and slipped a bit. I made an effort not to look guilty, but I was.

"Everything you asked for from the Berman is in the back of the truck, and the thumb drive is on your desk." I laid a hand over my skirt, holding the Wal-Mart sack still. "I'm headed down the hill to catch the last of safety class. I went ahead and changed clothes, in case the photographers are down there today. I think Mr. Singh said at yesterday's meeting that they'd be photographing the training now that everyone's in costume."

"I would imagine he's down there . . . amusing himself in his village," Tova muttered. I hadn't yet figured out what Rav and Tova's relationship was exactly, but it played out on a daily basis like some sort of strange war of the roses. According to Randy, they'd had a *thing* going on for years. I wondered if they still did, or if he wished they did, or if she wished they did, or if they both got some sort of warped satisfaction from the tango between them. Love, hate. Push, pull. Power play. Resistance and surrender.

I wanted no part of it—as a pawn or anything else. If Rav Singh had brought me into the cast of this project as a way of pulling Tova's strings, the smartest thing I could do was to steer clear. Not that I had a tender spot for Tova, especially after watching her torture Stacy the past couple of weeks, but having grown up with Lloyd as a stepfather, I had an intense dislike for compulsively controlling men. My mother couldn't drive to the store without Lloyd checking how many miles she'd put on the car.

"Stacy can see to the boxes." Tova assessed my costume with narrowed eyes, then she stepped away. "Actually, speaking of photographers, they just called up here from the village, looking for you. Something about media interviews that will be ongoing the next two days, and Rav wants to make certain you take part. As it turns out, the mother of one of your little *pretend* schoolchildren is, herself, a blogger. *The Frontier Woman*, I believe it's called. Perhaps you've heard of her? I hadn't." She had the look the evil queen gives the Magic Mirror when it selects Snow White as the *fairest of them all.*

"Oh," I muttered. I'd heard of *The Frontier Woman* blog. It was written by a former congressional staffer who had fallen in love, married, and moved to a ten-thousand-acre ranch along the shores of Moses Lake. Before we left Austin, Stewart had discovered the blog, and Kim had started reading it as part of her Wildwood research. Occasionally she shared bits of it with me. It was fun reading, but it gave me a healthy appreciation for what can happen to a city girl in the wild country. "I thought we were supposed to be in a media blackout until the end of the summer."

Tova's lip curled, flashing shiny white, dimensionally perfect teeth. "As did I. But Rav can never resist a pretty face." She shooed me toward the steps with an impatient backhand, her gold fingernails glinting in the sun. "Run along now, Allison—or I guess I should say

Bonnie Rose—before you get yourself in trouble."

I didn't wait for another invitation to leave. I was out of there, holding a wad of skirts, petticoats, and Wal-Mart sack. Most unladylike. The reenactment specialist had taught us that skirts hitched over ankle height in any circumstance were considered a sexual invitation—the measure of a loose woman. Right now I didn't care, as long as I made it to my quarters with my smuggled goods intact.

Once Tova was out of sight, I stopped to reposition my hidden package, then hurried over the ridge and down the other side to the village. Unfortunately, when I reached the schoolhouse, it was full of children. The historical specialist was teaching them more about 1861 school, while also delving into, judging from the blackboard, the safe handling of lanterns and other open-flame gear. In the front corner, Wren Godley sat by herself, looking bored and sour, as usual.

"Good afternoon, Miss Rose!" The kids broke into chorus as I tried to slip down the side aisle to my apartment door without disturbing their session. Why my quarters didn't have a rear exit like the empty room next to mine, I had no idea. I'd asked to switch, but I'd been unceremoniously turned down.

Since I'd interrupted the kids already, I stopped and offered a lopsided curtsy. "Good morning, adorable children."

Several of my favorites giggled.

The Wal-Mart sack crinkled as I straightened up. Alone in the front row, Wren offered a suspicious frown, her blue eyes narrowing above a starscape of freckles.

"Carry on," I joked and swirled my free hand in the air while sidestepping toward my doorway. The trainer chuckled and shook her head. She'd already figured out how completely unsuited I was to the life of a schoolmarm, being only slightly more mature than the kids myself.

Safely in my room, I peered in both camera holes to make sure they weren't in live test at the moment, then I looked for places to hide my stash. Places Wren wouldn't find when she was in the quarters with me.

My smuggled toiletries fit perfectly into a tin that was for storing flour. I rolled up the sneakers in the T-shirt and capris, then tucked them under my quilt between the mattress and the footboard. Plumped up, the feathers settled in around the forbidden items, hiding them nicely.

The iPhone was another matter. It required a safe, snug, dry spot where no one, but no one, would discover it. Being caught with a few contraband toiletries and clothes was one thing—I wouldn't be the first cast member to be forced to publicly surrender forbidden items to what security lovingly called *the confession box*—but being found with a cell phone was quite another matter. That was a security breach of epic proportions.

I finally settled for turning it off and tucking it underneath a small corner cabinet that held my very modest collection of dishes and foodstuffs. There was a shelf-like gap between the skirting and the slides of the bottom drawer. It seemed almost built for an iPhone, and even with the pink case, the thing was incredibly well hidden.

No one would ever find it there.

I tried to content myself with the idea that I wasn't just doing this for *me,* I was also doing it for Stewart and for Bonnie Rose. Stewart was so determined to dig up these last bits of information; it seemed wrong to leave him with no place to send them. But more important than that was the conversation I'd had with Rav Singh. The suppositions he'd made about Bonnie Rose seemed so sensationalized, so unfair. I couldn't shake them from the corners of my mind, and I wanted to disprove them, if I could.

The rationalization cycled in my head, struggling to become truth. It sounded so noble, so justified. Unfortunately, a guilty conscience rumbled louder than I'd ever anticipated it would. All evening it niggled me, and throughout the night I rolled around, listening to coyotes party on the bluff and worrying about what would happen if I got caught with the phone.

It was the first thing on my mind when I dragged

myself out of bed in the morning, exhausted and sore. I was cheating. *Cheating.* That wasn't me. I was the kind of person who did the right thing.

By the time I'd washed my face in the basin and struggled my way into my Bonnie Rose clothes, I was drenched in nervous sweat. Even the toothpaste I'd been so certain I *had* to have left a bad taste in my mouth today. If I couldn't give up shampoo, Aquafresh, and communication with the outside world, how could I possibly survive this summer?

Kim doesn't even want to be here anyway, now that she's in love. Maybe we should just . . . leave. Go home.

And then what?

Move back to Phoenix? Become a clerk in Lloyd's office? Go for the paralegal degree I didn't want? Give up on everything I really cared about? Prove that I really was as much of a loser as Mom and Lloyd thought I was?

Letting out a cleansing breath, I flopped down on the bed, hoops and all, and lay there liked a giant, tipped-over bowling pin. I was supposed to do *The Frontier Woman* interview after breakfast and then gather for cast and crew photos. They'd probably all take one look at me and know I was a cheater-cheater-pumpkin-eater.

I let my eyes fall closed, tried to think. *Calm down. Calm down. You're making too big a deal of all this.*

The air drifting through the cheesecloth screen felt like heaven, and I knew my mind was slowly succumbing, but I couldn't help myself. An Irish proverb from the Wall of Wisdom in Moses Lake floated through the last of my consciousness.

A good laugh and a long sleep are the two best cures for anything.

Maybe . . . just a little catnap. I'd get up again in a few minutes. . . .

When I woke, I had no idea how long I'd been there. The nap did help a little. It calmed the panic, and I felt ready again. Confident. Determined. There was no way I was running back home with my tail between my legs. If the real Bonnie Rose could survive here, so could I.

This was the last day we'd be provided food via the grub trailer that had been set up at the end of the street. When go-live started tomorrow, we'd be on our own to manage supplies, cooking, and food preservation. If the trailer was still serving breakfast, I should hustle down there and grab something, then go find Mallory Everson and knock out my *Frontier Woman* interview. After the cast photos at noon, I'd figure out what to do about the phone and . . .

Something caught my eye, bisecting the thought as I passed the window on my way to the water pitcher. I stopped to look out the glass above the cloth screen. There was . . . a guy coming up the path from the creek . . . wearing modern clothes and carrying . . . a black duffel bag? A member of the security team, maybe? They'd been chasing paparazzi and curious locals away for almost three weeks now. It's not every day an antique town and its citizenry rise out of the backwoods. Word gets around about a thing like that, despite all efforts to keep it quiet. The security guys had their hands full.

I imagined the man outside pointing at my window with a stern look, saying, "Allie Kirkland, come with me. You've been found guilty of breaching the laws of Wildwood."

And then . . . I recognized him. That wasn't a security guy. Holy cow! That was the *mystery cowboy*—Blake Fulton. So it *was* him I'd seen when I passed by the Waterbird yesterday.

Now here he was, skulking around behind the schoolhouse and carrying a black nylon duffel bag that definitely wasn't standard mid-nineteenth-century issue. He looked like he did *not* want to be seen. He wasn't in costume either—no surprise there. Once again, he was wearing camo pants, hiking boots, and a khaki-colored T-shirt that, I had to admit, fit rather nicely across his chest and strained just a bit, circling his upper arms. The black baseball cap was pulled low, and he looked . . . like he was definitely up to something. He stuffed his duffel bag under the edge of the porch, then stood up and glanced directly toward my window.

I ducked away from the glass.

Who *was* this guy, really? Did he know there was someone in here, or did he think he could come and go undetected?

Fat chance, mister. I peeked out just in time to see him forgo the steps and ascend the porch with one quick, athletic jump, then walk through the door into the room . . . right next to mine?

In two shakes of a lamb's tail (as Grandma Rita would've said), I was on my bed and crawling across the mattress, skirts bunched everywhere as I leaned close to the wall. He was in there, all right. The divider between the apartments was nothing more than studs and whitewashed tongue-and-groove boards. No insulation to muffle the sound. He was moving around the room and . . . whistling to himself?

Then shuffling again . . .

A grunt or two . . .

The *stomp, stomp* of boots on the floor . . .

More shuffling, a little walking around . . .

Something metal fell on the floor and clattered. Maybe one of the tinware cups like the set on the shelf above my cabinet? He stopped whistling.

There was an electronic beep. Then another. What was he *doing* in there? Bugging the place? Maybe he really was up to no good . . . perhaps a reporter of some sort. Or a disgruntled cowboy who'd tried to get a cast position and hadn't made the cut. Maybe he was here to . . . commit some sort of sabotage. It was a wild idea, but as usual my mind grabbed it and ran, inventing a scenario in which I, Allie Kirkland, saved the day and earned major brownie points by exposing a nefarious invader to the village.

Tucking my hair out of the way, I pressed my ear closer to the wood. The room had gone silent. No sign of movement, no electronic noises, no dishes being knocked off shelves.

Was he still in there, or had he left?

Or was he . . .

Crossing the porch and passing my window!

I scrambled away from the wall, tangled my knee in the quilt, and landed on the floor in an ungraceful heap of fabric. The boning in my corset temporarily incapacitated me, and by the time I made it to my feet, Blake Fulton was already headed down the path to the creek again.

The change in him caused me to blink and look again, and the scenarios in my mind morphed in a different direction. Suddenly, he was in full costume. He looked like any other cast member on this last day of dress rehearsal and pre-production photo shoots. He was wearing an unbleached muslin shirt—I recognized the seven-button, shield-front style as a pattern that Phyllis had ordered in a variety of fabrics from a reenactment store. He'd paired the shirt with civilian-style trousers with mule-ear pockets, and tall brown stovepipe boots worn outside his pants. He was carrying something in front of himself—the duffel bag maybe—but I couldn't tell for sure.

I had to follow him and find out, that was all there was to it. Whatever this guy's game was, I wanted to know it *now,* but if I took the time to go out the front way and circle around the building, I'd lose him. . . .

With a complete lack of forethought (the usual mode of operation when my mind was on a wild tear), I popped the cheesecloth screen from the window and prepared to exit. The opening was large enough and low to the ground, in keeping with authentic mid-century construction. Slipping through wouldn't be that hard. . . .

Halfway out, I suddenly understood why female operatives of the Civil War era weren't all that common. Yards and yards of fabric can be more than problematic, and a hoop has a mind of its own. I was quickly marooned over the sill . . . which, it turned out, wasn't very well sanded. I'd be picking splinters out of my skin all night, and given the lack of tweezers in the ladies' dressing kit I'd been given, that could be an interesting challenge. My hair blew over my face, and I couldn't see anything but a wall of red frizz, nicely highlighted by the morning light.

And then there was a sound . . . whistling . . . and it was coming . . . closer.

Panic set in, and I reversed course, struggling like a fish in a net and calling the window ugly names. I heard a small tearing sound and thought, *Randy is going to kill me, and when he's done, Phyllis and Michelle will kill me.* They were already so busy making adjustments to garments that didn't fit, didn't work, or had been damaged, that the entire costuming department was on the verge of a combined mental breakdown.

As far as I knew, though, no one had yet been stupid enough to end up stuck in a window. I pushed, pulled, and wiggled harder. Above my head, the window rattled in its sashes and slid downward as if someone had given it a good swift push. Fortunately, my neck and shoulders were there to stop it from crashing and breaking the glass. Unfortunately, it hurt, and I let out a yelp without meaning to. I'd just identified mistake number two in my plan. The trainer had told us to *always* put the brace bar in the window upon opening it. Frontier housing was most often not equipped with fancy window weights. Fingers and other body parts were not uncommonly lost in the windows of 1861.

Hair, too, apparently, because mine had been sucked into the frame as it came down. The window inched lower, and the hair pulled tighter. "Oww, oww, oww!"

Pressing upward with my shoulders didn't help. The window went cockeyed, pulled the captured hair tighter, and my head wedged against one side of the frame.

Good job, Allie. This'll make your record book of stupid human tricks.

Okay. Think, think, think.

There had to be a way to extricate myself from this situation before it got any worse.

Inside the room, I heard a telltale *beep, beep, beep.*

Too late. Things were already worse.

That was the sound of a camera about to do a go-live test, exactly ten minutes from now. Throughout the day today, production would be randomly taping for a behind-the-scenes reel to accompany *Wildwood Creek.* They were also testing the remote camera system and helping the cast members get accustomed to the cameras going on and off.

I was about to end up on film, inexplicably trapped in my own window.

Over my dead body. If I had to yank the hair out by the roots, I was . . .

"I must've missed this part of the pioneer manual." Blake Fulton's voice was easily recognizable, even from knee level. And yes, those were his boots, standing just a few feet away. "What page was it on?"

"The one . . . about . . . fire escapes," I ground out. "Didn't . . . you read it? I want to . . . ouch . . . be sure I'm . . . prepared, just in case." When all else fails, make fun of yourself. Stupidity does have a certain pathetic charm to it.

He squatted down, and I could see his face through the curtain of hair. "How's it working for you?"

"Well . . . other than the fact that my . . . scalp is slowly being sucked off my head . . . Not so bad. I made it halfway out."

He chuckled then. I caught a wide white smile through the wall of red frizz. "You realize there's a door on the other end of the room, right?"

"What if . . . the fire was in the . . . school? Ever . . . think of . . . that?" I wound my fingers into the trapped strands, tried to wrestle them free. Some hair, I could stand to lose—I had more than enough. But the skin covering my skull, I felt fondly attached to, and so did about a bazillion nerve endings, apparently. "I like to be . . . thorough."

"Next time you'd better get the kids out first. Save some innocent lives," he advised matter-of-factly. Funny guy.

"I'll remember that. I'm new to this . . . teaching thing."

The window slid a little lower and pretty little white fireflies danced around my eyes. "Owww. Help me out of here, okay? They just sent a ten minute go-live on my cameras."

There comes a time when picking the lesser of two evils is necessary. Right now, Blake Fulton, whatever his big secret deal was, seemed by far the lesser of two evils. I could already picture everyone up in the control center laughing their heads off, and me going viral on YouTube.

"Hang on a minute." Blake stood up and grasped the window frame. It lifted a fraction, taking my hair along with it, and I screamed like a banshee. The corners of my vision narrowed, twinkling with tiny stars. A whole galaxy of them.

"Hold on and let me get some tools. That window facing is just tacked on. I think I can pop it loose and . . ." All of a sudden, Blake was walking away.

"No! Oh no . . . wait . . ." But he was already crossing the porch. He came back with the duffel bag he'd stashed not long before. By then, I was making a last desperate attempt to free myself before the camera came on.

"This'll go better if you'll stop wedging yourself in there, tiger." At first, I thought he called me *tiger*. A weird little tingle went through me, and then I realized the word was *tighter*. *Stop wedging yourself in there tighter.*

"Just . . . trying to . . . make it as much of a . . . challenge as possible."

"You're doing a fine job of it."

"This is *not* funny."

"Darlin' . . ." He leaned close to my ear now, his long legs folding so that he was squatted beside the window, working his way up the facing. "Sometimes you can either laugh or cry, and you might as well laugh."

My mind did a quick hitch step. That was one of Grandma Rita's favorite sayings. I remembered it as the antithesis to life at Lloyd's house, where every misstep or social faux pas was a major tragedy and the impetus for a lengthy parental lecture about the importance of keeping up appearances and making a good impression.

Somehow, the mysterious Blake Fulton was channeling Grandma Rita. That was exactly what she would have said in a moment like this.

And exactly what I needed to hear.

How could he possibly have known?

He stood up again. "Close your eyes down there." The nails squealed as he manhandled the facing board loose.

Bits of wood drifted downward over my skin. I pictured what I must've looked like, high centered in the window, my skirts caught over the sill and my cheek crammed against the frame.

"You laughing down there, or turning hysterical?" Blake was laughing too.

I completely lost it.

Somewhere far, far beyond the laughter, I heard the beep of the camera going live.

It didn't even matter. When you're laughing hard enough, nothing does.

Chapter 17

Allie Kirkland
June, Present Day

No sooner had I gotten dislodged from the window than Blake Fulton disappeared into the woods and never came back. I probably should've reported the whole thing, but I figured enough of it had been caught on camera. Production could report it if they wanted to. From my standpoint, the less said the better. I was hoping the incident would go unnoticed—just another random camera test that no one was really watching.

I should have known I wouldn't be so lucky, of course. Even though no names were given, I was the talk of a last-minute morning safety lecture. *Someone tried to climb through a window without putting in the brace and got stuck this morning. Always use braces in open windows. Keep hair, fabric, ribbons, bonnet strings, and other dangling items well away from possible sources of entrapment. . . .*

I'd only begun to gather my tattered dignity when the set photographer showed up to snap pre-production photos of Wren and me in the schoolhouse. After that, Mallory Everson came to do the interview for *The Frontier Woman* blog.

The whole time all I could think of was the iPhone hiding under my cabinet and the need to be rid of it. I was relieved when the interview was over, and since I couldn't just leave Stewart hanging, it seemed that the best course of action would be to sneak off with the phone now, see if he'd sent me anything, and then let him know this was the last he'd be hearing from me until summer was over. I could hand the phone off to Stacy tonight, thereby removing further temptation and the danger of getting caught with it in the future.

Since engaging in illegal communication with the outside world definitely involved a hike, I shed my hoop, corset, and petticoat, then pulled my tennis shoes on under the skirt before leaving the schoolhouse with the iPhone hastily tucked into my skirt pocket. What I needed now was a secluded place—very secluded—and since photo ops were going on at the miners' camps scattered between Wildwood and the river, it only made sense to head beyond the brush arbor and find my way to the shores of Moses Lake, where no part of the production was set to take place. That was actually closer to civilization, so a cell signal was a good bet. If anyone found me, I could say I'd used the time after my photo ops to go exploring.

Escaping Wildwood unnoticed wasn't all that that hard, really: head down the path to the spring behind the schoolhouse with a water bucket in hand; ditch the bucket near said springhouse, where I could pick it up again later; follow the spring down to Wildwood Creek. Follow Wildwood Creek down to the lake-shore . . . because, what do small bodies of water do eventually? Flow into larger bodies of water.

I was impressed with my own rugged pioneer ingenuity. For a girl who'd recently gotten herself trapped in a window, I was doing exceptionally well. I even had the forethought to pull the back of my skirt up between my legs and tuck it in at the waist, creating mid-century genie pants. It made the hiking a little easier, though I decided that it would've been smarter to bring my T-shirt and capris along and leave the costume over a tree branch someplace.

Where it flowed downward toward Moses Lake, the waters of Wildwood Creek ran deep and wide through a limestone gorge roughly fifteen feet below. That part of the walk took a while, but it was worth it for the view alone. Along the lake-shore, a shady hidden spot beside a cedar tree provided the perfect frontier phone booth. With email in the palm of my hand and a jet drawing a slowly spreading trail across the sky, the modern world seemed just one comforting step away. A boat motored by on the lake, and I thought about Burt and Nester at the Waterbird store. Were they among the curiosity seekers security had booted out in recent days?

The cell phone found a signal and connected in less than a minute. Magic. Unfortunately, there was nothing significant from Stewart, just a note saying that the materials he was waiting for hadn't come in today. He was sure they'd show up in another day or two. *I'll be in touch as soon as I have more for you. I think I've found the missing link to Bonnie Rose.* He made it sound like we were spies, working together on some clandestine mission. *I'm on the case.*

Temptation nibbled, inconveniently compelling. It wasn't all that difficult to sneak off to the lake. I could probably manage it again after go-live started. Just . . . just one more time. *I think I've found the missing link to Bonnie Rose.* Had he? The possibility was too much to resist. All I had to do was keep the phone a couple more days. Just until I could see what Stewart came up with . . .

Maybe while I was here, I'd send off a quick email to Mom and Lloyd, let them know that my summer plans had morphed into something completely unexpected.

A little fantasy spun in my head—one in which they were excited by the news, impressed that I was trying to do this thing. For a minute or two, the altered reality felt good. Then I scanned through my in-box and realized there wasn't a thing from home—just as there hadn't been since I'd made my decision about working here. Same silent treatment. Same message. Play by the family rules or you're not part of the family.

It hurt to think about it, so I just turned off the phone and sat by the lake until I knew I'd probably been away far longer than I should've. I still had a long hike back, and I wanted to follow the little trail that ran alongside Wildwood Creek in the canyon, which would take longer. Tonight there would be a big celebratory hog roast in the village. I couldn't be late for that.

With the afternoon beginning to dim, it was time to abandon the real world and head back. Tomorrow, the Bonnie Rose life would hit me full-force. Suddenly, even as worried as I'd been about whether I could hack it, a part of me was relieved. The real world came with issues I couldn't just fix. No doubt Bonnie Rose's world did too, only hers were matters of survival, of life and death. Had Stewart really found the keys to her secrets? Would I ever know why she chose to come here and why she disappeared along with the others who'd lived in this place?

Beside me as I moved along, Wildwood Creek seemed to be keeping its secrets as well, its surface more of a long, narrow pool than a stream with intentions of going anywhere. Lines of debris along the rock walls testified to the fact that at some time this had been a waterway to be reckoned with, but right now the drought had choked the life out of it. If things got any drier, the little stream that had given our town its name wouldn't be flowing at all.

The soles of my sneakers crunched dully on the caliche ground as I walked, and in the water fish surfaced, their scales catching the last beams of soft sunlight. A tiny fawn lay hidden in a nest of grass and mustang grapevine. The two of us startled each other. I could've picked the baby up and carried it home, but thanks to Grandma Rita, I knew better. *Never touch a wild creature that looks healthy enough.* Her voice was in my ear now, her Texas drawl seeming right at home in these woods. *There's a mama nearby somewhere, and she'll come back for it, hon.*

A wishing-ache pierced me without warning. If only it could've been Grandma Rita stepping into one of those dowager lives in the Delevan house this summer. She'd fit right in there on the hill with Genie and Netta, taking her place among the grandmoms of Wildwood. We could be pioneers together, just like my ancestors on the Kirkland side. Who could say? Perhaps some of them had walked these very hills along with Bonnie Rose.

For a moment I slipped fully into the illusion of it, felt myself sinking into the past, into Bonnie's life. It happened at the strangest times now— when I was bent over a cooking fire, focused on corn pone cakes slowly frying in a pan, or learning to store milk and eggs in the spring-house along the bluff, or balanced on a stool trying my luck at milking a cow, or helping the school kids chase chickens into a coop. There were those odd moments when I felt as if Bonnie Rose may have been exactly in that same place, working at the same task, long ago. As if I she and I were in some way, one and the same.

When I finally climbed the narrow trail out of the creek bed, I almost expected to find 1861 waiting for me. There was nothing to say that it wasn't.

Overhead the jet trails were gone. Nothing but rustling leaves and sky. No power lines, no engine noises, no swoosh of passing cars, no faint hum of fluorescent streetlights. Not one sound made by machines. Just the deepening blue-gray of evening and a single first star insisting its way into the void, giving a warning that I'd dallied long enough.

Darkness would descend again, and another night in Chinquapin Peaks would take hold. The riot of coyote voices would start in the hills, echoing here and there, their raucous songs seeming to come from all directions. I'd gotten more accustomed to them in the past three weeks—all of us had—but when they ran through the woods near the town site, stirring up the dogs and causing the horses to pace their corrals, something primal still ruffled my skin. Hearing their calls now made me want to hurry home.

I quickly surveyed the hills to get my bearings

so that I could cut cross-country toward the village. It'd be faster that way. There was an old logging trail the production crew used for transporting men and equipment without making tracks through the set. If I could find it, I could . . .

Something stopped me short. I blinked, squinted, looked again. There were people among the trees, just visible against the shadowy branches. An old man and a little dark-haired girl. Her filmy white dress fell loosely from her shoulders and the hem danced around her calves, seeming to find a life of its own.

They stood on the hillside next to the logging road, looking downward into the village. For an instant, they seemed unreal . . . part of my 1861 fantasy. Ghosts of Wildwood.

A shiver of gooseflesh ran over my skin as I moved closer.

A mule brayed somewhere in the woods, and the man turned to look, and I knew I hadn't conjured him from my imagination. The stranger snatched off his ball cap and held it in his hands apologetically.

He closed the gap between us, the little girl trotting after.

"We w-w-wasn't b-botherin' unn-nothin'," he stuttered, struggling with each word. "Birdie j-just uww-wanted to see the t-town. She c-caught 'er some fire-fireflies f-f-for Nick."

The little girl held up a jar, her blue eyes rising

with it. "Grampa and me got 'em for Nick," she repeated in a whisper.

Nick, the little blond-haired son of Mallory Everson, the *Frontier Woman* blogger. Nick was the youngest of the students in our Wildwood school, only five years old, but pretending to be six and a first grader, in terms of village life.

Birdie pressed the jar toward me, and I took it. "I can give it to his mom for him," I offered. The jar certainly looked old enough to be part of Civil War–era life, though it probably wasn't. "Every-one's coming down for dinner in the village tonight. Nick probably won't be able to have this in Wildwood, but he can take it home with him." Little Nick was one of the few cast members allowed to come and go from the closed set. The ranch where he lived was providing some livestock for the production, so his parents were in and out anyway. Despite Tova's "pretty face" theory, that was the reason Mallory had been allowed to begin compiling blogs about the production, which wouldn't actually be published until after shooting ended in September. She was hoping to do a magazine series or a book as well.

" 'Kay." Smiling, Birdie reached across the space between us to touch my dress. "You're a princess lady."

I realized I still had the skirt tucked into my waistband. Some princess. "We start filming tomorrow. This is my costume." I turned to her grandfather. "No one's supposed to be around the area without a Razor Point ID, though. How did you get here?" There wasn't much chance they could've missed the plethora of *Private Property* and *No Trespassing, Violators Will Be Prosecuted* signs tacked to trees in all directions. Their presence here seemed innocent enough, though. I didn't want to see them get in trouble.

"We urr-rode the umm-mule." The old man paused, pointing across Wildwood Creek and upward, to where the hills of Chinquapin Peaks grew even steeper. From what I'd seen of this remote territory, life here wasn't very different from that on our reenactment set. The narrow gravel roads wound through a patchwork of lopsided cabins shored up with tar paper and ancient trailer houses with roofing held down by cement blocks or old tires. Here and there, derelict vehicles appeared to be serving as housing as well. Hungry-looking animals foraged in grass-bare yards and dogs on chains threatened passing cars. Chinquapin Peaks had the feel of a place that didn't welcome change . . . or strangers.

I wondered how this old-timer felt about our presence here, though he seemed friendly enough. "Over y-yonder we come. Birdie uww-wanted to s-see. My granny u-u-used to t-tell the t-tale about Wildwood t-t-town. Sing to us kids, 'B-be good, be good. Don' w-wander the forest udd-

deep. Bonnie Rose g-grab you up, and them she g-get she keep. Take you d-down, in the river d-drowned, leave your m-mama to w-weep.' "

A wild rush of righteous indignation swept through me, hot and furious and unexpected. "Your grandmother sang you songs about the schoolteacher kidnapping little kids and drowning them in the river? That's terrible!" I was offended for Bonnie Rose's sake. The young girl in that grainy photo of the Wildwood school, the girl who looked so much like me . . . what could she possibly have done to deserve to be immortalized in such a way? How could people say things like that about her? She wasn't much more than a child herself.

What had happened here in Wildwood? Was that rhyme, apparently handed down through generations, merely the hill folks' way of explaining the mysterious end of the village? Or was it proof of something awful—the dark, sinister reality that Rav Singh had alluded to as he coaxed me into Bonnie's life? Was this the Ballad of Wildwood?

"My umm-mama s-sung it," the man stammered, seeming embarrassed by my outburst.

"Grandpa Len don't sing it," Birdie assured me. "I ain't scared a' Bonnie Rose. I got Jesus watchin' over me." Slipping a hand into the neck of her dress, she pulled out a crudely painted wooden cross, the sort of thing we might've made in Vacation Bible School when I was in Texas for the summers. "We got Jesus, right, Grandpa Len?"

"Yes'm, th-that's urr-right. And udd-don't be f-forgetten it." Grandpa Len scratched his scraggly beard, giving the woods a concerned glance. "W-we ubb-best be ugg-getting back to the m-mule."

"Wait." I grabbed his arm impulsively. "What's the rest of the song? What does it say?"

His leathery features scrunched around his nose, conveying frustration. Finally, he pounded his head with the heel of one hand hard enough that it hurt just to watch. "Udd-don't know. My umm-mind ain't so ugg-good n-no more. Granny u-u-sed to s-sing it ubb-boiling them hen eggs, and let 'em g-go that ull-long."

Eggs . . . How long does it take to boil eggs? I'd just learned that during my frontier training. Five minutes, maybe? There was much more to the song than what I'd just heard.

The old man pounded his temple and alternately shook his head, trying to dredge up the rest. His little granddaughter grabbed his elbow to stop him. "It's okay, Grandpa Len. It don' matter. We can sing another song. Mrs. Zimmer taught us one in summer school th'other day."

Her grandfather gave an adoring smile, his face relaxing. "All urr-right. You c-can teach umm-me."

Birdie's eyes twinkled. "Okay. And tomorrow,

can we go see the caves down by the lake too?"

"If the w-water's down f-fer enough, we w-will. Them c-caves ubb-been c-covered lotsa y-years. Umm-might b-be a big ol' c-catfish in t-there g-get us ull-like this." Jutting out a hand, he nipped the little girl's waist before she could twist away, giggling.

"Well, be careful." I held up the jar of fireflies. "I'll give these to Nick's mom." Along with the promise came an idea. Maybe I'd mention the bit from the old ballad to Nick's mom. Perhaps she could dig up something online. I hadn't found any mention of it in the Wildwood research I'd done with Stewart, but who could say?

Birdie and Len turned toward home, fading into the shadows as I hurried back to the village. Fortunately, the press ops and photos were over for the day, and the schoolhouse lay quiet and empty, the heat of the afternoon slowly seeping out through the walls.

Back in my little room, I tucked the phone into the empty canister with my toothpaste and put it on one of the high shelves where Wren couldn't reach it. There were plenty of unused spaces among my kitchen goods. Even though I had gone through some of the domestic arts training with the historical experts, I wasn't expected to be cooking much. As the local teacher, my meals would be provided by various townsfolk as was customary for preachers and teachers in frontier settlements like Wildwood. I was counting on my kindly neighbors, as I hadn't been very adept at the frontier cooking lessons, and my limited teacher income wouldn't allow for much buying at the store, where the prices were exorbitant even by mid-century standards.

By the time I finally finished hiding everything and putting on my Sunday best outfit for the celebration of our last night before go-live, I could already hear music floating in the air above the village street. Someone out there was playing a mean fiddle. The bawdy tune wrestled a little jig from me as I opened the bedroom door with the firefly jar tucked under my arm.

The handle bumped into something soft, and all of a sudden, there was Wren Godley, looking undeniably guilty. Of what, I wondered?

"Ouch!" She rubbed her shoulder where the door had collided with it. "You should look before you come out. This is a schoolroom, right? There might be a *kid* here, *remember.*" She was her usual charming self. There was a reason why the grips and other cast members, including children, ran the other way when they saw Wren coming.

"School's closed," I reminded Wren. "Why aren't you out there with the other kids? I thought they were going to have games for you guys tonight." I tried to shoo her from the doorway, but she wasn't moving. Instead, she peered curiously into the apartment.

Her eyes squeezed upward from the bottom, and she crinkled her nose at me. "I don't *like* games." An obnoxious little head bob gave emphasis. "How come *you* don't have to be at the stupid hog roast?"

"I do have to be there. Actually, I'm looking forward to it, and I'm headed that way right now. Excuse me while I shut the door." I nudged her gently out of the way, and she sidestepped into my exit path.

"Well, where were you *before?*" She poked her nose out like a ferret sniffing for morsels. "Because you weren't in *here*. I checked in the window, and there wasn't *anybody* in here."

Now she was a Peeping Tom too? I'd have to be even more careful.

She noticed the firefly jar clutched under my arm before I could answer. "What are those? Bugs?"

"Fireflies. They're for Nick Everson. It's a long story."

"Ewww. What are they *for?*" Drawing back, she gave the jar a perplexed look, and it occurred to me that Wren Godley didn't know anything about gathering fireflies into a lantern jar.

A sudden and surprising tsunami of sympathy hit me, and I held the container out for her to see. "Well, because they're pretty. You enjoy their twinkling for a while, and then when you're done, you let them go. It's like . . . making your own lamp."

For just an instant, her face softened as she considered the wonder of fireflies. As quickly as it was there, the vulnerability vaporized, replaced by crossed arms and a sardonic eye roll. "Why don't you just get a *flashlight,* stupid?"

"Never mind." Since it was either say something inappropriate or move on, I chose to usher her out of my space and up the street toward the gathering of cast and crew. The festivities were already moving into full swing in the street outside Unger Dry Goods Store and Warehouse, the biggest building in town.

We hadn't gone far before Wren's mother apprehended her, and they veered off, the mom struggling to navigate the caliche gravel on five-inch heels while berating Wren for disappearing. There was face time to be had with important people, after all. Like Rav Singh, who had just arrived at the party. I could see him across the way, holding court on the loading dock of the Unger Warehouse. He was telling a story while a group of admirers hung on his every word. Wren's mother quickly elbowed her way to the front, maneuvering Wren into position.

I stood on the fringes and watched for a moment, wondering what it must be like to be Rav. To be surrounded at all times by people who wanted something, expected something, needed something, who were just waiting for you to notice them.

Did he thrive on it? Feed on it? Was he ever just . . . exhausted by it? How difficult would it be, never knowing if the people around you were real? How did my father deal with the culture of this business? Was I ready for it? Would I ever be?

What if, after all this, I found out that my father's passion, his ability to bring stories to film, had died with him—that I really didn't have it? What if my mother and Lloyd were right all along? What if I was just . . . nothing out of the ordinary? Not remarkably smart like Lloyd's kids. Not remarkably athletic like my half siblings.

Just unremarkable.

Insecurity nipped. Before it could take out a hunk of flesh, I wandered off to find Nick and his mother, so I could give them the firefly jar. Unlike Wren, Nick was delighted with creation and thrilled that his friend Birdie had brought it for him.

"Nick and Birdie adore each other," Mallory explained. "She's a couple years older, so it really works. She tells him what they're going to do, and he does it. She's like the big sister he never had. On top of that, she knows everything about bugs, fish, and little squirmy animals, as well as mules, chickens, and all the doodads boys like. Living up here, she's got a wealth of experience. Even though we're on a ranch, it's a whole different kind of life for these families in Chinquapin

Peaks. I'm sure Len and Birdie didn't mean any harm by coming to take a peek at the village, by the way. The hill people don't quite recognize private property rights, especially for something so foreign as a film project like *Wildwood Creek*."

Since we'd come around to the subject, I took advantage of the opportunity to tell her about the song Len and Birdie had mentioned and to discreetly ask if she could find out any more about it. "But if you'd keep it quiet, I'd appreciate it. I mean, I don't want to get you in any trouble, so if you'd prefer not to, I understand."

Mallory tucked her hair behind her ear, giving me a wry look. "Are you kidding? I love a good mystery, and it sounds like something I might want to do a story on, eventually. I'll see what I can turn up. My friend Andrea counsels for the Department of Human Services here. She could ask some of her older clients about it. If Len's grandmother knew the song, maybe other people do too. Folk music tends to be passed down. I'll see if I can find anything."

"There you are!" Kim was headed my way, hiking up her simple cotton skirt. "I haven't seen you in *forever!* That's the worst thing about this place—there's no time for girl talk. Okay, well, I take that back. The outhouse is the *worst* thing, my boss at the bathhouse is the *second* worst thing, but you're third. I miss you." She tackled me with a hug.

Mallory headed off to take pictures of the giant hog spitted over the fire pit, which I myself had been trying to avoid looking at. Something about seeing a roasting carcass nearby was . . . well . . . icky. But it did smell good.

Kim and I walked the other way, watching the kids participate in hoop-rolling contests and try their skill at walking on stilts, weaving pot-holders, bobbing for apples, and tossing little bags of river gravel into a cut-off barrel.

By the time the dinner bell rang, calling us to the serving line, I was warming to the idea of eating hog carcass. My mouth had started watering and my stomach sounded like a badger coming out of hibernation. With the go-live about to begin and our foodstuffs and incomes set to match that of our historic counterparts, the feasts were over after tonight, and everyone seemed to be aware of it.

Kim and I ended up seated near the end of a table with Genie and Netta. Tova and Rav wandered by with their plates, and I held my breath, hoping they wouldn't fill the last two empty seats at our table. Fortunately, they moved on, and the dinner slipped into a relaxed, friendly mode. Thanks to Kim, the conversation quickly turned to discussion of 1860s outhouses, chamber pots, and underwear. Not the usual table talk, but before long, we were all red-faced, laughing about each others' mishaps. Of course, my stuck-in-the-window story came up. Something that ridiculous doesn't happen just any day.

"Okay, okay. It wasn't one of my brighter ideas. It's hard to get used to needing a six-foot berth everywhere you go." I cleverly omitted the fact that it was Blake Fulton who had come to the rescue. What was there to say, anyway? The man had the most annoying habit of popping in and out of my life without explanation.

Kim frowned across the table, sensing something hidden. The girl could practically read my mind sometimes. "But what were you doing, *exactly,* climbing out the window?"

Leave it to her to home in on the obvious. I didn't have a great answer for that, but I came up with the best one I could. "Well, I just . . . was thinking about the fact that there's no rear door on my room and . . . what if there was a . . . a fire or something? I wanted to make sure I could get . . ."

"Hey, neighbor!" Of all people, Blake Fulton slid into a chair next to me without bothering to ask whether it was empty or not. As usual, he came out of nowhere. "You recover from that little wrestling match with the window yet? Heard you're famous up in the tech trailer now. I'll tack that facing back on for you tomorrow."

Across the table, Kim blinked, her eyes dropping open like the jaws on a steam shovel, ready to rake in the facts. Genie and Netta looked back and forth between Blake and me, brows rising speculatively.

"Yes, I did. Recover. Thank you." *Neighbor.* That's what he'd said. So, he *was* staying in the room next to mine? And if he was . . . where was he all morning during the photo shoots? I hadn't seen a sign of him, and I'd been looking.

To my complete horror, Kim requested the details of the window incident, and Blake Fulton obliged. My stupidity quickly became the stuff of amusing dinner conversation. He shoulder-butted me when he was finished, adding, "She was a good sport about it, for a girl with her head caught in a ringer. By the time the camera went on, she was laughing so hard, she didn't even notice."

Netta passed a playful look my way. "Well, you know, back in *my* day, if a gal wanted to get a young fella's attention, she just piled a few extra schoolbooks into her bundle, so it would look like it was more than she could handle. Then she'd stroll by the fella's house, a'course, and walk *rea-ul* slow."

A blush heated the upper half of my body. This conversation was taking a most disturbing turn. "I really don't understand why my room doesn't have a door to the back porch." *To change the subject just a little.* "It'd make it so much easier to go down to the springhouse for water, for one thing."

291

"And to practice fire drills," Blake offered. He was so helpful.

Genie threw her head back and laughed. "Oh, mercy! That was how I got the attention of my very first beau, back in the day—lugging a water bucket. He worked for a dairy up the road, so every day, just about the time I *knew* he'd be passing by on his bicycle, well, I'd be waiting there by Daddy's barn with a big ol' bucket of water to carry. Now, I was a farm gal, so I could heft that thing and lug it a mile. But as soon as I'd see that boy passing by, I'd start dragging it like my arm was gonna fall off. 'Course, when that boy stopped to rescue me, I'd invite him in for some fruit pie as a fair reward for all that rescuin', see?" She winked across the table at me.

Blake let his fork settle against his plate. "I didn't get any fruit pie when I rescued her." He turned an incredulous expression my way, as in, *What's wrong with this picture?*

The blush raced up my neck and suddenly the tips of my ears were burning. I probably could've shot a blood pressure meter completely off the charts. Seriously, who was this guy, really? And was he always this . . . this . . . flirty? Clearly, Netta and Genie were thoroughly charmed, much like the deli girl in the grocery store down the street from the Berman.

Across the table, Kim's eyes were like big blue baseballs.

Netta stuck her hand out and introduced herself properly, then smiled adoringly at Blake and added, "Hon', you come on up to the big house any ol' day and there'll be a pie there waiting on you."

Blake grinned, and I had to admit, the effect of it was dazzling. "Miss Netta, you can expect me for a visit."

Kim gave me another pointed look. She was obviously about to explode, the questions no doubt jamming up like commuter cars at rush hour. *I want details,* that look said. *What in the world have you been doing while I'm slaving away, learning the bathhouse-and-laundry trade?*

She'd just leaned across to introduce herself to Blake when the fiddle-and-guitar duo who'd been entertaining us suddenly stopped playing, and the sound system let out an ear-piercing screech. I looked up just in time to see Rav Singh step onto an old hay wagon, microphone in hand. He moved like a rock star taking the stage, lithe and confident, his head tipped back and his arms splayed out. A breeze whirled down the street and lifted the filmy black fabric of his shirt, swirling it in the amber light of lanterns and torches. Behind him, Chinquapin Peaks drew a dark, jagged line against a spill of stars and a full moon.

"Greetings, cast and crew of *Wildwood Creek*!" he said, and a hush fell over the crowd, the silence pregnant with expectation. "Welcome to the final night of the modern age. When you awaken in the morning, you will have stepped through time and been transported into *Mysterious History*, ready and willing . . . or not."

He paused, scanned the crowd. I felt as if the last part of that sentence might be aimed directly at me. He seemed to be looking my way, waiting for me to flinch as reality set in. Instead, I straightened in my chair. All my life I'd doubted my own abilities, and Wildwood was no exception, but I was going to do this or die trying. My dream, and my ticket into the business, depended on it. This was my chance to prove how much I wanted it.

Rav strode to the other end of the wagon, cutting a dramatic figure against the lamplight, the tails of his shirt dancing loose over his smooth brown skin, his long, sleek hair fluttering around his head like a curtain, parting and closing, then parting again.

"There is one detail I've not revealed until now. Many of you may have been wondering, what will be the secret mystery in this newest *Mysterious History* journey? What awaits you here beyond assuming the lives of those who came to Wildwood trusting their futures, their very survival, to the promise of gold?"

He paused, seeming to contemplate his own question as a murmur circled the tables. "There are so many questions about Wildwood, some of which you've already considered yourselves. Where did the people go? How can an entire community vanish with no record left behind? Did the people of Wildwood flee? Were they taken? Do they lie somewhere near here still, their resting places unmarked? Do they yet walk these hills and valleys, as the locals say?"

In the trees, the cicadas suddenly grew impossibly loud, their throbbing song rising to a deafening crescendo, then stopping all at once. Kim glanced over her shoulder, slanted a nervous look my way as the eerie speech continued.

"And what of the gold? A vast deposit that was, as we now know, never to be found. The vein that yielded the ore found near Wildwood was later determined to have been volcanic in nature. The mother lode that brought gold fever to these hills lay far beneath the surface, unreachable. But in 1861, it was the stuff of dreams and dreamers. A reason to leave behind all that was safe, all that was familiar, and to risk . . . all. It was the impetus of hope and courage . . . but was it also the spark that ignited the darker traits of human nature? Greed? Envy? Money lust? Perhaps murder? Mass hysteria? Madness? Does this explain the disintegration of Wildwood?"

Again, the cicadas lifted their song, and Singh waited, his shirt swirling around his waist. "We've no way of knowing, but perhaps through *Mysterious History*, we will learn. And so, my question now—*your* question as you *become* Wildwood—is how do we accurately re-create the emotions, the decisions, the driving forces— the beauty and the hideousness of *that* time in *this* place?"

An uneasy hum traveled the tables. A chill walked over me, and I rubbed away gooseflesh.

Across the table, Netta whispered, "I don't like the sound of that."

Beside me, Blake calmly ate another spoonful of purple-hulled peas and took a swig of lemonade, as if he hadn't the slightest concern.

Singh paced back to the middle of the wagon, stopped there, gazed over the tops of the buildings into the night sky, then slowly scanned the crowd, commanding a snap of instant and rapt attention. All side conversations stopped abruptly. "How . . . indeed?"

He ushered someone onto the platform, and I quickly recognized the woman who'd guided me through the dark halls of the Berman on the day of my initial interview. I'd seen her only occasionally during my months at the Berman. My suspicion was that she traveled with Singh. She handed him a sheet of paper, then stood behind him and to the right, statue-still, motionless, her hair bound so tightly that even the breeze couldn't tease it.

Singh held up the sheet of paper. "In the centers of your tables, you will each find a box. The box contains information needed for staking claims in and around Wildwood, and the price that will be required, in terms of your 1861 funding. Various sites along the river have been individually seeded with over one million dollars in ore — only fool's gold by the world's standards, but here in Wildwood, those with the fortitude and good fortune to choose their claims wisely may profit beyond their wildest dreams. In Wildwood, all that glitters is worth its weight in gold at the Miners Exchange. The locations of paying claims are not known to any among the cast and crew. And they *will not* be known . . . unless and *until* they are discovered by *you,* the residents of this town. The Claims Office will open in the morning for filing. I and Razor Point Productions wish you good luck and good hunting as you re-create not only the time period of Wildwood, but its mysterious history as well."

The crowd held silent in a moment of collective shock, heads turning slowly side-to-side, wives whispering to husbands, new neighbors looking across tables at one another, suddenly seeing something completely different. Potential competitors.

Singh descended from the wagon with his assistant in tow, seeming unconcerned by the murmur rippling through the crowd. Across the table, Kim was already wondering how much a claim might cost, and whether she could take her salary from the bathhouse and go into mining instead. "If I'm stuck here all summer, I want a chance at the gold."

"I knew that man had something up his sleeve!" Netta struck a palm against the table. "I can always tell. This isn't what we signed up for at all. We were supposed to spend two and a half months living like pioneers, not fighting each other tooth and nail for gold. It's not . . ."

I didn't hear the rest. I was busy watching Blake Fulton scoop up another spoonful of peas. One thing was clear enough. This news did not come as any surprise to him.

Chapter 18

Bonnie Rose
June 1861

Dear Ms. Rose,

I'd not thought, upon your departure from the New Ila, to inquire as to your permission that I might address you by your given name. I hope, in light of the distance between us now, that you will forgive my taking this familiar liberty. Many's the hour since watching you disappear into the distance, that I have cursed my lack of courage in not saying more. Indeed, were that scene to play itself out again, Bonnie, I would have committed whatever egregious breach of etiquette might have been necessary to prevent your leaving altogether.

It is my belief that trouble may befall you in Wildwood. I pray that I am quite mistaken. I pray that this letter reaches your hands, finding you unharmed and at the very least somewhat contented in your new position there. I pray that your gentle spirit and bold, independent nature are not dimmed by the realities of life in such a town as Wildwood.

I have long held concerns as to the nature of our in-common employer and his intentions for his holdings, as well as for those who are bound financially to his employment. With shots fired this spring at Fort Sumter, and the entry of Texas into the conflict as a Confederate state, animosities draw to a boil all around us. It may well be that I will soon be forced to scuttle the New Ila to prevent her from being conscripted as a tool in the Confederate cause. While I may not own her lock, stock, and title, she is my boat, and I will not see her used against the union of these United States.

If our employer should intercept this letter, if you should find it with the wax seal broken, it may be that I am already deceased, or otherwise detained. If so, my greatest regret, other than allowing you to disappear from my sight on that last day, is that I will not be capable of coming to your aid, as I had promised on our parting.

But know this, Bonnie. If it is a man's heart and his prayers that can preserve him and rejoin him again with another human soul, I will find you. Know also, that there is another in Wildwood who watches over you. If you recall our final conversation onboard the New Ila, you will and do know the identity of this person. Should the need of your rescue from Wildwood become imminent, go to him. He will help you to find a way.

Please, Bonnie, forgive my impetuous declaration of love in these words as I write. I have, many nights, struggled to reason myself from them. But there are times when a man's soul knows what his mind cannot yet comprehend.

If there is a possibility that I may find you again in this world, I will do it, if only you would bid it of me.

Could you ever love me, Bonnie Rose?

Yours affectionately,
James

I sit lookin' at the letter, touching my finger to the stroke of the pen, and inside, my heart flutters like a shore bird bound in a fisherman's net. I'm feeling I must escape and I must surrender, all at once. Alone in the darkness with Maggie asleep nearby, I read it again and again, hoping with one breath and fearin' with the next.

Could the eyes of love ever take away my scars, my shame? Could such eyes look at me and see the soul beneath the broken skin?

An ember lights inside, and I hold the letter close. I feel it flickering up. Hope.

An answer comes snarlin' and pantin' and nippin', cutting the hope from my mind like a lamb from the herd, driven off to the hills to wander. *No decent man could ever love you, Bonnie Rose,* the voice growls, sneers, and whispers. *None can look beyond the scars. None have until now, after all.*

He's only seeing what he believes to be true. He knows nothin' of your shame. If you've feelings for him in the slightest, you'll save him ever hearing of it.

I know it is true. I must bid him to go about his life without thinking of me. For a decent man such as he, there would be only guilt in knowing the truth and being forced, as surely he would, to rescind his proposal of love. Or worse, to honor it. A burdened heart, a soiled body . . . that's all I have to offer him.

I begin again to reply, to say what I must—that I've met another here in Wildwood, that indeed,

I've settled well into my position here and I've no fear of my own safety. None is true. Not a word. Quite the opposite, but I've only a few more hours to respond to the letter. I've only received it thus, because Mr. Hardwick was kind enough to hand it to Maggie May directly this evenin'. He could be bringing trouble upon himself by doing this, I know. But she has charmed him, my little Maggie May. Hers is the only face that can coax his smile. When he looks at her, I find myself believing he's seen the shadow of someone else he's known, some child he has loved, but I've no way of guessing who it might be. He's not a man to share his stories.

He has told Maggie, should she bring my letter of reply to him before the freight travels tomorrow, he will personally carry it with the post and deliver it to the *New Ila* himself. Both of us know, should such a letter pass through the mail in Unger's Store, I'll likely be among those who've gone away in the dark of midnight, leaving behind all their belongings as if they full well expected to wake and live another day in Wildwood.

I've lost count now of how many have vanished since the young woman from Red Leaf Hollow flung herself from the cliffs. Unlike that girl, whose body was fished from the river, many of the others have disappeared and not a trace of them found.

I fold the letter on the desk and lay my head

down upon it, not knowing what more to do. I want the answers to come clear, but they refuse, and time is running out. Mr. Delevan has been away this past week to one of his gatherin's of men who will raise troops from Texas to move east and join in the fighting of what's fast become a larger war. James Engle is no fool, for certain. From the *New Ila*, he's seen it growing clearly enough, swellin' like a fog that'll slip over us all before it's finished.

These weeks that've gone past since Essie Jane brought news of that young woman drowned in the river, Mr. Delevan's meetings have kept him mostly away from Wildwood. It's been a mercy for my own situation that he's had no time to devote his attentions toward me, but he'll be returning soon enough, and what then? Even now his men patrol the town, and there's no explainin' those who've disappeared into the night. There is only fear. And talk of monsters and men bewitched and renegades raiding in the night, taking only a few at a time.

I feel my mind asking the questions and drifting over answers I cannot bear. In a dream, I'm going the way of that poor girl from Red Leaf. Over the bluffs and down into the river, dead. And Maggie May along with me, or worse yet—left behind in his hands.

My dreaming mind sees that they've dressed little Maggie up for tea, paintin' red upon her lips and hanging baubles 'round her neck. She steals away down the kitchen women's path along the spring creek and comes looking for her sister, but I'm nowhere she can find me. I'm lyin' on the river bottom, and I see her there above, but I can't speak. He comes to find her then, slips his hand upon her shoulder, whispers to her, "Come away, Maggie. Your sister's gone and left you behind. You have only me now."

From the river bottom I'm screaming, but she can't hear me.

I wake to the feel of her shaking me, her fingers clutched tight over my arm. "Sister. Sister, wake up," she whispers.

I find her standing over me in her nightdress and cap. Outside the window, the day is risin' over the hills. I'm frightened of knowing what it will bring. Each morning, more disturbing news circles the town. More folks gone from their places.

Maggie catches my cheek with her palm. I'm soaked to the bone beneath my shift. My sweet sister doesn't trouble with asking why. She's found me this way many nights before, tossing and sweat-covered, drowning in a pool of my own fear. "You were callin' out my name," she whispers, and she curls herself over my shoulders, hugging away the cool kiss of the night air against my dampened skin.

"I must've fallen off and been gone in a dream. I can't remember a thing of it." I tell another lie.

There's no good in her knowing one more morsel that a girl of just nine years shouldn't. "I'm sorry for wakin' you."

"I don't mind it," she says. "I'll put the coffee on." She's giving me no trouble these days. No fuss about keeping shoes and stockin's on her feet, no wandering off in the wood. She's heard the talk around town. She knows the fear that's about. All the whispering.

"It's time for wakin' up, anyway." She nods toward the sound of the good reverend's door opening onto the porch. The man often goes outside and sits in his rocking chair, drifting into sleep at odd hours of the day, the bottle tucked in his breast pocket. But at night I hear him beyond the wall, shifting and murmuring in his bed, and on occasion crying out.

I wonder sometimes if his dreams are as troubled as mine. How could they not be? Each day he delivers a lesson in religion to the school-children, practically telling them that Mr. Delevan is seated at the right hand of the Father. It's their duty to obey Mr. Delevan's authority, to respect his decision that the men of this town come forth in support of mustering for the Confederacy now, rather than waiting for a draft order to begin. On Sundays, the good reverend seeks to instruct the adults of the same thing. Mr. Delevan's men force them to gather here on the Sabbath now. Outside, the slaves listen in, silent on the benches that've been placed 'neath the windows for them. There's no hint of their thoughts or even what understanding of these events they've been given. Only what the Delevans have told them, I suppose.

Big Neb sits at each service, his bulk making the bench seem a toy as he folds his hands and bows his head in prayer. He's the one the captain has told to look after me, I know it. But he'd be risking his life if he did anything to help me here. I cannot ask that of him.

Maggie notices the captain's letter, still waiting there on the desk. From outside the window, the first of the light catches the paper. I hear the sounds of the town coming to life. The day is beginnin'. My time for answering the captain is nearly gone.

"Have you written a letter for me to take to Mr. Hardwick?" Maggie is hoping for a reason to slip away from school and see her friend before he leaves Wildwood with his freight wagons today. Perhaps she knows more is at stake than just the writing of a letter, but I can't see explaining to her my reasons for rejecting his proposal. She needn't know more about my stains than she's seen already. Someday, perhaps, there can be a place in the world for her without the shame in it. There are no scars on Maggie May that anyone else can see. I pray that her beauty and her sweetness will one day bring a man to love her.

I'll not do anything to steal that hope from her.

"I may write later," I say. "For now we should be up and about. I've the lessons to study for the school day. Go out and fetch the butter and milk from the springhouse, and be mindful of snakes. Keep an eye as you go. Don't wander off the path. Only to the springhouse and back, Maggie May." Most mornings I walk there myself, but today I need a moment for reading the letter again, then hidin' it away in my pocket, where I can keep it close to me. "I'll watch out the window after you."

"Yes'm." She scampers 'round to make herself ready, pleased that I've let her have the task. For a moment she's forgotten about the trouble in Wildwood, and I am glad of it.

I watch her go, then stand at the window with the letter in hand. I read it again, my heart torn down the middle, and then I leave it unanswered.

We move through the rhythms of the morning, pretending today is another common day. When I ring Big Neb's bell to call the children in for school, one is missing. My heart falls and tears gather inside me, but I hold them away from the children. It's little Helma who is gone this morning. The tiny one with a crippled leg below the knee. Just a week ago, Big Neb added a brace to her shoe. Just yesterday, she was laughing as she played stickball with the children outside the school. She was finally able to run with the rest of them.

The others see that her space is empty. I'm hoping perhaps she's only sickly, home safe in her bed, but my heart fears something worse. Just days ago, her father presided at a meeting of the German folk, in secret in the wood. Maggie heard of it from the other children, but not of the subject of it. The children are careful around us. They don't know what to make of me, and they're takin' no chances. Each day my young students become more withdrawn and suspicious. The parents wouldn't be sending them to school at all if old Mrs. Delevan didn't insist that they must.

"Has anyone news of Helma Kalb this morning?" I ask, and little eyes flutter up, then down again.

"Anyone?" I'm trying not to seem as fearful as I feel. Little Helma won't survive the trip 'cross the wilds, if that's where her parents have gone in the night. She's a frail thing, and her mother not much better off, the family having suffered a terrible fever last year.

Please let them only be at home for the day, I hear myself askin'. I wonder if God has turned His back on this place. I've heard others say the same.

"Shall I take her lessons out to her when school is finished, do you think?" I ask.

I can see it in the children's eyes, the terrible answer.

"The river people took 'em." Little Brady

Riley blurts from the other side of the room where the Irish children sit. "They're Gonefolk now." Some of the older children have told tales to the wee ones, making them think that the river people have come from the water and lured away those who've left Wildwood. There's such terror in the children now. Some believe I am one of the river people—their queen, and all of this is my doing somehow. *Gonefolk* is what they're callin' the ones who've vanished.

But some of the German children say it's the Irish who've done it, hoping to take over the emptied claims. All those gone missing so far are German folk, save for the girl from Red Leaf Hollow who threw herself into the river weeks ago when it all began.

Now the Irish children sit on one side of the schoolhouse, and the German on the other. There's no mixin' of the wee ones nor the grown folk. Only worry, suspicion, and whispering. The number of Mr. Delevan's men grows by the day in Wildwood. They patrol the town and the country-side with guns—to keep the peace, he says.

Little Brady Riley's sister, Catherine, elbows the boy hard. "Shhh!" She hisses, lookin' at me, fearful.

Young Brady is rebellious this morn', though. He's seeking answers to questions his seven-year-old mind can't comprehend. Yesterday Helma was playing in the grass outside and today she is gone, with no trace left. "My da milked their cow this mornin', no sense it goin' to waste. Not a thing's been took from their place but the mule, Da says. Could be the river people drug it under too. Could be they drowned it and made a meal of it and hid the bones."

The children are watching me now, to see what I'll say about this, to see how I will respond to the news. They watch as if they half expect blood and sinew clinging in my teeth.

"There's not such a thing as river people, Brady Riley. They're nothing but a made-up tale, like wood fairies and sprites. A boy who sits in church on Sunday ought to know that much. If folks are leaving Wildwood, they're leaving of their own accord and on their two feet, not carried off by creatures that live in the make-believe."

But even as I'm saying it, I'm wonderin': Why would a family go without so much as taking a bit of canvas off the roof to carry along for shelter, a pot to cook in, food to sustain them on the trail, a skin to carry water? There's no sense in it. I'm seeing little Helma's face in my mind, and my stomach weaves knots.

"Or the Irish got her," one of the other children murmurs as I turn away.

"We'll have none of that," I scold and pass a stern look back. They freeze and fall silent as pillars of stone. In front, Maggie folds herself lower in her seat. I've moved her closer to me to stop all the tormenting. If they've decided that I am one of the river people, then they've named her one as well.

I try not to think of it as we move through the business of the day, but my hands shake mercilessly. There is little point to any of the teaching now, and my mind won't settle. I release the children early, and they run from the school like rabbits from the lion's den, not a one of them looking back. It is just as well. I'm planning to walk out to the shanty where little Helma lived, and it's best that none of them see.

"You keep yourself in the room and set the bar in the bracket," I tell Maggie May. "I have an errand to be about. If anyone should rap at the door, don't answer. Pretend you're sleepin' and haven't heard." I hurry to be off. It's nearly time for Mrs. Delevan to send her biddings for afternoon tea. Last night's dream presses my mind. Maggie, rouged and dressed in false finery. "Remember what I've said. If anyone should come 'round the door, don't answer."

Maggie asks to go along with me, but she doesn't argue when I tell her no. I'm down the path to the spring creek when I see Essie Jane walking from the big house. She's come to bring me for tea.

"Tell her you haven't found me," I plead, and I know she'll do it. "Tell her I've gone off after one of the students who was away from class today, to take the lessons out." I consider now that I haven't brought a book with me, and I should've thought of it, but I can't take the chance of going back.

"Yes'm," There's a small gash healin' beside Essie Jane's eye. I reached toward it, and she pulls away. "The massah be home dis evening 'fo dark-time. Asmae say he bringin' mo' men to chase off dem river people dat been draggin' folk away in the night." A shudder runs underneath her starched gray dress. Even she seems uncertain of me now, afraid to come close.

"Don't worry," I say. "I'll find out what is happening here in Wildwood. There is some way of explaining it, and it's not involving any river people."

I rush away into the trees, not catching a breath until I've left the sounds of town behind, and there's not a thing 'round me but the quiet of the wood.

I don't know what I'm expecting to find at the Kalb shanty—what answers I'm thinking will be there—but when I reach the place, there's little to tell the tale. The cow is trapped in the pen, the chickens shut up in their coop. The place is still as a picture, not a thing movin' but the canvas stretched over the roof beams of the little shelter dug against a rock hill.

I move closer, calling out to the family, telling them why I've chosen to visit. "It's only Miss Rose," I say. "I've come to ask after Helma, to bring her lessons to her."

The door hangs askew a bit. Through the gaps in it, there's not a thing but darkness. When I touch the latch, the wood shrinks away, the leather hinges foldin' in. It's all as young Brady Riley said—everything in place as it should be, from the blankets on the bed to the kettle by the fire pit. A schoolbook even waits beside the pillow on little Helma's pallet, the covers mussed as if she might've been readin' by the lamplight before she vanished. The larger bed above hers is still made up.

A coldness slides over my body as I stand looking. I can't bring myself to walk into the place. What's gone on here? What terrible thing?

The brayin' of a mule outside stands me up straight. If anyone should find me here, they'll only spread more rumors that this is somehow my doing. Were it not for the favor of the Delevans, for the number of times I'm called up to their home for tea, there would've been a witching party after me already, to be certain. I can't be seen near the home of those who've gone missing.

I press the heels of my hands to my forehead and try to think what I should do. Where I should go. Where I can run or hide.

The deep sound of a man's voice comes through the trees, and I recognize it. That's Big Neb, and in a moment, I see him leading the mule through the wood. My heart stills its wild fluttering, but I step behind the shanty and don't show myself

313

until it's certain there's no one but him and the mule.

"Dis here mule been foun' wanderin'." Big Neb indicates the animal, standing tuck-tailed just now. There's a trail of bleeding scratches over its flank, as if a mountain cat or a black bear's been after it in the wood. "He Mis'a Kalb mule. I put a shoe on 'im las' week. Look like he been on da bad end'a somp'tin las' night. I salve it up a bit befo' I bring 'im back."

"There's no one here," I tell him, but his face shows that it's dawnin' on him already. His gaze darts about the shadows, fearful now, and I understand the fear. "They've left the place. The cow wasn't milked this morning, and Helma was gone from school. Not a sign of them. Nor a word of where they might be."

Big Neb marks the cross over his broad chest and backs away a step, his eyes white rimmed. "Dis a bad place, miss. Dis a bad, bad place."

I lay a hand over my stomach and try to calm myself, to reason it out, but the panic wells up, tellin' me to bolt, take Maggie and run away. How would we do it? Where would we go? Whom can we trust?

Is there anyone?

Big Neb twists the lead rope in his hands, looking down at it. There's something inside him struggling to come out.

"Not a soul is nearby but the two of us," I say.

314

"I suspect that Essie Jane has told you things of me. Things of my . . . person, discovered by her onboard the *New Ila*." There were no secrets between Essie Jane and me as she nursed me through my sickness. She's seen the scars, but we've not spoken of it. "Things not known to all in Wildwood."

His downcast eyes say that, indeed, he is aware. Merciful heaven can only say what the two of them have made of it in their minds. Likely anythin' but the truth.

It matters little now. "If you've something to say, Neb, you must say it now." I wait, watching his courage gather like a storm brewing under his dark skin, straightening his body to its full height, tearing the bonds of restraint. I believe he'll snap the lead line any moment. Even the mule goes skittish, snorting and backing to the end of the rope.

"Dis family with da Gonefolk now, ain't dey?"

My stomach rises, and I swallow hard, nodding. "I fear the worst. Little Helma's too weak to have made a trip overland on foot. Her parents would've known that, and they loved her very much."

He nods grimly before regarding me with a directness I've not known from him before. "Cap'n say I'z to be watchin' aft'a you. He mighty feared when we lef' off da *New Ila*. He give you to my care, miss. Say I'z to get a message out wit' da freighter, dere be a need." He pauses then, cocks an ear toward a rustle that's caught the mule's attention. Only when it's passed does he continue. "I been prayin' ever' night. Seekin' da Way. Missus, maybe it be too late already, but you give me a message for Cap'n, and I get on dis mule right now, and I catch dat ox freighter 'fo he get far pas' da river ford."

"You'd be risking yourself." It drums in my mind, the terrible reality of what he's offerin'. I'm beset by pictures of what can happen to a slave who's thought to be running away. "If you're caught . . . Mr. Delevan's soldiers patrol in the wood, especially along the river."

He seems unafraid now, surprisingly so. "I gots me a way to go up Wildwood Crick. Be back fo' night come. Nobody know nothin', but dat I'z gone lookin' afta dis mule," he says, as if to persuade the both of us. "Cap'n, he a good man. He come."

"I fear there won't be time for it." It is difficult now to imagine that there could be. Whatever is afoot in this place, it grows by the day. Still, I slip the captain's letter from my pocket and turn toward the shanty. Inside, the darkness seeps over me like the soil of a grave. The only thing I find for writing is a bit of twig burnt off in the fire.

I lay open James's letter atop little Helma's schoolbook, kneel by her bed, and smell her scents—the mattress stuffed with leaves and sprigs of rosemary, the faint lingering of soil and summer grass, the scents of a child living close to the ground, knowin' all the tiny things the others don't see. A sheen of water covers my eyes as I turn over the letter and scratch carefully on the back of a page, *Come for us, James. Please.*

Bonnie Rose

I bring the paper to my lips, then kiss it softly and close my eyes, praying it may not be too late. I pray for the body and the soul of the child who lay only a day ago wrapped in this bed, and for all the others.

I pray that the Kalb family is safe.

In God's hands, either way.

Chapter 19

Allie Kirkland
June, Present Day

He was out there again. I rolled over, searched for the glow of my iPhone dock, then realized it wouldn't be there. No artificially lit digital display to tell me what hour of the night it was. Only darkness, moon shadows around the room, and grainy eyes proving I'd finally fallen asleep for a while.

I looked toward the window. Outside, the morning sun hadn't even begun to fade the stars.

For the past three days since he'd moved into the quarters next to mine, he'd kept the strangest hours. By extension, I had too. Between wondering about Blake Fulton next door, listening to coyotes howl, the scampering of tiny critters *inside* my room, and the schoolhouse creaking and groaning at will, the lack of a good night's rest was slowly driving me crazy.

Right now the wooden latch on Blake Fulton's back door was tapping against the frame. *Tap, tap-tap, tap-tap-tap,* the night breeze teasing it. He never closed it all the way when he went out there in the dark. With the walls so thin, I'd come to know his habits exactly—up, down, pacing the room, the ropes under his mattress moaning and squeaking as he tossed around, seeking sleep.

Every night since *Wildwood Creek* had swung into full go-live, he'd ended up outside like this. The man either had a sleep disorder or a guilty conscience.

I wanted to ignore the urge to get up and peek out the window. I really did. But even without looking I could picture him. He'd be standing in the open air, mopping off with a damp rag from the water barrel on the porch. One good thing since he'd moved in—I didn't have to haul water to the barrel anymore. It magically filled itself every morning . . . with the help of my mysterious neighbor.

Why did I feel so compelled to figure him out?

To discover who he really was and what kept him up wandering at night? His business here really wasn't any of my business. I guess it just bothered me that every time I subtly nosed around for details, he sidestepped the questions and changed the subject. The man wasn't one for offering straight truth.

Well, I'm just on hold for the time being was the closest thing I'd gotten to an answer. That was after I'd mentioned the schedule for the daily go-live of the cameras in my room. Everyone had a shooting schedule—a period of time when the cameras came on to record our struggles with the daily challenges of pioneer life and allow us to log video diaries, musing on how we felt about this whole experience so far.

I'd asked Blake what his shooting schedule looked like. He'd told me he was "on hold." I hadn't met anyone else who was *on hold*. In the village, shopkeepers worked to adapt to shop life, claim seekers waited in line at the land office and bought needed supplies at the Unger Store, the blacksmith sharpened pick axes, plows, and garden tools, would-be miners made their way into the woods to seek out gold-laden pieces of the promised land. Everyone here had a job. Everyone worked hard. Sunup to sundown, literally.

Yet Blake Fulton was "on hold." He'd circumvented all the normal costuming rigamarole and skipped the entire training class, but he did seem rather adept at this pioneer-living thing. He was cheerful about it, even. After wandering around all night, he'd be at his little cooking fire behind the schoolhouse in the mornings, happily stoking the coals, and by the time I was up and dressed, he'd be gone. Generally, I wouldn't see him again all day long.

He was in some way connected to Rav Singh— I'd figured out that much. I'd glimpsed the two of them from afar as I walked the kids up the street to turn them over to the production assistant who would shepherd them back to their various living places. Rav and Blake were standing just across what was referred to as *the blue line,* a row of stones that marked the edge of the on-camera area. No one out of costume was allowed across the blue line. Even production assistants, technical personnel, camera crew members, and Rav Singh himself dressed the part when coming into the village, so as not to break the continuity of a shot, should they be caught by one of the remote cameras.

When I saw Rav and Blake together, they were pointing and discussing. They seemed comfortable with each other.

That bothered me a little. Well . . . maybe more than a little. Something about Blake Fulton still didn't add up.

And then again, there was the revolving

question of why I cared. What I really needed wasn't *answers* but more *sleep*. The biggest shock of full-time pioneer life wasn't the lack of any one modern convenience, but how physically difficult it was every single day. I'd never been so weary by nighttime and so reluctant to crawl out of bed in the morning. I'd only become a frontier schoolteacher three days ago, and already I was wondering how in the world I would fill Bonnie Rose's shoes for two and a half months.

The wind picked up a little, the door tapping its frame until all I could think about was the noise. Finally I tossed off the quilt, stretched my legs over the side, and unfolded myself with a low moan before crossing the room. Outside the glass, the moon glowed above the cloth screen.

Standing back from the window, I checked Blake's location. He wasn't close by, so I leaned close to get a broader view.

Tonight he was sitting on the steps wearing his brown trousers but no shoes. His shirt fluttered in the breeze, unbuttoned around his midsection as his body hunched forward. Hands clutched into his hair, he seemed . . . in pain, almost. Such a contrast to his personality during the daytime, when he slipped into this whole immersion experience with ease, as if it were all perfectly natural. But something tormented him in the dark of midnight, that was clear enough. His fingers tightened around his scalp, and he seemed to collapse in on himself, a picture of suffering, of human misery.

I saw my own hand touching the glass above the screen, my fingertips landing soundlessly against the barrier that separated me from whatever plagued the dreams of Blake Fulton. Here behind the window, it felt safe to reach toward him.

I wasn't certain how long I stood transfixed. Finally he rose, his face tipped back, his eyes closed, the breeze off the bluffs sifting through his hair and pulling the shirt away from his skin. Slowly, he lifted his arms, held them up, his hands rising as if he were trying to catch the moonlight. I shifted behind the glass again, pressed close to take in his profile, saw his lips moving.

Who was he talking to out there? Himself? The shadows? God?

I watched, mesmerized and guilty all at once, conscious that I was intruding on a private moment, something that was, once again, none of my business.

Abruptly, he lowered his hands, turned around, and walked back to his room. I scrambled away from the window, tiptoed across the floor, and slid under my blanket as silently as possible.

In the morning, I awoke wondering whether I'd dreamed that vision of him. I'd barely gotten out of bed, pulled the hanging quilt across my little dressing corner, and wiggled my way into stratums of costuming, before there was a knock at the glass. When I went to the window, the familiar face of Blake Fulton was smiling and looking ridiculously chipper for so early in the morning. This version of him didn't mesh with the one who wandered the floors at night. It made me wonder, once again, what he was hiding and why.

Be careful, the little voice in my head warned. *This guy isn't who he seems.*

Then again, maybe Kim was right. She'd had a completely different take on the Blake Fulton matter after our dinner together at the big hog roast. *If you had even half a brain, Allie, you'd see that he's into you. Girlfriend, if I didn't have Jake waiting back home, I wouldn't be holding back, that's all I can say.*

I looked at Blake outside my window, smiling and holding up, of all things, two coffee cups this morning. An invitation? For me?

Kim's last words to me ran through my mind, *Stop being so careful. Let your guard down a little. What've you got to lose?*

I raised the window and lifted out the cheesecloth frame.

"Coffee?" he offered. "Figured I'd brew some up while I was bringing the water in." He motioned toward the barrel on the porch, undoubtedly full. My first chore for the day, already taken care of again. Making coffee was my second, and he had done that too.

"Thanks." I yawned behind my hand, waiting for the usual morning grog to wear off. Thank goodness I'd already deployed my forbidden toothbrush and tube of Aquafresh this morning. Frontier breath could be gnarly, and I hadn't even thought about hair yet. He was probably looking at Little Orphan Annie right now. After being up half the night I felt like I'd been run over by a truck. Wasn't he exhausted this morning?

"Don't forget to put the brace in the window," he said, grinning.

"Never." I couldn't help smiling back while I placed the bar.

He handed me one of the cups and I wrapped my hands around it, smelling the aroma before I took a sip. The liquid inside was thick, and black, slightly gritty with coffee grounds. "It's good."

"No it's not."

A little chuckle ruffled the liquid just as the cup touched my lips again. Coffee splashed onto my nose. I wiped it away and let the mug rest on the windowsill. "You're right. It's bad. But it's better than mine." I'd lit a fire in my stove and attempted coffee in my tin pot yesterday, and it was terrible. Aside from that, the stove had made the room unbearably hot all day, even after I'd closed the dampers and tried to smother the cook fire.

He took another sip, shuddered a little, and then sat down on the kindling box outside the window.

This was something different. Apparently, he wasn't in a hurry to be off to anywhere today.

Inside, I pulled up one of my little chairs and sat down, resting my head against the sash. "So . . . who are you, Blake Fulton?" The directness of the question surprised me, but frontier life has a way of whittling away the superfluous.

Hooking a finger through the handle of his cup, he shrugged. "Well, pretty much like I told you the other day, I'm on—"

"Yes, I know you're *on hold,* but I mean who *are* you? Where did you come from before this? Where did you grow up—that kind of thing? We all had lives before Wildwood, right?"

He lifted his cup again, his lips resting on the rim as he blew on the hot liquid. A smile danced in his hazel eyes. "We're not supposed to talk about those things, remember? It breaks continuity." He sipped, swallowed, and wiped a drip with his thumb. "Didn't you pay attention in the training classes?"

"You weren't even *in* the training classes." At least not when I was there.

"Maybe I've heard it all before."

"So, you work for Razor Point Productions, then?" Now we were getting somewhere. It all made sense—his coming in late, his association with Rav Singh. He was crew of some sort, not cast.

"Continuity," he reminded, then winked.

"There's no camera on right now. I don't have

go-live until after Wren shows up for the morning domestic routine."

A wide white grin answered, and he rubbed two fingers alongside an eyebrow, seeming to think. Then, as easily as if he hadn't been playing cagey all this time, he spun a picture. The all-American kind. Grew up in a small town in west Texas. Played football and baseball and all the other sports. His parents were ranchers. They raised and showed quarter horses and Black Angus cattle. The whole family still lived in his little hometown—mother, father, two brothers, one sister, grandparents, and so forth. From what I could discern, he was related to half of the community.

"What about you?" was the natural end to his tale. "What's a nice girl like you doing in a place like this?"

The question made me laugh, but it also made me wary. He was so polished at this. Did he do it often—move from production to production and romance the cast members here and there? "Trying to survive so far, I think," I admitted. "I'm a film major at UT, so that's how I got involved." Which was enough background to offer up.

In contrast to his storybook small-town history, I was a nerd who'd navigated the fringes of a giant high school with my head in a book, mostly trying to pass unseen. The Drama Department and the consumer sciences classroom were my refuges. I've never attended a single football game, but if there was a play, a choir performance, or anything involving a stage, costumes, and an audience, I was there painting, sewing, or rewriting dialog for actors.

It wasn't too impressive next to being the local football star, so I purposely turned the conversation back to him. We talked about his family a bit more, and then favorite movies. We were both *Star Wars* fans—go figure. I was living next door to a football star with a geeky side. He could actually quote lines from some of my favorite science fiction movies. He'd even seen one of my father's films. He was impressed when I shared that the film was part of my father's legacy.

"So, you're following in the family business," he assessed.

"Trying . . . sort of, I guess." It felt good to hear somebody mention it without sounding like it was an unfortunate affliction. "Although having one of us go into film wasn't in my mom and stepdad's game plan, so it's taken me longer than most. You can't run off and do internships when you're working to pay for your next semester . . . except this internship, that is. This is a great opportunity, if I can hack if for two and a half months."

"One thing you learn from football is that you need to play your own game." A crashing noise from the street caught his ear, and he leaned forward, sending a look of concern around the corner. "You'll get beaten up, playing someone else's."

"I guess that's a good point." I hadn't ever thought of it that way, but he was right. I couldn't let my family or anyone else choose my game for me. It wasn't my job to become something that pleased them; it was my job to become who I was meant to be.

Did Blake Fulton play his own game, I wondered? Or was he forced into someone else's? Was that what kept him up wandering at night?

The conversation died out, and we sat silent, me leaning on the window frame, and Blake kicking back on the woodbox, his long legs crossed at the knee, where his trousers were tucked into the stovepipe boots.

I took another sip of the coffee, grimaced, and swallowed it.

"You don't have to drink that if you don't want to."

Shaking my head, I tasted it again. It started to grow on you after your mouth got numb. "You forget that in less than an hour, the schoolhouse fills up, and before that, Wren comes for morning go-live. Wren Godley and caffeine withdrawals all at the same time are *not* a good thing."

"I get your point." His eyes took on a golden hue as the early rays of sunlight pressed over the bluffs. "She's a handful, isn't she. Poor kid."

"Poor *kid?*" The liquid in my cup splashed over the windowsill. "That's no kid—that's Atilla the Hun in a pint-size body. Without her, the school-teaching thing would be easy. Well, not easy, but it would be doable. Literally every time I turn my back, she's starting a fight with somebody over something. And if she's not, she's catching me in some corner where the remote cameras can't find us, and she's telling me *everything* I'm doing wrong."

"She's just looking for a friend." He pointed to a bluebird hopping across the dusty grass. The bird's feathers cast a flash of brilliant color as it flitted off. "Give her a little time. You'll win her over with your charm and undeniable enthusiasm for the teaching job." It took me a moment to decide that he was joking. By then, the part about *charm* had already flowed over me like warm water.

"You overrate the power of the force, Obi-Wan Kenobi."

A quizzical frown turned my way. "So why do you do that?"

"What?" I was instantly embarrassed. The *Star Wars* reference was probably dorky.

"Brush it off or change the subject when someone tries to pay you a compliment?" The intensity of his gaze made me draw back.

A half-dozen child psychologists would love to

know the answer to that question. My mother had been merciless about therapy after my father's death, even through my teenage years. As if there's something abnormal about a girl who can't let go of the father she loved and just . . . move on to a new father who never really wanted her around.

Blake didn't need to know all that, of course. It was ancient history.

Fortunately, I was spared from coming up with an answer. The front door of the schoolhouse slammed, and the noise rattled the building. A moment later, the apartment door burst open, and Wren waltzed in like she owned the place. She was scheduled to arrive a half hour before the start of school each morning so the cameras could do a short go-live of the beginning of the daily domestic routine that Bonnie Rose and Maggie might have shared.

I glanced at the small antique clock on the shelf above my cookstove. Morning go-live was in less than fifteen minutes. I'd been so caught up in the coffee conversation with Blake that time had slipped by.

Wren was late, actually, and she was a mess. Rather than having been neatly plaited into the usual braids, her hair was a wild frizz—like Einstein after a trip through a wind tunnel. I knew that look. I'd arrived at elementary school with it many times.

Outside the window, Blake stood up, calmly checking his pocket watch as Wren raced through the room in a tizzy and slammed a fabric-wrapped bundle onto the table. "Here's the stupid breakfast. I hope it's better than the last time. I think that lady who lives in the Hendrick house gave us her old leftover biscuits yesterday. I don't know why I have to pick up the breakfast stuff from somebody in the village instead of just bringing food from Crew Camp, anyway. It's way better than this crap."

Blake leaned in the window, pulling the string on the bundle and ferreting out a piece of bacon. "Good morning to you too, Wren." He smiled at Wren and winked at me.

Wren ignored him completely. "You gotta fix my hair." She handed me a hairbrush along with two blue ribbons. "I want these. And *not* two stupid braids either. One braid, over the shoulder, horsetail style. One ribbon at the top. One at the bottom. It's more mature. That's what they were wearing at the Emmys this year."

"I'm not much of a hair fixer, can you tell?" I offered up my own as an example.

Wren rolled a scathing look my way, surveying the extravaganza on my head, which I would somehow have to stuff into the snood in thirty seconds or less. Snoods, I had discovered, were amazing things. When I was finished in Wildwood, I intended to make it my life's work to bring snoods back into style. You could cram a tangled, dirty, frizzy thick mess into a snood, and it looked pretty good.

"Yeah, I can see that." Bracing her hands on her hips, she filled the room with pure adolescent attitude. The lovely warmth of morning coffee time was gone. *Poof.*

Blake checked his pocket watch again, then stepped away from the window, since he wasn't supposed to be there for go-live.

"Use the force, Luke Skywalker," he offered as parting advice.

A puff of private laughter slipped past my lips, and Wren shot an annoyed look toward the window, suspecting an inside joke. "What*ever*. Maybe *you* better go down to the claims office instead of hanging around here drinking coffee and *stealing* our bacon. Two guys already got in a fight down there this morning. I heard that people've been lined up since, like, three a.m. waiting for the thing to open, so they can get their papers and go digging for gold. I thought *you* were supposed to be Mr. Law and Order around here. Isn't that your *real* job?"

Blake blinked, surprised, his brows darting upward momentarily. Then he walked away without another word.

"So, what do you mean, his *real* job? How do you know why he's here?" I turned to Wren expectantly. Maybe I was finally going to solve the mystery of Blake Fluton, albeit through an unlikely source.

She made a show of checking her fingernails for dirt. "I look. I listen. I get around. You should try it sometime. You might learn something." Grabbing the ribbons again, she shoved them my way. "You better fix my hair before we're live. I can't go on camera like this, now *can* I?"

"If you don't stop talking to me like that, you can."

"What*ever*."

"You think I'm kidding, but I'm not." I had the sisterly urge to take the blue hair ribbons and use them to somehow tie her mouth shut. It really seemed wrong that a face so cute could spew such a constant stream of ugliness. "You know what, Wren? If you wouldn't insult people and boss them around and snap at them all the time, they'd like you a lot better."

"I don't *care*." A narrow-eyed look came my way as she turned her back to me. "Now fix my hair. Hurry up."

"Everyone *cares* if people like them."

She swiveled fully then, blinking at me, her lashes finally holding at half-mast. "*You* care too *much* if people like you."

"Maybe you can just figure out the hair for yourself, then. Since you're so *smart* about every-thing." She was sucking me in, pushing every button, and I knew it. This kid understood the psychology of insults better than anyone I'd ever met.

Then, for a fraction of a second, there was a flash of emotion in that freckled face—vulnerable, wounded, needy. "Well, maybe if my stupid *mother* wasn't totally out of it this morning, my hair would be done already. There *isn't* anybody else *but* you, okay?" The faintest quiver teased her mouth, the muscles straining in her neck.

Suddenly, I was an eleven-year-old girl, struggling to do something with my ridiculous hair that wouldn't get me laughed at in school, my mother too busy with new babies to worry about it.

A wave of sympathy came in, powerful and unexpected. "How about a snood? I have an extra one." Wren shrugged, looking down at her hands, and I added, "Snoods are very mature."

When the cameras in the room went live, Wren and I were fixing hair—a lovely, pastoral scene between sisters in the soft morning light, sweet as a dusting of powdered sugar.

As I smoothed her tangled locks and worked to twist and cram them into the snood, she chattered brightly about 1861 life, how interesting the school lessons were, the challenges of living without running water, and how much work it was carrying buckets, which to my knowledge she had never done.

Irregardless, she hammed it up for the cameras,

waxing nostalgic about the absolute darkness of the night sky here and the fact that, in the wilderness, neighbors were forced to depend on one another. Back home, she didn't even *know* her neighbors.

"Isn't it fun spending so much *time* with your *neighbor?* Like sharing *coffee* in the morning and things. Isn't that *awesome?*" She turned toward the camera, flashing her baby blues in total innocence.

"Mmm-hmn." I yanked the hair harder than I needed to, attaching the snood into place.

"Ouch!" She giggled good-naturedly.

"Done." I grabbed my own snood and rolled and stuffed my hair into it. "You look adorable."

"Thank you." Voicing the little nicety clearly hurt. *Thank you* was one of Wren's least favorite expressions.

We ate breakfast while she chattered on about life in Wildwood, offering lines that were far beyond the scope of an eleven-year-old. Her mom had clearly been rehearsing with her.

As we finished our go-live and gathered our things for school, I motioned to our reflection in the wardrobe door mirror. "Behold, the magic of the snood. The solution for bad hair days, antique-style."

"Great, now we look like *twinsies*." Things were back to normal now that the cameras were off. "This stupid thing itches."

"I could take it out." *Really, really fast. I could.*

"Well . . . it's already done now." On the way out the door, my pretend sister stopped one more time at the mirror to admire her snooded self.

Chapter 20

Allie Kirkland
June, Present Day

The school day was typical enough. Pretty good at times, something of a zoo at others. School hours were shorter than what would probably have been normal in the actual town of Wildwood. As usual, we ended with lunch pails around a wooden table outside. Two cameramen with handhelds stood nearby, and a grip held a boom mike overhead as the kids reviewed their lessons.

When they drifted away to play stickball, Wren was, as always, not invited to participate on either team. Typically, she wandered off behind the cedar trees to hide from the cameras, pretending to be headed to the outhouse.

Today, however, she followed me back into the school and sulked in a corner as I finished cleaning up and put things in place for another day. This afternoon, I needed to do laundry, a monumental chore, but on a teacher's salary, I couldn't afford to have it done at the bathhouse, and after only three days live, every bit of my daily wear felt sweaty, crusty, and disgusting.

"Why don't you get in on the stickball game? I'll go out there with you, if you want," I suggested.

"It'll mess up my costume. You don't have to try to get *rid* of me, you know. I'm not hurting anything in here." She rolled a petulant look my way.

"Never mind, then. I just thought you might have more fun outside."

"Stickball is stupid." A little sneer, and her head fell back against the wall. "Where's the dumb zookeeper? I wanna get outta here. I need a soda. Now."

"She should be here any minute." The production assistant was late coming to get the kids. Just yesterday we'd been reminded of the need for them to travel with a handler until they were back in their parents' care. A team of massive draft horses had spooked and careened through the set, nearly mowing down a little girl who didn't see them coming. It was a quick and almost tragic lesson in the dangers of nineteenth-century life.

Wren wandered through the schoolhouse door and onto the porch, scuffing her shoes against the rough wood.

"Hello! Holy cow!" Suddenly, she was jumping off the porch and running toward town. A moment later a completely foreign sound split the air, the noise out of sync with 1861.

A siren? I'd barely registered the thought when the two cameramen with handhelds and my entire group of kids bolted up the street, dodging wagons, pedestrians, confused cast members on horseback, and various dogs and cats that wandered the set.

I dashed after the kids, yelling, "Stop! Hey! You guys, stop! Now!" What were the cameramen thinking, letting the kids take off? "Hey! I said, stop!"

But no one was listening. We'd reached the edge of the chaos near Unger's Store before I caught up and started gathering my students into a group off to the side. The noise of the sirens had brought everyone in the village running. Nearby, horses balked and tugged their reins, loose chickens ran for the cover of crawl spaces under buildings, and two dogs got in a fight. A team of paramedics was coming down the hill from crew camp with a stretcher.

Nick's mom spotted us and hurried over to help with the kids.

"Mallory, what's going on?" I stood on my toes, trying to get a glimpse over the crowd, but all I could see were dresses, hats, heads, and people whispering. In the distance, the sound of another siren slowly grew louder.

Between two shoulders, I caught a flash of

someone dragging a man to his feet by a set of handcuffs. Was that Blake standing over the man? The crowd shifted, and I couldn't see anything.

Wren climbed onto a pile of crates to get a better view. "Whoa! The set medic has a guy on a body board thingy in front of Unger's Store, and he's, like, all *bloody!*"

Mallory leaned close to me. "I didn't hear all the details, but there was some kind of fight outside the land office this morning—something about claims. Security broke it up. They sent the guys away to cool off, but then the two of them got into it again this afternoon. By the time it was over, one man came after the other with a bowie knife, right in the middle of the set. This whole thing is way too authentic for me, especially with kids around." She rested her hands on Nick's shoulders with a look of concern. "If it's like this after only a couple of days . . ."

"They're messing with peoples' minds. That's what they're doing." Kim had threaded her way through the chaos and found us.

"It's seriously creepy, watching motives change." Mallory took in the crowd, perhaps wondering how she'd write about this as she documented the Wildwood project. "A week ago everyone was just excited to be here and to learn pioneer skills. It was all about neighbor-help-neighbor, about building a community. Now all anyone I interview can talk about is how fast they can get their claim staked and start looking for gold, and who's going to find it. The people who have town jobs —the ones who were *thrilled* during the training period because they get the more comfortable places to live—are mad now. They want a chance at the million dollars in ore. It's nuts, and to tell you the truth, even though all of this will make an interesting story, I'm not sure I'm ready to report a modern-day gold rush. For now I think I'll just take Nick back up to crew camp and hang out. He really doesn't need to see all this."

"I don't blame you." I looked at the rest of the kids, now trying to climb atop the crates with Wren so they, too, could get a look at the bloody man being prepared for medical transport. "I think I'll take the kids back to school and wait until the street clears, then walk them up to crew camp if the production assistants haven't come for them by then."

"I'll help you," Kim offered.

We gathered the kids and herded them down the street with Wren offering everyone a blow-by-blow of what she had seen. The others were wide-eyed, listening.

"That's enough, Wren. Everyone doesn't need to hear all about it."

She crossed her arms and stomped ahead of us, sulking when the other kids finally took off toward the school building in a loosely orchestrated footrace.

I moved closer to Kim, hugging my arms, a chill crawling over my skin despite the heat of the day. Suddenly, the atmosphere in Wildwood felt oppressive and strange. Dangerous. "What happened up there? Did you see any of it?"

Kim pushed her bonnet back, scratching her head. "I didn't see it, but I heard two guys got in a fight over gold claims. One of them actually pulled a knife, which was pretty stupid of him, because the other guy had a rock pick. Anyway, the one guy almost beat the other guy into oblivion. Your neighbor pulled him off and did a takedown on him in the street."

"Blake?"

"Yes, Blake. He probably saved the guy's life. Well, that's what I heard anyway. When I got down there it'd been over for a while. On-site medical was tending to the one guy, Blake had the other guy cuffed on the porch, and the county sheriff was on the way, along with the ambulance."

"That's awful." I thought about what Wren had said, about preventing fights at the land office being Blake's job.

Kim stopped walking before we reached the school, her blue eyes floating in a pool of tears. "I just wanna go home. I hate it here. I know I was the one who was all excited about it, but I'm really sorry I got you into this. I just . . . I don't think I have it in me. I'm tired, I'm lonely, I'm sore, I'm scared out of my mind I'll step on a snake or get eaten by a coyote every time I have to walk to the outhouse after dark. There are *mice* in my room at night. I smell awful, and I'm already sick of other people's laundry and disgusting tub water. My hands are so cracked up, they're bleeding. I feel like my fingers are gonna fall off. I thought this would be some great big adventure, but it's so . . . physically and mentally hard. I want to quit."

Taking her hands in mine, I looked at the damage. "I have some salve you can use on that. It's in my medical kit for the school." I tried to tamp down her panic as my own was rising. Even though she and I hardly ever saw each other in the course of a normal day here, just knowing she was nearby made village life doable. "You can't leave."

Her head dropped forward and tears trailed her cheeks. "I can't do it, Allie. I'm not as strong as you."

"Yes you are. You're stronger than I ever thought about being."

"The lives these women led in bathhouses and saloons were awful, Allie. They weren't anything like you see on *Gunsmoke*. It's sad to think that mostly these were just young girls. Teenagers. I don't know how they did it, but I guess there's not enough pioneer in me. Besides that, I miss Jake so much I'm going crazy. I just want to talk to him."

She was cracking. The part of me that loved my best friend desperately wanted to make it all better, and the part of me that didn't want to be left alone here was just plain desperate. "If you could talk to him, would it help?" The question was out before I really had time to think about the implications.

Kim wiped her eyes on her sleeve. "I don't want to be a quitter . . . I just . . . Wait, what did you say?"

"If you could talk to him, would it make a difference?"

"Why?"

I took a breath, then plunged into the story about the iPhone and Stewart. For half a second, Kim looked like she was seriously considering decking me with a left hook. We'd be the next two in handcuffs, facedown on the street.

"You have *got* to be kidding. You've been watching me go *crazy* all this time, and you had an *iPhone* hidden away? A *phone,* like I *asked* you to bring for me, and you *wouldn't?* So *Stewart* could give you some information about *Bonnie Rose.* Seriously? Some woman who died way back when means more to you than I do?"

"It was a last-minute decision. Stewart was so excited about something he'd found. I didn't want to disappoint him and . . . well . . . I want to know who Bonnie Rose really was, whether all the terrible things they say about her are true.

Maybe I can . . . clear her name or something. She deserves that, you know?"

"I do not *believe* you!" Kim got louder. Nearby, Wren trained a laser eye our way from her perch atop the picnic table.

"Just calm down, okay? So, here's the thing. So far, I haven't even been able to get off somewhere and check the phone again, anyway. Since go-live, there's not exactly any leisure time in the day. So, if you *promise,* and I mean, *really* promise, not to get in trouble with it, I'll give you the phone, and you can sneak away and call Jake. There's decent reception down past the brush arbor toward the lake. Everybody's so preoccupied right now, they won't even notice. It'll be a while before things settle back to normal, and if anybody asks where you were, you can just say you got upset and went for a walk or something." Why did I have a terrible feeling I'd end up really regretting this?

Kim's face brightened like the noonday sun emerging from behind a cloud. "I'll find a place where no one can see and I'll be quick, don't worry."

Checking the kids one more time, I led Kim through the schoolhouse and into my room. Something stopped me in the doorway. The chairs Wren and I had left askew this morning had been neatly tucked into their proper places, and atop the table a bouquet of freshly picked blue-bells sat in a tin cup. How had those gotten there, and when? And who'd put the chairs back in order?

Maybe a production assistant had come by and rearranged things while I was out? When? During all the chaos down the street? Why?

In the window, the cheesecloth screen was slightly askew, as if someone had been unable to properly put it back in place from outside.

"What's wrong?" Kim tried to peek over my shoulder into the room.

"Nothing." Surely those flowers weren't from . . . Blake Fulton? The idea lit a giddy little sparkler in my chest, which I extinguished immediately. Blake and I barely knew each other, and besides, he'd been busy breaking up fights, apparently.

I touched a finger to my lips as we entered the room, just in case anyone was still in the production center, monitoring cameras. Kim and I closed ranks in front of the corner cabinet, and I pretended to be loaning her the salve as I pulled the phone from its secret hiding place and held it in the folds of my skirt.

"Here it is. Be careful with it, okay? It's easy to get carried away and use it too much."

"Sure!" Kim was over the moon already. "I'll be careful, I promise." The iPhone quickly disappeared into the pocket along the side seam of her skirt, and she grabbed me in an impulsive hug. We rocked back and forth, sharing the embrace of pioneer women trying, as hundreds of generations had before us, to survive in the wilderness by bonding over important survival supplies . . . like iPhones.

"I can't wait to talk to him," she whispered against my ear. "I'll take good care of the phone, I promise. I promise. I promise. I promise. And I won't tell a soul."

"Shhh!" I moved away from her and checked the cameras to make sure they weren't running. "Okay, listen, I need to get back. I can't hear the kids outside all of a sudden." The two oldest schoolboys, Will and Nate, practically graduation age at twelve and thirteen, didn't necessarily cotton to following the rules. "Just don't get caught with it, okay? I know you miss Jake, but I can't get kicked off this project, and you don't really want to either." I leaned down and made eye contact, something I'd learned in my short stint as a pretend teacher. "You're hearing me, right?"

"I get it, Allie. I do. I would never, ever do anything to mess up your chances for film school. I know how much it means to you. You know I love you, right?"

"Yes, I know." *But I also know you're leaving me for a man.* "You'd better take off before things get back to normal and they expect everyone to be in their places again. While you're on the phone, check my email and see if there's any Bonnie

Rose information from Stewart, okay? If there's something good on there, copy it and paste it into my notes app so I can get to it without cell service. And tell Stewart thanks and I can't be in touch anymore, now that we've started go-live—it's just too hard to get away. I'll catch up with you later this evening to get my iPhone back. I'm going to turn it in when I get a chance to give it to some-one who won't rat me out."

I opened the door, and Wren was lurking on the other side. Clasping her hands behind her back, she played innocent, but her reason for being there was clear enough. My mind flew back over the last few sentences. Had the word *iPhone* been used?

"Well, hi, Wren!" Kim sashayed out the door, gave Wren a hug, then proceeded onward, her dress swaying as she went.

I hoped I hadn't just made the biggest mistake of my life.

"The zookeeper just came to pick up the kids." Wren frowned over her shoulder with a lemon-lipped sneer. "I told her to tell my mom I'm staying here with you. It's hot. I want to go down to the creek and swim, and there's no one else to take me. So you can."

I was dumbfounded. "Wait. Hold the phone a minute." *Oh man, did I just use the word* phone? "Wren, I don't have any plans for swimming today. I have laundry to do." It wasn't even that I minded going to the creek, but the idea of being saddled with babysitting Wren Godley was horrifying. This morning she had me doing her hair. Now, swimming supervision? Pretty soon she'd be moving in here full time.

What Wren really needed was to learn to get along with kids her own age so she'd have friends to play with. What she didn't need was another adult catering to her every whim.

Hands on her hips, she jutted her chin out and upward, a challenge. "If you *don't* take me, I'll tell *everything* I know about that cell phone. You think I didn't found out about that? *And* the tennis shoes, *and* the clothes you have hidden in your bed? How *stupid* do you think I am? I know *every-thing*."

My eyes flew open like kernels of popcorn in hot grease, and the next thing I knew I was bent over in a face-to-face standoff with an eleven-year-old force of nature. "Listen, *little sister*. I am not, I repeat *not* going to be bossed around by someone who is *still* in elementary school, thank you very much. I've had three older stepsisters strong-arming me and three little siblings yapping at my heels most of my life, and if you don't think I know how to fight back, well then, half-pint, you are sadly mistaken. You either lighten up, or you're going to find out just what kind of a big sister I can be."

Wren's cupid's bow mouth squeezed tighter, and

her blue eyes narrowed to slits. "See if I *care*. I didn't *want* to go to the water with *you* anyway. I just needed *somebody*." The muscles clenched beneath her freckled cheeks. She swallowed hard, a sheen of water rimming her eyes.

I felt like the world's biggest jerk. *This is not me. This isn't who I am.*

Right now Grandma Rita was probably giving me a smack from somewhere in the unseen realm of angels. *There'll come a day, Allie,* she was saying, *when we'll give an accounting of what we did with this one wondrous life. Be careful what you put in your book, darlin'. Don't let anybody or anything write in your book but you.*

"Okay, Wren, listen. Here's the deal. You and I are either friends, or we aren't. If we *aren't* friends, we don't do things like go to the water together, or hang out and fix hair in the mornings, or have little girly-girl chats about your favorite rock star or whatever you like to do back home. If we *are* friends, then you don't boss me around, threaten me, or talk to me like I'm the waitress at the Taco Hut and you've just been served a cold plate of nachos. Do you get me?"

Wren's stubby little fingers twitched in a moment of decision—draw down on me and take another shot, or cooperate and get what she really wanted? "Yeah."

"Yeah, we're not friends? Or yeah, we have an agreement?"

"Yeah, okay. I get it. Can we go to the water now?"

"As long as we're square."

"We're square."

"All right, then." Victory, I hoped . . . or at least a little battle won in the war of pretend sisterhood. The moment felt slightly Shakespearean. *The Taming of the Shrew* came to mind.

Wren and I discarded a few layers of unnecessary garments, I slipped my capris on underneath what was left of my skirts, and we departed the schoolhouse with what felt like a fresh understanding between us. The walk to Wildwood Creek was nice, actually. I knew the way, of course. I led Wren to the little spot near the water where I had seen the fawn before. She took off her shoes and stockings and I helped her slide out of everything but her chemise and pantaloons so she could wade. Stripping down to my chemise, I tucked the bottom in at the waist before rolling my capris as high as I could to produce what amounted to an unattractive bathing ensemble, encompassing a shameless mixing of centuries.

We chased tiny minnows and searched for the limestone fossils of sea snails, spiny urchins, and little round sea biscuits, distinguishable only by their shape, until you rubbed a dampened finger across the top and the imprint of a star magically appeared on the domed surface.

"My grandmother used to tell me that these are a lot like people." I held the stone in my palm, letting Wren pluck it up between two fingers to study the star. "You pass right by them, day after day, and a lot of them look plain enough from the outside. But the thing is, you never know what might be hiding under the surface until you stop and take the time to look. Grandma Rita told me the water is like love. Sprinkle a little of it on, and sometimes you're surprised what comes out."

Wren's face softened as she studied the stone, watching the moisture slowly evaporate, the exterior turning bland and dusty again. Leaning over, she dipped a finger in the water and wet the stone again. "My grandma says people get what they can, while they can . . . just like my mama. Last time we went to stay with *my* grandma, like, when we were in between stuff and the rent check bounced, she opened the door, and said, 'Oh no. If you don't wanna work, Tracie Godley, that's your problem. I'm not havin' it in my house anymore. You take your bastard brat and get off my porch.' And then she slammed the door." Wren's knobby shoulders shrugged, the bones poking upward along the chemise's lace edges. "But it doesn't matter. Because I got *this* job, and this job's gonna be my big break, and then we're gonna rub it in her big, stupid face like crazy." She swept the sea biscuit through the water again and lifted it, quicksilver streams pouring from her fingers in the afternoon light.

"Wren . . ." I waited for her to look at me again and saw someone I recognized. My lost, lonely, wounded self at nine, at ten, at eleven. Thank God for Grandma Rita. She taught me that I was worth something, that I mattered. Sometimes, just one person is enough to make you believe it.

"Whatever mess your family is in, it's not *your* fault. You can't let it become who you are. It's not your job to fix your mom or your grandma or to take care of them. Your job is to find Wren, and to make sure that when you find her, you find all the best things inside her, all the beautiful and unique things—just like the star on the top of the rock. God made you smart, talented, and pretty. Put that stuff on the surface. There's no reason to go around taking a swipe at people before they can take a swipe at you. Just give them a chance, and see how it goes."

A driftwood raft decorated with iridescent green, blue, and copper dragonflies floated by, and our conversation ended abruptly as we splashed down the creek to chase it.

When the afternoon was over, Wren and I walked back to the village, strangely at peace with each other. Bonded, in a way. I took her up the hill as far as the big house, where Genie and Netta were working in the garden they'd planted, along with Lynne Everly and her granddaughter, Alexis, who had stepped into the lives of Asmae and Essie Jane, slaves in the Delevan household. Andy, the blacksmith, was with them, taking a break from his shop to operate an antique hand cultivator.

They waved at me and invited Wren to help them in the garden. I told her good-bye, then stood and watched for a few moments as Netta gave Wren instructions for pruning the Seven Sisters roses that had been found growing native around the Wildwood site. It was nice to see Wren enjoying something for once. Maybe there was hope for the whole crazy bunch of us after all.

I felt good about the day, as I took the spring creek path to Bathhouse Row to retrieve the phone from Kim. Relief settled over me when I found her back at work among the massive open-air laundry tubs. Her dress was damp, and, understandably, she didn't have the phone on her. "It's hidden in a safe place, I promise." She glanced over her shoulder as she stood, bucket in hand. From the porch, she was being eyeballed by Annie, the forty-something ex–army ranger who ran the place with a slightly excessive bent toward authenticity.

"Just let me keep it a couple days, okay? It was so good to talk to Jake today—well, I only had enough tower strength to text, but it was so awesome." She clasped my forearm, trying to control a sudden rush of the giddies. "Let me talk to him a few more days. Then I'll get the phone recharged for you and give it back. But only if I can borrow it again in not too long."

I felt the parameters of our arrangement sliding dangerously toward the edge of a cliff. Kim's resistance to temptation when she really wanted something was practically nil.

"Kim, how, exactly, are you going to recharge the phone?" I was afraid even to ask.

"There's a grip up the hill who'll do it for me. . . . And don't look at me like that. He's a friend. He won't tell anybody."

Her shoulders jerked upward, and she gritted her teeth as her boss yelled from the porch, "This isn't picnic time! We've got customers to take care of. And they pay in gold." Annie had already raised the price of baths and laundry service for the miners, in anticipation of Wildwood's new gold-inflated economy.

"I've gotta go," Kim grumbled. "I'll take care of things, I promise. Oh, and you didn't have much information from Stewart. There was one attachment on an email—something about Bonnie Rose—but I couldn't get it to download to the phone, so I couldn't read it. Other than that, he'd sent a couple texts just sort of . . . shootin' the breeze and asking what it was like here. He wanted to know if you needed any supplies or anything, and he sent you some information that looked like it was out of a survival manual or something—how to preserve meat, and what kind of tubers you can dig up and eat, and that kind of stuff. He said he mailed a package to the village post office for you—something about a copy of *Jane Eyre* that had the information you wanted. Anyway, I answered him and just pretended I was you. I told him a little bit about life since go-live, that kind of thing. I figured, since I'm going to be keeping the phone for a few days, I can just keep checking your messages for you."

"Kim . . ." Right now, Stewart's emails were the least of my worries. What I did know was that I'd let a monster out of the box when I'd told Kim about the phone. "But listen, you need to give me the phone so I can turn it in. It's just going to get us in trouble."

"Well, it's not like I can go get it right now. Don't worry, okay? I'll be careful. I gotta scoot before Annie comes after me with a pitchfork or something. If I don't kill that woman before the summer's over, it'll be a miracle."

There wasn't much choice but to let her go back to work. Still, a bad, bad feeling lingered as we parted ways. I walked on toward the schoolhouse, counting the paths along the spring as I went, knowing where each one would lead. Above, the village played its evening melodies— kettles clanking, roughhewn wooden doors banging, wheels and axles singing bass and soprano, hammers adding rhythm, intermingling with a horse's high-pitched whinny, a dove's call,

355

a whippoorwill's song, the first raucous yip of a coyote.

The scents of suppertime meals tickled my nose and moistened the back of my mouth. I hadn't even thought about food, although there was a biscuit, butter, and muscadine jelly left from breakfast, along with few bites of bacon. I could get by without attempting to light a cooking fire and preparing something. It seemed silly, cooking for one in the evenings. Cooking and cleaning dishes here was so much work.

Smoke hovered in the air as I climbed the path to the school. When I rounded the cedar bushes, there was Blake Fulton, sitting on a chunk of log beside the fire, his boots propped near the ring of stones. I wasn't used to seeing him, other than first thing in the mornings. My stomach did a strange little flip-flop that had nothing to do with the smell of whatever was in the cast-iron frying pan he'd set over the coals. I remembered our conversation from this morning, how natural and easy it seemed.

Maybe he remembers too. I found myself entertaining a little fantasy that he'd come back here tonight because of our coffee time earlier. Silly of me, probably. Risky. The last thing I needed was to get involved with a guy who probably traveled around from production to production and had a girl in every location.

But despite the obvious reasons I should've

passed by and continued on to my room, I felt my dinner-for-one vision for the evening suddenly morphing.

A smile parted his lips when he saw me, and the strangest rush of sensations skittered through my body—a tingle of excitement, a strike of lightning, but also the soft, comfortable feeling of snuggling into an old quilt. Somehow the sight of him there at the end of the day felt so much more natural than it should have. Like I'd been waiting for it, hoping for it without realizing I was.

"Hungry?" he asked.

"Actually, yes." It occurred to me then that I was sans most of my proper 1861 underattire and still wearing my slightly damp capris pants beneath my skirt. I circumvented the fire, not coming too close, but trying to lean over and see into the pan. "What's for dinner?"

"Fish and beans. Camp food. Sorry, but I was afraid to try corn bread. I've never been much good with a Dutch oven."

"Me either. But I do have a biscuit leftover from breakfast." Actually, I had the makings of biscuits in my corner cabinet. Maybe when I got a chance I'd go to the big house and see if I could get a cooking lesson from the ladies up there. I'd never wanted to make biscuits to impress someone before, but suddenly I did. "And some muscadine jelly. I'll go halves with you."

"Deal," he agreed, and he seemed genuinely pleased with the plan to trade fish for leftover biscuit and jelly. I was definitely getting the better end of that bargain. The fish looked delicious. This guy had clearly cooked over an open fire before.

I hurried on inside, shed my damp capris, and did my best to put my clothes back together semi-properly before coming out again. By the time I did, Blake had finished cooking and was keeping the food warm alongside the fire pit. He'd brought out a Civil War–style folding chair and set it by the kindling box. Combined with the stump he was sitting on, it formed what looked like . . . an impromptu table for two.

"Where'd you have the biscuit and jelly stored? In the next county?" he joked, then grabbed the hook to take the bean pot off the fire as I set my contribution on the kindling box.

Something silly and flirty came over me, and the next thing I knew, I was doing a lousy Southern belle impression. "Why, sir, a lady nevah arrives for dinner without properly preparin' herself."

He blinked, then chuckled as I sidestepped to the folding chair, taking care to keep my skirts out of the fire. The weight of the fabric slid the chair backward as I attempted to lower myself into it. I repositioned, and the chair repositioned, and then I repositioned, and then the chair repositioned. For a minute, it was like a game of leapfrog in reverse.

"Here, Scarlett." Blake reached for the seat with one hand, then extended the other to me.

A giggle bubbled up my throat as his fingers circled mine. "Somehow . . . this looks so much . . . easier in the movies."

Blake's soft, low laughter brushed my ear, teasing escaped tendrils of hair there. "Everything does."

I turned to him and saw the firelight reflected in his eyes, heard the soft crackling of the flames, the faraway song of a mockingbird, the rhythmic chirring of night insects. A breeze skimmed my cheek and the warmth of his skin on mine suddenly felt hot, slightly electric.

My heart raced, then froze. The night swirled over me, my mind tumbling about completely unprepared.

A house cat growled somewhere nearby in the cedars brush, and we jerked apart, both of us turning toward the sound. Just before our gazes parted, I thought I saw in him a mirror of my own thoughts.

What in the world just happened . . . ?

Chapter 21

Bonnie Rose
July 1861

Four more are gone this morn', two being a young couple who were wed only months ago. Now I'm recalling that they passed by the schoolhouse not a week before this. He smiled at her the way a girl dreams of, as though the sun wouldn't rise to a world without her in it. There was the swell of a coming child around her middle. They spied me there, and he shifted her to the other side of the street, away from where I was. They didn't look my way, either one.

I wondered if they feared I'd put some manner of hex on the babe. Rumors fly 'round Wildwood like damselflies on a summer's eve, seeking places to light and molt into something new. Another girl from Red Leaf Hollow has gone missing day before yesterday. Last thing anyone remembers was her coming from the schoolhouse after stopping over to ask if I had any buck flour to spare. At least, that is the story they tell. In truth, I never saw the girl.

It could be that she came to the schoolhouse, though. Maggie May and I have gone out to forage in the woods as often as we can. With the declaring of martial law by Mr. Delevan, goods are scarce of a sudden, and the townsfolk are keepin' their extra for themselves. There's more talk around that this warring between the states will grow worse before it gets better. That it will become much more dire than Mr. Lincoln thought. The calls for a military draft increase steadily, strangers coming from other places in hopes of joining a well-funded regiment here in Wildwood and traveling east to fight. What little goods remained from our last freight are locked in a warehouse now, commandeered by Mr. Delevan's growing legion of men.

The town has the feel of a powder keg with a fuse burnt too close to it. And then there are the Gonefolk, the ones who've vanished from their homes and shanties. I pray they've run away, making their escape from Wildwood while they're still able.

"None so far this morn'." Maggie pokes her nose in from the schoolroom after she checks it. Folks are keepin' their children home, holding them close by, despite the directive that the children be sent to classes.

"Can you blame them, Maggie?" When Mr. Delevan's men discover the children truant, they give them a lashing and chase them to the schoolhouse. The children believe I've told the men to do it. "Can you blame them at all, with the parents tellin' the children that if I've mind to, I'll tempt them from their beds at night and drown them in the river? Who would say such a thing to a child? They're scared witless of me."

I've tried to discern for myself who may be behind this rumorin', but save for the kitchen women in the Delevan household, there's barely a soul who'll speak a word to my face in all of Wildwood. They've declared me to be the paramour of Mr. Delevan, a wicked enchantress of some sort, and just as much a devil as he. My scars have been found out as well, while I was doing our washing at the creek. It's all the more fodder for whisperin' and supposin'. Some believe I may have died once already and come back to wander as a spirit.

The sound of footsteps on the front porch turns Maggie 'round. I hurry across the room, catch her shoulders, and pull her behind me. I understand the fear the parents have, and their reasons for keeping their children away. They're worried that Mr. Delevan will use their own children against them, in more ways than one. I've been told to leave off all other means of educating them, and for now teach only doctrines supporting the rightness of raising a regiment and defending The Cause by any and all means. I'm to teach them from the Bible that it is God's way of things.

It's good that Mr. Delevan's men are well occupied with their patrolling of the hillsides and that no one supervises the lessons. I'll not be schooling children in such filth. I'll not be supporting the idea that a man made by God has not the rights of a man. That his body and soul can be purchased by another.

It's only a matter of time before the Delevans find me out. And then no telling what may happen. I fear that I sealed the fate for Maggie May and myself the day I first signed my name to his paper. There's not a citizen in Wildwood will help me, and I've seen no further sign of Mr. Hardwick since Big Neb gave him my message for the captain. Likely his freight wagons have been intercepted by the regiments scouring the countryside for more men and supplies to add to their numbers.

The school door opens, and a pair of children tumble in. This time, the men have ridden their horses onto the porch and simply thrown the little ones through the door. I rush forward to gather them up. They're sniffling and covered in filth, wide-eyed. The Riley children. Only a week ago they disappeared from school, and their father from his tannery shop up the street.

"Sir! What is the meaning of this? These are children!" I protest of the rider closest me. He can't be over fifteen years old himself, but I do not know him.

The children on the floor look as if they've not eaten in days, their cheeks gaunt, their noses crusted over. Just seven and nine years old, young

Brady and Catherine, cowering on the floor, weepin' for their lives.

The men on the porch are undaunted by me. The one farthest away delivers a hungry look in my direction. "Found these whelps hiding in the dugout with their mama along the river. No sign of their man."

They pull their horses away and the nags stagger and stumble from the porch. I'm left with nothing to do but comfort the children, yet they're scared mindless of Maggie and me. Even after I've washed them up and given them each a small portion of peas, still they shy away. They're afraid to eat the food at first, lest I might've poisoned it, but then their hunger compels them to take the risk.

They've finally begun to settle when more children are brought. Five altogether. I begin dividing the peas in smaller portions. They're the last I have. None of the children will speak of where they've been or what has happened to them. They're watching me now, wary as little animals. Their faces tell a tale I've known before. Their terror is that of Maggie May, just four years old as we're dragged away behind Comanche ponies, the rawhide lashed around our necks.

Klara Baum staggers through the doorway, bloodied and holding the seams of her dress together at the shoulder, and I cover my mouth to keep my stomach at bay. In her fourteen-year-old body, I see myself, and I'm at once wondering what has happened to her and also knowing by the shame in her eye.

I follow as she runs to a corner and hides her face. There's not a thing I can do but stroke her hair and try to comfort her. "You're safe now," I tell her, but such isn't true. Evil's come today, and I've no way of knowing what it's here for, but I know it's the end of the waiting.

"I see they found a few of the whelps." Mr. Delevan himself steps in the open door without warning. "It is impressive what the addition of a little bounty on their heads will do. Before long I'll have the parents bringing them in themselves. The Irish would sell their souls for the price of a keg of whiskey."

Klara cowers deeper into the corner, her fingernails scratching the wood and drawing blood as if she'd claw her way through. I rise up without thinking, and I'm to the door before I've caught up with my mouth. "What is the meaning of this? Those men! These are mere children." Inside I cling to a final, desperate hope that my employer knows nothing of what these men have done while he's been away to yet another of his war meetings.

He studies the children as merely a curiosity, then draws a clean white kerchief from his breast pocket to wipe a smear of blood from the door. I've no way of knowing whom the blood belongs to or how it has come to be there, but I watch it stain the white cloth, and I think of the day I signed the paper that brought me to Wildwood. That *sold* me to him. I'll not be making the same mistake again.

"They should not be truant from school, now, should they?" He carefully folds the bloodied kerchief and tucks it into his breast pocket. "And it is their parents who have abused them, not I. Have I not provided them with books, a school, and a teacher? Yet their parents choose to hide them out in dugouts along the river, under the floorboards of their homes, in the woods, and let them starve. With the storm brewing over the mountains today, they could have all been washed away, should the river come up. Such shamefulness. Such foolishness, don't you think, Bonnie Rose?"

He awaits my answer, and I know I am being tested. I bite hard on my emotions and tuck them down deep, as I've learned to do in my time on the prairie. A show of weakness only brought on the beatings. As did a show of resistance. Like all of those conscripted to a master, I've learned the value of displaying apathy. "I believe all children should be in school." I meet his eyes, and there is nothing in them but blackness. It is as I feared. He is not a man unwittingly caught by the terrible forces of a brewing war. This brutality is his doing, every bit. It is his nature.

"Very good." He stretches a hand across the space between us. His long slim fingers trail over my face, and I do not shrink away from it. Instead I hold steady. "You are so beautiful. It is no wonder that Mr. Hardwick was so taken with you."

Again, I am careful in my reaction. "I know very little of Mr. Hardwick, I can assure you." But my mind is racing. What has he been told? What has he discovered? I think of Mr. Hardwick and the captain. Have I brought disaster to all of us by answering James's letter?

"Interesting," he murmurs. His hand trails down my neck, his fingers coming to a rest on the ribbon, his thumb teasing the edge of it. I feel the fabric being drawn lower.

His eyes demand mine. "Remember where I found you, Bonnie Rose. There are few places in the world for a woman such as yourself, no matter how beautiful. *Please* me, and you will be well taken care of." He looks over his shoulder at Maggie May. I see her from the corner of my eyes, her mouth agape. "And so will she." His words upend my stomach. "Do not become a disappointment. I take care of my disappointments as well."

"Of course, sir," I say.

He seems well enough satisfied with the answer, with the sincerity of it. "Keep the children in the schoolhouse. Hold them into the evening, if need be."

"And if their parents come for them?" The simple question becomes a fearful thing. I'm dreading what the answer may be.

He's turning to leave now. "They shall not . . . anytime soon, I will wager. Hold the children until you hear otherwise from me."

"I'll keep them safe." But it's a promise I fear is beyond my ability. I know without a doubt that I've become a pawn in the devil's plan. This evil will swallow us all before its hunger is satisfied.

And then he is gone. Maggie runs to me, and we cling to each other, mindless of the children watching and the girl weeping in the corner.

"We must get away, sister," Maggie breathes against me.

"Shhh," I whisper to quiet her. She'll only frighten the others.

Outside, thunder rattles and rain begins falling. I think of the children who were found hiding with their mother along the river. If more are there, what'll become of them, should the waters rise?

I can't fathom whether to be hoping that Delevan's men find them, or that they don't. But it's not up to my wishing either way. As the day passes, three more are brought to me, one carrying a babe in arms, her tiny brother. I have no milk for the babe, who needs his mother's breast. He cries pitifully for hours before finally falling asleep.

There's no sound in the town at all, then. None

but the rain beating hard on the roof, the roll of thunder, the split of lightning. I try to reassure the children that their parents will be coming, but the day is almost gone out. The clouds smother the last of the light. There's been enough rain that by now the river may be rising. I must do something, I know.

The children have begun to tell their secrets, whispering stories of their parents being taken off by Delevan's men. Two of the older boys plot to find rifles and go after them. There was to've been an uprising today, a reckoning of sorts. Those who remain, who've resisted signing the loyalty oath and refused to serve in Mr. Delevan's regiment, made a pact to gather in force to demand they be allowed to leave with their livestock, their possessions, and their families. Many had hidden the women and children in the wood, so as to keep them safe if a fight ensued. But Mr. Delevan heard of it ahead, and his men began rounding them up. He's holding them somewhere, and these children in my care are no longer students, but hostages.

I tell the boys they cannot go. They are needed here to help with the younger ones. I must find a way of getting us out . . . but how?

The babe wakes again and wails bitterly, the sound filling up the schoolhouse, settin' all on edge. I take the tiny boy from his sister and walk the floor, trying to quiet him as the storm rages outside. He won't be still, poor thing, so I bring him to my room, hoping to find a bit of sugar to mix with water and a rag to suckle him. It's a trick Ma used with baby Cormie. I remember it now.

There's a clatter at the rear door while I'm searching, then a soft knock. I think first of the reverend, but three days've passed since I've seen a sign of the man.

When I open the door, it's Essie Jane on the other side. She stumbles in, nearly drowned from the rain, shrugging off the blanket she'd pulled over her head. It falls to the floor in a puddle.

"Essie Jane, why have you come?" No doubt, just as with myself, the slaves have been told to keep to their places. I search for something dry for her to mop off, and then hand over the empty flour sack I washed the day before.

She wipes her eyes with it, then wrings it tight around her hands, blinking as droplets from her headscarf fall into her lashes. "Asmae tell me come fo' you. Tell me come fo' you and the chil'ens. Somt'in happen. Somt'in pow'ful bad. He done somt'in, miss. He done some badness to dem peoples. Now he gone do what need doin' to get it hid. He even shot some a' his own men, Big Neb say—dem what wouldn't go 'long wit' the killin'. Miss Peasie in such a fit up to the big house. She got a simple mind, but she love dem little ones, love to watch 'em play. Asmae say we got to take the chil'ens. Get away befo' the

Massah come back outta the wood wit' his mens. Big Neb, he waitin' wit' a mule wagon and food up to the big house."

My senses depart me then, bolt like a panicked saddle horse with the reins tangled 'round its feet. "We'll never make it out. Not with all these children. Essie Jane, we'll be found and . . ." Horrible pictures torment my mind. "They'll put us to death, all of us."

Chapter 22

Allie Kirkland
July, Present Day

Through the wall, I heard someone breathing, someone moving, the light squeak of sneaker soles brushing against one another. The sound seemed startlingly loud. Too loud to be in the room next door.

I tried to open my eyes, but after a week and a half of sleeping in bits and pieces, waking to the sounds of Blake's comings and goings next door, suddenly tonight my eyelids felt impossibly leaden, my brain sluggish, unwilling to wake. I couldn't rise from the fog, couldn't see. There was only darkness and then the vague feel of weight against the feather mattress, a slight groaning of the ropes, the sound seeming far away.

Was someone here? Was I only dreaming?

A hand settled over my forehead, stroked my hair. I heard myself murmur, "Who . . ."

"Shhh . . ." The voice was just a whisper, and then the weight was gone. The ropes adjusted with soft moans, rising again.

Everything drifted farther away. The fog thickened, pulled me into blackness until there was nothing more. . . .

In the morning, when Wren burst into the room, bringing in both light and noise as she drew back the curtains, my head felt like it'd been the ball at a peewee league soccer practice.

"You and *loverboy* have a big time last night? You're not even up! We go live in less than ten minutes. And you better do something about that hair. You look *rough* this morning." The window protested loudly as she popped out the screen, then rescued a tin coffee cup waiting outside. "Looks like *sweetie pie* left you some coffee. It's cold, now, though. Smells nasty." She set down the cup, then leaned farther out the window, her stomach balancing on the sill. "Ohhhh, and look! Someone hid *flowers* behind the wood-box. And there's a tag too. How romantic."

I sat up, the room swirling around me. "I think I'm sick . . . or something." The memory of the night drifted through my consciousness, thick and strange. Misty. Had there been someone in here?

The idea brought a rash of chills, and my teeth

clattered despite the gathering heat of the day. "I must've dreamed it. . . ." Bracing my arms on my knees, I let my head fall between them. Why was my brain in such a fog? The last thing I remembered clearly was sitting on the porch steps with Blake before I went to bed. There had been complaints the past week from some of the show participants camping on their new claim sites in the woods. They'd seen someone sneaking around after dark. Blake was working quite a bit at night now, trying to figure out whether the interloper was a member of the cast or an outsider, trespassing.

"Ohhhh . . ." Wren cooed, setting a jar of yellow wildflowers on the table and reading the scrap of paper tied on with twine. "For the lovely Bonnie Rose. Ewww . . . special."

I tried to focus on the flowers, but my vision was swimming. I never slept this late. Usually I was up and dressed early in anticipation of Blake showing up with morning coffee. We'd fallen into a comfortable rhythm—early coffee chat at the window every day for a week now, occasionally a few minutes on the porch in the evening, if he wasn't busy working. Once in a while, I caught a glimpse of him beyond the blue line with Rav Singh or other members of the security team.

At this point, we were neighbors and friends. We flirted a little. But the flowers seemed a strange departure—last time and this time.

Despite our almost-kiss at the fireside the first night we'd shared dinner, we'd both been content to just let things amble along. It was easier than wondering whether it made any sense to get involved with someone under such strange circumstances as *Wildwood Creek.*

And now . . . flowers *for the lovely Bonnie Rose?*

That just didn't seem like Blake's style.

Wren opened the breakfast bundle, releasing the scent of food into the room. "Looks like corn cakes and jelly this morning. And beans. Who eats *beans* for breakfast? I told you that's the problem with having everybody else do your cooking. They give us the junk they don't like. Can I at least open a can of peaches? We have two left and you can buy us more at Unger's when you get your salary."

"Yes . . . okay. Don't cut yourself."

"I'm not *stupid*." Her high-pitched voice grated on my brain. She stopped moving, and I knew she was watching me. "You look like my mama with a hangover. You better get out of that position before the cameras go live." When I didn't respond, she came close, so that I was staring at the hem of her skirt. "Are you *really* sick? I mean, like *sick* sick? Want me to go get the set medic?" Her voice took on a note of tender concern. Something had changed between us since our afternoon at the creek. We had more in common than either one of us had ever thought.

The room stopped its carousel ride. "No, I think I just need to . . . eat . . . something. I had the weirdest dream last night, that's all."

"Was *loverboy* in it?"

"Take it easy on me this morning, okay?"

"Okay." She stepped in beside me, slipping underneath my arm as I wobbled to my feet. "Here. Sheesh, come sit down and drink your cold coffee." Moving me to a chair, she deposited me in front of the window, where I closed my eyes and let the sun and fresh air seep into me, clearing the fog from the night.

Wrapping my hands around the cup, absorbing the last bit of warmth from the metal, I looked at the jarful of wildflowers and thought of Blake. Was this his way of trying to . . . take a leap beyond just being neighbor-friends?

"Here, let me do something with your hair," Wren said with the exasperated tone of a mother dealing with an errant child. "You do *not* want to be on TV someday looking like that." She snatched up the snood and comb, then proceeded to rake my hair into submission. It would've been painful if my body hadn't been so numb.

When the camera went live, we were having breakfast, just like any other morning, except for the addition of the peaches. The conversation felt strangely remote, and I couldn't focus on it. I didn't even realize our go-live was finished until

Wren's tone of voice changed, and she pointed out the window.

"Looks like someone is trying to find you." I followed her line of sight, and Kim was on the spring path, a small pile of laundry in her hands. She motioned for me to come out.

"Hope she brought your *things* back finally." Wren added a conspiratorial smile as I stood up, the wobbling in my head finally settling to a vague dizziness.

I grabbed a blanket from the wardrobe and wrapped it around myself to cover my chemise, then hurried around the schoolhouse and down the path. If Kim had taken the risk of coming first thing in the morning when she was supposed to be getting bathhouse business underway, some-thing was probably wrong . . . either that, or she planned to beg for more days with the iPhone. I'd told her yesterday was it. Period. As soon as I got the thing back today, I was giving it to Wren to take up the hill.

But when we met in the cedars, Kim looked happy rather than distressed. I figured that wasn't a good sign. She was going to make excuses again. "Did you bring my phone back?"

"I need it another day." Her lips parted into a wide grin, and she had what I liked to call the here-comes-trouble twinkle in her eye.

"No. Just *no*. The phone goes back up the hill today. Did you email Stewart for me and tell him

I never did get the package he sent? Make sure he knows it's no big deal. I don't want him worrying about it all summer."

Kim raised an eyebrow, and I had a feeling we were about to jump tracks. "Yeah, about Stewart, you know, I've been keeping up with your texts from him. I figured I might as well, as long as I was hanging on to the phone for a while . . . you know, in case he came up with the big Bonnie Rose reveal you've been looking for. Anyway, he started sounding a little . . . *friendly*, if you know what I mean, so I—well, I mean *you*, because I've been being you—let it slip that you were dating somebody here. I thought it was a good idea, just in case he had the wrong idea about this little research arrangement."

"You told *Stewart* I was *dating* someone?" The last, last person in the world who'd be interested in my personal life was Stewart. Kim had probably embarrassed him to death.

"It seemed like a good idea. You know how you're always telling me not to give a guy the wrong idea if I'm not interested? And besides, it's not a total lie. There is Mr. Hotstuff next door. So, did he kiss you yet? Did you kiss him?"

"Kim . . ."

"Okay, never mind. So, just listen—because I have to get back to work before Annie catches me AWOL." Stiffening her arms, she pulled a breath, clearly trying to keep from going hoppy-jumpy about something. "We have a plan."

Oh, man . . . A little elf started hammering thumbtacks just behind my eye again. "Who's *we?*"

"Netta, Genie, and me . . . well, and the kitchen ladies. We couldn't do it without them, because they're at the big house too. And you, of course."

"I don't even want to know."

"Wait, listen. It'll work." She was talking rapid-fire now. A sure sign of approaching insanity. Mine. "So, as soon as you let school out this afternoon, Netta and Genie are gonna re-create one of the Delevan sisters' famous afternoon teas. They read about those in their bio pack. They've already been baking and planning and all that stuff. You're on the guest list, of course. Just think, you'll get to put on your Sunday-best outfit, eat tea cakes, and sip tea. It'll be fun. I'm on the guest list too. Only, *I* won't be there, because . . ." Her voice was bouncing now, and so was her body. Liftoff would occur any moment. "I'm going to meet Jake. There's a county road bridge not far downriver from here, and he texted me exactly how to get to it, and I just texted him back and told him when I'd be there. I'm actually gonna get to *see* him, Allie. I know it's just for a little while, but I'm so excited I can't stand it. And it's so *romantic*."

"It's not romantic, it's crazy." I'd hoped the

phone would make things better, not worse. Now she'd not only hatched a plan, she'd brought everyone in the Delevan house in on it.

She took my hands, squeezed them between hers. "Love *is* crazy, Allie. It's crazy and it's wild, and it makes no sense at all, but I am *so* in love. He's the one. This is it, I'm telling you. Sometimes you meet someone and you just know. Everything is just . . . right. When you're together, it's perfect. And when you're not together all you can think about is being together again."

When you're together, it's perfect. . . .

When you're not together, all you can think about is being together again. . . .

Why did Blake instantly come to mind? Why did her words make me think of the way I looked forward to his smile outside my window in the mornings, about the multitude of times I glanced toward the blue line hoping to see him there, even when I was trying not to think about him?

I understood the kind of infatuation that Kim was describing. I also understood that decisions based on runaway feelings rather than careful analysis could be the first big step toward disaster.

There wasn't any talking Kim out of this. I could see that. "Okay . . . But you realize, you're not going to be able to keep doing this. Aren't you afraid that seeing him now will just make it that much harder? Have you thought of that?"

"You know that I can only think of one thing at

a time." She was literally glowing with excitement. "And you think *too much*. Let loose and have a little fun with Mr. Handsome. We can both be in love at once. Come on, Allie. You can't go your whole life not getting attached to anybody because you might get hurt. I've watched you all these years, and every time a guy is interested, you close yourself off. Blake Fulton isn't your daddy. Love doesn't always end with someone being ripped away from you in the worst possible way. Your daddy didn't mean to leave you—he *died*. He couldn't help it."

"Don't psychologize me, okay?" I wasn't ready for this first thing in the morning. "We were talking about you."

"Just think about what I said, okay? I love you, Allie. You're my best friend. I want you to be as happy as I am."

"Go back to the bathhouse." Suddenly, I was exhausted and trying to change her mind was futile, anyway. "Please be careful this afternoon. Don't take any chances. Promise me."

"Promise! Pinky swear." She held hers up, and we hooked little fingers, and then she was off. Hiking up her skirt, she jumped a tiny yucca plant and dashed away.

The crazy cloud of enthusiasm left with her, and I did what I usually did when Kim came up with one of her wild plans: I started worrying enough for both of us. All through the school day and various go-lives, Kim's harebrained scheme was the only thing I could think about. When I saw Blake strolling by as I left the school to walk to the tea party, I almost spilled the beans and told him what Kim had in mind. Maybe it was the strange night I'd had, but something felt off today, and even the normal rhythms of Wildwood couldn't smooth the ruffle into place again.

"Well, don't you look just as pretty as a speckled pup?" He flashed a smile as he came my way. It temporarily burned off my lingering sense of doom, and I forgot about everything else. He did have the most incredible smile.

I performed a silly twirl on the schoolhouse porch. I was wearing my Sunday best—a green and cream madras plaid dress with piped seams and pagoda sleeves. The knife-pleated skirt was full and pretty—though incredibly hot—and even someone as un-girly as me couldn't help feeling special in it. The dress had been rented premade from a costumer at the last minute, but it fit perfectly. "Why, thank ye-ew, kind sir." My lousy Scarlett made Blake laugh.

He tipped his hat in response. "I do declare, ma'am, it would be my pleasure to escort you wherever you are headed."

"I was just about to stroll up to the Delevan house for tea." I realized I'd missed hearing his laugh this morning even more than I'd missed having hot coffee. The sound was deep, warm, and sweet. I really liked the way he laughed.

He offered his arm, I hooked mine into it, and we strolled up the street chatting about the school day. In the back of my mind, guilt niggled as we said hello to Andy outside the blacksmith shop, then started up the path to the Delevan house. The reality of what I was doing closed in on me. I was aiding and abetting Kim in sneaking off the set, a security breach of monumental proportions. Meanwhile, Blake was working night and day, trying to control security issues. If Kim was found out, it would look bad for Blake and the security team. How would he feel when he discovered that I was in on it? That I'd walked up the hill with him, chatting about school, when I knew what Kim was doing?

I wasn't a liar. How would I ever prove that to him, if the whole thing came to light?

At the big house, Netta and Genie were sitting on the porch in their rocking chairs, along with Lynne Everly and two other cast members living the lives of the kitchen women. Apparently I was the first guest to arrive, since there seem to be no one else around.

"Well, look who it is," Netta clucked, smiling at Blake. "You makin' sure the young ladies of Wildwood are safe on the streets today?"

"Yes, ma'am, I am." He tipped his hat. "It's a tough job, but someone's gotta do it."

"Doesn't look like yer sufferin' so much," Genie drawled, and the two women giggled at the joke. "Y'all come on up and have a bite. It looks like we fixed tea and cakes for nothin'. That little production assistant just came in and told us the power's gone down all over the place, and they don't know what's wrong or when it'll get fixed. Now don't that just put the socks on the rooster?"

"Yes, ma'am, it does." Blake's brows knotted, and he looked toward crew camp, suddenly all business.

Lynne Everly, the aging history professor who was now Old Asmae, lifted a platter off the table. "Try these tea cakes. It took us all morning to get these things right, and now they won't even be on camera. Hoo-ee, reminds me of baking for funerals in my mama's kitchen, that's for sure. Every recipe we made started with a pound a' butter."

Blake helped me up the stairs, then quickly made excuses to leave, grabbed a tea cake at the ladies' insistence, and headed off toward the crew camp.

I lowered myself carefully into a porch chair, muscling the hoops into place before accepting a teacup and cake. The sweet treat tasted like heaven, even though by modern standards it was somewhere between a cracker and a cookie. Not all that sugary.

"Pretty good, huh?" Lynne prodded. "That recipe is authentic 1860. Got it from an old journal."

"It's delicious." Oddly, after weeks of classes about the uncomfortable social structure of Civil War–era race relations, I felt like we'd be reprimanded any minute for enjoying cakes together and laughing on the porch. At times like this, I wondered how the African-American participants felt about life in the village. I'd asked Andy when I'd taken the school kids up to the blacksmith's shop for a science lesson. He'd simply shrugged and said, "How do you feel about being an Irish schoolteacher? It's history. It is what it is."

Nearby, Lynne's granddaughter, Alexis, was enjoying a break from the life of Essie Jane. She and Bella, one of my older students, had settled in on a rope hammock, giggling and using it as a swing.

Wren appeared from the general direction of crew camp and invited herself in for goodies. Since the chairs were full, she settled on the porch steps, her daisy-print cotton skirt spilling around her.

"They look like they're enjoying the break. I think I need one of those hammocks," I commented. The afternoon was warm and breezy. A perfect time to kick back and watch the clouds drift overhead—as if there were ever time for that on a normal day in Wildwood. There was always something to do in the work of daily life.

"You should ask your neighbor for one," Genie

offered. "He made us that neat little thang—just brought it by the other day and hung it up there in by the tree line. I do declare, that boy is handy as a pocket on a shirt. Some gal is gonna be lucky to snag that young fella." She gave me a pointed look, and I felt sweat dripping under my Sunday-best dress. Was it hot up here, or was it just me?

Netta continued the Blake Fulton brag fest. "Blake said he learned about making something out of nothin' while he was in Iraq. Why, he's a bona fide war hero—did you know that? He probably wouldn't tell unless someone asked, of course. He's so modest."

Wren batted her lashes at me. "You should ask him to make us a hammock, sissy. He'll do it if *you* ask. He'll do *anything* you ask."

I slanted a narrow look her way. "Don't you need to go sit in front of the air conditioner in your trailer or something?"

"I like it better here." A freckly smirk came my way. "Anyhow, the power's out, remember? It's hot up there in the trailers. It's a good day for swimming, and I want to wear my swimsuit this time. We can walk all the way down to the lake. I heard up in crew camp it'll be, like, *tomorrow* before they can get all the equipment back online, so we're just free as birds. *And* yesterday Blake told me that the drought's got the lake so far down that a *graveyard* came up out of the water. I wanna go see it."

Wren's story teased my curiosity. It also struck me in a way I hadn't expected, touching a tender place. Blake had spent time talking with Wren, telling her stories. He really was a nice guy.

With that came the usual measure of doubt. The voice of doom, warning that *nice* wasn't a guarantee of anything. Kim was right about me. Love and loss were so tangled inside me, it was impossible to sort one from the other. Both terrified me.

"Y'all go on and enjoy yerselves. No sense sittin' around here with us old gals." Netta fanned herself with a bit of embroidery in progress.

"Awesome!" Wren jumped up before I could answer. "I'll go get my swimsuit on."

"Make sure you tell your mom where you're going."

"Yeah, yeah, yeah." She jogged down the stairs and was gone.

I sat and talked to the ladies until Wren came back, this time wearing shorts and a T-shirt with a swimsuit underneath. She was trailed by none other than Blake Fulton, practically dragging him by the arm. "Look who *I* found," she teased.

"Afternoon again, ladies." Blake seemed a little confused.

Netta smiled. "Why, Blake Fulton." She stood up and straightened her dress. "You're just the man needed to protect a pair of innocent damsels from any-thang that might be lurkin' between here and the lakeshore."

A wave of consternation snaked across his forehead, lowering one brow and raising the other. "You look a little dressed up for swimming, Miss Netta."

"Not them, goofball. Me n' Allie," Wren protested, and Blake caught my eye with a wink. He knew. He was just messing with everyone. The usual little tingle went through my stomach. He'd already decided to slip away to the lake with us, and he wasn't doing it because Wren had dragged him along. He was looking forward to it.

How I could tell all that from a single look was beyond me, but sometimes it just happened between the two of us. It was odd, feeling that kind of connection with someone so quickly. If I didn't watch myself, I could tumble head over heels and be off my feet, just like Kim was. . . .

He grinned at me from beneath his hat, and the issues went out the window. All of a sudden, I wished Wren weren't coming along, which wasn't very kind of me, since it was her idea.

"You children go on and cool off. In fact, if y'all hang on just a minute, we'll pack you up some of these cakes to take along. Somebody might as well have 'em. Lord knows we don't need it."

"I'll go do it." Lynne rose from her chair. "It's my kitchen."

Genie hooked her arm through Lynne's as they started toward the door. "We'll do it together. I been waiting on people my whole life. This silly bit of having folks wait on me is making me crazy as a bullbat."

Lynne's laugh echoed high into the rafters. "Not me, sister. After raising five kids and seventeen grandkids, I'm ready for *somebody* to wait on me. You're looking at Princess Gran-gran. My grandkids don't call me that for nothing."

They disappeared through the door laughing, and Netta decided it was time for Blake and me to be on our way. "Y'all two go on down and rustle up whatever else y'all need to take to the water. Wren can stay here for the food and bring it to the schoolhouse in a minute."

I stood up, more than ready to depart the porch and the over-the-top matchmaking. My nerves did a little pirouette as Blake offered his elbow, and we descended the steps together, veering toward the spring path instead of toward town. "Shorter this way. But if you're worried that you might get your pretty tea dress dirty . . ."

I glanced up at him and had that melting feeling. "I'm not worried."

On the hammock, the pair of tweens sat up. "Hey, Blake!" Alexis called out, sending a wistful look his way.

"Hey, Alexis. How's the swing working out?" I'd noticed that Blake already knew practically everyone in the village, especially the women . . . of all sizes. The girls on the hammock were eyeballing him as if he were a rock star.

"Pretty good." Alexis dangled her long, thin legs over the side, idly kicking her feet, part woman, part little girl. "Hey, I saw that guy in the woods again last night. The ghost guy? He was there, I swear. I'm not making it up. I think you better come again tonight and stake out the porch. That's the third night in a row I've seen him, you know."

Wrinkles of concern formed at the corners of Blake's eyes. "Alexis, I looked all over the woods and didn't see any sign someone had been out there. You sure you two haven't just been telling each other too many stories up in the attic?"

"There's been somebody there. I'm not making it up." Alexis tipped her head up to one side, offering a short burst of teenage attitude.

"Did your grandma see him?"

"By the time she got all the way out of bed, he was gone. But he *was* there, I know he was. It's creepy. He walks around on the hill and then sometimes, he just stands there and looks."

Blake pulled his bottom lip between his teeth, scanning the trees. "Did *anybody* else in the house see him?"

"No. Nobody else would get up and look."

Blake nodded, unsurprised. Even I, who hadn't spent much time around the big house, knew that Carlton Danes, who played the town founder, wasn't nearly the pioneer he thought he'd be. He may have looked like Harland Delevan with his dark hair and handlebar mustache, but he was about as western as my mother. He couldn't handle the heat and spent his time between go-lives lolling around in his room.

"I'll come back and check it out tonight," Blake promised. "See if I can get a look at your ghost." He winked at her, and she pulled a little embroidered pillow off the hammock and threw it at him.

"I didn't say he was a ghost. I just said he *might* be a ghost. Or maybe he's one of those paparazzi sneaking around. You can chase him off like you did the other ones."

"I'll do my best." He snatched up the pillow and threw it back to her. "You guys should go down to the water. Hot day out here."

"That an invitation? Granny says we can't go unless we have someone to watch after us. She's all worried some creep might get us at the lakeshore or something."

Blake glanced my way, letting me decide. "Sure. Wren's in the house waiting for some picnic food. You can walk down to the schoolhouse with her."

"*Wren's* coming?" It was clearly a complaint.

Blake frowned. "Hey, if you're too good to go with us . . ."

"Yeah, whatever." The girls scooted off the hammock and ran for the house in a long-legged teenage footrace. Alexis was an athlete. She could fly. I wondered if her counterpart, Essie

Jane, ever had the chance to run freely through the grass on this hillside, or if her life was one of constant hard labor and abuse.

"What's behind that look?" Blake asked as we started down the path to the spring. "Something crossed your mind all of a sudden."

I felt strangely exposed. So much of my life had always been about keeping the wild meanderings of my mind to myself. I'd learned early on that sharing those things around Mom and Lloyd's house didn't bring good results. Strangely enough, the advice that came to me now was Wren's: *You worry too much about what other people think.* If an eleven-year-old could spot it . . .

"Do you ever wonder what they were really like? Whether we're getting any of it right? About the people who lived here first, I mean. Are we doing them any justice, or just making a farce out of their lives for entertainment's sake? It bothers me a little, I guess. People *died* here. Disappeared off the face of the earth, as far as we can tell. A whole town full of people. I don't know . . . I guess I just feel like . . ." I trailed off, searching.

"Like we owe them something?" Blake put words to my thoughts.

"Exactly. I feel like we owe it to them to get it right, to honor their lives, not just use them to put on a show or compete for a million dollars in gold. There's too much of that these days. It's like TV has become all about turning people into comic characters so we can ridicule them. I don't want to be part of that. *Something* happened to the residents here. They deserve for the truth to finally come out. I'm just not sure that's really what Rav Singh's goal is. He seems more about the sensationalism. This whole thing with planting ore and duplicating a gold rush . . ." I stopped walking and looked up into the trees, suddenly feeling as if the citizens of Wildwood were watching.

Blake studied me for a moment, seeming to muse on the question. "You know, I like that about you. You don't just go with the program. You think for yourself."

My eyes met his, and I felt myself falling, yet walking a tightrope at the same time. This feeling was a chasm so wide, so deep, so terrifying. If I kept stepping out farther and farther, sooner or later I was bound to take a misstep and tumble into the abyss. Everything in me wanted to believe that this was real, but I just couldn't get there. Trust is a muscle, and when you haven't exercised it most of your life, it atrophies like any other part of the body.

"Yeah, give me a door and a window, and I'll try the window," I joked, deflecting again. How pathetic, really.

He just shook his head and smiled down at me. "I was serious."

I stood there searching him. For what, I couldn't say. Proof? Some indication of how often he did this kind of thing? Did he charm everyone he met—like the deli girl and the ladies up in the big house? He was so easy with people, so seemingly unhindered, but was this really him? And why was I so caught up in wondering? I had my own plans for my life, my own dreams, and after this summer in the village, those dreams could start moving at light speed, compared to the past. I didn't need distractions . . . risks. Yet I was drawn to Blake Fulton like a moth to a porch light. Why?

"Listen, Blake, I . . ."

He reached across the space between us, touched the side of my face with the backs of his fingers. I closed my eyes, leaned into him with-out wanting to. My head was a mess, wave upon wave of thoughts and memories crashing on shore, splintering into droplets, chaotic and disorganized —my mother telling me what a screw-up I was, Lloyd looking right past me at a family dinner like he wished I wasn't taking up space, a child psychologist telling my mother that my oppo-sitional behavior was an attention-getting device, my father's friends and family spreading his ashes near a stream he'd loved as a child. The impos-sibility of comprehending that he was gone forever. The terrible, throbbing ache of always wondering whether I was doing what he'd want, whether I was honoring his life or just disap-pointing him.

"Blake, I'm just not . . ." *Sure of anything.*

"Shhh." He pressed a finger to my lips, stepped closer, and I lost myself in him. I knew he was planning to kiss me, and suddenly everything about it seemed right. The tide of worry in my mind went still, and a breath caught in my chest, then trembled out in anticipation.

"You know, I can't figure you out." His voice was low and intimate. His eyes held mine.

"Do you want to?" Who *was* this girl? This girl jumping in so completely, free-falling and not caring where she might land?

"Yeah, I do." His lips quirked slightly to one side just before his head inclined over mine, and my eyes fell closed, and I tumbled through space. His kiss was soft at first, but strangely familiar. In some part of my mind, I realized I'd been imagining this, and now it was real. I let myself drift into the strong, solid feel of him, the slight scent of woodsmoke, the taste of his lips against mine.

The questions didn't seem to matter then. They fell away, and for the first time in a long time, everything about the moment felt right.

When his lips parted from mine, he stood back and looked at me, his hand twined into my hair, the pad of his thumb sliding along my cheek. "Some things don't need to have an explanation, Allie. Some things just *are,* because they *are.* Because God made them that way. If we're meant to solve the mystery of Wildwood, we will. And if there's something meant for you and me, I think we'll know. Maybe that's why we're both here this summer. Maybe for us, it's about you and me."

If there's a girl in this world who wouldn't fall to pieces over words like that, coming from a guy like Blake Fulton, I hadn't met her yet. I laid my head against his chest and just hung on, because I didn't know what else to do. Nothing in my life had ever felt this incredibly powerful or deathly uncertain.

I wanted to believe in it. I wanted to grab the idea that all of this was meant to be, that it would last and travel beyond the confines of Wildwood, but as I clung to Blake, all I could see was my eight-year-old self, running after my father's car the day he drove away and never came back.

When you love people, they leave.

The chasm opened again as the heat of the kiss burned away, the gap quickly separating Blake and me. Love provided such a thin, fragile bridge. How could anyone trust it, even under the best of circumstances? And these were hardly the best of circumstances. What would we really be, out in the real world with all its distractions?

Some things just are, because they are. Because God made them that way.

Was God a big enough bridge? Was it really possible that this was meant for me? The answer to the prayers of thousands of lonely nights?

You may miss your daddy, sugar pie, and I know you do. You always will. But you got to remember, God's just one prayer, or one thought, or one hope away. Grandma Rita had promised me, holding my face at my father's funeral. *You lean on that when the world goes dark. Whatever big hurt you've got inside you, God can cover it over. Don't be afraid to open up and ask.*

But really, I'd never asked. I'd never believed that God had anything better in store for me than a life where you do your best to get by, to stumble along broken and wounded, never quite daring to hope for the really good things. But maybe I'd been wrong all this time. Maybe a tragedy is exactly that—a singular thing, a shadow we travel through on the way to a different destination. Maybe the bigger tragedy is the one we undergo by choice. The decision never to walk forth from the shadow and see what lies beyond it.

When Blake and I continued on along the spring path, I felt lighter, somehow. As if, all along, maybe it really could've been that simple. As if perhaps I could change the way I'd been looking at things.

The moment of clarity stayed with me as we returned to the schoolhouse, Blake disappearing into his side, and me going into mine. When I came out again, Blake was standing on the back porch in black exercise shorts and a gray tank top that fit rather well, I might add.

He frowned at my outfit, which I had reduced by several layers of petticoats and a corset, after trading out the heavy plaid skirt for my light-weight muslin daily skirt.

"You're going in that?"

I looked down, confused, my mind stumbling in a race from past to present. It hadn't even occurred to me to leave behind the costume and garb myself like a normal person. "I never even thought about it."

Blake grinned. "Not that it isn't fetching." He waved a hand toward the trees. "But no cameras today, Scarlett. No need to play the part. I know you've got clothes hidden in there. Your part-time roommate doesn't keep secrets very well. That might come as a surprise." He nodded toward the spring path, where the girls were giggling and looking at something under a cedar bush. For once, Wren was in on the game rather than just watching with a morose look. I wondered if she'd also leaked the information about the cell phone, but Blake seemed casual enough, so I guessed not. Thank goodness. Wherever Kim was by now, I hoped her plan to meet Jake had worked. I hoped she was being careful.

"Go on," Blake urged. "If we run into anybody, they'll just think you grabbed your clothes from crew camp."

"Good point." I hurried back to my room and returned in my closest approximation to swimming gear—capris, T-shirt, and tennis shoes. When I rounded the building again, I felt strangely underdressed as Blake looked at me.

Somewhere in the back of my mind, there was that realization again. We'd never spent real world time together, other than those confusing meetings in and around the Berman Theater. What if he didn't like me this way?

Doubt inched its way in, a summer cloud testing the determination of the sun as we walked to the water, the girls dashing ahead. I felt a shadow sliding along the ground, trying to keep pace. Did Blake feel it too? What if all we really had between us was the codependence of two people forced to live in close proximity, in a very strange situation?

He seemed quieter than usual as we sat on the rocks along the lakeshore, our legs dangling in the water while the girls enjoyed the magic of waves and sunshine. The motorboats slipping past seemed almost foreign now. Too noisy, too bright, too fast. Wildwood was a muted life, moving at the pace of a raft drifting down the lazy Mississippi. It took time to accomplish even the simplest of things. There was no multitasking, because so many tasks required the sum of your energy and effort.

At the end of each day, I was physically exhausted, yet mentally so much calmer than I'd ever been—as if my brain weren't trying to go a million directions at once, even in sleep. The past few evenings, other than that one strange dream last night, I'd slept like a rock, barely even hearing Blake come and go from his room as he worked the night shift.

"Kind of strange, isn't it?" He motioned toward a passing boat.

"Back to the future."

"Temporarily." The group of lakegoers toasted us with their beers as they went by. "Not getting tempted by the dudes with the luxury yacht there, are you?"

I shook my head, bracing my arms and leaning back, enjoying the sunshine. "Pppfff!" The kids on the boat looked about seventeen or eighteen, maybe. Too young to be turned loose on a party barge like that one. "Hardly. Why?"

He shrugged, looked out at the water. "You're kind of quiet this afternoon. Thought maybe you were considering making a run for it while you could."

I considered his observation. *I* was the one who was quiet this afternoon? Far away? Maybe it *was* me. On top of everything else, or maybe because of it, I couldn't stop thinking about Kim, and the fact that I was lying, and that this whole situation had the feeling of a snowball rolling downhill. This business with the cell phone, with doing something that could cause problems for Blake and trouble between the two of us, had to end here.

I wasn't letting this happen again, no matter how desperate Kim was to see Jake. Something inside me had turned a corner this afternoon by the spring creek. If there really was a chance of something for Blake and me, I was going to invest myself in it, no matter how shaky I was. It wouldn't help to build it on an undercurrent of lies.

Maybe I should just tell him the truth now. Get it all out in the clear . . .

I opened my mouth to do it, then lost my courage and diverted the subject instead. "So what about you? What comes next, assuming we make it through this long, hot summer in Wildwood?" I couldn't help picturing him after the docudrama finally aired, fielding offers for the next season of *The Bachelor.* "Do you go straight to another job for Rav Singh, or on to doing security for some-one else?"

"Depends on what my buddy and his wife pick up for us. Kevin and Leah pretty much take care of that end of the business. It's really Kevin's baby, even though we're partners." He plucked a little purple wildflower that was growing from a fissure in the rock, studied it. "The security business was his idea after we finished our last deployment and got out of the army. He had some contacts in Hollywood. He sets things up with the clients. I just look at logistics once I know what kind of a job we're taking on and where— calculate how many people we'll have to hire, what kinds of vehicles we'll need, what we can do to stymie the paparazzi if it's an event like a wedding or an awards show. Logistics is more my thing. Kevin and Leah like the PR end of it, so it works."

We'd suddenly stumbled into an area I'd wanted to ask about but been afraid to. "Is that what you did in Afghanistan? Logistics?" Was I overstepping by asking? Dredging up something that was hard to revisit? But I needed to know him. I needed to learn more about what made him tick. About who he really was inside.

He waited a minute to answer. "In a way. Security. Not always as well as I would've liked. It's a crazy world over there. When you don't get it right and things go bad, it's not just the tabloids leaking some wedding photo or a creepy fan getting a little too close for comfort—it's soldiers' lives. Little kids' moms and dads, people's sons and daughters. Someone's husband. Someone's wife. You don't stay one step ahead . . ." He let the sentence go unfinished.

"Is that what you're thinking about when. . . . I've seen you on the porch at night." I blurted it out, then immediately wished I hadn't. "I'm sorry. That's none of my business."

He handed the flower to me, our fingers brushing as a speedboat rushed by, three kids squealing in an orange inner tube. "It's okay. It's not something I talk about much anymore, but it's not something you just leave behind either. Any soldier who's been there can tell you that you don't come home the same. There's stuff in your head. A lot of guys didn't come back, or they didn't come back in one piece. The questions you ask yourself can drive you crazy—why couldn't you have done just one thing different on some certain day. Why couldn't you have made the difference? Why's another guy gone and you're still here? Why does God let things happen the way they do? Sometimes, the only option you've got is to just get quiet and ask. Just let it all go, you know?"

I did know, in a way. I understood that kind of regret. I'd always thought, if I'd gotten up and gone with my dad the day he died, maybe I could've kept the accident from happening. Maybe I would've been watching, seen the truck jackknifed in the road ahead. Maybe I would've begged him to stop off for doughnuts, and he wouldn't have been in the wrong place at the wrong time.

If only could drive you crazy.

"I know." It seemed strange to admit it after all these years, especially to a person I'd met such a short time ago, but somehow I knew he'd understand it. "It's hard to get past the idea that you can just . . . alter things. I did that for years after my dad died. I'd rewrite it all as I was falling asleep, and in the morning before I opened my eyes I'd tell myself that if I believed hard enough, it'd come true." I'd never told anyone about those desperate morning wishes before, not even my grandmother. "It was kind of a secret I kept, but Grandma Rita figured it out. When I was with her in Texas, in the summers, she'd take me to the church where my dad grew up and show me the murals he'd helped paint in the children's building. She'd tell me that, as pretty as they were, they weren't anything compared to what Dad and Grandpa John were seeing now in heaven. It helped me let go some."

Blake's hand found mine, his fingers a warm circle of flesh over flesh. "My granddaddy was an army chaplain in Korea," he said, "so he always understood. I don't think I knew how much the things he taught me really meant until I left home and went into the army. You end up in a situation where you might meet your Maker anytime, you think a whole lot about what you believe."

Our fingers intertwined, and suddenly I felt very . . . okay. Strangely vulnerable about something I had always kept inside, but okay. Not an oddball anymore. There was someone else who really *got* it.

We fell silent, and that seemed natural too. I've never been with anybody that way. Okay to just be my confused, tangled, conflicted self, still struggling to figure out God and my own life. No longer feeling the need to hide behind a mask. I'd never spent a day so completely comfortable with where I was.

The afternoon was waning by the time we walked the girls down a path to see the tombstones that had begun to emerge about twenty feet offshore in a grassy cove. Moss-covered, tilted, and forlorn, their rounded marble tips protruded from the water, hinting at names and stories.

"Eeewww! Can we wade out there and look?" Wren was fascinated.

Blake pointed to a thin brownish snake swirling its way through the water. "Depends on how you feel about sharing the water with that guy."

The other girls backed a few steps further from the bank, squealing about the snake, but Wren held her ground, fascinated by the stones. "I'm not afraid of him. He doesn't even have a viper head—he's a striped water snake. We learned that in safety class. He's probably more afraid of me than I am of him."

"Yeah, I bet he is," Alexis piped up, and Blake laughed.

"If he's got half a brain he is." Laying a hand on Wren's curly head, he checked his watch. "But, no, you can't go out there. We need to head back so I can catch Alexis's ghost-man tonight."

Alexis huffed and braced her hands on her hips, her long, slim arms still glistening with drying beads of water. "Don't even start with me."

Blake used Wren's head to turn her around and

steer her toward Wildwood. "Okay, everybody's had a look. Now we need to get home before the bears come out looking for an easy meal."

"There aren't any bears around here, and bears aren't nocturnal," Wren argued.

"She's got a point there," I teased, bumping Blake with my shoulder as we started back down the lakeshore.

"She's too smart for her own good," he joked. "You know what they say about curiosity and the cat."

"Funny." Wren cast a longing look over her shoulder toward the tombstones. "But are any of those from Wildwood?"

Blake shook his head. "Nah, they're newer. I talked to a couple of local fishermen about it when I was down here patrolling the other day. They said that's what was left of the original Mennonite settlement of Gnadenfeld. The Corps of Engineers flooded it when they built the lake."

A shiver slid over me. It had nothing to do with the heat of the day finally fading. "And they just left the people's graves?"

"Guess so." Blake took my hand, and I contemplated the tombstones as we walked. *In the end, it makes little difference what's printed in granite when you're gone. It's what you do while you're here that matters.*

By the time we reached Wildwood, evening was settling in. On the ridge above, there was no sign of the faint glow of lights coming on in the crew camp.

"Looks like the power's still out," Blake observed as we stopped at the schoolhouse. "Hard to believe they haven't gotten it back by now. I'll walk the kids up the hill. I'm on shift tonight, so I want to do some recon and see if there's anything to Alexis's man in the woods. It'd be easier if we weren't dealing with a power failure and all of our security cams down. Not that they've been doing much good. We keep realigning the cams, but if this guy does exist, we can't catch him."

He left me then, he and the three girls angling toward the Delevan house and crew camp, and me returning to the school, the warm comfort of the afternoon slowly fading into an evening that felt shadow-filled and strange. The nagging worry that had been circling all day came back, and it didn't take long to identify the source. Kim, of course. I should've checked on her before now and retrieved the cell phone.

The light was slipping toward evening as I hurried to Bathhouse Row. Kim's roommate was down at the spring, but she hadn't seen Kim since earlier in the day. "Everybody's everywhere, since we're off schedule. Last thing I heard, the power company had some kind of massive software problem, they thought. But then I also heard that some farmer with a tractor plowed through the power lines coming onto the property here. So I don't really know what's true. Anyway, some of the girls went up to crew camp to play cards and eat normal food, since it'll spoil with no power for the refrigerators, anyway. She's probably there."

I thanked her and started up the hill toward the trailers to look for Kim. I'd just made it to the parking lot when one of the grips spotted me and hurried my way, looking slightly breathless and wide-eyed.

He gave my capris and T-shirt a quizzical look. "Please tell me you know where Kim is." Squeezing his clipboard against his chest, he grimaced. "Mr. Singh wants us to make sure *everyone* is accounted for and back in place, in case they get the power on tonight." No doubt this was Kim's cell phone–charging guy. He looked like one of her usual victims: a little nerdy, a little too nice. Probably hoping that Kim would get over her fixation with Jake and decide a friendly grip just up the hill might be a better choice for a summer romance.

Right about now he was probably weighing the implications, should Kim be discovered downstream on a secret rendezvous aided and abetted by a forbidden cell phone and a neighbor on the crew. Rav would have this poor kid's head in about a minute and a half if word got out. Grips were expendable.

"I haven't seen her. I just checked the bath-house and then came up here to look."

The grip mopped his forehead. "She needs to show back up. Nobody's seen her since noon. I've asked."

A flash of neatly coiffed blond hair caught the corner of my eye, and I felt the instinctive flight response that indicated Tova was in the vicinity, even before I glanced toward the production trailer. She'd just come out the door, and she was moving in our direction at a rapid pace. I had a feeling our situation was about to go from bad to worse.

Her eyes narrowed as she took in my street clothes. "It looks like someone is drastically out of uniform."

The grip sidestepped her approach, tripping over a twig and practically landing on his backside in the weeds.

Tova ignored him. "Strange, how that could happen, when your belongings are still locked inside *my* trailer. Keeping a few forbidden items, are we, Allison? You might want to run back to your little schoolhouse before Rav sees you. He's in no mood to have one of his little birdies flitting around doing her own thing."

I backed up, a sense of impending doom seizing me by the throat. Before the grip could move away, Tova snatched his clipboard and thumbed through the pages. "Accompany Allison down to the village and make certain that her *extra* clothing finds its way to my trailer, where it *belongs*. We wouldn't want Rav to think she's been taking advantage of her *former* position in production to break the rules, now, would we? Such a thing could reflect poorly on those of us who have actually given our best efforts toward authenticity on this project."

The grip's eyes were like baseballs. For a moment, I was afraid that he was contemplating falling to his knees, confessing his crimes, and begging for mercy.

"Yes . . . yes, ma'am." His voice trembled like a leaf in a frigid north wind. As soon as we found Kim and the cell phone, this whole stupid business was D-O-N-E, finished. Before we ended up in any more trouble.

But I had the nauseating feeling that trouble had already found us. Tova had scented blood.

"Well." She smacked her lips apart, glancing up from the clipboard. "Look who *else* is missing. A certain ditzy person of vaguely blond nature. How peculiar, Allison, that it would be *your* friend."

She shoved the clipboard at the grip, and he caught it in the chest with a muffled cough, quickly withering under Tova's glare. "If you haven't found her by dark, inform me directly. It isn't *my* job to baby-sit, but Rav should be told if there is a problem."

"I'm sure she's here somewhere," I piped up. "We've been offline for hours. People have been down to the lake and whatnot."

Tova smirked at me. "And no one was supposed to be going any farther than the lakeshore, now were they? And the lakeshore has already been checked, has it not? I believe I saw a security guard on an ATV coming back from there, not fifteen minutes ago." She swiveled toward the grip. "If she is here, you won't have a problem turning her up. Either way, inform me."

She turned on her heel and walked away, leaving the two of us to writhe in the pool of acid left behind.

"She's gotta be here," the grip whimpered, smacking himself in the forehead with the clipboard. "She said she'd only be gone a couple hours. She promised."

"Okay, okay . . . Let me think a minute." With Kim, reality so often defied logic. Would she take off with Jake? Go AWOL on purpose? She had to know what kind of trouble the rest of us would be in.

But she'd been so lovesick the past few weeks. *She wouldn't, would she?*

Possibilities began weaving a strange tapestry in my head. Several of them, actually. What if Kim had suffered some sort of accident on her way back to Wildwood? What if the guy that Alexis said she saw lurking in the woods was more than a figment of a teenage imagination? Someone real? Someone dangerous?

In reality, anyone could be in these woods . . . or under the highway bridge where Kim planned to meet Jake.

And there was one more scenario. One I didn't even want to contemplate.

How well did Kim really know the man she had sneaked away to meet? The headlines were full of stories of women who'd been duped by predators online. Men who hung around, looking to meet unsuspecting women on classified ad sites. Guys who seemed too good to be true.

"I have to go find Blake." Like it or not, there was no choice but to confess this whole thing and ask him to get on one of those four-wheelers, go down to the river, and see if he could locate Kim before it was too dark to look.

Chapter 23

Allie Kirkland
July, Present Day

Blake still hadn't come back to his room. Tossing and turning in my bed, I listened for the night air to carry his footsteps through the screen. I wanted to talk to him, but things had been strained after he couldn't turn up any sign of

Kim. His security crew had spent hours frantically trying to make sure she wasn't hurt or lost in the woods, even though that seemed unlikely. The river was easy to find and easy to follow.

At this point, it looked like she'd made a spur of the moment decision that she couldn't quite own up to. In the morning, hopefully we'd hear from her. She and Jake had probably run off to some nearby wedding chapel, and they were spending their honeymoon night at a lakeside cabin.

I wanted that to be true, and at the same time, I wanted to kill her.

Didn't she care about the trouble she was causing? About breaching her contract? About breaking her promise to me? Would my best friend really just run off without saying a word? The idea stung in ways I couldn't stand to contemplate, but even that didn't hurt as badly as the shocked look on Blake's face when I'd confessed.

He'd stared at me like he didn't know me at all. He'd looked hurt, and I didn't have any idea how I was going to fix things.

This was such a mess, and it was my fault. I was the one who'd brought the phone here in the first place, who just had to chase after the story of Bonnie Rose, to hang on a little longer and see what else Stewart could come up with. Once again, letting my mind get lost in a daydream had produced a monumental screw-up in real life.

I just wanted Kim to be okay. *Please, please, let her check in tomorrow morning. . . .*

A wildcat screamed somewhere in the hills, the sound splitting the night air, slicing through the screen, sitting me upright in bed. Shuddering, I rose, dipped a cup of water from the pot on my stove, took a sip. It tasted tinny and strange, but I drank it anyway, then stood at the window watching for Blake and listening to the cat's cry. Resting my head on the sash, I swallowed the prickly lump in my throat, and my mouth felt dry again.

Blake wouldn't be coming with coffee tomorrow. The whole thing was over. In the morning, security would no doubt be knocking on my door, but it wouldn't be Blake; it would be someone telling me to pack my stuff and leave. Both of the men who'd gotten in the fight outside Unger Store had already been dropped from the cast, along with their families. They'd disappeared as quietly as the original citizens of Wildwood.

Sleep tugged at me, sudden, almost dizzying, insisting that I return to bed. The rope supports groaned softly as I pulled the quilt over the T-shirt and capris I'd kept on, unable to shed the feeling that I'd need to rise in the night and go find Kim. . . .

I dreamed of a day with my father. A perfect day, when he had taken me to the Santa Monica pier. A father-daughter excursion filled with

Ferris wheel rides and carousel horses, sand and surf, and time to build castles and watch them wash away in the tide. In the dream, I was small again. Safe because my father was near. . . .

Allie. Allie, wake up. The voice was my father's. He was shaking me. Trying to rouse me from a nightmare.

There's a monster under the bed, I whispered, still groggy from sleep.

His arms circled me, held me against his chest, made me safe.

Then he faded even as I tried to cling to him, even as my mind grasped for the precious memory.

Blackness slipped in and thickened until there was nothing more.

I was falling, spinning down, down, down. I tried to cry out, but there was no sound, only a surrendering.

And then, nothing at all.

My head pounded, the pain so incredibly intense that I only wanted to sink into the blackness again and make it go away. My eyes throbbed like they were bulging out of their sockets, and when I tried to open them, everything was filmy, blurry, and gray. Water dripped somewhere nearby, the sound echoing and seeming to drill into my brain. *Plink, plink, plink.*

A shudder rattled through me, beginning in my

stomach and radiating outward. I was so cold . . . shaking. My skin grated along something frigid, rough, and hard, my head bouncing against what felt like solid rock.

Where was I? What was happening? Was I still dreaming?

I blinked, then blinked again and tried to bring the world into focus, to decide what was real, but there was only a blur. My lashes tugged downward again. The blackness drew over me like a blanket, heavy, the weight suffocating.

Wake up, Allie-bear. Wake up, my father demanded.

Daddy? My voice was nothing more than an unintelligible groan. I looked for him in the darkness, but I couldn't see.

Wake up, Allie-bear. Wake up now.

I pushed through the ink, swimming upward like a diver submerged in some immeasurable ocean, trying to find my way out, fighting for air and light before it was too late. The awareness of danger teased my senses, but I couldn't define it. What was the last thing I remembered?

The night sky, the porch, the window. Blake wasn't out there. . . .

I went to bed. . . .

Why was I on the floor now? No . . . not the floor.

My fingers slid over the dampness around me, discerned the cold unevenness of stone. And water. It was dripping nearby, splashing outward in tiny droplets. Icy cold.

Something was crawling on my arm. The sudden realization forced me awake. I jerked away, felt tiny legs dash across my wrist as I dragged my eyes open and tried to see.

Stone. There was stone all around. White sandstone, like the inside of the schoolhouse, but not blocks. No mortar. Just stone. My body was stiff and uncooperative. I hurt everywhere, the cold and pain a strange mix, sleep clinging to me, my stomach acid-filled. When had I felt this way before?

Yesterday. Yesterday when Wren came into the room and woke me.

Was that yesterday?

I was underground now . . . in a cave or something. Light flickered against the wall, barely enough to see by. Beyond its edges, impossible darkness swallowed any details.

A tiny creature skittered past the rim of my vision and disappeared under the tangle of red hair strewn beside my face. Gasping, I pushed upward, but the movement was slow and clumsy. A centipede as large as my index finger tumbled out and dashed away. Another shudder traveled through me, rattling my teeth and making my head pound.

This had to be a dream. A nightmare . . .

Pain drummed in my head, and blackness closed

around the edges, tiny sparks dancing in empty space as I struggled to my hands and knees. Blinking, I fought to shake it off, to see what was out there, to finally rise to my feet and stagger to the wall, then brace one hand to keep myself upright. An agony of pin prickles shot through my legs with each step. My bare feet were so cold, I couldn't even feel the rocks underneath.

The source of the flickering light was nearby. A lantern sat perhaps ten feet to my left. Not an old kerosene lantern like the ones we used in the village, but the modern propane type. The guys in crew camp carried them occasionally.

Was this all part of the show? Some kind of weird, twisted punishment for what I'd done? Was Rav Singh behind it? Had this project, his obsession with Wildwood, somehow driven him over the edge? Had someone else in Wildwood finally completely lost it? How closely had they checked the backgrounds of the people here?

I opened my mouth to call out, then stopped. If there was someone nearby, I needed to stay quiet to figure out what was happening, discover how I'd ended up here. I was okay as far as I could tell, just chilled and bruised.

I had to find a way out. Now. Before whoever had brought me here came back. Was I alone?

What was hiding in the darkness outside the lantern's glow? One step, then two, then three. I squinted into the void beyond. Was someone watching me even now?

A movement teased my ear as I reached for the lamp handle. The soft echo of a woman's voice. It was gone as quickly as it came, then, silence again, save for the water dripping. Maybe I'd only imagined it. . . .

The flame hissed and flickered as I grabbed the lantern. Its warmth melted over my stiff fingers, and I lifted it so that the light spread farther. Seeing more of my surroundings told me little more than I already knew. The chamber was perhaps twenty feet in height and roughly the same length, slightly narrower in width. Eerie shadows manifested on the walls, ghostlike as they outlined odd shapes carved into the limestone by flowing water at some time in the past. Nearby a small spring bled through the rock, its passage creating a waxy crystalline dome as it trickled downward and fell into a pool on the floor.

On either end of the chamber, darkness stretched toward what seemed to be narrower passageways. Which would lead out? How far was I from the surface?

The woman's voice came again, faint and then gone. Was that someone outside I was hearing? Maybe someone who didn't even know I was in here? I had to be near the lake or the river. Was it daylight out there? If it was, people might be close by, boating or canoeing, hiking or picnicking. Would they hear me if I called out?

The lantern flame danced and spit sparks as I inched toward the sound, shivering and crouching, picking my way carefully along the floor, slick and mossy beneath my feet. Something rustled in the shadows as I reached the room's end and extended the light in front of myself so I could see down the tunnel. It was the larger of the two passageways, and it seemed logical that the larger passage might lead out, the cave narrowing as it went farther underground.

But there was no way to know. I could just as easily be going deeper.

Water trickled under my feet, icy as I crept along the shaft, bracing a hand on the wall to keep my balance. I was still so dizzy, my brain slow and foggy.

There was another chamber ahead. No light, other than what the lantern cast. If this was the passageway out, I was still far from the surface, but the tunnel was widening again, the lantern painting a wavering half circle that grew as I moved. Too late, I realized it would announce my approach to anyone inside. Pressing close to the wall, I covered my mouth, trying to stop my teeth from chattering as the water grew deeper, covering my feet. My toe collided with something, and it rolled away. Bending over, I groped for it blindly, circled my fingers around it. A stick or rock, slightly curved. Not much of a weapon, but it was something.

Sound emerged from the chamber, louder, easier to make out now that I was closer. A woman moaning, trying to say something. The pulse in my ears sped up, pounded wildly. My senses became stark and acute, my thoughts focused on defense and survival.

The moaning increased in desperation as I stepped into the chamber. My fingers tightened around the stick, and the lamplight flickered outward. A rush of nausea and dizziness whirled over me, clouding my thoughts, making me struggle for balance, for reality. Around me, images spun like fins on a pinwheel. Limestone walls, strange shadows, bones, a remnant of fabric. Calico, the colors time-faded. A shoe—the black lace-up sort the women and children wore on the production, but this one was old, largely disintegrated, the layers of the sole fanned out like pages in a book.

A spill of hair, reflecting the light.

A groan.

Movement.

A hand covered with bleeding blue-white flesh.

I saw my own fingers, wrapped around something white with a ball-shaped end. A socket. A bone. My fingers jerked apart. It fell, clattered.

The noise echoed through the room, escaped among the corridors, the vibrations telling me there was no way out of this place other than the passage that had brought me here. This was the end. The deepest part of the cave.

I turned toward the sound of the woman, letting the light discover her as her moans intensified.

Kim?

Her body lay splayed in the dirt, unnaturally twisted, her brown dress torn and bloodied.

"Kim." I rushed toward her, set the light just beyond the spill of her hair, and knelt down. Her skin was like the water seeping from the rocks, damp and frigid to the touch.

"Leee," she murmured. My name, I thought. Her fingers opened slightly, seeming to beckon mine.

Something chalky white at the edge of the lamplight caught my eye. A skull, resting against the wall like a movie prop, the remains of a bonnet still clinging to it, a ragged hole in the dome of the forehead.

I could only stare, clutch Kim's hand, and think . . . *This isn't real.* My mind searched for an explanation, any explanation, however irrational.

How could this be happening? How long had Kim been here? How long had I?

Someone had brought me here. But who? Why? Did Kim know?

I touched her face, tried to rouse her, but she barely responded. "Kim, wake up." I checked her injuries. The blood seemed to be largely from scrapes and scratches and a small gash on her forehead. Beneath it, her skin was purple and swollen. Had someone hit her, or had she fallen? Her legs lay bent behind her body. Were they broken?

"Kim, what happened? How did you get here?"

She didn't answer but seemed to sink farther away, suddenly quiet.

What now? Did I keep trying to wake her? Search for a way to safety and bring back help? I couldn't possibly carry her out of here. How far underground were we? Were we alone?

My mind circled around again like a roulette wheel slipping past the same numbers over and over on every rotation. Who would do something like this? Why? This couldn't be random. There were over seventy cast members in Wildwood, as well as an entire crew. It couldn't be a coincidence that someone had brought both Kim and me here.

I stood, raised the lamp, and let it burn away the darkness, illuminating the debris along the walls. The shapes were covered in dusty sediment, some sealed partially into limestone formations created over countless years as water dripped through stone, leaching minerals slowly down-ward, build-ing conical stalagmites and perfect domes over protruding bits of bone.

The evidence was unmistakable. Those were human beings, or they had been once. Their remains lay scattered like random debris, the surfaces dotted with a ragged scrap of faded calico, the brim of a disintegrating bonnet, a bit of leather, a length of rope, the wire frame of a pair of spectacles.

Who were they? How many? How had they ended up here?

Were these the citizens of Wildwood? Had they been here, hidden beneath the earth all this time?

A breath of must and silt shivered through my lungs, pressed a cough into my throat. I swallowed hard to silence it.

Behind me, Kim groaned, a sound of wrenching pain. Squatting down again, I leaned close and touched her forehead, then whispered against the chill of her skin, "I'll be back. Don't worry. I have to find a way out."

The lantern hissed and threatened to die. I held it up, for the first time noticing how light it felt. The fuel canister was probably almost empty. If I didn't go now, while the flame was still burning, we might never get out.

Holding the lamp low to quell the arc of light, I crept back through the passage to my original chamber, passed by the mark my body had left on the silty floor. That could have been my final resting place. It might be, still.

The darkness seemed to close around me as I entered the boulder-strewn passageway on the other side. My heart thudded painfully, trying to break free of the trembling cage of my body, crowding my ears as they strained toward every sound. Was someone out there? Did I hear breathing, or was it just the air panting from my own lungs?

The bone. The weapon I'd found earlier, I should have brought it with me. But it was too late now.

The passage continued, the tunnel seeming as endless as the catacombs of the Berman Theater in my dream. Kim's sounds faded and disappeared, and a sense of aloneness overwhelmed me. The lantern spit sparks, burning low. The darkness beyond was impenetrable, terrifying.

Please, please help me. The plea whispered through me, and I thought of Blake's words. *You end up in a situation where you might meet your Maker anytime, you think a whole lot about what you believe.* I understood it now—that kind of faith that's born on the battlefield, the reason Blake went outside alone at night when he was haunted, the reason the original citizens of Wildwood gathered to worship when they could have been focused on all the hard work of surviving in the wilderness.

It was also the reason it had always been so easy for me to slide away when I left Grandma Rita's each year. My life hadn't been nearly as tough as I'd thought it was. Life had never brought me to the breaking point, to the point of either giving up or reaching outside myself.

Now here I was, and I knew beyond a shadow of

a doubt that I couldn't find the way on my own.

Moving downward in the tunnel, I quickened my pace, ducking under formations in the ceiling, squeezing past outcroppings of rock, my feet leaden and numb, save for the stab of a thousand tiny needles brought by each step.

The sound of water grew louder, from drips and trickles to a stream, the echo telling me of a chamber ahead even before the tunnel opened into a boulder-strewn slope. Inching forward, I held up the light, looked into the widening cavity. In front of me, the slope led at least twenty feet downward into a pit. A stream of water flowed along one side, moistening the coating of dried moss and lime that painted everything but the chamber's ceiling. Clearly, the area had been underwater fairly recently. The bones of some sort of enormous fish lay along one edge. Bits of driftwood dotted the rocks leading into the pit, and up the slope on the other side, a long snakeskin lay diaphanous as a bridal veil.

The passageway on the far end seemed to hold the faintest light of its own. Sunlight, or another lantern? I had to be close to the surface now. The only way out was through the pit . . . and through whatever lay beyond.

Below me, the surface of the water sat black and ominous. How deep was it? What if I stepped in and there was no bottom? What if I lost the lantern while trying to cross?

Just go slow. Just go slow. The voice of survival was in my head as I started down the slope, crab-crawling on the loose rocks but trying to hold the lantern level to keep it burning.

A strange sort of calm eclipsed all else. I could do this. I *would* do this.

The water was warmer than I'd expected. The stream running down the rocks had to be coming from outside, from the lake, rather than leaching in from an underground spring.

A faint rumble rattled the chamber around me. Thunder. The water seemed to tremble, circling my knees, then my thighs, slowly growing deeper as I felt my way across the pit. It was raining outside. If the lake rose, Kim could end up trapped back there. The front end of this cave had been below the surface before, probably for years. Only the recent drought had exposed it.

The thunder died, and the sound of movement somewhere above caused me to freeze and hold the lantern close to the pool, shielding the light with my body. A ripple circled my leg as if something had passed by below the water. The urge to scream welled up, and I covered my mouth. What might be living in here?

Everything in me wanted to run for the opposite shore, but I couldn't. There was no choice, other than to move as silently as my stiffened body would allow. My legs were softening slightly now, growing more cooperative, warmed by the water, but I was still too off-balance, too weak to run. If someone or something waited up there, I'd never get past.

The slope on the opposite shore was moist, slippery, hard to navigate. The cold air of the cave teased my skin as I left the pool, climbing carefully, bracing the lantern ahead of myself, pausing and holding my breath as loose rocks slipped and bounced downward into the water.

Each time, no sound from above. No evidence that anyone was up there waiting.

The muscles in my arms and legs burned, and my breath came in short, ragged gasps, my head swimming before I finally reached the top of the slope. Pausing momentarily, I lay against the rocks, pulling in air, trying to clear my thoughts.

I was so tired. So cold. The wet clothes clinging to my body felt like a layer of frost. My brain wanted to surrender, to sink into sleep. . . .

Outside, the rain fell in earnest now, and along the sidewall, the flow of water had swelled, weaving its way over the rocks and down to the pool. There wasn't time to waste. I had to keep moving.

Please, please make me strong enough. Please help me. . . .

Pushing upward, I peered over the tumble of debris lining the pit. There was definitely light somewhere beyond the chamber ahead. Not much, but enough to see by, to find my way.

Abandoning the lantern, I crawled upward, finding my footing on the cave floor again. The rocks were slick, a cold mist of condensation seeming to cling to everything. The air smelled fresher. I couldn't be far from the entrance now.

Curling my arms around my waist, I moved toward the next chamber, doubled over, shivering, fighting to keep my teeth quiet as I worked my way closer to what looked like an old rockslide that might have sealed off the rear of the cave in the past.

A sound caught my ear. Feet splashing in water? Then it was gone.

Chapter 24

Bonnie Rose
July 1861

Essie Jane's eyes shift toward the schoolhouse door, then return to me as we stand together in my tiny room. "Asmae say we gots to do it. Now, while the missus gone out to see what Massah done in the wood. Fo' she go, she say to Miss Peasie, *'If the dog's gone, gots to be somt'in done 'bout gettin' rid of the whelps.'* Miss Peasie, she beside herself up to the big house. She a gentle soul, miss. She don't never want to hurt dem chil'ens."

Essie Jane reaches for me then, touchin' my arm, her skin cold against mine as I clutch the babe who has finally cried himself out. The chill wakes me from the feeling that I've fallen into a nightmare dream and none of it is real. "We gots to go get 'cross the river now. Big Neb say he know how to find Missah Hardwick. Big Neb say we get pass the river ford wit' dat mule wagon fo' it fill up too high, den we keep on and pray dat rain keep comin' and wash out the crossin' fo' Massah figure where we gone and come afta us."

Fear arises and covers me. I know Essie Jane is speaking true, but it's a truth too horrible for imaginin'. How can such a thing be? They're coming for the children? Can it really be so?

But I know it in my heart. I know it from all that's happened today. From the man's words to me, himself. This is a nightmare come to life. I cannot let these children be taken by him, but the moment I resist, my death is certain as well as theirs. And Maggie May's. We must run. But with ten children and a babe? And in the storm? How can we do it? How much chance do we have of success?

I close my eyes, hug the babe close, and whisper the most desperate prayers of my life against its downy head. *Heavenly Father, if you'd hear one such as myself, hear me now. We need nothin' short of a miracle. Save this babe and save the rest of us. Deliver us from evil, for thou art the kingdom and power* . . .

Then there's no more time, so I turn to Essie Jane. "Help me gather the little ones. Don't speak a word to them of what's happened to their folk. They must have their wits about them, or we've no chance at all."

"Yes'm," she says, and together we hurry to the schoolroom.

"Quickly, children." I rouse them from their hiding places. "We'll be leaving now, and I want no questions about it, do you hear me? Put on your coats and shoes if you have them. You older ones help the little ones." I point to Aiden and Tomas, who've talked for hours now of seeking rifles and heading out. They're like two half-grown strays, working up the courage to challenge the butcher for a pound of sausage. At thirteen and eleven, they haven't a chance of survivin' but to flee with us, whether they care to admit it or not. "No arguin', you two. You must think of the others now."

What else? I wonder. *What more?* But my mind races as fast and wild as the lightning streaks outside the window. "Maggie May, take everythin' from our room. All that can be used for keeping warm and for travelin', and from the pastor's room as well. Hurry now, as fast as a wink."

I give the babe over to his ten-year-old sister. He's gone soundly himself to sleep again, thankfully. Maggie returns with the preacher's frock, and I wrap it over the both of them. "Keep the babe dry as best you can. You must be a little woman now, Corrie. It's what your ma and da would need from you, do you understand?"

She sniffles and nods, poor thing, her chin quivering, her eyes round and wet. It's too much burden for a child of just ten, but the babe knows her scent the best. I pray he'll remain settled, but should he cry, there won't be anyone hearing him over the storm. The devil has unleashed his horses in the sky now, and he's cracking the whip over them. They thunder like madness as Maggie and the older boys garb the other children. Essie Jane flits to the window to seek after any sign of Mr. Delevan's men coming for us.

In the corner Klara Baum still whimpers like a kitten. She presses closer to the wall as if she'll melt herself into it. I go to her last, crouch close, look into her eyes. "Listen to me." Her hands are bleedin'. She's torn the fingernails bare in her grief and terror. "Hear me now, Klara Baum. Staying here is as sure as dyin'. You must get your wits and rise now. You must follow on, help with the younger ones. Those men are coming for you again, and this time they'll be taking more than they have already. Do you understand me, child?"

She nods and climbs slowly to her feet, her head bowed, her arms wrapped tight over the blanket I'd used to cover her torn dress. She limps as she moves. "My cloak for her. Give her my cloak, Maggie May."

We wrap her in the last of the clothing we have, and I look around. What else must we take? We haven't any food nor a weapon, save for kitchen knives.

"We bes' be gone, Miss Bonnie." Essie Jane's eyes are dark bits in circles of white. "He comin'. I feels him comin'."

"Get the lantern." I gather the children near the back door to go out. I count down each one, making certain we've left none behind before I lift the latch. Behind it, the door rattles in the wind, and soon as the latch is gone, the door blows inward, bringing the storm with it. The children scream and some plead to stay where we are, and I tell them we mustn't.

The storm rages, and we've no choice but to run into it. It's the lesser of the two opponents.

Overhead, the trees bow and sway as we file out. The rain drives in, cold and blowing side-ward, soaking us before we've even descended the steps. There's water over the path already, but not so much that we can't walk it.

"Take a hand! Take a hand!" I scream to the children, but the storm steals my voice away, so I turn my back to the wind and rain, stand against it, and link the children together, big, then little, big, little. Essie Jane goes in front with the lantern and the oldest boys. Maggie and I take the rear.

We move slower than we'd like, our heads against the wind, Essie Jane finding her way only because she knows it so well. The lantern is no match for the storm, and before long, we can only grope through the darkness, Essie Jane finding the path in each flash of light.

The creek swells by the minute, it seems, and I wonder if we've any chance of making the river ford, even now. Beneath our feet, the caliche mud turns wet and slick, and the children slide and fall and pull one another up. Thank goodness for Aiden and Tomas. They're strong young men, and many a time they straddle a watershed in the path with the angry creek at their backs, so as to help the rest of us through.

Big Neb finds us on the path, and he grabs up Essie Jane's hand and leads us the rest of the way. We tumble onto the Delevans' porch, wet to the bone already and near drowned, each of us.

Miss Peasie herself runs out, meeting us there. She's gathered food in a basket, and she thrusts it into my hands, cryin' fitfully, "Oh, the children! Oh, the children!" She moves from one to the next, pulling them to her, soakin' the front of her dress, trying to ease their pain or her own, or both. "I can bring them something dry. Something pretty for the little ones."

"There isn't time for it," I tell her. "We must go now, ma'am. We've no time."

"Oh, but to the babies in the storm . . ." She

433

paces toward the door, then back. "Oh . . . oh . . ." Raking her fingers through her hair, she tears the ribbon loose, and a patch of long gray hair comes with it.

Big Neb takes her hands and stoops eye-to-eye. "Miss Peasie, we done talk about dis. We done talk, you 'member? Massah, he gone done dat ter'ble thing, and it gone go bad for dese chil'ens, he come back. You 'member now? We gots to get down the wagon road. Gone lock you and Asmae and the other womens up in the attic, so can't be said you had none to do wit' it. Massah track down anybody, it gone be me and Essie Jane. We only ones takin' the risk. You 'member, dat's how we decide it?"

Peasie looks long at him then, her mind coming and going from it. I feel the moment ticking by as we wait, frozen. Asmae slips her arm around her mistress's shoulders. "Come 'long, now, missus. We gone back inside. We gone up top, and I give you yo' medicine, so you be sound 'sleep soon. We gone wait out the storm, and we ain't tell nobody what happen here dis night. Jus' we all pow'ful feared by the storm. We don' know nothin' mo'. You come wit' old Asmae now."

They disappear into the house then, and Big Neb sends Essie Jane after them to see to the locking of the upper door. He dashes away through the rain to the wagon shed and soon enough we can't see a thing of him. Again I feel the time passing.

It seems forever before the wagon rushes 'round, a team of Mr. Delevan's mules sliding in the mud ankle deep. Their tracks are gone in the water as quick as they come, which will be God's blessin' to us if we're able to get off. It'll take Mr. Delevan's men a bit before they find the wagon missing and discern where we've gone.

We load the children as the rain ebbs a bit. Aiden and Tomas aren't willing to climb in.

"I'm not leavin' my ma and da and my sister," says Aiden. "Tomas and me are goin' back after our folk."

"Your folk are gone," Big Neb yells above the rain. "Ain't nothin' you can do fo' dem now. But we get dis here wagon bog down in the mud, I'm gone to need you boys on the pry bar."

"If you stay here, you're given up for dead, and perhaps all these little ones as well," I plead with them as the rain pours over us. "You listen to me. You must help with the wee ones. There'll be no one going back. Not any of us." And I know it is so. There is only one way out of here for the lot of us. One way that doesn't include the shedding of more blood today.

Overhead, the attic window opens and the frantic voices of the kitchen women challenge the storm as it rises up again. "Lights on the hill! Lights on the hill!" they cry out.

"Up with you now," I tell the boys, and the three of us climb in together. Big Neb takes Aiden out again. "You come hol' the brake fo' me. Keep dis wagon off the mules when we gone down the hill." Aiden scrambles out, then, and Big Neb closes the wagon gate, pulling the tarp down behind us.

Moments later the brake releases, and the wheels lurch forward, sucking out from the mud and sliding down the hill too fast as Big Neb wrestles and calls to the mules. I hold the children close and whisper prayers over all of us, and the rain breaks free again. We've no way of knowing yet whether it'll be a blessing or a curse. A crash deafens the air, and I wonder if it may be thunder or a rifle shot.

Is it salvation or the devil on our heels? There's nothin' more we can do but hope the angels carry us as we skid 'round the corner and run break-neck away from Wildwood, praying we make the river ford in time.

Chapter 25

Allie Kirkland
July, Present Day

Outside, thunder exploded as I crept past the rockslide and into the chamber, trying to discern its edges in the dim glow cast by a larger passage-way beyond.

I didn't see him at first, in the shadows near

the wall. My heart pitched in my chest when he stepped out, an unmistakable human form. He was tall, thin, slightly stooped over. Something dangled in his hand, pointing toward the floor.

A flashlight. He clicked it on, and the beam illuminated his dark, tight-fitting pants and a pair of combat boots that seemed comically oversized.

Something about that was familiar. . . .

He stepped forward. My mind registered his profile, the way he walked, and relief swelled inside me. Help had come, even if in a strange form. Thank God. Everyone we knew must be out looking for us.

How long had we been missing?

"S-stewart?" My voice was weak and hoarse, almost inaudible over the noise of the rain outside the cave. I rushed toward him as he turned. "Oh, th-thank God, Stewart. Thank God s-someone f-found us!"

He stumbled backward, surprised, the flashlight beam bouncing toward the ceiling, then turning my way, blinding me. I threw a hand up, peering through my fingers to adjust to the brightness.

"Allie." He hurried to me, wrapping me awkwardly in his arms. "You're okay."

A sob pressed my throat, and I felt myself collapsing into him. Finally, I wasn't alone. Help was here. He shifted, then something slipped around my shoulders, heavy, warm. A coat that smelled of rain and woodsmoke.

"What *happened?*" He patted my back awkwardly, bracing his feet apart to steady me as I swayed. "We've been looking everywhere for you. I came as soon as I heard you'd gone missing. It was just pure luck that the map of these caves was in my research." His voice was a welcome comfort. A promise of rescue.

"I d-don't know . . ." I stammered, the words vibrating with my teeth, almost unintelligible. "I was asleep . . . in my b-bed . . . the last thing I remember . . . and then . . . I woke up here. How l-long . . ."

He tucked my head under his chin, his arms wrapping more tightly. "I have to get you out of here." I felt him twisting to lift me from my feet. "The water's coming up. This place could flood if the lake level rises any more. It isn't safe."

I pushed away, stumbling a couple steps toward the passageway and the pit. "Wait. Kim . . ." My head swam, and for a minute I lost my balance, then doubled over, catching the coat around my shoulders and letting the blood flow into my head again. "Kim's . . . b-back there. She's in bad shape. We . . . we have to g-get her out." Clarity burned away the fog, and the floor came into focus beneath my feet, the shadows evaporating.

Stewart slipped a hand beneath the dangling coat, his fingers circling my arm, supporting me. Turning toward the light of the entrance, he guided me with him. "We'll send more help. There's a search team nearby. I need to get you out of here first. You're in no condition to . . ."

We stumbled forward, Stewart half lifting and half dragging me. I thought of Kim, far back in the cave, the water possibly rising. "No!" His grip broke as I spun away, finally stumbling to a stop against the wall of the cave. "I'm not leaving Kim. We c-can get . . . get her out. I'll help you. We can't leave her here." If Stewart was wrong about a rescue team nearby . . .

His body stiffened suddenly in silhouette, the line of his back straightening under the black T-shirt, his shoulder blades jutting against the fabric, his fists clenched.

"Stewart?" A strange, primal reaction ran through me, quick and sharp and visceral, burning away my dulled senses.

The growl started low and grew into the chamber, fierce, animalistic. I realized it was coming from Stewart. When he whirled around, his teeth caught the glow of the flashlight, his lips drawn back. "It's *always* her, isn't it? It's always *her,* or your work, or some *guy* you met next door. You don't think I knew about that? You don't think I saw?"

I steadied myself against the wall, sidestepped away, but I was moving in the wrong direction, toward the interior of the cave, toward the pit. "Stewart, w-what are you . . ." I tried to find his eyes in the darkness, to understand what was happening.

He threw the flashlight my way, and I jumped as it struck the wall nearby, the sound echoing into the chamber, the beam shining on him, turning him into an actor on a strange, twisted stage.

His long, thin arms flailed crazily. "I *let* you go away for the summer, and this is how you *repay* me? Mess around with some guy? Some man you just *met?* Throw it all away for *him?* You don't think I *knew?* I was watching. I saw you with him by the lake and behind the cabin, sipping your little coffee cups in the morning." He raised a finger, pointed it. "Cheating on me!" His voice grew and filled every corner of the chamber.

My mind raced backward. The nights I thought someone was in my bedroom . . . the times Alexis saw a lurker near Wildwood . . . the day things were moved around in my quarters, the chairs straightened, the flowers that were left behind the tinderbox . . .

"You were . . . you were there. . . . It was you."

"You're *just* like all the rest of them. Just like them. Just like them. No different." His chin jerked downward, his face disappearing into the mop of curly hair. He advanced a step. I backed up another. "I would've let you save her, you know. I would've let you call and tell them where to find your friend, once we were away. But now it's ruined. All ruined. And it's *your* fault. It's all your fault."

Survival instinct scrambled inside me, looking for a toehold. He'd brought Kim here as a means of convincing me to leave with him? "Stewart, wait. I'm sorry. We can just go . . ." If I got out of here alive, I could send help for Kim. At least there would be some chance. There had to be people around the lake, people who really *were* looking for us. Was that why Stewart hadn't gone forward with his plan? Was that why he was still here, pacing like a caged animal?

I had to calm him, to get him to take me outside. In here, he could do whatever he wanted, and nobody would know. I imagined myself and Kim, our bodies left to slowly fade, nothing remaining but a mystery.

"All lies." His voice rose as he strode back and forth. "All lies, all lies, all lies. All you do is lie."

"No, Stewart." A movement behind him caught my eye. I recognized the bulk of a form sliding through the shadows near the wall. Andy . . . the blacksmith from Wildwood? He brought a finger to his lips, then circled it in the air, motioning for me to keep Stewart talking.

A glint of sunlight on metal flashed nearby. Someone else was here, too, passing along the opposite sidewall.

Stewart stopped pacing, froze and studied me, then swiveled to look over his shoulder.

"Stewart," I said, trying to draw his attention. "Where? Where could we go? I mean, is there a plan? Someplace people won't bother us? Where my family can't find us? Because . . . b-because all they care about is turning me into an unpaid nanny." I realized now how untrue that was, how broken my mother, my siblings, and even Lloyd would be if a police cruiser came to the house, disturbing a perfectly ordinary day with the most unthinkable news. Whatever differences we had with each other, we were still a family. I still wanted to see them—to be part of their lives and have them be part of mine. There were worse things than having a family that didn't understand you. So many worse things.

Stewart rotated slowly toward me again, looking confused, pulling his hair away from his eyes, nodding frenetically. "I know places." He stopped, leaned in, his face jutting close to mine, his breath thick and foul. "But I don't think you can do it. You see, while your milquetoast parents were raising you on Starbucks and lobster tails, mine were teaching me how to survive in the woods. You don't kill your food, you don't eat. Isn't that the natural order of things? Kill it before it kills you? *A thing that can't survive on its own is worthless, isn't it, Stewart?*" The last sentence came in an eerie, high-pitched voice, an imitation of someone else. His mother? His father? I couldn't imagine what had been hiding all this time inside the shy, withdrawn college student next door.

"I can do it. I can." I forced as much volume as I could, not only to command his attention, but to cover any noise behind him. "The trainers taught me. I've learned everything in Wildwood. How to get by without electricity, what kinds of food we can gather, how to purify water, how to make a fire. It's perfect, Stewart. They gave us everything we need to know. We can go somewhere where no one, not even my parents, will find us."

He let his hair fall, his shoulders drooping forward. "Do you think I'm *stupid,* Allie? Do you know, really, where they've estimated my IQ? Do you have *any* idea? Look around you. How many years have people been trying to figure out the mysteries of Wildwood? Yet . . . here we are. It didn't even take me all that long. A little research, some trips up here exploring. I knew it had to be someplace where the entrance was covered with water when the lake was filled. Someplace . . . inaccessible, even before that. They were *meeting* here, you know. To make secret plans. To plot against him. To *betray* him. He gave them everything, yet they turned on him."

Stewart stepped toward me, taking something from his pocket, pointing it my way. A gun? A knife? "Sounds familiar, doesn't it?"

"No, Stewart . . ." My hands flew up to stop

whatever was coming. Behind him, Andy had moved into the light now. The second figure came out of the shadows. Blake. I couldn't see his face, but his careful stride across the floor was unmistakable.

"Stewart, listen," I pleaded. "I never meant to hurt you. You didn't tell me how you felt. I didn't know. I want to hear more about where we can go. The place you know about. How do we get there?" I forced myself to focus on Stewart, not to glance toward Andy and Blake. They were less than ten feet away now, almost within reach. "Tell me more about it. Is it in the mountains? I've always liked the mountains. A place with snow. Not like Texas. It's so hot here. I'm sick of the heat." For once, my ability to babble was a life-saving skill.

Stewart tipped his head to one side, seeming almost mesmerized by the picture.

"Is there a cabin? A lake, maybe? I've always had that in mind. A place to get away from everything. No Internet, no phone calls, no TV . . . just quiet. Doesn't that seem almost perfect? Just quiet and . . ."

A rock crunched against the floor, and suddenly everything was happening at once. Blake lunged forward, Stewart whirled, the gun exploded, I screamed. I felt myself falling, a stabbing pain, and then darkness.

Grandma Rita was there as the light faded. *You did a good job, darlin'. You did all you could do.*

She stroked my hair. *You're a Kirkland, and our people pioneered this country. We don't take guff off nobody.*

Then even she was gone, and there was nothing.

Overhead, a patch of blue shone through a void in the clouds, the color perfect and brilliant, the edges outlined in radiant streams of golden light.

Heaven?

An airplane flew across the open space, drawing a vaporous line. Did they have airplanes in heaven? Was I still here?

Movement at the edges of my vision came into focus. I recognized faces. The fishermen from the Waterbird, Burt and Nester. Mallory from Wildwood. Birdie's grandpa, Len. Andy stood above him, and strangely enough, Rav Singh and Tova.

Tender concern etched their expressions.

"Move back, give her some room," a sheriff's deputy in uniform commanded.

No one retreated.

Blake was sitting over me, his face near mine. "Welcome back to the world." His hand moved my hair from my forehead.

Somewhere nearby, water stroked the shore, soft, rhythmic. Far in the distance, thunder purred, the sound receding now, harmless as a contented cat settling in for an afternoon nap in a sunny window. We were near the lake, but I was lying on something soft.

I tried to reach for Blake, but my hands were strapped down.

"Just stay still. They're getting ready to take you in the ambulance."

Panic flickered. "W-was I . . . was I . . . d-did he . . . shoot?" My voice was barely a whisper. Blake leaned closer to hear.

What if I was dying, right here? Now. The life seeping out of me?

Please, God, no. There's so much I need to do. So many things I want to change. So much I need to fix. I'd lived my life as if I had all the time in the world—time to think about relationships, time to understand why I was put on the planet, time to make my life count for something, time to make a difference. I'd never really understood that at any moment, time could run out.

"It's not that bad," Blake promised. "You tripped and fell. You hit your head."

My lips trembled upward, my body filling with relief, with gratitude, with determination toward all the things I had left untended.

I had time. A future.

"Fig . . . figures." Laughter pressed, bubbled out with the word, ended in a groan. I hurt all over. "I c-can't even . . . do . . . k-kidnapping right."

Blake gave me a stern look, not appreciating the joke. "You did it just right, Allie. Falling when you did probably saved your life."

"K-kim?" I whispered.

"They're with her now," one of the sheriff's deputies reported, grabbing his radio for a status update. "They should be bringing her out soon. You girls are darn lucky. We've been combing these hills looking for you for two days. It's a good thing these old-timers know Chinquapin Peaks and that they'd noticed a guy camping nearby this past week. The entrance to that cave is just big enough to get through, and almost impossible to see. If Len hadn't spotted where this jerk's camp was and helped track him to the cave, we never would've found you in time."

The information landed in a jumble, like bits of a newspaper shredded to confetti. I struggled to put it together into a story that made sense. "Stewart's been here a *week?* He was planning . . . ?"

I looked at Blake, and his face took on a hard expression. "He's been fixated on you for months, Allie. He had a bunch of your things packed in a duffel bag at his camp. His fingerprints were all over your apartment in Austin and all over your room in Wildwood—even at the Berman. He had a Razor Point Productions crew shirt in his backpack, maps of the Wildwood set, architectural renderings of the Berman. His computer was full of hacked messages from your cell phone and your email. He's been monitoring you, telling his co-workers you were his girlfriend—that the two of you were getting married. The text that brought Kim down to the river was from Stewart, not Jake. Kim's boyfriend left town on a business trip three days ago."

"From *Stewart?*" Even now, it was still almost impossible to assimilate those things with the quiet, seemingly harmless guy next door.

"You don't know how close you probably came," the sheriff's deputy added. "We picked up a report that he was investigated in Mississippi. A co-ed he tutored there disappeared ten months ago, and they haven't found any trace of her yet."

I tried to rise again, but the straps held me in place. I was angry now. Angry and terrified.

"Shhh . . ." Blake soothed. "That's enough information. Just rest." He leaned down, his lips touching my forehead and lingering there, his hand finding mine. "You're safe now, Allie."

"Don't leave me," I whispered.

He rose and looked into my eyes. "I'm right here, Allie. I'm not going anywhere."

Chapter 26

Allie Kirkland
August 1, Present Day

The wedding dress was beautiful. The costuming crew had spent hours searching through patterns of the time period, looking for just the right ivory fabrics and French and Belgian laces. They'd poured over the designing, measuring, cutting, basting, and building of the final dress.

The women of the village had even created a sewing circle at the Delevan house and begun to bond while doing the fine handwork on the dress. In reality, having a special wedding outfit devoted to only one day of wear would've been unlikely for a bride of modest estate in 1861, but the fact is that every bride dreams of her wedding day and imagines that special dress.

Sometimes, allowances must be made, even in re-creating history. After everything the cast of *Wildwood Creek* had been through so far this summer, it seemed only right that this celebration of the glorious bonding of man and wife be nothing less than a perfect moment.

A real preacher had even moved into the room behind the schoolhouse. The impending nuptials and the trauma surrounding the kidnappings had evidenced the need for any society, even a temporary one, to have a strong moral compass. Reverend Hay, the small-town minister from Moses Lake, and his wife were excited to be filling the position of Wildwood's pastorate for the next few weeks until the production reached its closing point.

"Oh, don't you just look pretty as a museum painting?" Netta cooed, handing me a bouquet of antique roses as she stepped into our impromptu bride's room, the downstairs parlor of the Delevan house. "These are for the bride."

I took the roses and felt the slightest hint of their thorns through the blue embroidered hanky that had been used to wrap them. Their scent danced upward, and I thought about the history of the plants brought long ago across seas and prairies by hardy pioneers. Even as Wildwood had faded into dust, the roses had rooted and survived for generations, growing untamed and untended where human lives had come and gone. They would stay here after we moved on, too, their lacy blooms greeting the schoolkids who would come to visit this place to learn about life in a frontier town and to study the tragic history of Wildwood.

"They're beautiful." I glanced toward the bedroom, where Kim was getting dressed with the help of Mallory, who'd been documenting the addition of each piece of clothing, bit by bit, for her *Frontier Woman* blog. "I'll give them to the bride, if she ever comes out."

"I'm coming! I'm coming!" Kim yelled. "Perfection takes time!" At this point, she was somewhere between a giddy girl and bridezilla. In any given moment, there was no telling which one would gain control. I couldn't blame her. The stress of a wedding in front of the cameras, in full period dress, with the entire village and her friends and family decked out in rented costuming, was a lot to handle—even for a girl about to marry a wealthy banker who'd come west to propose to his true love, marry her, and set up shop in Wildwood.

At least until the end of the production.

It's not every day a girl gets the whole fairy tale, and the thing about fairy tales is, there's a need for everything to be perfect. Throughout the whirlwind planning of the wedding, Netta and Genie had been reminding both Kim and me that some of the unexpected moments in life are the ones you remember the most.

When Kim squeezed through the bedroom door in her hoop, corset, pantaloons, petticoats, and new silk chemise, delicately hand-embroidered for the wedding night by Netta, she looked beautiful enough to be a bride already.

Tears stung my eyes, but they were happy tears. When you love someone—*really* love someone—that person's happiness becomes your own happiness. I had finally figured that out. Life isn't about protecting yourself, it's about tearing the box wide open and letting other people in. The people you meet come with lessons to teach. Kim had taught me to be bold. To take risks. To jump in with both feet instead of always standing on the shore worrying about getting my shoes wet.

Jake was a great guy, and if I hadn't believed in love at first sight before, I did after watching the two of them at the hospital. Jake loved my best friend in the way of fairy tales and happily-ever-afters. Some of us are a little slower to recognize it than others, but when the right person steps into your life, you know it.

So now Jake was entering the world of *Wild-wood Creek* . . . a concession made by Rav and the producers after all Kim had been through. An unconventional wedding and honeymoon, but it seemed to fit the couple just fine.

"Oh, look at you, Allie. You look so pretty." Kim pressed her hands over her mouth, then fanned her face, holding back tears.

"I put on my Sunday best for you." I did a quick twirl, being sure to show her the roses Netta had woven into my hair that morning.

"You're so skinny," Kim lamented, then grinned at me.

"What about you?" Between all the hard work in the bathhouse and the time in the hospital,

Kim looked like a model getting ready for a shoot in an extremely retro bridal magazine.

Bracing her hands on her hips, she twirled her shoulders side-to-side and sashayed into the room. "My goal is not putting all the weight back on, now that I'm gonna be a lady of leisure."

We giggled like little girls, and Mallory reminded us that we were already late for the wagon ride to the cliffs above the river, where the camera crew, the cast of Wildwood, and invited guests were already gathering for a sunset wedding that had been kept top secret to prevent the interference of paparazzi. With the breaking of the story about Stewart, the production had drawn national attention. Now that the commotion was finally starting to die down, no one wanted to get it started again, including me. One thing a near-disaster will do is bring families together, and after days of hovering over me in the hospital, it'd practically taken an act of Congress to keep my mother from following me home to Wildwood. She'd even flown back here for the wedding and brought Lloyd and the younger kids along. *Who knows when they'll ever be able to participate in something like this again,* she'd said. *It's a fabulous opportunity they shouldn't miss.*

It's strange how just a few new words can chip away old walls. Nothing I'd ever done had been classified in the realm of fabulous opportunity. It felt really . . . good. For the first time we all seemed to be looking forward to an experience together, even if it was just for a few hours during the wedding. After that, Wildwood would be locked down again, the village drifting back to its normal routines for the final four weeks of production.

The door opened, and Wren poked her head in, her face flushed from marshaling the kids in the wedding party. Perhaps due to the mature hairdo, she had managed to assume control of the group. I'd probably never get my snood back now. "We need to *go*. The little twirps are getting restless. Mallory, Nick says he's *not* walking up the aisle with the ring pillow in front of all those people. You're gonna have to talk to him."

"Yes, ma'am." Mallory flashed a look my way, and I lifted both palms as she headed for the door. With Wren, the social skills were slow in coming, but even when you're eleven-going-on-thirty, it is possible to grow and change. Maybe that was the deepest lesson I'd learned in Wildwood: that life should never be a stagnant thing. That just like the rivers, we thrive when the water flows in and washes away the silt of the past. All the debris we cling to doesn't keep us afloat, it kills the life within us.

If I had learned one overriding lesson from Bonnie Rose, whose eventual fate it seemed I would continue to wonder about forever, it was that I had a little more pioneer blood in me than I thought.

"There's someone out here for you too, Allie." Wren's berry-tinted lips pursed into a smug smile. "*Lover boy* wants to see you. Isn't that, like, bad luck before a wedding?"

"Not if you're just the maid of honor." I hurried from the room and out the door, suddenly as giddy as Kim. Blake was waiting on the porch, leaning casually against one of the pillars.

My heart did the little flip-flop it always did when I saw him.

"Aren't you supposed to be at the wedding already, doing crowd control, chasing away nosy photographers in helicopters, or shooting laser beams at boaters on the river who're trying to get a peek?" I intertwined my hands behind my back, feeling coy and cute. Something about being in love made foolishness seem normal.

"When you're the law in town, you can get away with a few things." He smiled that sweet, slightly careless smile that I'd come to anticipate and adore. "I thought the prettiest girl in Wildwood shouldn't just ride to the big event with the rest of the wedding party." He stepped aside and motioned down the hill, indicating a black horse hitched to a two-person surrey.

"Why, sah, I just don' know if that would be prop-ah . . ." The Scarlett in me emerged at the strangest times. "Travelin' all the way to the rivahside with a handsome gentleman such as yourself."

"Oh, but I come bearing gifts." From behind his back, he produced a small bouquet of wildflowers. "Beauty for a beauty." Even though he overdramatized the sappy line, it made me blush as I accepted the gift. Reaching into his breast pocket, he pulled out a manila envelope. "There's a little something else too. But keep it mum for now—and you didn't get it from me. It came from the DA's file on Stewart's case."

"You stole something from the DA's files?"

"Procured a copy," he corrected. "It was on Stewart's computer. He'd done mountains of research on Wildwood."

I didn't even want to think about Stewart. He didn't belong in this day or anywhere in my life. I wouldn't let what he'd done steal one day of my future. "I don't want it, okay? I'm sorry, but if that has anything to do with Stewart, I don't want to go there right now."

I tried to push the envelope back, but Blake only shook his head, his gaze meeting mine. "You'll want this."

"What is it?"

"Maybe you should sit down."

A sense of dread crept in as Blake guided me to one of the rocking chairs. I imagined the envelope containing some sort of twisted manifesto. At the same time, I knew Blake wouldn't do that.

Especially not today. Whatever he'd brought, it wasn't meant to hurt me. Blake would never hurt me.

I perched on the edge of a chair, being careful not to wrinkle my Sunday best. Blake sat on the table next to me, waiting.

My fingers trembled as I opened the envelope. I felt the stiff, thick edge of something inside and slowly drew it out—a sheet of seemingly harmless cardstock, blank.

"Turn it over." Blake leaned close so that he could look at it too. "Trust me."

I did as he asked, taking in the reprint of a web article titled "Quarter Milers: Foundation Sires of the Quarter Horse Breed." There was a faded reprint of an old photo at the top—a woman in a black dress, holding the reins of a gray horse ridden by a young man. Two young children stood beside her—a girl and a boy. *Wildwood Rose, circa 1870,* the article read. *A champion early-day sprint racer and foundation sire of the Quarter Horse breed, pictured here with owner Bonnie Hardwick and her children.*

Bringing the photograph closer, I looked at the cloudy image of the young woman, her bonnet hanging loosely around her neck, her curls blowing in the wind. Bonnie Rose. "She survived."

"She did."

"But how?"

"I'm not sure we'll ever really know. We might

find out more, if we can track the history of the horse once we get back home." Blake tapped a finger to the page. "My daddy had a few broodmares that went back to a Wildwood Rose line. They were ranch stock out of Montana . . . and race stock, apparently."

A lightness came over me, and I relaxed in my chair, mindless of the dress. "She had a life after this. A good life."

"She rode good horses, that's for sure. That's a fine animal." Blake laid his hand atop mine. I turned my hand over, and our fingers intertwined, the habit as natural now as so many others I'd learned in Wildwood.

"It figures you'd notice the horse. I noticed the kids. She had children. She had a family after this." From one answer, so many questions. Was she happy? Where did she live? How did she live? Whom did she marry? Was she in love? How many children? Did she live to be a grand-mother, to see her granddaughters gain the right to vote, to see the West slowly settled and tamed and changed?

Maybe it didn't matter. Maybe this was enough. Sometimes it's only after you've learned to accept the mystery that God reveals a bit of the answer.

Then again, sometimes one answer leads to another. . . .

Sighing, Blake moved to the edge of his seat. "What's that look about?"

"I was just wondering . . . you know, about the rest of it. Everything else that happened here."

Blake stood up, leaned over my chair, and braced himself with one arm. "Stop." He smiled down at me, shaking his head.

"I can't. You know how I am."

He leaned closer, his eyes twinkling with a light that both accepted the questions and burned them away. "Yes, Allie Kirkland, I do know how you are." He breathed the last words against my lips. "You never settle for just one piece of the story."

Epilogue

Allie
August, Present Day

It was the stillness that seemed so out of place. No dogs barking, no horseshoes grinding against the caliche gravel street, no wagon wheels and harness hames singing their long, lonesome tunes. No voices, no clanging pots, not even the snap of drying clothes flapping in the wind. Just silence. Like the quiet of a graveyard on a day when no funerals or visits have been planned.

A hundred stories whispering, but none you could hear. You have to *know* the stories to hear them after the people are gone. Wildwood, it seemed, would always be a graveyard with no one to tell its tale. I felt guilty about leaving it this way, even though our time here was up. The cameras had been dismantled, the fiber-optic cables pulled. Up the hill, semitrucks and heavy construction equipment were already rolling in to move away the crew trailers.

Yet there was a part of me that still couldn't accept the mystery. I didn't want to leave Bonnie Rose behind, just a bit of legend and lace, part woman, part myth. I had imagined her escape from this valley a thousand different ways since Blake had shown me the photo of her. Dreamed of it, even.

Maybe this was how she would have wanted it, after all. No ties to bind her to this place, other than a song no one could even remember all the words to anymore. Mallory had tracked down bits and pieces, but even the old-timers in these hills no longer sang "The Ballad of Wildwood."

Standing in the schoolhouse for the last time, I listened for the air to whisper it, but it wasn't there. Even so, I couldn't help lingering, just looking, just thinking.

I wasn't the only one. Around the village, there had been a fair bit of lingering, as we closed down these temporary lives we'd lived. After three months of investing ourselves here, of living this life, it was difficult to just walk away. Several winners had amassed small fortunes in gold, but it was still hardest to leave behind homesteads that had become homes, gardens that had grown to produce table food, livestock that had become like part of the family. An existence you build with your sweat and your hopes and your hunger doesn't just go away instantly. Tears were bound to be part of the process. I had shed quite a few of my own. More than I'd ever thought I would.

But I was looking forward to Bluebell ice cream and Dr Pepper. Preferably combined . . . in an air-conditioned room.

Still, I hoped I would never really leave Wildwood behind. I hoped to carry it with me wherever I went. One day, maybe Blake and I would sit around a table somewhere, sharing a wild story of how we met and found a strange connection to the famous sprint horse Wildwood Rose. I pictured telling the story at holiday dinners and class reunions, places where one tale led to another and another and another until a whopper was generated and everybody wondered if it could really be true.

There was so much to think about between here and there. So many choices life offered, including those tucked inside a folder of reference letters and scholarship information for the University of Southern California. "Rav has already spoken to a contact for you," Tova had said when she gave me the folder along with my final review. "You've done quality work this summer, Allison. I must admit, I may have somewhat underestimated you. But a job well done is the best reward, isn't it?"

Then she handed over the folder, and that was that. No hugs. No shared smiles. No cheers at the prospect of our leaving the wilderness. Just the faintest hint of an uptick in the corners of her lips before she turned away. And three little words: *Don't lose touch.*

Now, standing in the schoolhouse, I looked at the folder and it almost seemed surreal. My ticket to the future. The golden ticket. It had finally happened. The thing I had hoped and prayed for all these years had finally been just . . . handed to me. But like so many answered prayers, it had come with the knowledge that I had stored up my treasure in the wrong place. The important thing isn't proving you can achieve a goal, but living every moment along the way, even the side trips.

Perhaps, especially the side trips.

"Regrets?"

I turned to find Rav Singh in the doorway, his profile eerily familiar in the fading afternoon light.

"None," I said, holding up the folder. "Thank you for this. Tova told me what you did, making a contact at USC for me."

"Top-rated film school, and we support a number of endowments there." He moved a few steps further in the door. "You seem surprised. I am a man of my word, and that was our bargain."

Bracing his hands on his hips, he looked up into the rafters, and suddenly I had a feeling he was lingering here for the same reason I was. It's hard to create an imaginary world and then say good-bye to it. Maybe it never got easier no matter how long you were in the business.

"No regrets at all, then?" He seemed to be challenging me, to know why I made it all sound too simple. "Yet you're still here, and up the hill the buses are leaving."

"I'm riding back to Austin with Blake. I wanted to stop in Moses Lake and thank the fishermen who helped find Kim and me. They probably saved our lives." That small portion of the summer was still so hard to think about. I'd done my best to push it from my mind, but the reality of it waited in the outside world. Stewart's trial still lay ahead. More time in small white rooms with investigators and lawyers and FBI agents. But Kim and I had made a pact we would get through this together, and neither of us would give Stewart any more than he had already taken. What he had done wouldn't change the way we lived the rest of our lives. "I guess I wish I'd been a better judge of people—that I'd picked up on Stewart before things happened the way they did. That's a regret."

"Some of our best moments are born of the worst." The statement came out of the blue, seeming strangely sentimental for Rav Singh. "In film, and in life, the highest point arrives just after the lowest."

I gaped at him, slightly stunned. He was comparing what Kim and I had been through to plot points in a film? Sometimes I wondered if he had any concept of reality—of the fact that the people in these shows had to go home, process, and deal with not only the experiences they'd had, but the fact that millions of people would now share in the carefully edited perception of it. Life would never be quite the same for any of us.

Seemingly unaware of the whirl of my thoughts, he slipped something from behind his back. An antique book of some sort. "This was apprehended in a package to you earlier in the summer and kept in the holding area. As you know, all incoming packages were checked for materials not appropriate to our time period. This copy of *Jane Eyre* was carrying a bit of cargo—not so cleverly hidden, I might add."

"Stewart's package?" My throat tightened, a heaviness settling on my chest.

Rav nodded, extending the book my way, urging me to take it. "Yes, but strangely enough, this one came bearing gifts . . . beyond the slightly mutilated reprint of *Jane Eyre*."

I forced myself to take it, to lay it in my palm and look at the cover.

"Open it."

I took a breath, flipped open the cover, felt

something shift deep inside the pages. They parted slightly near the center of the book, and I slid a thumb in, laying the spine flat and exposing a cutout section with something small and silver inside. Electronics of some sort. "What is it?"

"A recording. Something he must have discovered while researching for you." He stood back, clasped his hands behind himself, and smiled at the book, seeming pleased. "As I said, you'll find in life, Allie, that the pattern of struggle and triumph is so often tightly interwoven. And what we each must decide for ourselves eventually is, are they random, or is there a weaver at work? It is, in fact, the great mystery that underlies all the smaller ones."

"I've already decided." I knew it was true. This summer had changed me in ways I never thought it could.

"I leave you to your final discovery in Wildwood, then." He went out the door, stopping on the porch to survey the village and breathe in the stillness before descending the steps and disappearing.

I sat down in one of the pews, trying to work up the courage to push the button. I was still there, staring off into space when Blake came looking for me. And then I knew: That was what I'd been waiting for. I'd been waiting for him to come.

"Stewart sent this over the summer. They had it at the mail lockup. He wanted me to listen to it."

Blake's eyes narrowed warily. "Do you need me to take care of it?"

"No." But I handed it to him anyway. "I guess I want you to push the button and just sit here with me."

Outside, a mourning dove called as Blake slipped into the seat beside me. "I can do that." His arm circled my shoulders and pulled me in close, sheltering me in that safe place I had come to both trust and rely on. I laid my head on his shoulder, and he kissed my hair, then pushed the button. "Here goes."

Whatever happened now, I knew I wouldn't be alone.

At first there was only static, the scraping sound of a needle on an old phonograph.

"The Slave Narratives." An announcer's deep voice pressed through the static of the recording. "As recorded in December 1938, by extension of the Federal Writer's Project under the authority of the Works Progress Administration and President Franklin D. Roosevelt."

Outside, the mourning dove stilled its call, as if it were pausing to listen too.

I closed my eyes, let the stress seep away as a breeze combed the live oaks, causing their branches to softly stroke the roof overhead. The scents of water, stone, and growing things wound through me. Timeless scents, the very ones that would have surrounded Bonnie Rose, here in this place.

I felt her nearby, listening with me, waiting for a voice to press its way through the static again, to insist on being heard after these endless years of silence. Finally, they came. Words, steeped in the hum of background noise, slowly floating to the surface like the leaves in a cup of tea, ready to be skimmed up.

The interviewer spoke first, and within the first few words, I suddenly understood that like everything else that had happened since my coming to Wildwood, this moment, too, had been sent with a lesson to teach.

Interviewer: "This is the slave narrative of Essie Jane Porter. Session two.

"Essie, thank you for joining me today to share more of your personal story. As you know, our purpose is to record the living history of slavery before it disappears. Can you tell us your age at the time of this recording?"

Essie Jane Porter (laughing): "You done as' me that yes'aday. But I ain't 'shamed to tell it again. I seen ninety-one-and-a-half year in this world. Long time."

Interviewer: "Thank you, Essie Jane. That's no small feat for anyone to achieve. Yesterday, you told us of your young childhood on the Blevins Plantation in Lousiana. I wonder if, today, you could share more about your adult life? For instance, when and how did you leave your parents' home? Where did you go after that?

Where were you when the conflicts that eventually led to the Civil War began, and what were you told about those events as they were happening?"

Essie Jane Porter: "I'z thirteen year old when hard time hit on the Blevin Plantation. Cotton come in bad, and Lou'siana gone into secession, and Massah figure they gone be some fightin' fo' too long, so he take us down to town and sell off the las' three a' us they is. That be me, my mama, and Big Neb. After that, Big Neb and me, we owned by a man name Delevan. We ain't never seen the man, but we told we goin' to be his. I'z scared that day, I don't mind to say.

"I guess tha's when I become a big girl, thirteen year old but a woman now, all-same. End up sent to work on the *New Ila* steamboat, owned by Massah Delevan. Big Neb, he frightened like a little chil', 'cause he don' swim. The first mate on the boat, he take one look at Big Neb, and he tell him, 'You give me any trouble, I throw you in the watah, and you be drown dead.' So Big Neb work loadin' and unloadin' that boat, and I work down b'low, seein' after the passenger-folk with the cook women and cleanin' up they messes in they staterooms.

"Now, the *New Ila*, she a beautiful thing, but the first mate, he ain't a good man. He known fo' usin' the women slaves hisself, and the cap'n don' know one thing 'bout it. You don' dare tell nobody, neither. You find yo'self slit throat and dump in the river, and they jus' say you jump off and run away. That the first time I see how mean life can be. My mama kep' a lot of that off me, back home.

"It on that boat, I meet a woman gone change all they is about me. Firs' time I see Miss Bonnie Rose, I think, she got the face of a angel, and hair like fire, long and curly and red, down far as her waist. But she 'bout scared as me. She try to hide it, but I can see. She scared to death a' them fine folk on the boat. Scared to death a' everythin'.

"Cap'n, he noticed she beautiful too. He start keepin' a eye on her. Tell me, 'Essie Jane, you watch aft'a her special.' I didn' know Cap'n knowed my name even, befo' that.

"So I do what he say, and it Miss Bonnie what gets that first mate t'rowed clear off the *New Ila*. I'z glad that day, and Big Neb too. Figure we can work for Cap'n jus' fine. But when that boat get where it been goin', I fin' out we ain't travlin' back with it. I ain't never gon' see my mama again. I got no way to know how to follow them rivers all a' way back home, even if I was to run away. Big Neb, he gon' to be with me though, so I jus' little less afraid, but still, I wonder how it gon' to be, this place we goin', call Wildwood.

"Bonnie Rose, she goin' too, and her lil' sister, Maggie May. Cap'n, he tell Big Neb n' me, 'You look after Bonnie Rose. If'n trouble come in

Wildwood, you get me a message with the freighter, Missah Hardwick.' He don' want no bad to hap'n to Miss Bonnie. He in love wit' her by then, I figure, but she don' have nothin' to do wit' all that. Don' trust it. She got secrets she keepin'.

"So off we go then, into the open country, where they's Indians and all kinda dangers. Lordy, I never pray so much in my life, as then. And if I ain't growed before then, Wildwood turn me into a woman. Strong woman, findin' where my own mind is. They ain't no other way a' life in Wildwood. Ain't no place fo' the weak. You don' get strong, you be ate up after-while.

"Massah Delevan, he pure bad. He a bad, bad man, and his mama bad too. Wildwood they town. They own ever'body and ever'thing in it.

"They so much evil in that place, I feel it wrappin' 'round, minute I come to town. Bonnie Rose, she feelin' it too, I can see. But she won' say. She got secrets, and she trapped as me.

"They's some secrets meant fo' carryin' to the grave. Some secrets kept fo' the livin', and some fo' the dead. Some ain't never to be told. But I reckon it okay to tell this one now. She long gone now, Miss Bonnie Rose. Live to the ripe old age a' eighty-two, up in Montana Territory. Her kids mos'ly gone by now too, I 'magine. I outlive 'bout ever'body I know, 'cept my gran'chil'ens and two of my chil'ens. Som'tin' wrong wit' dat, but I had me a good life. A good, good life, so I

ain't complainin'. My life been a' adventure—
wit' pain, hard work, love, and blessin's. Lord
give me everythin' I need, day by day, and the
blessin' part is, I knowed that while it was
happenin'. Didn' go 'round wantin' mo', way
these young folk do today.

"All that wantin' make you pow'ful unhappy. I
learn that early, so I jus' spend my life thankin'.
Thankin' the Almighty fo' everythin'. Good Lord
give me a fine man, give me seven babies. Give
me a life where I never had to put a babe a' mine
in the ground, till long after they had they own
long lives.

"In Wildwood, he give me a miracle too.

"He deliver me from evil, just like the Bible
say. Bad, bad time come to Wildwood, not three-
month after I get to that place. War brewin' heavy
to the east, den. Regiments gatherin' in Texas to
go to the fight. Massah Delevan, he got plans to
raise him one. Got the money fo' it too.

"But they Irishmen and Germans folk in
Wildwood, mostly. Fair number a' them, they don'
want nothin' to do wit' no secession or no goin'
off to fight them North states. They immigrant
folk, come from up north, mos'ly. Got they
families and they people back there. They don'
cotton to fightin' they homefolk. First a' all, one
speak up again' it, then another. Then they gone
all-sudden, they whole families. Jus' gone.

"Fear come circle 'round Wildwood. All kind a'

fear. Folk runnin' off and hidin' in the wood. Folk talkin' 'bout monsters in the wood, Indians sneakin' round, and river people come up outta that water to drag down mens and womens and childs, eat 'em up whole. Some say Miss Bonnie Rose done it, dat she be queen a' them river people herself. A river witch, and she be stealin' people's minds in they sleep.

"Fear travlin' everywhere, then. Fear got faster feet than truth, sometime. Folk jus' want to get 'way from Wildwood, but Massah's men, they don' let nobody go. Some a' the townfolk, they make a plan, they gon' to band together, take over the town, get they belongin's and they families and run fo' Mexico.

"But Massah Delevan and his bunch, they find it out that bad, awful night. Catch them men and start roundin' up all the families that's dug in, hidin'. Gon' to make them peoples sign that oath. But befo' it be done, fightin' break out, and they kill mens, womens, even boys that ain't growed they whiskers yet. Massah Delevan covered in innocent blood when he come stumblin' back into that big house.

"His mama, she know. She know what he done. They got to hide it, she say. Hide it so's the tale don' never be told."

Interviewer: "Essie, I can see this is very upsetting. Shall we rest a bit before we go on?"

Essie Jane Porter: "No'm. I tell it all, while I

can. Get it outta me. Might be I's the only one lef' knowin' how them chil'ens a' Wildwood been saved. Massah Delevan's men corralled the chil'ens up at the schoolhouse to make they parents mind. After Massah and his mama leave, we know them little babies gon' to be next. Massah don' want nobody lef' to tell the tale.

"When Massah and his mama gone, Miss Peasie and Asmae gather up Big Neb n' me, help us to get what we gon' to need. She a good woman, Miss Peasie, but soft in the head. Like she a little chil', but she won't hurt nobody. She love them little chil'ens in Wildwood. Love to sit on the porch a' the big house and watch them play. Even she understand what gon' to happen that bad night.

"Miss Peasie tell me, 'You run get Bonnie Rose and the chi'dren, and get gone, far as you can go.'

"I scared outta my mind. A big storm come that night, and I know what happen to a runaway if they get caught, but I do what Asmae say. We get them chil'ens and them bags Miss Peasie and Asmae pack up, and we load it on a mule wagon, and go racin' off in the storm.

"God give us a miracle that night. He deliver us from evil, jus' like the Lord's Prayer tell it—the evil of men agains' men. Of murderin' them who's innocent. The Lord bring us outta Wildwood, get us 'cross the river, and then He rise up the watah, keep them bad men back, same way He stop Pharaoh chasin' the Israelites outta Egypt.

"Big Neb and Miss Bonnie, they get us through, all the way to Missah Hardwick, and he take us on. We keep runnin' till we safe."

Interviewer: "So, you were able to escape with the children and travel north, away from the fighting?"

Essie Jane: "Yes'm. Missah Hardwick, he hear tell that sometime soon, President Lincoln gon' to sign a paper where folk can claim public lands in Montana Territory, jus' fo' homesteadin' on it. Missah Hardwick, he say he don' know if that mean free Negro folk too, but if me and Big Neb hep him get to Montana, he figure out a way fo' me and Neb to homestead land next'a his, and it be ours someday.

"We can't even think it in our mind, Neb and me. Land that belong to us! Lord have mercy!

"But we got so many new things to learn. This a new life, and it come wit' all kinda lessons. Got to learn not to call no man massah. Got to learn to count money. Got to learn to figure up what we gon' need and get it fo' a fair price. I never done that befo' in my life. Never look a white woman in the eye, neither. Got to learn to hold my head up, stand straight, act like a free woman, not no runaway slave.

"Like I been born again in a whole new world, dat's how it is. Like God lift me outta Egypt and drop me in the promise' land. I figure that Montana Territory gon' to be somethin' to see.

"Miss Bonnie, she school me in readin' and writin' and numbers while we wait and get us all ready to join a group gon' to go north, next spring. I learn right 'long wit' little Maggie May and them eleven kids we brung outta Wildwood. Mos'ly, they's no finding they families, if they got any still livin'. Back in them days, ain't like today. Got no FBI, no telephone. Can't do nothin' but take them babies in to raise, and so Miss Bonnie, she do it. She and Mr. Hardwick say they gon' to marry. They fill up a hole inside each other. They good together.

"Me and Neb, we figure we might as well too. 'Neb, if we gon' to homestead together in dat Montana Territory,' I tell him, 'I ain't gonna be livin' in sin. You gon' marry me fo' God, or you can forget about all that.'

"Travlin' preacher, he say the vows befo' we head off wit' a group of folk gon' to Montana. We cross rivers, climb mountains, fight off Indians, even. But mos'ly, just put one foot in front'a the other, and keep walkin' from pas' to future, one step at a time. That's all God ask of folk, if'n you think about it. Step out on the trail, and have faith that He gon' to lay it down, mile after mile, make you strong enough to walk it.

"I live all my life in Montana, mos'ly. We got the money fo' what we need to make a start up there. On the trail, when we open up them bags Miss Peasie pack fo' us, in there wit' the food, they two bags a' gold coin. It ain't enough to get rich off'a, but it get us west and keep us goin'. We figure it ain't stealing, since it been give to us, but they's not a one a' us like keepin' a thing from Wildwood. That place like a nightmare we all need'a forget.

"We don' never talk about it no more, even wit' the chi'dren. We keep that secret for they sake, much as our own. For lotta years, we lookin' over our shoulder, 'fraid maybe Massah Delevan fin' out where we gone, and he come afta us fo' stealin'. And finally, that secret don' even seem real no mo'. Them kids grow up and start makin' they own lives, and it like Wildwood never been at all.

"Miss Bonnie, she love Mr. Hardwick in her own way, I think. They smooth the rough edges off bad mem'ries.

"But I know. I know they another man she always think about, when she ride off to the hills on her own. I see her sittin' up there sometime, starin' off into the faraway. She and Mr. Hardwick try for babies, but babies never come. I know she missin' that too.

"And then, when she still a young woman, not twenty-six year-old, Mr. Hardwick ol' roan horse miss a step and slide down the mountain wit' him. They raisin' horses by then, and got a reputation fo' a stallion fast as lightnin'. Missah Hardwick name him Wildwood Rose, afta Miss Bonnie.

Neb break the colts and shoe the ridin' stock, and Mr. Hardwick sell 'em far and wide to them settlers and gold seekers pourin' in. But afta that accident, Mr. Hardwick, he gone from pneumonia in two month. He die on Christmas Day. Ground so froze, we can't even dig a grave.

"In the spring, we finally get to bury him, and Miss Bonnie say good-bye. I don' know what she gon' to do after that, but she just keep on livin' day by day, runnin' that ranch with some a' them kids they's raised. The big boys, they mens by then. They take that stallion to the match races on Sat'aday nights. Old Wildwood Rose, he win ever-time.

"Miss Bonnie, she ride him up on the hill some evenin's and look out into the distant. I know what she lookin' fo'.

"I make up my mind to write me a letter. I ain't good at writin', don't care fo' it much, but I can put together enough to say what need be said. I write one letter, and I put another inside it, and I send it off.

"The steamboats, they done had they day by then, but I figure, if the cap'n survive the war, he still gon' to be workin' on the water. He got that big, long river in his blood. I figure, somebody at that riverport know where to find 'im, if he still alive.

"I don't tell nobody I make that letter. Even Neb. We got us a settlement near enough then, and I just go and post that letter my ownself, but befo' I do it, I stop off, and I get on my knees, and I pray over it hard, hard. Send out that letter and the prayer, all in one.

"Come summer, me and Miss Bonnie out hangin' the clothes one day. We always gets us together and does the washin' and ironin'. We laughs and talks and watches after the babies. Neb an' me, we got them comin' one right after the other. Five by then, in only eight-year, and we figurin' we gone have to stop sometime soon, but they so cute. Miss Bonnie, she love 'em ever-one. They like her own grandbabies, even though she young yet.

"And then that day, we doin' the wash, and they come a man walkin' in the far-off distant. I figure he must a' jump off the freight wagon up the trail a piece, come to get him a good young horse. Miss Bonnie, she stand up and shade her eyes. Look over her shoulder and check fo' the rifle, jus' in case. But he don' get too close befo' I know who he be. Some men, you can tell from a long way off. He a walkin' mountain, that one, like my Neb.

"I feel it all up inside me. The Lord, He my friend and my helper. My steady rock. My maker a' miracles. 'Cause that what it be. I seen it right off.

"My prayer been answered. A whole lotta prayers, I reckon. Miss Bonnie been offerin' them

478

up on that hillside fo' a long time now. I reckon Cap'n has too, or he wouldn't be travlin' all this way.

"When Miss Bonnie finally see who that is comin', she don' say nothin'. Not one word. Jus' drop that white petticoat she holdin' and let it fall right in the dust, and she scream out and go to runnin'.

"I don' say nothin', neither. I just fall on my knees, and thank God, thank God, thank God.

"He a God of miracles and wonders. And love the greatest one of all.

"This big ol' world can't never, ever get enough of it."

Discussion Questions

1. Both Bonnie and Allie are young women who find themselves in challenging circumstances in pursuit of a dream. Have you ever been forced to face what seems like insurmountable odds to achieve a dream? How did you react?

2. Allie finds herself caught between family expectations and an artistic passion that doesn't fit the family structure. How do families unconsciously limit and/or nurture dreams, especially big dreams that may seem impractical? Is there a "black sheep" in your family who struggles to fit the mold?

3. When faced with the reality of confronting her worst fears by moving to the frontier again, Bonnie confesses, "Fear changes nothing. A circumstance is still a circumstance." How does fear affect our decision-making? Should it? Have you ever made a decision out of fear and then regretted it?

4. Allie works diligently at her job with Razor Point Productions, but like many young hopefuls, finds herself unappreciated and often

talked down to. In part, she uses humor to overcome. Have you ever experienced a similar circumstance? How did you overcome it?

5. Allie struggles to be happy for Kim when Kim decides she is in love. Why do you think she feels this way? Why do we sometimes struggle to be happy for the people we care about?

6. Part of the history of Bonnie Rose is preserved in the "Ballad of Wildwood." How does your family preserve history? Do you have a favorite family story? If a ballad were written about your family, what would the title be?

7. After beginning life in Wildwood, Allie discovers that, while the days are physically hard, her mind is far less cluttered and busy. Do you think we're too busy and distracted with all of our gadgets and demands these days? Is it possible to simplify our modern lives? What good examples could we take from the lives of our ancestors?

8. Would you like to become a modern-day time traveler? If you could visit any era in history, which one would you visit? What modern convenience would you have the hardest time giving up?

9. Because of what's happened in the past, both Allie and Bonnie have trouble trusting the possibility of new love. How can previous pain limit our ability to be open to new people in the future? How can we overcome this?

10. Bonnie fears that God might not be able to love or hear the prayers of a "soiled" woman such as herself. How do you see God's love as different from human love? Why do we sometimes feel we're not "good enough" to be loved by God?

11. Kim lives by the seat of her pants, stepping out boldly into new situations, while Allie is the worrier and much more careful or doubtful. What are the problems of each approach? What are the advantages? Which character are you more in line with?

12. When mentoring Wren, Allie realizes how much Grandma Rita did for her and notes that sometimes one person who speaks good things into you can change your self-image. Did you have that one person? Have you been that one person for someone?

13. Allie realizes in the end that "All the debris we cling to doesn't keep us afloat, it kills the

life within us." Have there been times when you've clung to debris for too long? When and why? What were the effects? What happened when you let go?

14. In her narrative, Essie Jane observes, "My life been a' adventure with pain, hard work, love, and blessin's. . . . The blessin' part is, I knowed that while it was happenin'. Didn't go around wantin' more. All that wantin' more make you powerful unhappy." How do our own expectations blind us to the gifts we've already been given? How can we become more aware of the golden moments in life as they're happening?

About the Author

Lisa Wingate is a popular inspirational speaker, former journalist, and national bestselling author of several books, including *Tending Roses*, *Talk of the Town*, *Good Hope Road*, *Dandelion Summer*, and *Never Say Never*. She is a Christy Award finalist, a seven-time Carol Award nominee, and the winner of the 2011 and 2012 Carol Awards. Her work has been selected among Booklist's Top 10 of 2012 and 2013, and she was recently honored by the Americans for More Civility for promoting greater kindness and civility in American life. Lisa and her family live in Central Texas.

Visit *www.lisawingate.com* to sign up for Lisa's latest contest, read her blog and excerpts from her novels, get writing tips, contact her, and more.

Center Point Large Print
600 Brooks Road / PO Box 1
Thorndike ME 04986-0001 USA

(207) 568-3717

US & Canada:
1 800 929-9108
www.centerpointlargeprint.com